To A, for believing in me

The Hating Game © Talli Roland 2010

Published in paperback 2011 by Prospera Publishing
© Talli Roland

All rights reserved in all media. No part of this book may be reproduced or transmitted in any form by any means, electronic or mechanical (including but not limited to: the Internet, photocopying, recording or by any information storage and retrieval system), without prior permission in writing from the author and/or publisher.

The moral right of Talli Roland as the author of the work has been asserted by her in accordance with the Copyright, Designs and Patents Act 1988.

e-ISBN 978-1-907504-10-5
Paperback ISBN 978-1-907504-03-7

Cover design © Prospera Publishing Inhouse
Cover photograph © Torvald Lekvam @sxc.hu
Cover image © Barunpatro @sxc.hu

All characters and events featured in this book are entirely fictional and any resemblance to any person, organisation, place or thing living or dead, or event or place, is purely coincidental and completely unintentional.

Set in Palatino Linotype.
Printed in the UK by CPI Antony Rowe.
Contact: editor@prospera.co.uk.

Acknowledgements

Thank you to everyone at Prospera for their continuous support and efforts to make this novel the best it could be! A massive thanks goes out to my wonderful network of blogging buddies and fellow Tweets, who so enthusiastically participated in helping the book reach bestseller status – I can't tell you how grateful I am. Thank you to India Drummond, writer and friend extraordinaire, who's been with me on my writing journey from the very beginning. And most of all, to the wonderful Jennifer Keay and to my parents, who have always encouraged me to go for my dreams no matter how far-fetched they may sound at the time: thank you.

CHAPTER ONE

*Half of all work-related flings end within one month.
One quarter of work-related marriages end in divorce.*

'IF I GET PNEUMONIA, HE'S GOING to pay,' Mattie Johns muttered as she gripped the chains of the dunk-tank swing and looked down into the murky water. Several unidentifiable floating objects bobbed on the surface and the water had a funky yellow tint. Bonus if she got diphtheria! She'd sue Stuart for all he was worth, saving her company and putting the loser out of business in one fell swoop.

Shame you couldn't sue for boredom, she sighed, shifting her frozen bottom on the swing. Watching TopRank Media's Family Fun Day was about as exciting as watching the company's CEO clip his toenails – which, unfortunately, she'd had the pleasure of witnessing first-hand. As hideous as that display was, Stuart's toenail manoeuvres had been infinitely more entertaining than the bedroom moves that had followed. Any male sporting man boobs and a muffin top should be banned from dancing naked to Barry White – stuffed penguin prop or not – no matter how many millions he had.

A withered man with an adventurous comb-over lumbered towards her and tried to get a look up her skirt.

'It's not Family Porn Day, you perv!' she hissed, trying to cross her legs. The swing swayed ominously over the water and she grasped the chains even tighter.

'Stuart!' she yelled, scanning the gathering crowd. Where the hell was he? He was the one who'd stuck her up here on the dunk tank of doom, promising the whole thing would be over within minutes. Just do me this favour, he'd said. Show me you're really on board with TopRank Media. Then we'll talk business.

If he needed to dunk her in the water to make her pay for not calling him back, fine, she'd thought as she climbed up the ladder and onto the swing. Pathetic, but fine. As long as he renewed his contract, too.

'Cold?' Stuart appeared around the front of the tank.

Mattie made a face. Looking down, she could see the beginnings of a bald patch on top of his head and the buttons on his boring checked shirt strained to keep his belly in place. She'd really had her champagne goggles on when she'd agreed to accompany him home that night.

'No, not cold at all!' Mattie tried to keep her rattling teeth together – no way was she giving him the satisfaction of seeing she was about to become an ice sculpture. 'Listen, Stuart, before the fun begins, can we have a chat first? I have some great ideas to extend the scope of your contract with Mattie Johns Media Recruitment.' She tried to smile but her lips were numb.

Stuart looked at her steadily. 'You know, Mattie, when I started TopRank Media, I asked myself what kind of people I wanted on my team.'

Here we go, Mattie thought. Boring, boring, *boring*. She started to hum a little tune in her head to entertain herself – just like when they'd slept together.

You'd think two bottles of rubbish award-show champagne would have provided enough of a buzz. Stuart had succeeded at dulling even that.

'Would I want someone who isn't considerate? No. Who divulges personal information in front of potential employees? No. Who shows a lack of professionalism the likes of which I have never seen? No, no, no.' Stuart smiled and tapped the side of the dunk tank. 'You're perfect for this, though. Enjoy!' He walked away.

'Stuart!' she screeched. But he was already out of earshot, corralling more troops around the dunk tank. What a nerve, getting her to perch up here, all the while knowing he wasn't going to renew the contract. Kind of surprising; she hadn't expected to find an ounce of guts lurking in that slovenly frame.

His loss, Mattie sniffed, as she tried to get a foot on the ladder leading down to the ground. It wasn't her fault one of the candidates she was vetting for TopRank Media overheard her on the phone to Jess last month, describing Stuart's toenail rituals. And who would have thought the silly employee would report it back to Stuart? If you asked Mattie, she'd done Stuart a favour. Maybe he wouldn't ask the next girl to file his toenails before getting busy.

And she *was* professional, much more than him. True professionals never let their personal feelings interfere with business and that's exactly what he was doing now. He could learn a lot from her.

'Okay, everyone.' Stuart clapped his hands and silence descended. 'Many of you came to TopRank through Mattie Johns. Now's your chance to express your thanks for her *wonderful* services!' His face twisted and he laughed but it sounded more like a cackle.

'Wait!' Mattie yelled at the advancing crowd,

feeling more and more like a witch about to burn at the stake.

She swung a foot out, hooking her heel onto a rung of the ladder.

'Stuart, I'm getting down. You can find someone else to boost your ego. Maybe file your toenails, too!'

'Come on, everyone,' Stuart shouted, a maniacal look in his eye. 'One, two, THREE!'

A flurry of balls hurtled through the air towards her as the gathered crowd let loose.

'Oh, shit!' Mattie reached for the ladder. But before she could grasp it, there was a thump and she felt the metal bar give way. She plunged into the cold murky water, her foot still hooked on the ladder rung and her skirt floating around her head.

She tried to haul herself upright, water streaming into her ears and nose, breaking the surface to the sound of laughter. Above it all she could make out Stuart's goofy guffaws.

'And she's up!' Stuart yelled through a megaphone. 'Let's get her back on that bar again, folks.'

'No way.' Mattie shook her wet head, hair whipping across her face, and climbed down the rickety metal ladder on the side of the tank. She'd almost drowned, not to mention ruined a thousand pounds of prime wardrobe along with showing off her knickers to a hundred nerdy individuals. All to make an idiotic fool feel better about himself.

'Thanks for coming out,' Stuart said sarcastically. He strode over to where she stood dripping onto the asphalt. 'But we've just signed an exclusive deal with another agency. I believe you might have heard of them. Kyle Cook Recruitment?' He met her eyes triumphantly. 'Kyle speaks very *fondly* of you,' Stuart sneered.

Mattie stared back, anger blocking any retorts from

springing to mind. Of all the agencies to lose business to, of course it had to be Kyle's. Not that it surprised her – he'd already taken more than half her clients. As if cheating on her wasn't bad enough! He wasn't going to stop until she was completely ruined. At the rate she was going, that would be any day now.

She squared her shoulders and plucked a strand of wet hair from her cheek. 'I hope you two have a very fruitful partnership.'

Emphasis on *fruitful*. She'd never seen two such pathetic men. They could file each other's toenails, she smirked, trying to stop her brain from flicking through what losing TopRank's account would do to her bottom line.

'Oh, we will, Mattie, we will,' Stuart said. 'We have one thing in common, anyway.'

Mattie turned and squished off. She could think of many things they had in common. Pea-sized brains – and other miniscule appendages, for a start.

'We both hate you!' Stuart shouted.

She stuck up her middle finger and kept walking. She had been such an idiot to trust Kyle – to *love* Kyle. Her mother was right: no man could be trusted. Look how things had turned out between her parents! Twenty years later and her mum had only just managed to pay back the debt her father had left behind when he'd run out.

Mattie clomped over to the bus stop to get the bus back to the tube. God, she missed her Mini Cooper. She'd had to sell it almost a month ago to keep her business landlord off her back and most days she still looked for the keys before her Oyster card.

'Thanks for coming, Mattie!' Stuart yelled out the window of his predictably dull black Lexus as he flashed by the bus stop. Mattie made a face at the back of the car as it zoomed away, then slumped down onto a gum-covered bench.

In the grimy glass of the bus shelter, she looked a fright. Her black bob was plastered against her head and her cheeks were so pale she could pass for a corpse. Add to that blue lips and sodden clothes, and she resembled something the gutter had thrown up.

The bus lurched over and Mattie climbed on, digging her payment card out of her dripping blazer. She touched it on the reader, then sank down onto a seat, head propped up against the window. Much as she hated to admit it, she'd really been counting on Stuart's business. Now what was she going to do?

'Miss!' the bus driver called.

Mattie sighed and lifted her head. 'What?'

'Your card didn't work. Can you try it again, please?'

Mattie got to her feet and stalked over to the bus driver, then touched her card to the reader. 'There. Happy?'

The driver shook his doughy head and turned to face her. 'No. I'm sorry. It's not working. Got any cash?'

Mattie's insides twisted. If she had cash, would she be on this smelly bus with the rest of society's rejects? 'Of course I don't have cash. That's what the card is for. It's not my problem your reader's broken.' She turned away and went to sit down, staring out the window and praying for him to just leave her alone.

There was a noise beside her and Mattie looked up to see the driver looming over her. His round body was a larger version of his head.

'Miss.' He twisted his hands anxiously, his eyebrows moving so much they looked like they were trying to escape his face.

'What?' Mattie gave him her harshest look, the kind her mother used to bring men to heel.

'You must pay or get off. And as you can't pay. . .' He gestured towards the door.

Mattie snorted. 'I'm not going anywhere.' Never back down was always her mantra – especially with blobby bus drivers. Besides, if she got off now, how the hell would she get home?

'I don't want to call the transit police,' the driver said, locking eyes with her. Mattie stared hard at him, wondering if he'd actually go that far. Probably not, but did she really want to take the risk? She could only imagine the rumours that would circulate if anyone ever got wind of it. And things were bad enough as it was.

Mattie got up. 'Okay, okay. Don't get your size eighty knickers in a twist.'

The driver's face sagged with relief and the other passengers broke into applause as she climbed down the stairs. The cold hit her like a slap in the face and she stood on the side of the road, watching as the bus disappeared. Crossing her arms to keep warm, she began the long trudge towards the town centre.

CHAPTER TWO

Seven per cent of married couples met at secondary school reunions.
Twenty per cent of these were married to others at the time.

'DID YOU GET THIS?' JESS MCKENZIE burst into Mattie's office later that afternoon, holding an envelope in her hand. Her chest was heaving up and down and she was puffing as if she'd run a marathon.

Mattie looked up from yet another letter stating payment was overdue and grabbed a tissue to wipe her streaming nose. It had taken her an hour to walk to the nearest tube station and she probably had pneumonia by now, if not tuberculosis. Her clothes had steam-dried in the sauna-like tube but she was still freezing. Stuart better hope she didn't get sick. She'd come down on him like a ton of bricks.

'What is it?' she asked. Jess got excited about flyers from Tesco's offering price reductions on toilet roll but judging by the deep red flush on her face, this must be something big. Ever since they'd met in Year Seven, Jess's chubby cheeks went red when she was excited or embarrassed.

'School reunion next month! God, can you believe it's been ten years?' Jess's large green eyes were even wider with excitement. She pushed a clump of long brown hair away from her sweaty face.

'You ran all the way from your office to tell me that?' Mattie shook her head as she sifted through her remaining post. Bank, bank, bank . . . here it was, the letter from Staines Secondary School, inviting her to a Hawaiian-themed reunion dinner to be held in the cafeteria. Everyone was to come in costume! Hors d'oeuvres would be served! Live music would be played!

Someone clearly had a little too much rum punch already. Mattie couldn't think of anything worse than hanging out with her former classmates, wearing flowers and eating limp pineapple appetizers.

'Are you going?' she asked, although it was obvious Jess had already bought into the exclamation-mark enthusiasm of the invite.

'Yeah!' Jess said. 'Don't you want to see how everyone turned out? Anyway, I read in *Heat* that reunions are a great place to reignite old flames.'

Mattie rolled her eyes. Old flames, as if. Jess was *such* a romantic. 'There are quite a few people at that reunion I don't want to reconnect with, ever again.'

'Come on, Charlie probably won't even be there.' Jess put on the whiny, pleading voice Mattie hated. 'The last I heard, he was living in Ibiza, if you can believe that! No one will even remember what happened, anyway.'

'*I* remember,' Mattie spat through gritted teeth. Her already shortened fuse sizzled as she recalled finding Charlie – her boyfriend at the time – snogging Kwong, the Korean exchange student, at the secondary school prom. She'd only managed to save face by grabbing the mic and dedicating *Let's Get it On* to Staines' hottest new couple, outing them both to the whole school in one go.

'And maybe Adam's going to be there?' Jess pondered.

Mattie chortled. 'Stumpy? He's probably size thirty-six now. I've never seen anyone inhale biscuits like he did.'

'He goes by Adam now,' Jess said, a little too quickly. 'And he's really successful. Started this amazing video game company. There's, like, a hundred people working for him or something!'

'Fat old Stumpy, successful. Imagine.' Mattie shook her head. Just went to show how unfair life was. She expected him to be in servitude somewhere along the M25, asking: 'Do you want fries with that?'

'Well, he is.'

'I didn't know you two kept in touch.'

Jess toyed with the invitation as a guilty look slid over her even features. 'Yeah, we talk every once in a while. He always asks about you, you know.'

'God, he needs to get over it. Year Ten was, what, a million years ago.' Mattie shrugged. People didn't change. If Stumpy didn't wow her then, he was unlikely to do so now, no matter how much cash he had at his disposal.

'Nope, I'm not going to this thing.' Mattie crumpled up the invite and deftly threw it in the bin. 'A reunion with anyone remotely related to my love life is the last thing on my agenda.'

*

Nate Reilly was late for his appointment. He'd had a hell of a day on the set of *Jungle Jangle*: screaming kids, dogs with trigger-happy biting tendencies, and a bucket of slime that had landed on the pristinely-dressed guest celebrity instead of the presenter. Every excrement-filled episode made him more determined than ever to leave behind the wonderful world of children's television. It was time for a grown-up gig – one without vomit clean-up in the job description.

He ran down Shaftesbury Avenue and onto Earlham Street, checking his GPS quickly. Here it was: number thirty-seven. He pushed through the open door and up to the second floor where Mattie Johns Media Recruitment was located, striding purposefully into the reception. Hang on. Where was everyone? Hmm. He'd heard some disconcerting things about Mattie Johns lately, but they related to her dubious personal life – he assumed she was still doing business. Collapsing into a trendy metallic chair, he tried to control his heart rate, but his shirt was now damp and clung to his back like a second skin. Even seated, his legs shook from the unexpected exercise.

Christ, he really needed to hit the gym. He needed to *join* a gym. As soon as he got a new gig, he promised himself. Then he'd lose his love handles, try to tame his Afro-like hair and – he pushed up his giant Mr Magoo-style specs – maybe even get contacts.

Nate crossed his legs, then uncrossed them and slung a foot over one knee in a casual pose he'd noted from a fellow assistant producer in the meeting last week. Before the assistant producer got promoted, he thought bitterly. Why did Nate have to waste his time in what everyone knew to be the loser zone of television when other people got promoted almost instantaneously? Well, no more. If SiniStar Productions didn't appreciate his skills and experience, some other company would.

Suddenly he heard laughter. Through a half-open door to the right he could see a woman wearing a severely tailored suit with a business-like bob, skin stark white against the black of her suit. She was beautiful, in a terrifying, harsh kind of way. That must be Mattie, he thought. He'd heard through colleagues she was a real ball-buster; guaranteed to get you the post you wanted.

He turned his attention to the other woman in the room. With her cherub-like cheeks and open expression, she seemed charming – a comforting respite from Mattie's angular features.

Even though Mattie was half the size of the woman beside her, everything about her screamed power and control. Rumour had it Mattie's ex had recently done a runner, taking most of her clients with him, and in the process practically destroyed her business. Nate shuddered as he considered the man's bravery. He certainly wouldn't want to cross her.

Mattie made an abrupt move and Nate jerked his head away from them. Wouldn't do to be caught eavesdropping. He grabbed a *Media Today* magazine from the glass coffee table and tried not to listen in, but as more laughter drifted towards him he decided they couldn't be discussing business. He was about to cough to let them know he was here when Mattie mentioned something about not wanting to run into past love interests.

His ears perked up. Along with her reputation for getting people the jobs they wanted, Mattie was also renowned for being a man-eater. Nate had learned not to listen to the waves of gossip that washed over the sets of TV shows, but he couldn't help hearing from several colleagues Mattie had placed that she'd provided a few with *other* services besides recruitment.

One told Nate he'd tried to call her afterwards, but she'd completely blanked him. 'She used me, man, like some kind of *dude*,' the disbelieving camera assistant had said. 'She out-duded me. At least I give the birds a courtesy call afterwards.'

Nate listened with interest to the two women discussing their ex-boyfriends and what sounded like an upcoming secondary-school reunion. He pictured Mattie facing a firing line of all the men she ditched in secondary school – from the sounds of things, there'd been quite a few.

Just how many exes did Mattie have? Imagine if he corralled them all into one room. Would she give any of them the time of day or would she douse them with petrol, light a match and fan the flames? He'd bet on the latter, but it'd be an interesting scenario. It would certainly make an entertaining show.

Nate sat up straight. Hang on! It *would* make an interesting show. Something like *The Dating Game* – but with exes. A second chance for romance! One woman. Three, maybe four exes. And she chooses one to have another go at a relationship.

Nate stood up, heart beating fast. This was it. *This* was what he needed to make an impact at SiniStar. A great concept; an exciting idea. There was nothing like it on TV! It would be new, it would be fresh and it would be all his. He even had the perfect contestant – if Mattie's business was suffering as much as he'd heard then she'd jump at the chance to get some juicy prize money.

Nate considered his options. He'd pitched ideas to SiniStar's managing director, Silver Hatchett, before and been chucked out within seconds. This time, though, he had a feeling she'd listen.

Screw the new job, Nate thought as he ran back down the stairs, trying to keep his puffing to a minimum lest he alert Mattie to his presence. Finally, he had an idea to make Silver sit up and take notice. Heady with the thought of his future success, he decided to throw his weekly budget to the wind and lash out on a cab. After all, it was only a matter of time before things turned around. He was sure of it.

CHAPTER THREE

One in three people has a pair of lucky dating pants.
One in fifteen men admits to never washing them.

'WHAT THE—?' NATE CRACKED OPEN an eye, then stretched out his arm to throw the buzzing alarm clock against the wall. It was only five a.m., for Christ's sake!

Then he remembered. This was it. The day his life was going to change. Despite the foul-smelling wrapper from last night's kebab stuck to his cheek, he couldn't help smiling. This was the day he wouldn't have to watch others get promoted while he cleaned up slime; the day when people would finally respect him. Nate Reilly, executive producer.

If only Kira could see him now!

Stop, he admonished himself. Don't think about her. No need to get down on the big day, right?

Nate rolled out of bed and headed for the desk, grabbing his saggy underwear before it fell to his ankles. He'd been working on the treatment for *Second Chance for Romance* since arriving home last night and it was almost, *almost* done. He read it over for the hundredth time, grinning giddily.

'Picture this,' Nate intoned in a game show announcer's voice. 'One woman. Four men. A second chance at true love. But these aren't just any men.' He shook head. 'Oh, no. Just imagine the look on the woman's face when she finds out – one by one, choosing blindly each night – that the men are her exes!'

Nate stood up and paced around his studio flat. 'The great British public rates each date. When the dates are done – and all the exes revealed – the ex with the highest rating gets a second chance for romance, spending two weeks alone with the lady in a romantic location.'

He spun towards the mirror. 'After two weeks and a daily dose of specially designed Relationship Repair activities, will they choose to be together? Will it be a *Second Chance for Romance*? Or the reunion from hell?' Nate hummed the theme from the *Love Boat* and crashed onto the sofa.

Brilliant. It was bloody brilliant: the perfect mix between dating game show and reality show! What was *not* to like? Silver had to love it – or at least not chuck him out within thirty seconds like she had the last time he attempted a pitch.

Right, just a few loose ends to tie up. He clicked on Mattie's website and downloaded a severe photo of her in a black suit – did that woman wear any other colour? Now for the final detail: how much prize money to award? Two hundred thousand pounds had a nice ring. Enough to be significant, yet peanuts for a major network. Nate added the details to the file and hit save. Done!

He threw on his lucky T-shirt and a pair of relatively wrinkle-free jeans, smushed down recalcitrant curls and settled horn-rimmed glasses on a rather wide nose. Pretty good, considering he barely made enough to keep him in takeaways and beer. He might not be executive producer yet, but he was on his way. At best, Silver would ask him to shoot a pilot episode to pitch to the networks, but that would still buy him some respect with his workmates.

And if the show did get picked up . . .

Nate grabbed his keys and rushed down the stairs, holding his breath as he passed the door to the kebab shop on ground level. Once I'm executive producer, I'll buy a flat in Chelsea or Notting Hill, where all the media people live, he thought, dodging screaming schoolkids on his way to the Wood Green tube. I might even meet someone, someone much better than bitchy Kira – someone who doesn't feel the compulsion to bankrupt me. London flashed by care of the Piccadilly Line as Nate daydreamed his way into Soho Square and SiniStar's offices.

'Earth to Nate!' Ginny, Silver's assistant, snapped her fingers in his direction. '*Hello!* I said, Silver's ready for you!' She rolled her eyes and flipped bleached-blonde hair over a skeletal shoulder.

Nate swallowed, unable to respond. Suddenly his throat was dry and he could feel sweat beading on his forehead. What if Silver hated it? What if he got booted out as unceremoniously as the last time?

'She's waiting!' Ginny screeched, dropping all pretence of politeness.

'Right.' Nate quickly opened the glass door to the MD's office and walked in.

'Whatever you want, you've got one minute.' Silver waved him into a chair in front of the desk, then shoved back her short grey hair and fixed him with iceberg-blue eyes. 'Fucking crisis here. Bloody tree-hugging gardener just pulled out of his show at the last second, gone back to live in his heap-of-manure farm in arse-end nowhere. I've got to meet the network this afternoon. And do you think any of my idiot producers have something decent to fill the slot? Incompetent slobs.'

Nate sat up, unable to believe his luck. Silver needed a show urgently and he had one. A great one!

'What the hell's wrong with you? Are you constipated? Not surprised, with all that shit you eat.'

'Well, I, er, um . . .' *Come on, Nate!* he told himself, struggling to remember the opening line of his pitch. *Pull it together.*

Across the sharp-edged glass desk, Silver pursed her lips with impatience. Next to the crimson lipstick, her white teeth looked like fangs. 'What are you trying to say? Moron!' she barked.

'Right,' he began. His voice sounded reedy so he cleared his throat. *You can do this. You* need *to do this! No more slime!*

Silver huffed and crossed her legs. Nate tried not to look at the scary three-inch black patent stilettos she was sporting.

'Right,' he repeated, his voice stronger this time. 'I have an idea. For a show.' *Shit.* That wasn't how his pitch was supposed to start.

'Aw, Christ. Not some hippy loser uncommercial crap again. I don't have fucking time for this.' She jerked back her chair and spun to look out the window. 'Of course you have an idea. For a show.' She mimicked his tone. 'Do you know how many people tell me that every day?'

'Dozens?' Nate replied weakly. She'd given him this same speech when he'd dared ventured in with his last idea a few months ago.

'Exactly. Dozens, Nate. Dozens like you, who think they have something different, something unique. Well, I can tell you, I've heard it all before.'

'But mine *is* different!' He hated the pleading tone in his voice and took a deep breath. 'Just listen. You said you needed a show. It can't hurt to hear it. Especially with the network meeting looming.'

Silver turned back towards him, cocking an eyebrow, and Nate rushed ahead before she could respond. 'One woman. Four men. The series kicks off with a live show, where she chooses the first man. The following day, she goes on a date with him, then heads back to the studio for a taped segment where she picks the next man. We edit the date highlights together with the taped segment and air it later that night – and the audience rates each date.'

Nate paused to gulp in air. 'After all the dates, the man with the highest date rating spends two weeks with her in a romantic location, where there's a daily activity designed to bring them together. After the two weeks are over, they decide to have a relationship ... or not.' Nate let out his breath. It didn't exactly have the drama he'd practised at home, but at least he'd got the basic format out.

Silver tapped her claw-like nails on the desk and squinted. 'A dating show? That shit's been done a trillion times before. Didn't I tell you not to waste my time?' She waved a hand towards the door. 'Go.'

'Wait!' Nate's heart was beating so fast it felt like it was going to burst out of his chest. 'I forgot to mention, er, these aren't just any men. They're guys she's ditched. Her exes.'

Silence filled the room. Silver leaned back in her chair, eyes locked on his. 'Go on,' she said finally.

Nate nodded. 'Yes, exes. And here's the thing: she won't know the men are her exes until they're revealed, one by one.' That was the best bit! Silver couldn't resist that, could she?

'Hmm.' She grabbed a cocktail sausage from her desk drawer and bit it in two. The sight made Nate cross his legs uncomfortably.' You need to get the right woman. The whole thing could fall apart if you have some ugly loser no one could care less about. And it needs to be someone who can hold it together when her exes are revealed.'

Nate's heart pounded. Thank God she hadn't dismissed it outright. 'Yes, I've thought of that and I've got a great contestant lined up already.' He tried to sound confident as he slid Mattie's photo across the desk. He hadn't exactly signed her up, but he'd do whatever he could to convince Silver this was something worth developing. Right now, he didn't care if she kept him working up sizzle reels or budgets for weeks. He just wanted a chance.

Silver glanced at the photo, then shrugged. 'Not bad. More Cherie Blair than Katie Price in that Joseph suit, though. We'll need to sex her up.'

Nate nodded, hope leaping inside him. She was actually considering it! 'No problem.' It might be difficult to get Mattie to agree to go on a reality show, let alone turn her into a porn star. But he'd cross those bridges when he came to them.

'What's this going to cost?'

Nate put the full treatment he'd worked up on the table. 'Not much. The preliminary breakdown's here, but the main cost is the prize money awarded to the woman at the end of the show, along with a nominal appearance fee for the men.'

Silver grabbed the report and scanned it. 'Two hundred thousand, eh?' She ran her tongue along blood-red lips. 'Shouldn't be hard to get a network to agree to that.'

Then her expression went blank again. 'But of course there are a lot of holes in the concept. Leave it with me.' She gestured towards the door. 'I'll keep you posted.'

Nate stood up. 'So are you going to pitch it to the network? The one that lost the gardening show?'

Silver smirked. 'Like it is? Forget it. It's got *limited* potential – I'll give you that – but right now it stinks like a sack of shit. I'll have to put some work into it.

Then we'll see. Don't worry, Nate. You'll be the first to hear if anything happens.'

Nate took another deep breath and forced the words out. 'This is my concept. If anything happens, I want to be executive producer on this.'

'Or?' Silver asked, looking amused.

'Or I take it to another company.' He felt like he was about to collapse, but he knew the idea was strong and he had the perfect woman – desperate and broke – to front it.

Silver laughed. 'You're getting a bit ahead of yourself, aren't you? Let's just wait and see.' She looked pointedly toward the door.

Nate nodded and walked out on unsteady legs. Today's batch of slime might not be the last he'd ever mix. But Silver hadn't rejected his pitch – yet. At least there was hope.

*

Mattie threw the TeknoNerds bill in the office's overflowing rubbish bin. She wasn't going to pay a bunch of incompetent losers five hundred pounds for messing up her laptop instead of fixing it! Massaging her throbbing head, she tried not to think about all the other companies waiting for payment. Three hundred pounds for the phone lines, two thousand still pending on her credit card . . . not to mention rent for the office and the mortgage on her flat. How much longer could she hold out before bankruptcy came calling? She needed new business and she needed it fast.

She wrinkled her nose as a foul odour drifted towards her. What the hell was that? Pushing back her chair, she tracked the sulphur-like smell to the office's tiny loo, fumes burning her eyes. Oh, gross! The floor was slathered in coffee-coloured liquid bubbling out from the toilet – and the level was rising, fast. Backing away, she ran to her laptop, quickly Googled 'London plumbers', then punched the digits into her mobile.

'I need a plumber – now!' she shouted, when someone picked up.

'It's two hundred pounds for the call-out plus the cost of the job,' a voice informed her. 'We can have someone there in thirty minutes.'

Two hundred pounds *plus* the cost of the job? Jesus, were they bringing her lunch from The Ritz, too? Mattie stared disbelievingly at her BlackBerry, then ducked back to the loo. Cloudy water was now seeping into the reception-area carpet and a large dark patch was expanding quickly.

'Fine,' she said, defeated. What choice did she have? She gave them her address and hung up, shaking her head.

This was it. She was now officially in the shit.

CHAPTER FOUR

*Eight in ten men don't brush their teeth before a date,
compared with one in fifty women.*

'WE NEED THE FERRET, NATE! NOW!' The producer of *Jungle Jangle* sounded anything but pleased.

'Coming!' All day, Nate hadn't been able to think about anything other than his pitch to Silver, let alone ferrets. He struggled to reach the animal that was now crouching behind a discarded fish tank in the jumble of junk backstage. Grabbing the tank, he turned it upside down, managing to trap the ferret underneath. Too late Nate realised it still held some water. The ferret was soaking wet and looking extremely retaliatory.

'Shit!' Nate lifted a corner of the tank and stuck a hand in, grabbing the animal as firmly as he dared. He drew out the squirming creature and ran onto the set, blinking against the lights. 'Here you go,' he said, holding out the ferret that worryingly had stopped struggling.

'I'm not touching a rat!' Tabitha Trittley, the host, squealed. 'Ew, it's wet!'

'It's not a rat. It's a ferret.' Nate looked around the set. 'Does anyone have a blow-dryer?' Blow-drying a ferret, he sighed. I can't believe I'm about to *blow-dry* a bloody *ferret*! Not only that – he grimaced – the ferret had peed in his hand.

'Nate!' A runner burst onto the set. 'Silver wants to see you. Now!'

Nate wiped his hand on his jeans and swallowed. Could this be it? He'd only pitched Silver the day before but the network *was* desperate for a show to replace the boring old gardener. Nate sent up a silent prayer thanking whoever Greenfingers was for breaching his contract, then raced off set.

'Go in,' Ginny grunted, not even bothering to look up from the computer screen.

Nate took a deep breath and entered Silver's lair.

Silver stood at her floor to ceiling windows, gazing out on London.

'Nate. Sit down.' She spun around and waved him towards a chair, her pale blue eyes locked on his brown ones.

'Any news on *Second Chance for Romance*?' The words slipped out of his mouth before he could stop them. *Ease up, man. Careful.*

Silver slipped into her chair, inserted a cocktail sausage in her mouth and chewed. 'Actually, yes. There is some news.'

Nate waited for her to continue speaking but she just kept chewing.

'What?' he asked, when he couldn't stand it any longer.

Silver swallowed. 'X-ACT is interested.'

'X-ACT?' Nate squeaked. He coughed to cover his excitement. They were one of the biggest TV networks in the UK!

'That's great!' He tried to sound nonchalant. 'So when do we shoot the pilot?'

Silver shook her head, tapping expertly finished fingernails on the gleaming desk. 'No pilot, Nate. Actually, they've bought the show. We start production next week.'

Nate's mouth dropped open. No pilot! Filming next week! This was even better than he'd hoped. His life *was* going to change. No more ferret pee, no more slime. He was finally going to be executive producer, quite possibly on a top-rating show.

'Just one thing, Nate. One thing you need to do before I can promote you.'

'What?' Nate asked eagerly. He'd do anything.

Silver threw a stapled sheaf of papers at him. 'Take the contract. Get the woman signed up – fast. Then come see me and we'll discuss.'

Nate swallowed. What did she mean, *we'll discuss*? They'd already agreed he'd be executive producer, hadn't they?

But Silver was standing up and shrugging on her coat. 'I'll see you later this afternoon. With the signed contract.' She stalked out.

'Of course,' Nate said to the cocktail sausage stash on her desk.

'No problem.'

A few hours later, Nate was circling round and round the piazza at Covent Garden, lips moving as he rehearsed his pitch to get Mattie on board. Only thirty minutes, then he'd know if he'd bagged the promotion or not. Thank God Mattie agreed to meet this afternoon.

His stomach rumbled as he passed Mick the Slick and his Dog Stand. He'd skipped lunch and right now he could think of nothing better than a hotdog with onions; maybe some of those sugared nuts . . .

Focus! If you nail this, you'll be executive producer! He puffed out his chest and straightened up from his usual slump, putting on a serious *I'm an executive producer* expression.

'All right, mate?' Mick the Slick gave him a funny look.

Nate let out his breath. 'Fine,' he muttered, backing slowly away from the hotdogs.

He continued marching around the cobblestones, running snippets through his head. Prize money . . . good PR for business . . . prize money . . . A woman clutched her baby closer and gave him the evil eye and Nate realised he'd been muttering aloud. But he didn't care. He was almost a big-shot executive producer now! He returned the woman's glare with one of his own, feeling victorious when she looked away first. Ha!

He walked towards Mattie's office, determination flooding into him. This was it. The last step before he had everything he'd ever dreamed of. There was no way he could mess up now.

*

Staring at her empty inbox, Mattie couldn't help but notice the dearth of appointments. There was only one – Nate Reilly – on the agenda for this afternoon.

Where had she heard that name before? She almost called out to Jude, the receptionist, before remembering she'd had to let Jude go last month to save costs. It was for the best, anyway. Jude had witnessed Kyle's sleaziness first hand and the last thing Mattie wanted was someone around to remind her of his treachery.

Mattie pushed away the familiar pang at the thought of Kyle. Where was she? Oh yes. Nate. That was the guy who hadn't even bothered to show up a few days ago. Loser, Mattie snorted. She hated people who took up space in her agenda, then didn't even have the common courtesy to ring and cancel. When she saw Mr Nate Reilly, she'd give him a piece of her mind. It would feel good to let off some steam.

The familiar sound of the un-oiled door reluctantly

giving way alerted her to the fact that someone was in reception.

'Come through!' she yelled, grimacing at the sight of a lumpy man about her age, dressed in baggy jeans and an oversized T-shirt. His hair sprung off his head like an aging Orphan Annie gone wrong and horn-rimmed glasses clung fast to his nose, as if keeping it in place in the middle of a blobby face. She remembered from his file that he worked on kids' shows. The way he looked, he probably fit right in.

'Have a seat.' She waved him towards the Philipe Starcke chair in front of her desk, trying to keep a straight face as he squirmed not to fall off the edge. She'd deliberately chosen the most uncomfortable chair she could find for her office. Watching candidates' discomfort was both useful in giving her the upper edge and, depending on her mood, highly entertaining.

'So.' Mattie fixed Nate with a glare, noting with satisfaction that he already seemed nervous. 'Thanks for taking the time to show up on Tuesday.' Just the right level of flippant sarcasm, she congratulated herself.

Nate shifted on the chair again. 'Um, yeah, sorry about that.' His round open face coloured.

'Sorry about that?' Mattie mimicked. 'That's all you have to say? Consider yourself lucky. Normally I wouldn't offer someone like you a second appointment. I had a last-minute cancellation – someone who bothered to call – so I decided to give you another chance.' She was enjoying the shell-shocked look on his face. God, some men were just too easy to wind up.

'Um, thanks.' Nate leaned forward in the chair and nearly slid off the edge again. 'Look, I didn't come here for a job. I've got a business proposition for you.'

Mattie almost snorted. A business proposition – from a toad like him? 'Really?'

Nate sat up straight. 'Seriously. I'm a producer for SiniStar Productions and I've just been talking to our MD.'

'So?' Mattie tried not to roll her eyes. Was he going to tell her what he'd eaten for breakfast too? By the looks of things he'd downed ten bacon butties followed by some McMuffins.

Shifting uncomfortably, Nate cleared his throat. 'Well, SiniStar's launching a new show, a spin-off of *The Dating Game*.'

A new show! Mattie's heart-rate quickened. Was he here to ask her to drum up some crew? Maybe she could pay her rent this month if she upped her usual commission?

'I'm pretty busy but I might be able to help you with your recruitment needs. Of course, it will take some time to put together a list but I should be able to have it to you by tomorrow. If you're lucky,' she added.

Nate held up his hands. 'No, no.' Beads of sweat were forming on his broad forehead. Mattie watched one burst and run down the side of his face. 'We don't need you to do the recruitment.'

Her heart plunged. 'Why are you here, then?' This better not be some joke courtesy of Stuart.

'We want you to be on the show,' Nate said.

Mattie stared. Was he on drugs?

'You're the perfect package.' Nate's voice was shaking and Mattie looked at him closely. Maybe he *was* on drugs – that might explain the bloating.

'You have a great look for television, a strong persona and I've no doubt men find you attractive.'

She rolled her eyes.

'Think how good it would be for your business,' Nate said quickly. 'You could raise your company's profile in the media. You could show how well you understand the needs of your clients, because you've actually been on a game show. Not to mention the prize money.'

Mattie's ears perked up at that. 'Prize money? How much?' She couldn't believe SiniStar wanted her on a dating show. Obviously they had no idea what her track record was like. But if there was money to be made, she wasn't about to inform them of her love 'em and leave 'em past.

'Let me tell you what's involved first.'

'Go on.'

Nate quickly explained the format. 'And if you stick it out to the end, there's two hundred thousand pounds waiting for you.'

Her mouth dropped open at the sum but she snapped it shut. Two hundred thousand pounds! That would cover all her debts and leave some for savings. She'd finally be back in the black! And the time away from work wouldn't matter much. She looked out at the empty reception. It wasn't like she was in demand, was it?

Sure, she'd have to deal with cameras and the media but that wouldn't be a problem. She was a natural performer. Whenever they had the Christmas pantomime in primary school, she'd always got the lead role. Except for that one year when the new Head refused to take her mother's 'contribution'. Mattie sniffed, remembering how she'd been relegated to wearing a hideously striped tea towel on her head. Her mum had reacted by calmly stating the Head was a chauvinist – Jesus could have been a female, after all – then getting him transferred elsewhere.

Bringing herself back to the present, Mattie decided all would be fine if she just stayed in control and didn't let down her guard. She'd caught a few glimpses of *Big Brother* and it always amazed her how people behaved, knowing a camera was watching them. Burping, kissing . . . sex in some festering hot tub. She shuddered. No, she'd behave as she always did: professional and businesslike. And Nate was right. It was a great opportunity for her to promote her company, too. All in all, it was a win-win situation.

'Well, what do you think?'

God, the man was almost quivering in anticipation of her answer.

She looked straight into his Play-Doh face and smiled. 'Where do I sign?'

*

Nate scuttled out of the office and around the corner to the nearest pub for a drink to calm his nerves. Mattie scared the shit out of him, if he was being honest. Her mocking eyes and dismissive tone reminded Nate of his Granny Edith, who was forever grabbing handfuls of his puppy fat and cackling.

Still, he couldn't believe it'd been so easy to convince Mattie to go on the show. Maybe he was smoother than he thought – or she was in bigger trouble than he'd heard. She couldn't be yanking his chain, could she? What if she didn't sign? No, she was desperate. Desperate people did anything for money, didn't they? He took a deep breath and wiped his face, letting the built-up tension from the day drain away.

Well done, Nate-o, he said to himself, sipping his pint. The business angle had definitely been the right way to get her hooked. He just hoped she wouldn't walk when she found out who the other contestants were. But Mattie could handle herself, he was sure, and if she really did need the money then she'd stick it out. And how cool would it be if she actually ended up with one of her exes when the show was over!

Nate downed his pint then headed back to the office, feeling like he'd just scored the winning goal at a World Cup football final.

Womanising sleazebag extraordinaire Baz Jonson clapped him on the back as he crossed SiniStar's foyer towards the lift.

'Hey, mate. Long time no see!'

Baz's hair was gelled so high it added a good three inches to his height and his crisp white shirt made Nate feel like a bum with his in-need-of-a-wash tee and jeans.

Nate checked behind to make sure Baz actually was talking to him and not some director or hot-shot producer. Nate had worked with Baz for almost a year before Baz got promoted to *Naked or Not*, but Baz had never even so much as sneezed in his direction.

'Hiya, Baz. All right?' Nate tried to sound casual.

'Good, mate, good. Listen, a group of us are going out for drinks tonight. Movida.' Baz winked. 'Top totty. You in?'

Despite the uneasy feeling Baz was setting him up, Nate didn't hesitate. 'Sure, Baz. Sounds good.' Well, why not? He hadn't been out clubbing for ages, plus he had something to celebrate now, didn't he?

'Cool. See you there around nine.' Baz waved and strode confidently from the building, his gelled hair defying the wind tunnel outside.

Nate drifted into the lift, wearing a goofy grin. Baz wanted to hang with *him*? Obviously word was out about Nate's new show. He looked in the mirrored panel and ran his fingers through his hair, fixing it like Baz's. No. Ugh, he looked more like a giant turnip with an Afro than a hip media type. Maybe it was time for a fresh image – something more befitting his great new job.

First chance he got he'd hit the shops and get himself all geared up for his future.

Who knows, he might even pull a girl!

Or two.

*

The minute Nate was out the door, Mattie pounced on the contract he'd left behind. First things first: the money. She turned the pages, looking for the pound sign. There it was, two hundred thousand pounds, the juicy prize in all its glory.

Leaning back in her chair, she stared at the number. Sure, there'd been years when she'd made a whole lot more than that – in fact, the business often raked in that amount in one quarter. But right now, two hundred thousand pounds would be her saviour.

Skimming the fine print, she began looking for catches. Production companies could be notoriously cheap, she knew that from dealing with them on behalf of her clients. But they'd never been able to talk her down, Mattie thought victoriously. That's why people kept coming to her. Or used to, anyway.

Now it seemed they preferred Kyle's soft touch.

Bastard.

Whoa! Her eyes flicked from the prize money to the section below. What the hell was this?

Please list, in chronological order, the names and dates of any previous relationships.

Screw that. There was no way she was divulging that information to God knows who. Like she could remember all the names, anyway!

She left the section blank and scanned the remaining pages. Health and safety, rules and regulations, blah blah blah. As long as the prize money was in the bag, she could deal with everything else. She signed and dated where indicated, bundled a copy of the document into a courier bag and sent it off.

Done. She looked around the empty office and took a deep breath. The business and her reputation would remain intact; no one would be able to say Kyle had ruined her. Just thinking of the rumours that circulated after the incident with Kyle made her clench her fists again.

Bastard!

She stretched out her fingers and tried to relax.

All she needed was to get through the next few weeks, collect her two hundred grand and life would return to normal.

CHAPTER FIVE

The average British woman has twenty sexual partners in a lifetime; the average British male, ten.

NATE STRUGGLED INTO THE OFFICE the next day just in time for his eight a.m. meeting with Silver. After a stellar night with Baz and the blokes, his head ached and his tongue felt furry. The hang-over was more than worth it, though. It'd been bloody brilliant.

Determined to measure up to Baz, before hitting the club Nate had made a beeline to Firetrap for some cool new threads, forcing himself not to think about the equivalent hoard he could net at the trusty Marks & Spencer outlet he frequented. Kitted out in a trendy shirt and loose fitting jeans, he'd popped into Punkz for a trim. His usual number three buzz didn't seem to be an option, so he just sat back and let the butch red-haired woman – more like a dominatrix than a hairdresser – take charge. He emerged with something which to him looked like he'd just got out of the shower but which made everyone else in the salon nod approvingly.

He got to Movida early and downed a few shots to ease his nerves. Then Baz showed up, told a cluster of hot girls he could get them work on reality shows and the girls were all over them – even buying *him* drinks! Nate left the club buzzing and happy, clutching a handful of mobile numbers.

Now it was back to work, and his new career.

Almost skipping, he appeared in front of Ginny.

'Go on in,' she said, not even looking at him.

Self-assuredly he pushed through the glass doors of Silver's inner sanctum.

Silver was attached to her BlackBerry and waved him into a chair. Was that Mattie's signed contract on top of the pile on her desk, just next to the half-eaten cocktail sausage? Nate's lips lifted in a smile. *This* was it, surely. The moment he became an executive producer. He leaned forward in anticipation.

'We have a problem, Nate.' Silver fixed her steely eyes on his.

Nate blinked. That wasn't what she was supposed to say. 'A problem?' he croaked. 'Didn't she sign?'

'See for yourself.' She threw the papers at him.

He reached to grab them but missed and they fluttered to the floor. Nate bent down to retrieve them, already feeling damp patches spreading under his arms. Turning to the last page, he saw Mattie's signature, scrawled so determinately it almost tore the paper.

'But she signed,' he said, looking up at Silver and wondering what was wrong.

'Sure, she signed all right. Well done.' Silver's mouth twisted around the words. 'But she didn't fill in the most important bit!'

Nate was confused. 'The most important bit?'

'The men!' Silver hissed. Spit and a fleck of sausage flew from her mouth and lay glistening on the glass desk. 'She didn't complete the part on her ex-boyfriends. Without that, how are we supposed to do the show, Nate? Tell me that. TELL ME!'

'I'll sort it out,' Nate mumbled, his eyes moving back and forth across her face as if the answer was written there. 'I'll talk to her. Right now.'

Silver grimaced. 'That's just the problem. You can't

talk to her about it, can you, Nate? If she gets any whiff of interest in her exes, we could blow it.'

'I'll come up with something,' Nate babbled, his mind desperately trying to formulate a plan.

'We don't have time for you to monkey around.' Silver locked onto his glasses with distaste. 'X-ACT has already started selling advertising slots for the show. As EP – and believe me, if you want to stay one – you'd better find out who those men are, asap.'

Nate nodded. EP! *Executive producer!* He'd done it!

He sat up straight, a broad grin stretching across his equally broad features.

'I don't know what the hell you're smiling about. Just track down her exes. And she'd better have a long list to choose from. The audience needs to care, to invest in these men as much as they do Mattie. If they're all duds like you – if there's no chemistry – forget it.'

'Oh, she has plenty of exes. Don't worry about that.' And by the sounds of things, the difficulty would be narrowing down the list.

Silver rustled around in her desk drawer. 'Here.' She handed Nate a business card. 'Ring him up and tell him I told you to call. He'll help.'

Nate stared at the card. *Harry Horne, Private Investigator. Because ignorance isn't bliss.* Was Silver for real? Nate hadn't thought anyone other than jealous TV housewives used PIs. Especially ones called Horne.

'Go get those men. And if any of them need a little extra – shall we say, *incentive* – to come on the show, tell them they'll get half Mattie's prize money. If she chooses them, of course, and if they stick out the two weeks together until the end.'

'Half the two hundred thousand? But I already told Mattie she'd get the money. And the contract says–'

'The contract says she only gets half the money.

Didn't you read it?' Silver bared her teeth in a smile. 'It's all in the fine print, Nate, in the Health and Safety part. Nobody reads that shit.' Silver grabbed the contract and flipped to that section. 'See?' She pointed to a clause and handed it back.

Nate squinted. Yes, there it was, right underneath the bit about the mandatory pre-show psychological assessment:

In relation to the financial reward, the Contestant shall forfeit half the total amount to the winning Male Contestant to ensure his continuing mental and physical wellbeing.

Wow. Nate never would have thought to read the Health and Safety section for information on the prize money. Obviously Mattie hadn't either.

'The network and I agreed there needed to be a bit more *punch* to the concept. This isn't kids' TV any more.' Silver looked at him closely. 'If you can't handle it, you should go back to La La Land.'

Nate held up chubby hands in protest. 'No, no, it's fine. Great idea!' As executive producer he'd get behind it one-hundred and ten per cent, even though his gut was feeling a bit queasy. He probably just needed to eat breakfast. Or another breakfast, anyway.

'Now go get those men. I need them signed up by Friday. And don't let me down.'

'Friday?' Nate stared. That was only two days away!

'Friday, are you deaf?'

'No Silver, yes Silver, consider it done.'

There was a pause.

'Then get the hell out of my office and do it!'

Nate rose and scurried from the room. Two days! This Harry Horne bloke better work fast.

*

'Oh my God.' Jess's eyes bulged out of her head. 'You're not?'

Mattie nodded and eyed the buzzing crowd at Boheme. Leaning back on the leather banquette, she sipped at her whisky, letting the smoky smoothness burn her throat.

'Why is it so hard to believe?' She raised her eyebrows, enjoying Jess's reaction.

Jess continued staring. 'You. YOU! On a dating show! How on Earth did that happen?'

Mattie shrugged. 'The producer just said I had everything they were looking for. Charisma, good looks, the sort of things TV stars have. I couldn't argue with that, could I?' She winked at a nerdy guy in brown polyester who was attempting to squeeze in beside them on the banquette. He flushed and gave her a small nod in return. 'See?' she said to Jess.

Jess snorted and shifted to make room for the man, who was busying himself with the menu and desperately trying not to make eye contact. 'I think you scared him. Do they know you've gone through more men than there are in, I dunno, Scotland?'

'Come on, Jess. More like Ireland. Give me some credit.' Mattie grinned. There was nothing shameful about dating lots of men. Anyway, it wasn't her fault if they always turned out to be such morons.

'I bet you can't even remember half of them!' Her friend shook her head and sipped a lychee martini.

'Too right!' Mattie laughed. 'Funny, the game show contract asked me that too. They wanted to know all the names of my exes for, like, ever! As if!'

'I hope you didn't try to write a list!' Jess dropped her eyes. 'It might make you look a bit, well . . .'

'What?' Mattie gave Jess a challenging look. So what if she'd had a lot of short term – okay, miniscule term – relationships. It didn't mean there was anything wrong with *her*! All it meant was there were loads of idiot men roaming about.

'Unstable,' Jess said finally. 'Like you can't commit. And it's a dating show, right? They'll want to know you're at least *open* to a relationship.'

'I am open to a relationship.' Mattie jerked the glass to her lips. 'It's not my fault all those losers had something wrong with them. And what about Kyle? I was going to commit for life. He screwed it up, remember? Fucking *Chloe Collins*.' Her mouth twisted. She'd never forget that blonde bimbo's name.

It was hard not to give in to the hurt and anger. Kyle was the one man Mattie had been with longer than a month – they'd lasted two years. He was the only man who made her feel comfortable; the only man she knew would never interfere with her ambition because he had it too. Together, in business and life, they were unstoppable.

Until he cheated on her.

Staring hard at a watermark staining the table, she couldn't stop her mind from flipping back to the moment when she had walked unannounced into Kyle's office to find him throwing himself at Chloe on his sofa.

Kyle had argued over and over again he hadn't done anything; that Chloe had pounced on him. But Mattie knew better than to believe that load of tosh.

Never trust them, her mum always said. *Look at your father. Would a man who really loved his family bankrupt us for his own selfish dream?* And Mum had been right – her father hadn't loved them, running off soon after declaring bankruptcy.

Mattie had been smart to get rid of Kyle.

'Anyway, I can remember most of them,' Mattie answered, trying to push Kyle out of mind.

The ruddy-faced bloke beside them leaned in closer. God, was he listening?

'Can I help you?' Mattie asked, loudly. He blushed an unfortunate shade of purple and turned away. 'Loser!' she muttered.

'Yeah, there are the major ones, like Adam, from secondary school.' Jess shook her head sorrowfully and Mattie rolled her eyes. Jess really needed to get over feeling so guilty about that whole thing. Sure, she'd encouraged Adam to ask Mattie out, for some inane reason only Jess knew, but she hadn't known it would end so badly.

'And Charlie, of course,' Jess continued. 'Disaster. Then didn't you have sex with some bloke in his student digs at UCL?' Jess wrinkled her brow. 'I remember something about *Star Wars* . . .'

Mattie grimaced as the memory flooded back. Determined to exorcise the prom trauma caused by gay Charlie and his Korean-kissing ways, the second she got her hands on some birth control pills, she was on the hunt for a man to 'dominate her womanhood', as her mother so romantically phrased it. Her first week at university, she and Jim had forged a bond over putrid vodka jelly shots in the student pub. They'd gone back to his room, where he'd huffed and puffed his way into her as she stared up at his *Star Wars* poster.

'His name was Jim,' Mattie said, impressed by Jess's memory. Then again, it wasn't like Jess had a long list of her own to remember. Poor girl had only had two or three serious relationships since secondary school, usually with strays she'd adopt for a few weeks and clean up as pet projects. After a time under Jess's wing, the men would take off when the first fake-tanned bleached blonde cocked her finger.

'Jim, right, and then there was that super-hot guy. The one with the really big feet.' Jess smirked.

'Duncan.' Dumb as a doornail but he'd still been great sex.

Jess laughed. 'Ah yes, Duncan. Hard to forget that one. But what about after university?'

Mattie thought back, rattling off a dozen or so names of men she'd seen pre-Kyle. Now for the post-Kyle bit. There'd been the foreign fling – what was his name? Giancarlo or Giovanni – on her trip to Italy right after the whole Kyle thing. And then Sean, Kirby, Stuart, of course . . .

'And I think that's it,' Mattie said finally, draining her whisky. 'See? I can remember after all!' The man sitting beside them got up and pushed past, knocking the table with his leg.

Jess laughed as she mopped up the drops of spilled drink. 'See, you *did* scare him, with your long and distinguished list!'

'Well, at least I'm not boring!' Mattie shot back.

Jess flushed and looked away. Oh shit. Mattie reached out and touched Jess's hand. 'Sorry – you know I didn't mean you.' Although really, she did. Jess had about as much excitement nooky-wise as a bed-ridden pensioner.

'That's okay, I know you didn't.'

Whatever. The past didn't matter. It was the future that counted. And right now Mattie's future held two hundred thousand pounds, financial freedom and a newly successful business.

What more did she need?

CHAPTER SIX

Two in ten admit to feigning a sexually transmitted infection to escape unwanted sexual advances.

'HELLO? ANYONE HERE?' NATE'S TIMID voice floated through Mattie's empty reception.

'Shit,' Mattie muttered, looking up from GetToned's bill for photocopier toner. She shoved it into the drawer and pulled out her Gucci compact, dabbing at the bags under her eyes. What the hell was Mr Potato Head doing here? She slicked on some crimson lipstick, trying to inject a bit of colour into her face. If he saw her looking like death warmed over, he might have second thoughts about the show – and there was no way she was going to let that happen.

'Come in!' she yelled, not moving from her chair.

'Hello,' Nate said in a deep voice. His voice cracked and Mattie couldn't help sniggering. Something about his round face and comical specs made him difficult to take seriously.

Nate sat down gingerly on the chair opposite her desk. 'All set for this afternoon?'

Mattie tried to keep her face neutral as her brain rushed through her schedule. 'This afternoon?'

'Yes, the psychological assessment? The details were all outlined in the contract.' He brandished a copy at her.

Aw, Christ, Mattie groaned. The last thing she needed was some Freudian obsessive trying to pull her apart, telling her she needed a father figure in her life. Still, if it had to be done for the show then she didn't have much choice – not that she was going to let Nate off easily.

'I'm busy.' Mattie went back to her laptop and started drafting an email to – she scanned the empty inbox – herself.

Nate fidgeted, the chair creaking under his weight. Mattie waited him out, sure he (or the chair) would crack. 'Um, it needs to be today,' he squeaked. 'Before we finalise your participation, we just need to make sure you're psychologically fit.'

Mattie rolled her eyes. 'I'm not going to have a meltdown because of a stupid dating game show, you know.'

'My boss says you have to do it.' Nate cleared his throat. 'I mean, as executive producer, I'm afraid I have to insist.'

Mattie snorted at his pathetic attempt to look powerful. 'Okay, okay.'

Nate handed her the address and name of the psychologist and fled. Mattie watched his flabby rear wobble its way out of her office, then sank back into her chair and scanned the paper. What kind of a quack had a name like Dr Wheestle? Sounded made up. By a two year old.

The stack of unopened bills on her desk reminded her it was imperative she did well at this psycho appointment. Obviously she could pass any mental-health assessment with flying colours. But what if they delved into her dating history? Could having too many failed relationships hurt her chances on the show? And would a silly psychologist somehow think the reason she couldn't find a man had something to do with *her*? God, what if he recommended the show find someone else? Someone more like, well, Jess.

Mattie swivelled to look in the full-length mirror she'd installed behind the door. That morning, she'd thrown on one of her many black trouser suits along with pointy knee-high Kurt Geiger patent leather boots. She could only imagine how a psychologist would judge her: aggressive, man-hating, pushy . . . she'd heard it all before from the men she dumped. Her mum always told her to take it as a compliment; that men just didn't know how to deal with powerful women.

But she didn't want to turn off the show producers. She had to look and behave in a softer fashion; feminine. More 1950s housewife than twenty-first century ball-breaker.

She didn't have time to change her suit, but the boots . . . She scrounged beneath her desk for a pair of French Sole ballet flats she remembered kicking under there, way back when she and Kyle were still together. Brushing the dust off them, she tried not to think about when she'd last worn them.

Memories of her and Kyle, laughing as they crunched across the gravelled pathways of Blenheim Palace, flooded her head. They'd gone there for lunch one Saturday and ended up spending the day, wandering through the grounds and lounging on the lawn. It had been sunny and perfect. Mattie shoved the images out of her mind and flung off a boot with anger, then jammed a foot into the unfamiliar flats.

She looked in the mirror, already missing the extra two inches the boots provided – whenever possible she liked to ensure she was looking down on men. Nothing could be done about the severe black suit, but she scrubbed off her crimson lipstick and put on some clear gloss, then puffed up her poker-straight bob so it floated softly around her face.

There.

Not her usual eat-you-alive appearance. She could pull it off for an afternoon, anyway.

The cab pulled away from Mattie's office on the short journey to Harley Street.

'What's the number again, love?' The cabbie smiled at her in the mirror.

Mattie almost responded with her customary snap. But the sooner she got in her demure role, the better. 'Seventy-seven,' she said pleasantly. 'Between New Cavendish and Weymouth.'

'Oh, right. Sorry – me old ears are going.' He tapped the side of his head.

'No problem,' Mattie replied, noticing she was smiling back at him. God, she'd have to watch it. Her mother always said there was nothing wrong with being nice to men – if you wanted to let them walk all over you.

'Here we are.' Ten minutes or so later the driver stopped in front of a brick townhouse. Mattie handed over some money and climbed out. Stupid shoes, she grumbled as her arches protested the change of footwear by sending shooting pains up her calves. She ignored the pain and mounted the steps.

Inside, the snooty receptionist barely looked up. 'Name?'

'Mattie Johns.' Mattie smiled sweetly but the receptionist remained po-faced.

'Matilda Johns? Oh yes. Sit down,' she grunted, pointing to a chair.

Mattie's cheeks flamed at the sound of her full name. No one – not even Jess – knew her name was Matilda. She only used it in legal documents like the show contract, where she had no choice. Gritting her teeth, she thought for the thousandth time how much she wanted to kill her mother for forcing 'a strong and unyielding' name like Matilda on her. Matilda!

Mattie plastered a smile on her face to cover her embarrassment and sauntered over to a lumpy leather chair, lowering herself delicately onto it. She grabbed *The Financial Times* before quickly replacing it with *The Sun,* more in keeping with her current persona. Ugh, look at the Page Three model, practically hanging out of her swimming costume. How could women let themselves be exploited like that?

'Matilda Johns?' A man with a wispy coiffure and ill-fitting suit appeared. Another pathetic creature who couldn't even dress himself properly, Mattie sighed as she lowered the newspaper and fixed him with a bright, vacuous grin.

Despite the antique furniture and the oil paintings on the wall, the office he led her to was dingy and smelled of stale sweat. Mattie folded her hands in her lap, held her breath and hoped the session would be over quickly. She wasn't sure how long she could keep up the facade before internal combustion.

'So, Miss Johns,' Dr Wheestle said, opening his file. Mattie bit back the reply that she preferred 'Ms' – her marital status was no one's business but her own. 'You're here for a psychological assessment to ensure you're mentally fit to withstand the pressures of a reality dating show.'

Duh, Mattie said in her head, but she nodded demurely in response, hoping her expression conveyed wonderment at just how clever Dr Wheestle was. 'I'm very grateful for the time you're taking out of your busy schedule.' Barf, she added silently as she considered his droopy eyes, hoping she hadn't gone overboard.

Dr Wheestle just exposed his tobacco-stained teeth in a wide smile. 'My pleasure, my dear. My pleasure.'

He took out a fountain-tipped pen and a notebook. A fountain pen. How old was he? 'Why don't you begin by telling me why you want to be on this show?' He gave a long look which started at her ballet-shoe clad feet and ended up at her chest. Mattie watched incredulously as his small tongue darted out to moisten his lips.

Perv! He deserved a good swift kick to the balls – if he had any. But there was nothing she could do about it, verbal or otherwise, she reminded herself. Two hundred grand was two hundred grand. She cleared her throat.

'I just really want to meet a man I can make a life with,' she twittered. 'And I figure a dating show can find me some great men!' She inserted an excited upward inflection at the end of her sentence.

Dr Wheestle – *Weasel*, Mattie thought – tore his eyes away from her chest and scribbled some notes on the pad in front of him. 'Uh-hmm.' He patted his thinning hair and Mattie watched with disgust as he then wiped his fingers on his trousers.

'And your general relationship with men?'

Mattie stared for a second. General relationship? What a stupid question. 'I love men,' she simpered. 'They're strong, they're . . .' – she wracked her brain – 'they're, um, supportive . . .' She tried not to grimace. Those were the last words anyone could use to describe men like her father and Kyle.

Weasel tapped the file. 'It says here your father abandoned you when you were eight.'

How on Earth had he found that out? Bloody Nate, digging into her background. What a silly word, 'abandoned'. It was as if she'd been left at the side of the road or something, instead of – let's face it, better off, as her mother kept saying.

Her dad's face on the night he'd left flashed into her

mind. He'd pulled her close and hugged her so tightly it hurt. She could still smell the spicy aftershave of that embrace, even today. He'd let her go only when her mother had come into the kitchen and told him to get out; that she never wanted to see him again. And although he'd tried to get in touch through countless phone calls and letters, Mattie never had.

She shifted in her chair and tucked the ballet flats beneath her, trying to keep her face from showing the jumble of emotions swirling inside.

Finally she lifted her head. 'Yes, that's right.'

Silence filled the room and Mattie stared steadfastly at Weasel. If he wanted her to say more, he was going to have to ask.

'Well.' Weasel dropped his eyes to her chest then looked up at her. 'I think we're just about done here, Matilda.' He patted his oily hair again and smiled. Mattie tried not to recoil even further from him. 'But I'd love to talk to you some more; perhaps somewhere a bit more comfortable? Maybe over drinks tonight? Say, seven?'

What an absolute wanker! *This* was why she didn't dress like a sodding milkmaid or act like an idiot without brains. If she'd been her normal ballsy self – instead of a beaming bimbo – Weasel wouldn't have even dared look in her direction. Mattie felt her face flame with anger but she covered it up by giggling and looking down coyly.

'Really?' she said through lowered lashes. 'Me on a date, with a real doctor?' She widened her eyes, trying not to be sick as she took in the full horror of Weasel. 'I'd love to! I just have to go to the Well Woman clinic first.' She put a hand to her face, pretending to be embarrassed. 'I can tell you, I guess, since you *are* a doctor.' She met his eyes. 'Gonorrhoea,' she whispered.

Weasel jerked back as if she'd slapped him. 'Ah. Yes. Gonorrhoea. Dreadful thing.' He cleared his throat. 'You know, I just remembered I have a lecture to go to tonight. So another time . . .' Before Mattie could reply, he stood up. 'Thank you for coming in, Matilda. I'll contact the producers today to tell them you're fit for the show.'

Grinning at his shocked reaction, Mattie forced herself to hold out her hand. 'Thank *you* so much.'

Weasel shook it quickly and she turned to leave the office, nearly tripping over her feet in haste. Outside she gulped fresh air and shook her head.

Imagine, him having the nerve to ask her out on a date!

That's what happens when you give an inch, she reminded herself grimly.

A man will take about forty-five miles.

CHAPTER SEVEN

*One in twenty relationships ends with a restraining order;
one in two-hundred thousand ends in murder.*

AS HE WAITED FOR SILVER to deign to see him, Nate stared at the list of Mattie's exes that Harry Horne, the private investigator, had given him. The list was long – it had about forty names on it – but with such a short timeline, Harry had only been able to provide contact details for four of the men.

There was a guy called Adam Higgins, CEO of some gaming software company, who lived on the outskirts of London; Charlie Robbins, a British ex-pat in Ibiza; an Italian named Giovanni Costa (bit of foreign blood was good, mix it up a bit); and finally Kyle Cook, the man who'd apparently taken half of Mattie's clients.

Nate wiped the sweat forming on his brow. Was he supposed to just ring them up out of the blue and ask them to go on a game show? What if they said no? Thank God Silver had buried half of Mattie's prize money in the contract as an incentive.

'She says go in,' Ginny snapped, pointing at the door.

'Er, yes, thanks.'

He had barely made it inside before Silver swooped. 'Give me an update.'

'It's going great.' Nate tried to sound more confident than he felt. 'I've got a list of names here. Just about to contact them.'

Silver grabbed the list. 'Looks to me like you only have four real possibilities. I thought you said there would be loads of men to choose from.'

'We only have contact info for the four. But there are plenty of men, look at the list! If we had more time—'

'Well, we don't *have* time, do we?' Silver interrupted. 'Get on the phone. Now! Get those men signed up. Any less than four and the format's not going to work. You'd better hope they all want to do it.'

'I'm sure it will be fine,' Nate said, pulling his face away from Silver's menacing finger. A bead of sweat rolled down his cheek and he grabbed his BlackBerry.

'One more thing,' Silver said before he started dialling. 'You need to arrange a promo shoot for Mattie. You have talked to a photographer, right? Get her styled up, throw some pics to the media. Asap, Nate. And make her sexy. Make her someone men would *want* to go out with. Remember, these are the photos we're using to sell the show to the public. And sex sells.'

'Of course, asap,' Nate echoed lamely.

'Well, get out then,' Silver ordered, patting the pile of papers on her desk, looking for leftover cocktail sausages.

Nate scurried away and headed for his cubicle, checking the time, panic rising. Christ, he hadn't even booked the studio or the stylists for the promo – or told Mattie, for that matter. He cringed, thinking of her reaction. How was he supposed to do all this stuff at once? On *Jungle Jangle* the most stressful item had been booking the guest animal for the next day!

He took a deep breath. Calm down, Nate-o. This was what EPs did, juggle balls in the air. First things first, call the men. Then get onto the promo.

Nate considered the list. Who to start with? Italians were supposed to be friendly, right? And maybe this

Giovanni bloke fancied a trip to England. He punched in the numbers and listened to the foreign ring of the phone.

'*Pronto*! Villa Costa.'

Villa Costa? Was Giovanni some kind of Italian royalty? 'Um, *hola*,' Nate stammered, before remembering *hola* was Spanish, not Italian.

'You wish to book? Make-a de reservation?'

Ah, it was a hotel. Thank God they spoke English. 'I'm looking for Giovanni Costa,' Nate said.

'*Si, sono* Giovanni Costa. I am he. How can I help?'

Nate explained why he was calling as fast as possible before Giovanni could think to interrupt him.

'You want me to be on the television programme? In *Londra*?'

'Yes, exactly.'

A long pause, then: '*Si*! No problem!'

Nate's eyebrows flew up. That was easy. Had Giovanni understood what was going on? Did he even remember Mattie?

'I will send you my portfolio,' Giovanni was babbling. 'You want da nude?'

'Nude?'

'*Si*, how you say, fulla frontal? I send.'

'No, no.' Nate made a face. That was the last thing he wanted. 'It's a dating show, you know, with women.'

'You want I make sexy film with woman?'

Nate gave up. As long as the guy turned up, any misunderstanding could be sorted out later.

'Yes, sort of. Listen, do you have a fax? Good. I'll fax you the contract. Just sign it and send it back, along with a photo or two. With clothes,' he added. 'We'll be in touch with all the details.'

'*Si, buona, fantastico*!' He could almost imagine Giovanni kissing his fingers like a fat chef in a spaghetti advert.

Nate hung up. There. That wasn't so hard. One down, three to go!

*

Back in her office, the shrill ring of the phone jolted Mattie from her catnap, head snapping up as she jerked awake. Jesus, dealing with Weasel and his moronic questions must have really taken it out of her. Fury snapped inside as the memory of that greasy-haired slime-bag asking her out came to mind.

'Yes?' she barked into the BlackBerry, before remembering it could be a much-needed client. 'How can I help?' she added in a softer tone.

She listened incredulously as a timid voice squeaked out she'd been scheduled to do a photo shoot tomorrow, somewhere in godforsaken Shoreditch. Shoreditch! She'd expected Notting Hill, at the very least. Who knew what she'd catch all the way over in grimy East London? No wonder Nate had got some lackey to do his dirty work, telling her about the session.

'What kind of photo shoot?' she asked, hoping Nate wouldn't be pulling double-duty as a stylist. His ideal woman probably looked more gorilla than human.

'Just some head shots for the media,' the voice said. 'A car will pick you up at two p.m. tomorrow.'

Mattie clenched her teeth. 'Great. I'll be ready.' If Nate thought he was in control, he had another think coming. She'd show him who really called the shots.

*

It was almost five and Nate's day had been brilliant. After Giovanni, he'd rung Charlie Robbins in Ibiza. Nate had asked him question after question about his relationship with Mattie, but all Charlie said was he couldn't wait to catch up with Mattie again after all these years. One mention of the potential prize money and Charlie was immediately on board – babbling non-stop about his plans to open a spa back in Ibiza.

Nate couldn't believe how easy the first two had been. Amazing how strong the lure of the television was for some people . . . and maybe, just maybe, the two of them really wanted a second chance with Mattie. Well, Charlie, anyway. Nate still wasn't sure if Giovanni even understood Mattie was involved.

Adam had been a bit more difficult. No, not difficult exactly, just *creepy*. Nate had paid a visit to Snake Software, Adam's company headquarters in Staines. It was like walking into a video game. Everything was gleaming white and chrome; employees darted around wearing headsets. Nate had noticed several cameras tracking him as he crossed the vast lobby.

Dwarfed by his massive steel desk, Adam was a younger, larger version of the Wiz, running the whole company through a bank of monitors and mics. With his jet-black hair and pale skin he looked as if he'd never seen the light of day, like some sort of pudgy vampire.

Even though Nate was pretty sure it was a lost cause, he quickly explained the show's concept. Why would Adam go on a dating show when he was clearly such a success, work wise? Sure, he wasn't the best-looking guy, but Nate imagined his loads of cash attracted all sorts of girls. Women always liked rich successful men, didn't they? Nate grinned. He'd know that feeling soon enough.

But Adam had listened calmly, nodded his agreement and scrawled his signature on the contract within minutes. No smile, no grimace, no expression had crossed his face or entered his voice the whole time Nate had been there. He'd been downright robotic – even Stephen Hawking's voice simulator sounded more human! Nate couldn't figure out why the hell Adam would even *consider* going on a dating game show, but he wasn't about to argue.

So with Adam signed up, Nate was on his way to Charlotte Street to meet the last man: Kyle. Of the four, Kyle was the one Nate was most worried about. From all accounts, Kyle's business was flourishing and whatever had actually happened with Mattie, chances were if you angered her you'd be lucky to escape with your testicles intact. But you never know, Nate thought, trying to be optimistic; he hadn't bet on Adam signing on either, and he had.

Ringing the buzzer for Kyle Cook Recruitment, Nate waited for the door to click open. Entering the reception, he was struck by how different it was to Mattie's barren lair. Every chair here was filled, and two receptionists were passing around what appeared to be forms for various candidates to fill out. Comfortable-looking sofas lined the far wall, the inviting smell of fresh coffee drifted through the air, and the soft sounds of lounge music came from speakers in the ceiling. It was more like a coffee shop than a recruitment office. No wonder people preferred this to Mattie's torture chamber.

'I'm here to see Kyle?' Nate said to the receptionist. He had to admit he was curious to meet any man who could bear Mattie Johns for more than five minutes. The guy must have balls of steel!

'Nate.' Kyle was out of his office before Nate even had a chance to sit down. They shook hands. 'Come on through.'

Nate settled into a roomy leather chair and nodded his thanks as Kyle handed him a glass of water. Tall and blond, he was definitely good-looking, but Nate wouldn't have pegged him as Mattie's type.

The guy seemed too *nice*.

'So you said on the phone you have some kind of business proposition for me?' Kyle asked.

Nate nodded. He'd decided to use the same pitch he had with Mattie, and he launched into it full force. Kyle listened quietly, his eyebrows flying up as Nate explained the show format.

'Mattie agreed to this?' Kyle asked.

Nate cleared his throat. 'Yes.' He wasn't about to tell Kyle that Mattie didn't know about the exes.

'Hmm. That's interesting.' Something like hope flickered across Kyle's face. 'I don't know what she told you, but I never cheated on her, you know. We were going through a sort of difficult patch, yes, but I never cheated.'

Nate stayed silent. A difficult patch? Nate couldn't even imagine. He wouldn't blame Kyle if he *had* cheated on Mattie.

'I tried to tell her, but she just wouldn't listen.' Kyle looked up at Nate. 'I know she seems tough, but underneath it all, she's actually really vulnerable.'

Nate nodded and tried to keep his poker face. Mattie, vulnerable? Yeah, right. The same way grizzly bears were vulnerable. He'd noticed something in the PI's report about Mattie's father taking off, but from what Nate had seen, it hadn't made her vulnerable. Quite the opposite.

'But maybe now she'll listen.' Kyle sighed. 'If I go on the show, I might just be able to convince her I still care.'

Nate held his breath.

'So yeah.' Kyle stuck out a hand. 'Count me in.'

'Great.' Nate tried to keep the jubilant grin off his face as he took Kyle's palm. He'd done it! All four were signed up!

Thank God. He didn't even want to think what

Silver's reaction might have been if one of them said no.

Nat pushed the contract towards Kyle. 'Just sign here.'

*

Back home in his luxury flat, Adam made a beeline for the safe under his bed. He quickly punched in the code – MATTIE – and drew out his graduation yearbook, turning the pages to Mattie's photo. He'd fingered it so much that most of the colour had worn off and the paper was tissue thin.

Oh, Mattie. Twelve years had passed, and she was the only woman he had ever asked out, the only woman he had dated. And she was still the only woman he wanted.

For the one week in Year Ten they were together, Adam was walking on air. He loved fetching Mattie's books, queuing up for her food at lunch and doing her homework – in short, he loved making her happy.

Then she dumped him, without warning or reason. He begged her to take him back, saying he loved her. To prove it, he hacked into the school's computer system so all the screen savers in the IT labs said *Adam loves Mattie*, with a cute Photoshopped picture of Mattie in a bikini. He'd even managed to splice together their photos so it looked like their lips were touching, with a colourful sunset behind them. The height of romance, he thought.

But she'd just laughed, saying she'd never kiss a boring, spineless blob like him; that she'd only gone out with him to have a servant do her bidding. Adam had run out of the school and hidden behind the skip where... He shook his head, still unable to believe he'd actually started howling uncontrollably. Thank God

Mattie's friend Jess was the only person to witness it.

That last year of secondary school was spent downing Jaffa Cakes. As his weight ballooned, he waited, just waited, for her to notice him again. But she never had.

He flipped over to his photo. There he was, Adam 'Stumpy' Higgins, in all his adolescent glory: raging acne, excess flab and hair that never could achieve the much-coveted bed-head look no matter how hard he tried. No wonder Mattie wouldn't take him back again.

In the past ten years he'd worked hard to be a success, throwing himself into developing video games. People loved the hero he created for his games – a thinner, more handsome version of himself. His hero got the heroine in the end, despite the obstacles.

Funny that the heroine always ended up looking like Mattie. It wasn't a conscious act, but whatever he did, Mattie was on his mind. Sometimes, he even found himself driving by her flat or hanging out in the off-licence down the street just so he could snap a shot of her.

Adam hadn't been able to believe his luck when Nate showed up. He'd had to work hard to wipe every trace of excitement and emotion off his face – to stay cool and in control, just like his video-game characters. Inside, though, his heart was pumping. This was his chance to make Mattie fall in love with him!

But how? His appearance hadn't radically altered since she had last seen him. The word 'blobby' still sent a pang through his heart. Come on, he told himself sternly. You run a multi-million pound business. Losing a bit of weight isn't beyond you. Winning Mattie back wasn't out of the question. After all, he had the money – now he just needed the looks.

Filled with determination, he walked over to his

kitchen and, taking a deep breath, methodically dumped packet after packet of Jaffa Cakes into the bin. From now until the show began, he'd have nothing but vitamin shakes. And he'd get a personal trainer for twice-daily sessions. That should help him get fit quickly.

He examined his face in the mirror, grimacing at pock-mark legacies of the acne that erupted after Mattie dumped him. Racing back to his state-of-the-art laptop, he Googled furiously until he found a solution: a few chemical peels should do the trick. Plus he could smooth the perma-scowl that had developed on his forehead with a bit of Botox while he was at it.

Finally at peace, Adam smiled. If he played this right, the audience couldn't help but choose him to spend those two weeks alone with Mattie.

And then – finally – Mattie would be his.

CHAPTER EIGHT

The average woman spends sixty minutes primping for a date.
The average male, ten.

'WATCH IT!' MATTIE YELPED AS a dollop of red splashed her cheek. Her head was pounding and the cloying smell of the hair dye wasn't helping.

She was *so* not in the mood for this. The useless pipsqueak who'd rung her yesterday had neglected to mention that before the photo shoot, she'd be subjected to a torturous makeover by a long-haired Fabio-wannabe with a rather dodgy Italian accent. She'd tried to call Nate several times to complain but the idiot hadn't answered the phone and before she knew what was happening, Fabio had smeared her dark bob with a foul fire-engine red dye.

'Good idea, just blind me so I don't have to look at this hideous colour,' Mattie grumbled, wiping the goo from her face.

'It's fab-u-lous! You gonna look great.' Mattie stared as Fabio lobbed another lump of colour onto her head. Did she detect a hint of a Liverpool accent? Probably wasn't even Italian, she snorted. Barely human, in fact.

Just remember why you're doing this. Two hundred thousand! Two hundred thousand! It was her mantra now.

'Now we just letta sit for thirty minuti. I'll be back to check on youse.' Fabio disappeared behind a curtain in the back where she could hear – and smell – him eating some kind of fishy sandwich.

Mattie looked around the small space for something to read but the room was bare. It wasn't even a real salon – apart from the battered old chair she was perched on, there was just one basin. Surely SiniStar could have plumped for a proper hairdresser, not one who'd trained at the *Sluts R Us* academy. Only prostitutes had the colour she was going to end up with.

'How we doing, eh?' Fabio finally reappeared, poking and prodding at her hair. His breath reeked and the heavy gold medallions around his neck clunked her in the face as he leaned over.

'Great,' Mattie grunted, following him over to the basin where he doused her hair in cold water, ignoring her protests.

'Gorgeous, darlink. Gorgeous!'

Mattie rolled her eyes. The accent was morphing into Hungarian. 'Give me a mirror,' she demanded as he plonked her back in the chair again.

Fabio smiled. 'No, no. No!' He waggled a playful finger in her face. 'You're not done yet. Next – extensions. We givva you gorgeous longa hair. You gonna love it!'

'I don't want long hair,' Mattie argued. She liked her hair the way it was – short, tidy and no fuss. She hadn't had long hair since . . . well, ever. Her mother had always kept her hair short, and Mattie had pretty much maintained the same style. Bobs never went out of fashion, anyway.

'Sorry! Production says extensions, we do ex-ten-sions.' Now he sounded more French than Italian.

'I think you got your accents mixed up,' Mattie said snarkily, but Fabio had already disappeared. For the next few hours Mattie sat like a concrete block as the minions buzzed around her, braiding revolting-looking clumps of hair to her head. She was going to kill Nate. No, not kill. Torture. Lock him in a closet with no food or drink. Mattie had read somewhere that the combination of starvation and dehydration was the most painful death to endure. And Nate had enough extra flesh to last for days. At least he'd die skinny, she sniggered to herself.

'There, we done-a! Now we just do some-a make-up and you ready for your photo shoot!'

Mattie grimaced. 'Great. Thanks. Not that I had any say in the matter.'

Fabio flicked his curls back. 'Maybe this make you 'appy.' He patted her knee, blowing fishy fumes over her. 'I think this make-a you happy.'

Mattie shrugged his hand off. 'I am happy, you faux-Italian. I don't need extensions to make me happy.'

Fabio held up his hands and backed away, his rings glistening in the light. 'Yeah, you're a proper ray of sunshine, innit?' The Italian accent had disappeared, replaced by a full-on Scouse twang that rang out loudly as he shook his head. 'Make-up will be out in a second. Good luck to them.'

Idiot. How deluded to think long hair could make you happy. Anyway, she *was* happy, when she wasn't being transformed into some game show monster. True, she hadn't been in the best mood lately, but that was understandable with her business going downhill, wasn't it? Mattie strained to remember when she'd last been happy. With Kyle, yes. And before that?

As a Cyndi Lauper lookalike started smearing Mattie's face with hideous beige foundation, her mind flashed back to a time before her father had left, when she and her parents had visited Brighton. They'd mooched along the pier, gone on the rides, and got some ice cream. The sky had been so bright it had hurt her eyes and her parents hadn't argued once. Mattie could still remember skipping across the pebbled beach while her parents walked on behind her. It had been the perfect day.

Shame her father had gone and screwed it all up by quitting his job at the bank and trying to start a birdhouse business. Imagine remortgaging your own home to provide houses for birds!

'Done!' Cyndi twittered. 'Would you like to see?'

Duh. She limited her response to a curt nod.

Cyndi passed over a mirror and watched eagerly for her response.

Mattie stared at her reflection. Everything inside froze as she took in the long copper hair falling in corkscrews past her shoulders, the sparkly green eye shadow and the false eyelashes. Mattie Johns had disappeared. And in her place was some sort of clown-type creature who looked like a recent escapee from a freak show. She couldn't tear her eyes away from the horror.

'I know,' Cyndi said. 'It's crazy, right? You look amazing! The power of make-up.' She shook her head and thumped her chest. 'Gets me right here, every time.'

Mattie didn't answer. How on Earth was she going to go outside looking like a trashy burlesque dancer, let alone appear on TV in front of the whole nation!

'Aw, hon.' Cyndi patted her knee. 'It's so cool, isn't it? I mean, I saw what you looked like before. All pale, as if you were dead or something. And now you've come to life!' She reached down and hugged Mattie.

Mattie shoved her away. Why did these people keep touching her? Was everyone who worked in TV a perv? 'Can I go now?'

'Ouch!' Cyndi rubbed her arm where Mattie had rammed her. 'No, you can't go. Production needs a few promo shots.' She reached behind her and threw some clothes onto Mattie's lap, smile replaced by a scowl. 'Here. Put these on.'

Mattie's mouth fell open as she held up the skin-tight gold lamé top and PVC leggings. No. *No way!* It was bad enough that her hair screamed slut. She wasn't going to dress like one, too.

She pulled out her mobile and rang Nate again but the phone just kept ringing. If he knew what was good for him, he'd stay hidden. So much for showing him who was in control. Next time, she vowed.

Two hundred thousand pounds, she sighed as she pulled on the top and leggings – she just needed to keep that number front and centre. She hobbled over to the mirror, barely able to walk in the skin-tight black material. Every curve of her body was visible and her chest was straining to escape the top's plunging neckline. Thank God Mum was away on her annual *Mind over Soul Control* cruise. If she saw this get-up she'd disown her!

Mattie stepped into the platformed red stilettos and lurched out into the studio. To keep her business afloat, she could handle a little objectification, no sweat.

*

'Wowee! Who's that?' Baz whistled as he stared at the photos of Mattie the photographer biked over. Mattie was smiling – or her lips were, anyway; her eyes looked furious – and her chest was almost spilling out of a skin-tight gold top. Bright red hair cascaded past her shoulders and shiny black leggings revealed every contour of her body.

The promo team had done a great job, Nate thought as he looked at the photos again. She could be on cover of *GQ* – or even *Nuts*!

'Um, that's Mattie Johns. The lead contestant on *Second Chance for Romance.*' Nate loved saying the name of the show. He could hardly believe he'd come up with something so clever.

'I'll give her more than a second chance for romance,' Baz said, moving his hips back and forth in the air. 'A third, a fourth, a fifth . . .'

'Yeah, mate,' Nate said lamely, rocking his hips like Baz. 'Know what you mean.' There was no way he'd get anywhere near Mattie without donning full protective gear, but she'd be the perfect bait to the exes he'd signed up. If they'd been eager to see her before, imagine what they'd think when they saw her now. 'I've got a meeting with Silver,' he said, grabbing the photo out of the still-drooling Baz's hand. 'Catch you later.'

He ran to his desk to get the exes' signed contracts and headed towards Silver's office, rehearsing the men's names in his head.

Adam – successful CEO, Mattie's boyfriend from Staines Secondary. Kind of lumpy, not so telegenic with his pock-marked face, but he'd be good to offset Giovanni's flash appearance.

Charlie, who'd also dated Mattie in secondary school. Nate shuffled through the paperwork to the photo Charlie had sent him. He looked almost aristocratic, with his thin face and floppy sandy hair. A nice contrast to Giovanni and Adam's dark looks.

Nate flipped over to Giovanni's photo – the only one in which he was actually wearing underwear. Nate grimaced as he remembered the scene by the fax machine when Giovanni's images had come through. The woman who watered the plants had started whooping, and within seconds every female in the office had gathered around the fax, laughing and grabbing as more nude photos spilled out.

Sure, the guy was good-looking, but he barely spoke English. And it was pretty obvious he'd only signed up to the show to be on TV, not because he was interested in Mattie. But he'd signed the contract and that was all Nate cared about now. Mattie wasn't there for the men, either.

Then there was Kyle, the one bloke Nate thought was a pretty decent guy. Nate couldn't imagine him and Mattie together, but underneath Kyle's friendly exterior Nate sensed he might have the balls to take her on. Shame he'd had to mislead Kyle into thinking Mattie knew he'd be on the show. But maybe they *would* get together? Imagine the ratings! The network could cover the wedding, too, along with the birth of their first child. Nate would be a network hero. He could even start his own media production company on the back of it!

'Hi, Ginny,' Nate smiled as he walked into Silver's office. He was an EP now – surely he was entitled to more than Ginny's usually grunt. 'How are we today?' He tried one of those cool winks he'd seen Baz do but closed both eyes instead of just one.

Ginny stared, then snorted. '*I'm* fine, Nate. Don't know about you, though.'

'Could I have a glass of water?' he asked, trying again.

Ginny waved a hand in the direction of the water cooler. 'Water's over there.'

Snooty cow. She was a secretary, after all. And he was an executive producer. It wasn't like he was asking her to mine gold or something. He stared at her pointedly but she just kept clacking away on the keyboard.

Nate slumped back in his chair for a second then straightened up again. All he needed was one successful show, just one. Then the women around here would be swarming over him like he was one of Giovanni's photos.

'Nate,' Silver yelled from her office. 'You better have those signed contracts.'

Nate stood up and marched into Silver's office, clutching the contracts triumphantly. He dropped them with a flourish onto her desk. 'They're all signed up, Silver, all four, just like you asked.' He met her flinty eyes.

Silver looked down at the papers he'd plonked on her desk. 'Get those *off* my sausage.'

Sausage? Nate scrambled to remove the offending pile, uncovering a plate of what looked to be tiny chorizos. He hadn't even seen them there.

'Sorry.'

Silver popped a whole finger-shaped sausage in her mouth and swallowed without chewing. Nate watched as the lump moved slowly down her throat.

'Let me see the contracts.'

He handed them over, shifting his bulk from foot to foot as she flipped through.

'Fine, fine, yes, they're all fine. Good variety, different enough professions, and you even got a foreigner in here.' She looked up. 'Did any of them ask for more money than what we offered?'

Nate shook his head. 'I just told them they'd get half the prize money if they won and that was fine.' He still felt weird about that one – Mattie thought she'd get it all – but if that's how the game was going to be played he didn't have much choice. Anyway, it wasn't like she'd get nothing. He'd kill for a hundred thousand pounds.

Silver flipped through the pages. 'Any good potential here for conflicts? We can edit to make things interesting if we need to, of course, but it's always better if it's genuine. We need to keep the ratings up.

And the only way to do that is to make every date explosive.'

Nate stared. 'Conflicts? But the purpose of the show is to get Mattie back together with an ex. *Second Chance for Romance*, you know . . .'

Silver rolled her eyes and swallowed another sausage. 'It doesn't matter if they want romance or if they want to club her over the head! Love and hate are the best emotions for driving ratings.' She tapped her finger against her chin. 'Get these men into the psychological assessment with Wheestle, and tell him to really dig. I want dirt. I want to know everything about them. Then we can come up with some great storylines for dates.'

'Storylines?' Nate had thought Mattie and the men would just go out on dates with the cameras filming them.

'Jesus, Nate. Yes, storylines. You don't think we're just going to jolly around with a camera, do you? We need to make sure there's action. And drama. Remember, we're in control here. Mattie and that bunch of idiots are all pawns on our chessboard.' Silver shoved another whole sausage in her mouth. 'If you don't get that, I don't know what the hell you're doing here.'

*

'You can stop laughing now.' Mattie threw one of her Liberty-patterned silk cushions at Jess. It was the night before the live kick-off show, and Mattie had invited Jess over to her flat for a much needed ego-boost after her slut-tastic makeover. But Jess was having the opposite effect. One look at Mattie's new hairdo and Jess had burst into giggles.

'It's not *that* bad,' Jess said, after collapsing onto the

gleaming resin floor to catch her breath. She tilted her head to the side. 'Actually, the colour's pretty good. It's just that you don't look like *you* any more.'

'I know,' Mattie sighed. 'I don't feel like me, either. I haven't done any work all week, I've been wearing PVC leggings, and then *this*' – she tugged at a curl and made a face – 'I don't even know what to do with long hair.'

Jess scooted over and dug an elastic out of her pocket. She grabbed a handful of Mattie's extensions and quickly twisted them up into a knot, letting a few strands hang down around her face. 'There. That looks quite nice.'

Mattie walked over to the mirror above the faux-fireplace. 'Not bad.' With most of the sausage-like curls out of her face, it wasn't *quite* as dire as it had been.

'So you ready for tomorrow?' Jess asked, plopping back down on the sofa.

Mattie shrugged. 'I guess. I mean, what is there to be ready for? I meet the men and I pick the one I want the first date with. No biggie.'

'There must be more to it than that,' Jess said. 'Otherwise, they wouldn't be making such a big fuss. Haven't you seen those big billboards on the M4? It's *a new spin on dating*.' Jess lowered her voice dramatically.

'Oh Jesus.' Mattie couldn't think of anything worse than being splattered across a giant board next to a motorway. Next thing she knew she'd be on Page Three! Thank God her mother was safely out of the way in the middle of the Indian Ocean. For the amount of fuss they were making about the series, you'd have thought it was freaking *Top Boot* or whatever that silly car show was called.

'I wonder what the spin is?' Jess asked.

'I hope it's that they've found the last few intelligent

men left in the world. They definitely seem to be a rare species.' Mattie shoved the remaining tendrils of hair into the bun on top of her head.

Jess sat up. 'What if there is a really cool man there? You know – someone clever and handsome, with a good job? Maybe you can meet someone!'

'I'm not there to meet men,' Mattie said, shaking her head at her friend's naivety. 'I'm there for one thing: the money. The men can be convicts for all I care.' Maybe that was the twist – a dating game show in a prison, where she had to choose from a selection of criminals. She could just imagine it: *Date an Inmate*. Hopefully they'd kit out the cells with all the mod cons.

'Shame you're going to miss the reunion,' Jess said. 'But I guess everyone there can just watch you on TV!'

Mattie groaned as she pictured all those secondary-school losers watching her every move on the small screen, night after night. She took a deep breath. It would be fine, though. She'd go through the motions, get the money, and leave those rejects behind in the dust just like she had when she'd escaped from Staines all those years ago.

Whatever she had to deal with in the coming weeks, it would all be worth it in the end.

CHAPTER NINE

*Three in five women say wearing a new item of clothing
boosts their confidence on a first date.
Two in three men admit they rarely notice a date's attire.*

ONE HOUR LEFT UNTIL THE LIVE KICK-OFF show and Fabio's slut machine was in full gear. Mattie had entered the studio without a stitch of make-up, her hair pulled back to within an inch of its synthetic life. Minutes later and it was teased into a beehive high enough to accommodate half the Earth's insect population. Her face was slathered with so much oily make-up spots were already forming, and her eyelids struggled to support the sparkly green shadow that would make her 'eyes pop', according to her new frienemy – the teeny, tiny Cyndi Lauper lookalike from the other day.

Taking a deep breath, Mattie rubbed her shaking hands together. She wasn't nervous; she'd just had too much coffee earlier and not enough to eat. Her stomach shifted uncomfortably. She wished she'd thought more about what this 'spin' might be, rather than just brushing it off. What if they made her poledance or something equally embarrassing? Thank God Jess would be in the studio audience so there'd be one friendly face.

'Here's your wardrobe, honey.' The nasal tone of one of Fabio's minions pulled her back to the dressing room.

Mattie stared at the low-cut sequined top and

the short skirt on the rack in front of her. 'What, I can't wear this?' she asked, plucking at her best silk Aquascutum top.

The stylist snorted. 'Maybe if you were going to a make-believe tea party at Kensington Palace. This is a reality show, babe. Time to get real.'

'All set?' Nate burst into the dressing room. He stared at Mattie in horror. 'What are you wearing? You need to get dressed!'

Nate's cheeks were flushed and his hair was standing even more on end than usual, thanks to what looked to be at least half a tube of gel. He'd ditched his usual tee for a starchy green shirt, with a collar straight from the seventies. At least his jeans weren't bell bottoms. He was twitching so much Mattie almost asked him if he needed the loo.

'No.' Mattie shook her head and pointed to the clothes. Now was the time to show him just who was boss. 'I'm not set. Promo shoots are one thing, but I'm not going on national telly looking like I'm about to perform a handjob on a street corner.'

'It's not that bad. Designer stuff, check it out.' Nate held up the skirt, which was about the width of a belt, for her perusal. Mattie caught sight of a Primark tag. Designer, her arse.

'It. Is. Not. Happening.' As the star of a live show – with only minutes to the start – she'd take full advantage of her fierce bargaining power. She cocked her head and waited for Nate's meltdown to begin.

He shook his Afro violently, heavy horn-rimmed spectacles nearly flying off the end of his nose. 'No, no, no way. My boss would kill me. Please, you have to wear that.'

'I don't give a toss what happens to you, Nate,' Mattie said. Jesus, what a loser.

'Look,' his voice quivered, 'if you want that

hundred thousand pounds, you have to wear what we tell you.'

Mattie froze. Did he just say *hundred thousand?* 'What do you mean, hundred thousand?' she asked, her voice deadly calm.

Nate's fleshy lips formed a silent 'o'. 'No, no, I meant two hundred thousand. Two hundred!' He cleared his throat.

Mattie advanced on him. 'Too right you meant two hundred. I'm not here for a piddly hundred thousand.' He backed away from her with every step.

'Of course. Of course! Two hundred thousand.' Nate flashed his fingers in the air as if he was signing out the number. His chest was heaving up and down and he looked like he was about to pass out. 'Fine, keep your trousers, just wear the top,' he puffed finally.

Mattie shot him a victorious look. Paired with her MaxMara tailored black trousers, the sequined rag might not look *too* trashy. 'I'm the star here, Nate,' she said, keen to drill the pecking order into his thick skull. 'I call the shots. And don't you forget it.'

His head wobbled back and forth. 'Sure, sure. So anyway, here are the questions you need to ask the men,' he said, handing her laminated cards. 'Follow Seamus Leary's lead and you'll be fine.'

Mattie's eyes bulged. 'Seamus Leary's the host?' He'd risen to TV stardom after a disastrous cosmetic surgery split his upper lip. Rather than repair it, he used it to springboard him from a D-list TV personality all the way to the host of *Family Secrets*. He'd harassed a ninety-year-old granny so much last year that she'd battered him with her crutch before collapsing from a heart attack, all to the cheers of the studio audience. The show had been cancelled soon afterwards, but it had secured Seamus's place in TV history. He'd even made a special appearance on *Judge Judy* in America before checking into a detox facility. What the hell was a feral creature like him doing on some stupid dating game show?

Nate nodded. 'Yeah. Pretty cool, huh? He even cut his detox short to be here for the kick off.' He looked at his watch. 'We're on in ten. Please, just put on the top. Then have a look through the questions and someone will come get you when it's time.'

Mattie shrugged, trying to keep her face calm. Inside, her heart was picking up pace and she could feel sweat breaking out on her forehead.

'Break a leg!' Nate gave her a dorky thumbs up and disappeared.

Mattie grimaced. She'd rather break his leg, actually. She pulled on the sequined nightmare, then flipped through the question cards.

What's your favourite colour, Bachelor Number One?

If I was going to cook your favourite dish, what ingredients would I need?

Okay, nothing shocking there. She let out a breath. Could the spin be that they were making the most snore-worthy dating game show ever?

A roar rose from the studio and Mattie glanced at the clock. Eight p.m. – the show was starting. Her hands began to shake again and she glanced down at the silly questions to calm her nerves. She could deal with this with her eyes shut. She could, she told herself for extra emphasis.

This is it, Mattie thought, breathing deeply. It's show time.

*

Jess took her place in the front row of Studio 1 just as the doors were closing. She'd been late leaving home – unable to decide between good jeans and sparkly top or the H&M jumpsuit she'd purchased last weekend. In the end, she'd settled on the safe combo of jeans and top. She wasn't used to high heels, though, and had nearly broken her ankle trying to run for the tube.

She jammed her handbag under the chair, heart thumping, unable to believe she was right up front at the live taping of a game show. She studied the set in front of her. The right side was carpeted in a vivid red and a high metallic stool stood beside a gleaming steel podium. To the left, four egg-shaped pods shone under the bright lights – where the men were going to be, obviously, out of sight from both the audience and Mattie. Maybe that was the twist? But wait a minute, hadn't Cilla Black done something similar on a show once?

Jess peered into the darkness offstage but there was absolutely no movement. God, was Mattie scared? Jess herself would be petrified if she were about to appear live on a dating game show. But when Mattie had rung her a few hours ago, she'd been her usual self: dissing the men and the show; making cruel fun of the whole thing. To be fair though, ever since the whole Kyle episode the only emotion Jess had seen from Mattie had been anger, with a little bit of sarcasm thrown in.

Mattie had never been the biggest proponent of the male species – probably because of what had happened with her father – but Kyle's alleged cheating had pushed her over the edge. Jess couldn't even remember the last time she'd actually had *fun* with Mattie. Each session out usually turned into a rant against men, with Jess nodding mutely as Mattie went off on one of her diatribes. And it was hard watching Mattie chuck man after man, while Jess was still waiting for just *one* to notice her.

Still, she and Mattie had been friends ever since Mattie had taken down the three boys who dared mock Jess's Scottish accent when she'd first moved to Staines. Mattie had been Jess's only friend for the first few years of the horrendous transition from sheep farm to suburbs, and the two of them had remained close ever since. Jess was sure Mattie would snap out of her hyper-angry state eventually.

The lights onstage suddenly got brighter and a trio of burly men took up positions behind giant cameras. A pudgy bloke with fuzzy hair lumbered onto the set, talking into his headset and squinting into the lights. He motioned off-set and Jess leaned forward. Was Mattie coming on?

Oh my Lord! Jess's heart plunged when she saw just who they were bringing on: Seamus Leary, wearing his trademark Hawaiian-print tie and an ill-fitting shiny suit.

Did Mattie know he was the host? She was in for a tough ride – Jess could only imagine the kind of cracks he'd make at Mattie's expense. Mattie would pretend she didn't care, that being labelled a chick with a dick was actually a compliment, but Jess had seen the hurt in her friend's eyes too many times to believe the jibes wouldn't sting.

Jess watched the pudgy bloke try to manoeuvre Seamus into position behind the podium. Oh Jesus, Seamus could barely remain upright – he was swaying back and forth, looking completely sloshed.

Maybe it wasn't too late to warn Mattie. Jess rooted around for her mobile and slumped in her seat as she dialled Mattie's number. But the phone just rang and rang. Jess snapped her mobile closed as another man with a headset counted down the remaining seconds and the on-air light began to flash above the stage.

Seamus swivelled towards a giant camera that was lowered from the ceiling.

'Hello! And welcome to *The Hating Game*!' he

slurred. A big screen with the show's name in purple letters flashed up in the background.

Jess's mouth dropped open as she scanned the logo. *Hating* Game? Mattie hadn't told her anything about that. What on Earth was *The Hating Game*? Whatever it was, it certainly didn't look good – the word 'hating' seemed even more ominous surrounded by the flashing hearts and curlicues.

'So what's *The Hating Game*, you ask?' Seamus said, scanning the audience with a leer. 'Well, imagine this.'

*

'Ready?' A girl sporting a natty headset stuck her head around the dressing-room door.

Mattie got to her feet, flexing her sweaty fingers to stop them shaking for just a minute. The unfamiliar top pricked at her skin, and a trickle of sweat was already snaking down her back. She followed the girl's very unattractive camouflage trousers through the corridors and over an obstacle course of electrical cords until they came to a flimsy grey swinging door, guarded by a man with a headset and clipboard.

'One minute,' he said, crossing his arms over the clipboard as if it were a matter of national security.

In the silence backstage, Mattie could just make out the drone of Seamus's voice on set but she couldn't identify exactly what he was saying. Given the boring questions, though, most the audience had likely fallen asleep by now.

'Thirty seconds,' the man said.

Mattie nodded.

*

Jess gulped in air as she waited for Seamus to explain.

'Imagine a woman goes on a dating game show, thinking she's going to meet anonymous strangers. Strangers who know nothing about her past, nothing about *her*, at all.'

She let out her breath. Okay, sounded normal enough. But the way the infamous host was raising his eyebrows and the quivering of his split lip indicated he wasn't finished.

Seamus dropped his chin and lowered his voice. 'But what if the men weren't strangers? What if they were the woman's ex-boyfriends, back for another go at a relationship?' He tried to spin to another camera and almost tripped. 'Or *revenge*?'

A dramatic sigh went up from the audience. Jess slapped her hands to her burning cheeks. Oh my God. Exes? Would the show really spring that on Mattie? Was *that* the spin – that Mattie would come face to face with her exes?

Her eyes flew over to the steel pods on the stage, mind racing as she ran through Mattie's list of exes. Was Kyle in there? Or Adam? Poor Adam; Mattie would rip him to shreds! Jess stared hard at the four pods, wishing she had x-ray vision.

Seamus was now walking unsteadily towards the audience. 'Their relationship crashed and burned the first time around, and now these boys are back for more. But is it love or hate? *You* decide!' He stabbed the air for extra emphasis and nearly fell over. '*You* determine who deserves a second chance for romance.'

What did he mean, *you* decide? The audience could control who Mattie dated?

Jess swivelled to look at the people around her. They were staring at Seamus hypnotically, eyes shining darkly, and for a second they reminded Jess of zombies – or girls waiting for the doors of a TopShop sale to open.

Seamus lurched back to the safety of his podium. 'Here's what happens.' He gestured towards the pods. 'There are four exes, right here, right now, waiting in these pods.'

'Ooooh,' squealed the zombies.

'And there will be four dates, to reunite each ex with our sexy single lady. The ex with the highest Date Rate – as decided by you, the audience, in a phone-in vote – spends two weeks alone with the lady in question in a romantic location.' Seamus paused. 'And together, they could win two hundred thousand pounds!'

The zombies rustled and nodded appreciatively.

'But here's the thing.' Seamus wiped his split lip. 'When our single lady comes on in just a few seconds, she won't know the men are her exes. Even their voices will be disguised!' He rubbed his hands gleefully.

Jess sunk deeper into her chair. Oh God. Poor Mattie.

'So she'll ask each of them two questions, which they'll answer – truthfully – but without giving away too many details. And at the end of this show, she'll choose which one to date first!'

Seamus swung around to a camera. 'And night by night, as she chooses the next ex to date, she'll find out it's *not* just another dating show. She'll discover she's playing *The Hating Game* – whether she wants to or not!'

The zombies roared as the giant screen with *The Hating Game* logo lit up again and started flashing. Jess took a deep breath to stop the rising nausea.

'Tune in every night this week at eight p.m. right here on X-ACT to watch our sexy single lady give her exes a second chance, one by one. Then, every night after the show, you out there in TV land call to register your Date Rate!' Seamus laughed heartily, spotlights illuminating the spittle flying out of his mouth.

'This Sunday night, when all the dates are complete, we'll reveal the ex with the highest Date Rate: the one who will spend two weeks alone with our sexy single lady – and the one who gets to try to win her heart again.' He turned and winked at the audience, his split lip gaping to reveal glowing white teeth. 'Or to make her life a living hell.'

'Will it be love or hate?' He turned towards a camera inches from his face. 'Let *The Hating Game* begin!'

The zombies roared and Jess held her head in hands, feeling dizzy. Her heart thumped in time to a psychedelic remake of the *Jackson 5* tune *I Want You Back* blaring from the speakers.

'So let's meet our single lady. Ladies and gentlemen, I give you . . . Mattie Johns!' Seamus yelled.

Jess lifted her hands from her temples and watched the stage for her best friend. It was like knowing there was a massive car crash waiting to happen and being forced to watch it in slow motion.

The zombies around her cheered wildly as the silhouette of her best friend appeared against the studio lights.

CHAPTER TEN

One in five men purchases flowers for a date.
Half of all women admit to preferring chocolates or alcohol.

UP IN THE CONTROL ROOM, Nate stared unseeingly at the monitor. *The Hating Game*? He hadn't approved that script! Where had that come from? He glanced at Silver. Her face was as poker-like as ever as she examined the monitor in front of her.

'What happened to *Second Chance for Romance*?' Nate blurted. His heart was beating so fast he felt like he was about to pass out.

'What?' Silver waved her hand as if he was an insect to swat away. 'Oh, yes. We had to change the concept. Make it more dramatic, you know. Yours was too *fluffy*.' She said the word with disdain.

'But I told the men it was *Second Chance for Romance*!' Not that Giovanni or Adam would care, but Kyle definitely would. Imagine when Mattie found out he'd signed up to something called *The Hating Game*. Kyle's chances of getting back together would be completely ruined.

'Don't worry, Nate.' Silver looked amused. 'You're still EP.'

Nate turned back towards the monitor where Seamus was spraying the front row of the audience as he painstakingly explained the rules of the game yet again. Executive producer was great and all, but what about his concept? This *Hating Game* thing wasn't *his* full and complete creation, was it? Maybe it was naive to think he'd be consulted on any changes to the concept. Naive or not, he'd need to embrace *The Hating Game* and show Silver he was totally on board if he wanted to stay in the frame. He didn't want to be one of those EPs who faffed around with nothing to do except look forward to seeing their credit at the end of the programme.

'Sorry I'm late.' Baz strolled in and took a seat on the other side of Silver. 'Hey, mate.' He raised a hand for Nate to high five.

What the hell was Baz doing here? Nate stared as Baz's hand wilted in the air until he finally shrugged and turned to face the bank of monitors.

'Baz is producing the series,' Silver told him, not even bothering to look in his direction.

'Producer?' Nate croaked.

'He'll help out with storylines and day-to-day details,' Silver said, still glued to the nearest monitor, 'and you'll both report back to me.' She swung around to face them. 'I want to know when the contestants break wind, what they had for breakfast, *everything*. The more we know, the more we can poke them and create some great TV moments. I expect the two of you to make it happen.'

Nate's face went hot as he watched Baz nod eagerly. 'We will, Silver.' He punched Nate playfully in the shoulder. 'Hey, Nate?'

Nate nodded limply. 'Yes, yes of course. We will.' He shifted on the chair and wiped his forehead.

He couldn't let Baz take all the credit; run away with his show. Somehow he'd have to show Silver *he* was the one in control here.

*

Mattie crouched behind the door, waiting for her cue to go onstage.

'So let's meet our single lady. Ladies and gentlemen, I give you . . . Mattie Johns!' she heard Seamus Leary shout. The audience roared and the girl with the headset shoved her through the door and onto the set.

Heart pounding, Mattie took a deep breath, tugged up her top for the thousandth time, then marched onto the stage. Squinting against the bright lights, the audience swam before her like a giant heaving, clapping mass. She tried to force her trembling lips into a smile as another trail of sweat ran down her spine.

'Come sit over here by me, Mattie.' Seamus Leary patted the stool, a pervy smile exploding on his face. With his shiny suit gleaming under the lights, he looked more used car salesman than game show host.

Mattie crossed the crimson carpet and climbed up onto the metal stool beside the podium. She scanned the audience hoping to spot Jess, but all she could see were a hundred pairs of eyes shining back at her.

Where were the men? Probably haven't crawled out from whatever rocks they're hiding under yet, she snorted to herself, just as she noticed oval-shaped metal structures on the other side of the stage. Oh Lord. Mattie rolled her eyes. How unoriginal – the men were in soundproof booths or whatever and she had to choose one blindly. Was that the spin? About as inventive as beer at a barbeque.

'So, Mattie! You're here looking for love?' Seamus leaned too close and Mattie instinctively jerked away. He absolutely *reeked* of gin.

'Um, yeah, I guess. Looking for love, that's me.' She knew she sounded snarky, but come on, what a stupid thing to say. For a man renowned for getting underneath the skin of his guests, he was certainly coming out with lame statements. Must have lost his thorny touch.

Seamus bore down even more and Mattie began to breathe through her mouth. 'Well, you've certainly had *plenty* of chances for romance, haven't you?' He didn't sound so nice this time.

Mattie shrugged and tried to keep her face blank even though she could feel sweat breaking out on her upper lip. Where was he going with this? And hadn't he heard of mouthwash?

Seamus circled her slowly. 'Haven't you been in multiple relationships – all ending in failure? Wouldn't you *really* like a shot at happiness in love?'

How on Earth did he know about her multiple relationships? Mattie swivelled her head to try to read his expression, but he kept twisting about.

He finally stopped circling and swayed behind the podium. For a second Mattie was afraid he might fall over but he gripped the podium's sides with his meaty fingers and steadied himself. 'Well, in these soundproof pods are four men. Four men who can't wait to meet you!'

Applause swelled from the audience and Mattie tried to see into the mass again. Where was Jess? She shifted on the stool, nearly sliding off from the sweat that was pouring from between her skin and tight, cheap top.

'Tonight you'll have the chance to ask them two questions each – then you'll choose one lucky man for your first date. And after your date tomorrow, you'll be back in the studio to select the next fortunate fellow for a second chance at romance!'

Mattie rolled her eyes again. The whole thing sounded completely idiotic. No matter how much drama Seamus tried to inject, it really was another boring old game show. He probably had to get drunk just to sound excited about it.

Seamus handed her a familiar-looking stack of laminated question cards. 'So let's get started! Mattie, choose your question and your bachelor.'

A hush descended over the studio as Mattie sifted through the cards, her sweaty fingers leaving marks on the glossy surfaces.

Do you like cats or dogs better?

If you were a cocktail, what kind would you be?

Same old boring questions! God, the show would probably be cancelled before the first commercial break. And if that happened, Mattie would be down two hundred grand. No way was she going to let that happen. Time to spice things up a little.

Mattie smiled at Seamus. 'My first question is for Bachelor Number One.'

The first pod to her right started flashing bright red. 'Go on, he can hear you now,' Seamus said.

'Bachelor Number One. What's your best bedroom move?'

Lights around the pod continued to flash as the audience waited for Bachelor Number One's answer. Mattie stole a glance at Seamus to see if he'd noticed her changing the question, but his eyes were drooping and he looked like he was about to fall into a coma.

'I'm more of a giver than a receiver in the bedroom,' a robotic voice from inside Pod One finally said.

Mattie jerked her head towards the flashing sphere. So they were disguising the men's voices, too? Not that it mattered – they were probably all monosyllabic morons anyway.

'I like to make sure my partner is happy first,' the voice was saying.

Mattie made a face. He was probably one of those

blokes who always tried to cuddle after sex. She shuddered as she recalled one man, post-Kyle, who pinned her in his sweaty arms and gazed at her with bovine eyes for what felt like hours.

'Thank you, Bachelor Number One.' Seamus was nodding as if he completely agreed with the answer but Mattie suspected he had no idea what had even been said. His earpiece dangled from his ear and Mattie could hear it squawking. 'Mattie, next question?'

Mattie looked towards the pods. 'Bachelor Number Two. What's your favourite lingerie item on a woman?'

Red lights started flashing on the second pod. And kept flashing.

Seamus cleared his throat. 'Bachelor Number Two? Can you hear me?'

'Um, yes,' came another robotic voice, slightly deeper than Bachelor Number One's. 'What is this *lingerie*? Is it food?'

Oh, dear Lord, Mattie muttered to herself. Where had they found this idiot? On Mars? Who the hell didn't know what lingerie was?

Seamus looked just as disbelieving as Mattie. 'Lingerie,' he said, spit flying everywhere. 'You know – corsets, brassieres, panties, stay-ups . . .' he stopped as someone yelled so loudly into his earpiece that it hurt Mattie's ears.

'Why don't you just tell us what your favourite colour is?'

'Ah, yes,' said the robot voice. 'I prefer the woman to be wearing nothing. Naked.' Although the monotone voice was flat, the cadence of his words made Mattie think he was a foreigner. Either that or he had the IQ of a lump of coal – something she wouldn't be so quick to dismiss given that Nate chose him.

Mattie turned back towards Seamus and racked

her brain for another risqué question. In spite of her best efforts, this was getting so predictable. She'd have to come up with something that would really make men squirm.

'Next question, Mattie?'

'Bachelor Number Three,' Mattie said. 'How many women have you slept with?'

The crowd rustled and murmured.

There was silence, then: 'I've not slept with a woman yet. I'm saving myself for the perfect one.'

The muttering from the audience swelled and Mattie's eyebrows nearly reached her hairline. Imagine, in this day and age, saving yourself for one woman. That idiot man probably thought it was romantic. Obviously he didn't realise women would actually run screaming, probably to the nearest airport, when they found out he was a virgin. Of course, there was the distinct possibility he resembled the missing link and finding a woman desperate enough to sleep with him was as unlikely as that tubby Nate developing a fashion sense.

God, this was really tiresome. 'Bachelor Number Four,' Mattie said, without waiting for Seamus, who was now becoming overly familiar with his host's podium. 'When did you last cheat on your girlfriend?' Because they all did, of course.

The lights on Pod Four had only just started flashing when Bachelor Number Four said: 'Actually, I've never cheated on a girlfriend. She thought I did, but I didn't.'

Mattie rolled her eyes. Yeah, right. Same old pathetic story. She plodded through another round of questions, trying her best to spice things up as Seamus got progressively droopier. The control room were shouting blue murder through the earpiece, which he still hadn't bothered to put back in.

Finally, when she'd questioned all the men for a second time, Seamus straightened up. 'So, Mattie, which one will it be for tomorrow's date?'

Mattie shrugged. Who cared? They were all equally foul sounding. 'Number One, I guess.' If she remembered correctly, he was the 'giver', probably the easiest man of the four to walk all over. She'd have no problem dealing with him.

'Bachelor Number One! Come meet Mattie Johns . . . again!'

Again? What did that mean, again?

Applause and cheers from the audience swirled around her as Mattie swivelled towards Pod One.

The pod door swung open and a wiry man with floppy hair emerged. From where she was sitting, Mattie could only see that his shoulder-length hair had highlights – a sure sign of a preening prima donna.

He turned towards her and Mattie's mouth dropped open.

It wasn't some hideous anonymous stranger Nate had pulled out from under a rock. It was hideous *Charlie*. The boy (now man) who'd humiliated her in front of the whole school by getting busy with Kwong at the prom. The *gay* man she'd outed!

She snapped her mouth closed and arranged her face in a smile as he walked towards her. It had been ten years since she'd last seen him, but even encased in a designer suit he looked as juvenile as ever. Back in secondary school, he'd have fit right in with a quiff-sporting boy band, but now he just looked like an overgrown teen trying to dress like his dad. He was carrying a bizarre-looking clutch of deep-purple flowers she'd never seen before. *Those* were meant to impress her? They looked like weeds.

'Hello, Mattie,' he said in his soft breathless voice, the same voice that used to drive her mental.

She looked down at the hand he extended and took his soft palm in hers. He was even better moisturised than she was! She squeezed his hand and thumped it up and down.

'Charlie. It's been awhile, hasn't it?' She tried to make her voice sound normal, conscious of all the cameras around her, but it came out sounding slightly strangled.

Bloody Nate, springing this on her. Then again, it did make sense. These kinds of shows always had an ex pop out at some stage, didn't they? They certainly could have done a lot worse than Charlie. Nate was obviously missing the gaydar gene, she sniggered to herself.

'It's been too long.' Charlie's thin lips were smiling but Mattie noticed his eyes were hard. Maybe he had manned up after all, she thought. She'd never seen Charlie get angry; even when she outed him, he'd just run off without confronting her.

'Here. This is for you.' The audience oohed and awed as he handed her the bunch of flowers. Their scent was foreign and she wondered if they were popular with the gay community. She struggled to keep the smirk off her face as she remembered Charlie's words about being 'the giver'. It was obvious what he'd meant by that now!

'How sweet.' Seamus leaned his weight on the podium and wiped his mouth with a loud slurping sound. 'So our sexy single Mattie Johns has chosen Bachelor Number One, Charlie Robbins, for her first date. Tune in tomorrow at eight to learn more about Charlie, watch their date unfold, then make your Date Rate! Plus see who Mattie chooses for her next date!'

Seamus burped. 'Thank you for watching . . .'

'The Hating Game!' the crowd screamed, egged on by the floor manager.

The audience continued to cheer as a giant monitor Mattie hadn't noticed before lit up with *The Hating Game* written across it in a sickly sweet purple font – the same shade as the flowers she was holding.

What the hell was *The Hating Game*? Wasn't the show supposed to be called *Second Chance for Romance* or something equally insipid? She cast a suspicious glance towards the other pods on the stage. Oh no. Who else was in there?

'Do you know who the other men are?' she hissed at Charlie, smiling into the camera as the floor manager counted them out.

But Charlie didn't answer. Useless as ever, Mattie thought, looking at the wilted flowers in her hand. Revolting things.

'And we're out!' the floor manager yelled as the on-air studio light switched off. The bright lights onstage dimmed and for the first time Mattie was able to see beyond the gleaming eyes of the audience to where Jess was sitting in the front row. Thank God! Mattie couldn't wait to dissect the show and talk about just who else might be in those pods – if she didn't find out first by getting Nate in a headlock.

Jess's face was bright red – a sure sign she was anxious about something – and she was motioning that she'd wait for Mattie outside the studio. Mattie nodded as a production assistant wrestled Mattie's mic out from under her skin-tight top.

When she turned back, Charlie had disappeared and Nate was helping Seamus off the stage. It was now or never, Mattie thought, edging towards the pods.

'Hello there!' she heard a voice behind her. 'You must be Mattie.'

Shit. She turned to face a man with hair that looked like it had been suctioned up by a Hoover then spat out again. So much for her sleuthing mission.

'Yes, and?' Mattie's lip curled reflexively. She'd worked with enough idiots to spot one coming from miles away. Shame this one was only a few metres from her and rapidly advancing.

'I'm Baz. I'm producer on the series.'

Mattie shrugged. 'Here, take these.' She shoved the purple flowers towards him. He stepped back and the flowers fell on the floor.

'Sorry, I'm allergic to flowers,' he said.

Mattie eyed the blossoms. Was there a reason this fool wouldn't touch them? What kind of flowers *were* these exactly?

She bent down and snapped off a blossom, shoving it in her pocket. Jess was into flowers and gardening, all that stuff. She might know.

'Just don't, er, eat it,' Baz said.

'I'm not going to eat a fucking flower, mate,' Mattie said. 'Nice to meet you, now bugger off.'

But Baz didn't move. 'Actually, we need to run through what's happening tomorrow. Let me get Nate.'

'Oh, yes please. Get Nate. You can both explain to me what the bloody hell *The Hating Game* is!' Mattie couldn't wait to let the two of them have it for changing the contracted show *and* bringing Charlie on!

'Nate, where the hell are you?' Baz said into his headset. 'We need you, now.'

Nate lurched over, his man-boobs jiggling as he panted. Dark patches stained his shirt under his armpits. Mattie grimaced. If there was one thing she hated more than a fat man, it was a fat *sweaty* man.

'Sorry, sorry,' he said, running a hand through Chia-pet hair and pushing up his spectacles. 'Seamus was sick and I had to get him cleaned up.' The smell of vomit wafted from him and Mattie stepped back in disgust. Could this evening become any more vile?

'Jesus.' Baz wrinkled his nose and moved beside Mattie. 'Right, we need to go through tomorrow. Nate, you and the cameraman . . .' Baz glanced at his clipboard, 'ah, Ram, will pick up Mattie in the car. You'll do the brief Q&A with Mattie on her history with Charlie as you drive to the site.'

'Um, hello?' Mattie waved her hand in front of Baz's face. 'You're both assuming I want to carry on with this fiasco. After everything that's happened tonight, I'm not sure I want to continue.' There was no way she was going to drop out, of course, but she wanted to show them they couldn't just spring surprises like Charlie on her.

Nate's face flushed even redder. 'You have to!' He scrambled around in his pocket then thumbed through the papers on his clipboard. 'I can't find it. You show her, Baz. Show her the contract.'

'Screw the contract,' Mattie said as Baz quickly flipped to it and pointed out a line that said she had to adhere to any and all filming schedules for the duration of the series, and that SiniStar reserved the right to change the series title at any time.

'But you have to comply! It's a legal document!' Nate looked like he was going to have a heart attack.

'Shut up, Nate,' Baz said. 'She'll be there tomorrow.' He turned to Mattie. 'We'll pick you up at nine.' He gave her a sickly smile. 'And don't worry, we'll go over everything then.'

Mattie rolled her eyes. Bloody idiot, like she'd trust Spaz – or whatever his name was – as far as she could throw him. Thank God for Jess. She'd grill her tonight for every last detail *and* watch the playback. When tomorrow rolled around, she'd be the one in control, just wait and see.

Mattie snatched the sheet from Baz and strode off the set without another word.

CHAPTER ELEVEN

Ten per cent of women duck out on a date if
the man fails to live up to expectations.
Twenty per cent of men ditch a blind date the second they see her.

NATE DARTED INTO THE MEN'S toilet and splashed cold water on his face. So much for being in control, he thought, water dripping down his cheeks. He'd just let Baz tell him to shut up, without even defending himself. And he hadn't even got the chance to have a go at Mattie for changing all his questions. God only knew what Silver would say about the questions Mattie *had* asked.

Nate sighed as he plucked his damp T-shirt off his skin, grimacing as a foul odour drifted off it. He'd thought this job wouldn't involve any more puke – what a joke. Of course, as EP, it shouldn't. As usual, he ended up doing the dirty work, while someone else – Baz – got all the glory.

You'd think after Kira, you'd smarten up, mate, he said to himself in the mirror. Stop letting everyone walk all over you.

He considered his tired puffy reflection, wondering for the millionth time if Kira had actually seen anything in him except money and a chance to move to London. Probably not: fat and floppy, he was more Johnny Vegas than Hugh Grant. Kira, on the other hand, was like a life-sized Barbie. Despite the fact she had to keep asking him the entry code to the flat they shared (1,2,3,4!) and had a tendency to pinch anything that wasn't securely locked up, one look at her and he felt like the luckiest man on Earth.

It had been a stroke of luck meeting her – or so he'd thought. An old uni mate had invited Nate beyond the boundaries of Wood Green, all the way to a stag party in deepest Essex. With nothing better to do that night than plough through his large vindaloo curry, Nate had turned up to the local primary school, where half the village – and their offspring – had come out to watch the *Barbie Babes* bump and grind to *The Cheeky Girls' Greatest Hits*.

Kira had been the fourth bumping Barbie from the left, and Nate hadn't been able to take his eyes off her. She'd winked and when their set was over, she made a beeline for him. They'd squeezed into the same chair and swigged beer from a paper cup. Kira asked him where he lived, and when he said London, that was it: they went back to his flat in Wood Green that night. She was ready to give up the touring rigours of the *Barbie Babes* and settle down, she told him.

Nate hadn't realised 'settling down' meant taking his credit cards, running up a load of debt and spending half the night out at 'auditions' as she tried to break into the world of musical theatre. It wasn't long before he ran out of cash, and he came home one day to find his flat empty and Kira gone. All she'd left him – apart from his battered futon and saggy sofa – was a note in childish handwriting that said *Laters!* with a wonky happy face beside it.

Nate had stared at that happy face, confusion swirling around his mind. He thought he'd been exactly what she had wanted. He'd provided a home for her, made her happy and catered to her every whim. But nice guys came last, didn't they? What had happened just a few minutes ago more than proved that.

Well, he wouldn't be Mr Nice Guy any more, personally or professionally. Bounding up the stairs for the post-show meeting with Silver, he threw back his shoulders, then opened the door to the control room.

'Hello,' he said to Silver and Baz in a deep voice, selecting a chair purposefully and pulling it into the space between them.

'Glad you could make it.' Silver fingered a cocktail sausage, then bit off the tip and laid it down on the plate beside her. 'So who changed those questions?'

Nate's mind worked frantically. If he said Mattie, he'd look like he had no control. But if he said it was him then Silver would bite off *his* head, just like that cocktail sausage.

'Must have been Nate,' Baz held his hands up.

Nate jerked towards him. Baz knew Nate had no more to do with it than Silver's headless sausage! But tossing the blame in someone else's direction was a good tactic to avoid it himself. Nate filed that away for future use.

'Well, I liked it. Ramped up the tension and played out well.' Silver devoured the remainder of the sausage with satisfaction, while Nate sagged with relief. He couldn't help smirking at Baz's defeated expression.

'Just don't do it again, Nate. I need to know *everything* that's happening. You might be EP, but I'm the one paying you. Remember that.'

Nate nodded. 'Sure thing, Silver. Of course.'

'Initial ratings for the live show are good so far. Now we have to keep it up!' She popped another sausage, this time whole, into her mouth. 'So we've got the gay guy tomorrow, right?'

Nate's mouth dropped open. Charlie, gay? Nate had thought he was just one of those floppy-haired posh blokes. 'Sorry, Silver, I–'

'I don't care if he's an alien as long as you make him interesting. Vengeful love-sick puppy, whatever.' Silver turned to Baz. 'What do you have planned?'

'Well, Mattie and Charlie both went to secondary school together. So we're going to take them back there,' Baz said. 'I've got a dance instructor all lined up who'll give the two of them lessons in the gym.' He leaned back in his chair.

Nate stared. When had all this been organised?

Silver nodded. 'Good, good. Just make sure to get him out of running. The last thing we want is a gay man stuck with Mattie for two weeks. Jesus, imagine the ratings.'

'Oh, don't worry.' Baz gave her a long, slow smile. 'I've got it all worked out.'

Nate opened his mouth to ask if it was really necessary to push out poor Charlie so soon but he snapped it closed just in time. No more Mr Nice Guy, he reminded himself.

Silver pushed her short hair back behind her ears and stood up. 'I'll see you both here tomorrow. And remember, boys, ratings!'

Nate bobbed his head. Ratings, he repeated to himself. Just remember: ratings.

*

'Faster, faster!' Adam muttered as his legs churned over Waterloo Bridge after the show. A group of babbling tourists nearly fell over the side of the iconic structure as he shoved to get past them but he wasn't about to slow down. He'd only been able to get in ninety minutes of weights this morning instead of the prescribed two-hour workout, and he had to make up for lost time. Chucking those Jaffa Cakes would not be in vain.

Not that Mattie would know how good he looked quite yet. Adam increased his pace to a jog, new shoes pinching his feet. Stupid bloody pods! He'd spent hours getting ready to face Mattie for the first time after all those years. Then that fat slob of a producer had herded him into a stuffy pod where he'd sat and sweated for a good two hours.

Afterwards, the producer rushed him through the studio and onto the street like some kind of criminal. He hadn't impressed Mattie, he hadn't impressed the audience and he hadn't even been able to check out his competition – although given their lame answers they weren't likely to put up much of a fight.

But maybe the pods were a good thing, after all. Given extra time, he could shed even more weight; boost the biceps a little more. His protein-shake diet and killer workouts would all pay off. Adam touched his face. So would that chemical peel and three hundred quid haircut.

Mattie would see him soon, and when she did, he'd do everything possible to make sure she fell in love.

*

'Here's to two hundred thousand pounds!' Mattie raised her glass of whisky and clinked it against Jess's daiquiri as they settled onto a brightly patterned sofa in the nearby bar at the British Film Institute. Her head was still throbbing from the dazzling onstage lights, but she wasn't anywhere near ready to head home.

It was past ten on a Sunday night but the bar still buzzed with media types who'd barely given her a second glance, even though she'd just made her screen debut. They'd all beat down her door for recruitment soon enough, though, once she was properly back in business. All the palaver of the show would be worth it. Anyway, it couldn't get worse than what they'd pulled with Charlie.

She waited until Jess had sipped her drink. 'So tell me *everything*. What the fuck is *The Hating Game*?'

Jess lowered her eyes, dragging her straw through the frozen drink. 'Well, um . . .'

'For God's sake!' Mattie snapped, rubbing her head. It felt like someone was poking behind her right eye with a knife. 'It can't be that bad. Just tell me.'

Jess sighed and raised her eyes to meet Mattie's. 'Well, all the men . . .' She took a deep breath. 'They're your exes.'

Mattie shook her head. 'What?' It was too loud in here to have a normal conversation, especially with that group of pin-striped idiots braying next to them.

'Shut up!' she barked in their direction, then swung her eyes back to Jess. She must have misheard. Jess couldn't have said they were all her exes, could she?

'They're your ex-boyfriends. That's what Seamus said.' Jess crossed arms over chest to protect herself from Mattie's coming eruption.

'Not just Charlie? The other three are my exes, too?' Mattie couldn't believe her ears – or the absolute *nerve* of Nate and Spaz. She'd thought it was perfectly clear she wouldn't stand for any more surprises and they hadn't thought it relevant to fill her in on this little bit of news? Cowards!

'Oh my God,' Mattie blurted as a thought entered her mind. 'You don't think Kyle would be there, do you?' The jabbing behind her eye intensified. She wouldn't be surprised; he was an expert at making her life hell. Why not go the whole hog and torture her on live telly, too? She could deal with it, of course. She'd just rather not have to.

But Jess was shaking her head. 'I don't think he'd want to make things any more difficult for you.'

Mattie rolled her eyes. Jess would believe Hitler if he said he wasn't a bigot. 'How the hell did they manage to track down my exes, anyway?'

Jess shrugged. 'I don't know, but it's television, right? I'm sure they have a whole team of people checking into your background.'

Mattie rubbed her head. Between the whisky and the headache, she was beginning to feel nauseated. It wasn't really that shocking – they'd managed to find out about her father, after all. And the loser men she'd dumped were probably frothing at the mouth to get their ugly mugs on TV, like all pathetic people with nothing else better to do.

She rummaged through her purse to buy another shot of whisky and her fingers touched a wilted flower. 'Oh yeah.' She drew it out and plopped it on the table. 'Do you know what this is? It's from the bunch Charlie gave me. One of the producers acted like it was poisoned or something. He wouldn't even touch it!'

Jess squinted at the purple blossom. 'Looks like deadly nightshade. It *is* poisonous – but only if you eat it.' She stared at Mattie. 'I can't believe Charlie gave you poisonous flowers!'

Mattie snorted. 'I reckon Charlie had nothing to do with it. It's such a stupid gimmick, that idiot Baz the Spaz must be behind it.' She fingered the limp flower on the table. 'At least it's not poison ivy. All I need is a Herpes-style rash on live TV.'

Jess patted her shoulder gently. 'Are you sure you want to continue with the show?'

'Absolutely.' Two hundred thousand pounds, Mattie repeated to herself, crushing the flower on the table.

She'd shown those exes the door once already.

She could do it again.

*

It was three in the morning, but Jess couldn't sleep. Every time she closed her eyes, Adam's face floated into view. She hoped he knew better than to go on *The Hating Game,* but she guessed he'd jump at the chance to see Mattie again. Poor Adam. Even though he was a big-shot businessman now, he'd never really got over what had happened back in secondary school.

Jess would never forget the look on Adam's face after Mattie dumped him. He'd run out of the school and she'd followed, finding him shaking with sobs behind the school skip. She'd tried to hug him but he'd roughly pushed her away. Made sense; she was the one who'd encouraged him to ask out Mattie. Mattie was between boyfriends at the time and Jess had thought dating Mattie might help Adam come out of his shell. Instead, the break-up had driven him to binge eating and reclusiveness.

Even now, whenever they met up for coffee or dinner, he spent at least half the time asking about Mattie. It was so sad, and Jess's heart ached for what she'd done to him.

Jess slid off the sofa and tiptoed to where she'd left her mobile on Mattie's glass coffee table. After the bar, they'd come back to Mattie's where they'd downed a bottle of Pinot Grigio and watched the show on playback. Mattie had asked her to stay over before collapsing in a drunken stupor. After much coaxing and dragging she had managed to tuck Mattie in bed. Since then, Jess must have tried Adam at least fifty times, to no avail.

Jess sighed as she checked for messages and missed calls. Still nothing.

Why didn't he reply?

Could he really have been one of the men in those

pods? Was he desperate enough, after everything he'd been through, to go back for more?

Jess dialled Adam's number one more time, hanging up when it clicked through to voice mail. She crept back to the sofa and shoved a pillow under her head, trying to sleep as the tinny beat of *I Want You Back* rang in her head. She'd try him again tomorrow.

CHAPTER TWELVE

*One in fifty high-school sweethearts get married.
Of those marriages, half end in divorce.*

'CIAO BELLA! HOW YOU LIKIN' *les extensions*?' Fabio breathed oniony fumes all over Mattie as he played with her curls.

She shook her head and shifted in the chair, barely able to move in the tight jeans the wardrobe department had so *thoughtfully* provided. It was the morning of her date with Charlie and she was back in the studio for hair and make-up. Her head pounded after last night's post-show drinking session with Jess, which was why she couldn't be bothered telling Fabio *les extensions* was French, not Italian; and that he was a fool.

Mattie closed her eyes. After having drunk herself to sleep, the faces of her exes had drifted through her dreams – and one ex in particular featured repeatedly. Although Jess insisted Kyle wouldn't go on a show like *The Hating Game*, Mattie wasn't so sure. It was good PR, and Kyle had never been one to miss a trick when it came to business. Mattie had admired that about him – until he stole all her clients.

She'd barely had time to drag herself from bed and get showered before the car arrived to whisk her to the studio to get ready for the big date. She snorted. Big date, as if! There was hardly a second chance for romance with a gay guy! Charlie probably planned an outing to a tranny club in Soho or a day trip to Brighton.

'All right, Mattie?'

Mattie looked up. 'Ah, Tweedledee and Tweedledum.' Nate and Baz were standing there looking like booby prizes at a speed dating session for halfwits. If she *was* in the mood for something today, it was bringing them down a notch or two for springing those exes on her.

'Nice hair, did you get caught in a wind tunnel?' she asked Nate, watching as he flushed and tried to straighten his wilted curls into the spiky hairdo Baz sported. Why someone would actually *want* hair that looked that way was beyond her.

'So, you ready?' Baz asked, eyeing her top's plunging neckline, then looking down at his clipboard. 'Nate and a cameraman will go with you to the location. We'll film you meeting Charlie there.'

'No, I'm not ready.' Mattie stood up, shaking off Cyndi's mascara wand. She swivelled to face Nate and Baz, noting with satisfaction how Nate jumped back as though she might bite. Which, given the mood she was in, was a definite possibility.

She took a step closer. 'I think you two should do the date – more up your streets, if that hair is anything to go by.'

'And afterwards we'll go back to the studio to film you choosing the guy for your next date.' Baz carried on as if she hadn't even spoken. And *nothing* pissed her off like men ignoring her.

'Let's get something straight here, Spaz,' she said, feeling her ringlets bounce as she spoke. 'When I signed up to this thing, I had a pretty good idea it wasn't just a normal dating show. I thought those men might be my exes. So your little surprise stunt last night didn't fool me at all.'

She was bluffing but she had to make them believe they hadn't pulled one over on her.

Baz smirked and she wanted to punch him. 'Oh, good. We're happy you're happy, right Nate?' he sneered. Nate nodded his head. 'Now, let's get this segment underway, shall we?'

Had all that gel clogged his eardrums? Mattie squinted, anger clouding her vision – not that she really wanted to see Baz, anyway. 'But what I don't need is two brain-dead idiots trying to push me around.' She spun away from them and tossed back her curls. 'In fact, I don't need this show at all. Find another *sexy single lady*.' Ha! That should terrify the duo into compliance. They'd never pull her from the show at this point.

In the mirror, she could see Nate shooting Baz a worried look. But Baz just strolled over to where she was standing, hands in his pockets. 'No worries, Mattie, no worries,' he drawled, rocking back and forth. 'If you don't want to do the show, we've got someone else lined up.'

Mattie turned towards him, a small thread of fear weaving its way into her anger. 'Oh, yeah?' She stared, trying to read his mind. They couldn't really have a backup, could they?

Baz nodded. 'Yeah.' A woman Mattie hadn't seen before walked by the open door, and Baz nodded in her direction. 'Actually, that's her.'

'Sure, Baz. Sure. Whatever.' Mattie rolled her eyes to pretend she didn't believe a word of it, but . . . what if they *did* have someone else stashed backstage? Could she really risk losing the prize money? Red pound signs flashed before her eyes as she totted up all her debt.

Signing inwardly, Mattie strode out the dressing-room door, the TweedleDuo scrambling after her.

She'd do the show because she had to, but she wasn't going to roll over and play the brainless bimbo. They wanted a ball buster, and they had one.

'What are you waiting for?' she barked over her shoulder, trying not the picture their triumphant expressions. 'Let's get this over with.'

Half an hour later, Mattie and Nate were in a black limo heading to whatever godforsaken site the date was to take place. A squat cameraman – who, with his grimy baseball cap, nicotine-stained fingers and gold chains, seemed better suited to the role of mafia hitman than TV operative – climbed in beside them. 'The name's Ram,' he said, offering his collection of ragged fingernails to Mattie to shake.

Mattie ignored him and turned towards the window. The less she had to do with anyone else on this production team, the better.

'Um, Mattie?' Nate's voice interrupted her thoughts. 'I need to film you answering some questions about Charlie now.'

'Nate, tell me who the other exes are.' She fixed her laser glare on him and watched as he squirmed like a bug pinned to a wall. 'Tell me, or I won't answer your questions.'

Nate pushed up his spectacles and shook his head. 'No, no, I can't. Baz and Silver would kill me if they found out.'

'Come on, Nate,' Mattie said. 'Grow some balls! It's not like I'm going to tell them, is it?' Jesus, what a wuss.

But Nate just quivered and held his clipboard against him like a shield. 'Mattie, I can't. Please answer the questions. Or we'll have to stick with the information we have . . .'

The nerve! Was he trying to blackmail her? What exactly did they know about her and Charlie? 'Maybe you should run what you have by me first, before I answer any questions. Just to check for accuracy.' She leaned forward to get a look at the clipboard but she couldn't see anything around Nate's massive mound of belly.

'Er, Baz has all that information,' Nate said, shrinking back against the side of the car. 'But we do know Charlie's gay. That must have been quite traumatic for you.' His bushy brows knit together in a look of faux-sympathy that didn't quite work, given his flushed, sweaty cheeks.

Mattie raised an eyebrow. So they *did* know Charlie was gay. Just how many more sordid details had he spilled? The only way to find out was to hear Nate's queries – and at least she'd be able to give her side of the story.

'Fine,' she snapped. 'Ask your silly questions. But make it fast.'

Nate nodded to Ram, who lifted a massive camera and trained it on Mattie. She flinched as a bright light hit her. For once she was grateful for the caked-on make-up.

Nate looked down at his clipboard. 'Can you tell us what you liked about Charlie when you first met him?'

What a stupid question. As if anyone really chose their secondary school boyfriends for reasons that extended beyond how cool their hair looked or what kind of trendy shoes they wore with their uniform. But if this was going to be on TV, she'd better try to come up with something semi-intelligent. God only knew what Charlie was saying about her.

Mattie smiled at the camera. 'What an interesting question. Well, what wasn't there to like about

Charlie? He was so giving, so kind.' That much was true, anyway, she sniggered, remembering his answer the night before. And he *had* always given her little presents here and there, leaving notes in her locker with her favourite crisps: prawn cocktail.

'So why did you split up?' Nate asked.

Mattie stared into the camera. Didn't he know? Well, if Nate hadn't ferreted out all the gory details behind the break up there was no way she was going to give him or Charlie the satisfaction of making herself out to be the baddie. She'd only done what was necessary to protect herself, but with all the political correctness around these days she knew the public might not see it that way.

She shrugged. 'Oh, you know. I was going off to London for university and Charlie had other things to pursue.' *Like Kwong,* she added silently.

'We're here,' the driver said through the intercom as the car pulled up in front of a low, red-brick building.

Oh my God, Mattie breathed to herself, trying to keep her expression neutral for the camera only inches from her face. She couldn't believe she hadn't noticed where they were driving! It had been years since she'd been here, but the sprawling 1970s-style building looked exactly the same. The sign spelling out *Staines Secondary School* still had the blue splatter from where Danny Llewellyn had shot it with a paint gun when Mattie was in Year Eight.

Nate looked at his watch then consulted the clipboard again. 'Right on time. So Mattie, you stay here. We want a shot of you getting out of the car. Then you'll enter and meet Charlie in the reception area. Just hang tight and we'll get you sorted out with a mic.'

Mattie nodded, thoughts swirling through her head. Was this Nate's doing, coming back here, or

Charlie's? For the life of her, Mattie couldn't figure out why Charlie would *want* to revisit this scene. Surely he couldn't be upset about the fiasco ten years ago?

Well, whatever happened she was determined to come off the better person. Nobody liked an angry gay man.

Ram finally swung the camera away from her and got a small wireless mic out of his camera bag. He handed it to her. 'Put this on. You can clip the battery pack above your arse and put the cord up under your shirt. Need any help, just ask.' He winked.

'Back off, perv!' Mattie hissed. She didn't need his beefy hands all over her.

Ram raised both palms. 'Don't you worry, sweetheart. You ain't me type.' He got out of the car before Mattie could retort that his type probably had scales.

She threaded the wire under her tight top as best she could before attaching the pack to the waistband of her jeans.

Nate knocked on the window. 'Ready?'

She nodded and took a deep breath. For some stupid reason she felt all shivery and her palms were clammy. Must be because I haven't eaten anything, she told herself as she climbed out of the car, conscious of the camera trained on her. She heaved open the metallic blue doors of the school and walked into the reception. God, it even smelled the same: a mixture of body odour, bleach, dust and lemon wax. Charlie was examining the trophy case. He turned, running a hand through floppy hair.

'Hi, Mattie,' he said, *sotto voce*. He fiddled with the collar on his suit, remarkably like the TopMan one he'd been wearing when she caught him sucking face with Kwong. She'd never forget that sight, the back of his head plastered against Kwong's.

Mattie leaned in and placed a kiss on his cheek for the benefit of the cameras. His cheeks were just as soft as his hands had been.

'Excellent choice for our date! So many great memories!' she trilled, watching him closely to see how he reacted to her words.

A flicker of anger showed on his face. 'Yeah. Great memories.' He started down the hall. 'Come on, follow me.'

So much for polite banter, Mattie thought, trailing behind him down the corridor and through to the gymnasium. One corner had been transformed into a sort of dance studio, with wooden flooring covering the linoleum tiles and mirrors lining the walls.

Mattie turned to Charlie. 'Dancing? I don't dance.' Her mum had never really encouraged it, enrolling her in computer camps while the rest of the girls her age were learning ballet.

Charlie raised an eyebrow. 'I figured a few ballroom dance lessons would be nice.'

Mattie forced a smile. 'Great!' She'd show him. Give her five minutes and she'd be gliding about like . . . one of those famous ballerinas, whoever they were.

'Hello, my dolls!' A man in a sparkly purple jumpsuit burst through the gymnasium doors and glided over to them. 'Welcome to my studio!' He gestured to the corner with a flourish and Mattie rolled her eyes. Men over fifty should be banned from wearing tight-fitting Spandex, particularly those with pot bellies.

'Is this your boyfriend?' she hissed at Charlie. His face flushed red and he ignored her. 'You've been trading down, not up!' Too late she remembered the mic under her clothes. Nate surely wouldn't use that – would he? She'd have to remember to watch what she said. She wanted to come out the good guy. Girl. Whatever.

'I am Dennis Driver!' the man said with a flourish. Charlie clapped and reached out to shake Dennis's hand. Mattie stared. Dennis Driver? Was she supposed to know who he was?

'Former British Ballroom Champion!' Dennis announced, staring at Mattie through piggy eyes. She stared back and shrugged, not about to applaud some fat old has-been.

'You both look way too tense. You must be relaxed to dance!' Dennis started to shake his legs and arms and Mattie tried not to watch as his belly and other appendages began quivering under the shiny material. 'Please, turn to face each other and hold hands.'

'Oh, for God's sake,' Mattie muttered. She smiled right into the camera Ram had set up on one side and grabbed Charlie's hands.

'Very nice,' Dennis said, still jiggling disconcertingly. She noticed a corner of Charlie's mouth lifting and she caught herself almost grinning too. 'Now, look each other in the eye and breathe deeply three times. In . . .' – Mattie watched Dennis's belly shrink – 'Out . . .' – and expand. Gross.

'Okay, dolls!' Dennis clapped his hands. 'Let's get dancing!'

The gymnasium lights went off, plunging them into darkness. Mattie's hands reflexively tightened around Charlie's before she realised what she was doing and pulled out of his grip.

'Aw, shit,' Ram's voice came through the dark. 'Nate, give me a second here.' They could hear him fumbling with something and then four massive spotlights shone down from some rigging above. Mattie shielded her eyes and looked up. Jesus, it was like being on *So You Think You Can Dance*. Except she was pretty certain she couldn't.

She sighed as she remembered her father putting

on Frank Sinatra and trying to waltz her around the room. Mattie had almost tripped him several times, but he'd just scooped her up and spun them through the kitchen and down the hall. Even her mother had laughed and over the giggling protests he'd pulled her mum into his arms and they'd kissed passionately. Sandwiched between her parents, Mattie had felt so safe, so protected. And then the next year her father was gone.

'Today we will start with a simple waltz.' Dennis was already moving back and forth as if he had a partner in his arms. Where had Nate and Spaz dug him out from, Mattie wondered?

'Right, now, Mattie and Charlie, you face each other again. Mattie, put your left hand on Charlie's shoulder.' Mattie did, trying not to look at Charlie. 'Now Charlie, put your right hand on Mattie's waist.' Mattie struggled not to grimace as he put his hand on her waist so reluctantly it was as if she was contagious.

A hideous half hour of torture followed. Dennis would shout right – she'd go left. Charlie would step forward the same time she did, his size tens stomping all over her patent stilettos. Even when Dennis finally gave up and just blared the music in hopes of improving their moves, it was obvious they were a disastrous combination.

'I thought gay men were supposed to be good dancers,' Mattie whispered into Charlie's ear.

'I am,' Charlie said through gritted teeth. 'But you must be genetically programmed to turn any occasion to shit.' Through the swells of the Viennese waltz she could barely believe he had the guts to say it but the look on his face showed he definitely meant it. She stamped on his foot and he yelped.

'Mattie, why don't you take a break,' Dennis said. 'I'm going to show Charlie the next set of moves. You can practise the ones you've learned over there.' He pointed off set.

'With pleasure,' Mattie said as she slunk away from the spotlights and into the back of the dark gym. The two of them deserved each other and anyway, she was starving. If memory served correctly, there used to be a vending machine in the corridor right outside the gym door. She pushed out into the hallway, blinking in the light. There it was – and it even had prawn cocktail crisps! Bonus! She opened the bag and crunched her way through a few, leaning against the wall.

God, it was weird being back here. Secondary school seemed so long ago – it had been ten years – and she was a different person now. Sure, she was still bombing through boyfriends. That hadn't changed. But back then, she had still had *some* hope not all men were like her father. That her mother could be wrong – some men wouldn't let you down. Well, after Kyle, she knew differently.

Thank God for Jess, who had always stuck by her, ever since they first met in Miss Larsen's tutor group right around the corner from here. A finger of guilt prodded her crisp-filled gut. She hadn't been that nice to Jess lately, sort of snappish and impatient. When this whole thing was finished and she had the prize money, Mattie was going to take Jess on a road trip back to the Scottish Highlands. Jess loved walking the hills and although nature made Mattie queasy, it would be worth the effort to show Jess how much she valued their friendship.

The music inside the gym shifted abruptly from waltz to tango. Dennis and Charlie dancing the tango? Now this was something she had to see! She gobbled the remaining crisps and was about to go back inside the gym when a movement down the corridor caught her eye. Under the screeching strains of the music, she could hear the low murmur of male voices. Who was down there?

She edged her way down the corridor towards the reception where she could see Nate's back crouched over a monitor and headphones clamped on his ears. Baz was beside him, and the two of them were staring at the small monitor perched on a table.

'See? I told you! Look at that!' Baz was crowing.

Nate shrugged and mumbled something Mattie couldn't hear.

Mattie inched closer. What were they looking at? She peered at the monitor and her face twisted in disgust. There, under the lights, Dennis was clutching Charlie close, running his meaty hands up and down Charlie's body in time to the swelling strings. Dennis's face was positively orgasmic and although Charlie looked like he was struggling against the older man's clench, his skinny frame was no match for Dennis.

Jeez, the man was stronger than he looked, Mattie thought as she watched Dennis fling Charlie outwards then draw him in close again, nuzzling his neck. The music finally stopped and Dennis spun away, leaving Charlie panting in the middle of the makeshift studio. Baz high-fived Nate and the two of them took off their headphones. Mattie scuttled away down the corridor.

What the hell was that all about? *Had* Nate and Baz known what had happened with Charlie way back in secondary school? Had they invited him on the show just to humiliate her all over again by recreating the scenario? Would they really go that far for a little bit of drama?

Mattie marched into the gym and over to Charlie who was wiping his dripping face. 'You two make a lovely couple,' she said.

'He just grabbed me and started dragging me around! Old queens are the worst.' Charlie glared at

Dennis who was serenely pirouetting and smiling at his reflection in the mirror.

Mattie shrugged. 'They got the whole thing on camera, you know.'

Charlie's face went pale. 'Alistair will kill me if he sees me dancing with another man!' Charlie streaked over to Ram. 'Can I see? What exactly did you film?'

Ram shrugged and heaved the camera to his shoulder again. 'I just do what they tell me. They wanted me to get some good close-ups. So I did.'

'Oh my God.' Charlie sagged to the floor. 'Turn it off, turn it off!' he shrieked as Ram trained his camera on Charlie again.

Nate and Baz burst through the gym doors. 'Is something wrong?' Nate asked. Mattie motioned towards Charlie on the floor.

Charlie jerked to his feet and ran over to Nate. 'Please don't show that film. Please! My family don't know I'm gay. I don't know what you're going to show, but . . .' He paused. 'I beg you. Please.'

Silence fell and Nate slowly shook his head and took a step back from Charlie. 'I'm sorry,' he said in a low voice.

Charlie started shaking. 'You know what? I'm done. I'm done with this show!' He ripped the mic from his chest and turned towards Mattie. 'I never should have come back here, even for the money.'

Money? Of course, they must get an appearance fee, she thought. Charlie probably wouldn't get his if he bowed out now.

Tears dripping down his cheeks, Charlie threw his mic on the floor then ran through the gym doors.

Mattie watched him go. Imagine, coming back to the scene of your first public outing and being groped by a man twice your age – then outed again on national telly. Whatever Charlie had expected to get out of the show, she could bet he hadn't counted on this. Mattie almost felt a little bit sorry for him.

'Did you get all that?' Baz was saying to Ram.

Ram nodded. 'Oh yeah. Lighting might be a bit wonky but you should be able to fix it.'

'Ace,' Baz said. 'And Nate, the press release is all set? Our official statement is ready?'

Mattie's mouth dropped open. 'Wait. You *wanted* him to leave?'

'Well, yeah, we were hoping,' Nate said. 'I mean, he is gay and everything, so–'

'I don't think it's appropriate to discuss this with a contestant,' Baz interrupted, smiling ingenuously at Mattie. 'Mattie, why don't you wait in the car? We'll take you back to the studio so you can choose your next date. Fun, right?'

Mattie grimaced. 'Yeah, fun. What are you going to do to the next guy, maim him?' After what had happened today, she wouldn't be surprised.

A small pang of sympathy shot through her as she recalled Charlie's devastation. 'You aren't really going to show all that groping on TV, are you?' she asked. 'I mean, now that Charlie's left, there's no reason.' Not to mention it was a real turn-off – watching prima donnas get busy couldn't do much to increase ratings, surely.

Baz snorted. 'No reason? That's prime footage, right there.' His mouth snapped closed as if he realised he'd said too much. 'Anyway, what do you care? It's one less man for you to worry about.'

Mattie didn't bother answering as she climbed in the car then leaned her head back against the leather seat, gazing out the window away from the school.

One ex down, three to go.

*

Nate heaved a sigh as he packed away the monitors at the school. The plan had worked – even better than they'd hoped. They'd banked on Charlie dropping out after the programme aired that evening. Charlie leaving now was a bonus; they could try to get an exclusive interview with Charlie's partner and feed the story to the tabloids to boost ratings.

Baz had already rung Silver to tell her the good news. Judging by the smug expression on his face, he was now the golden boy. Again. Next time there was a chance to stir up some conflict, Nate would go for it for all he was worth, show Silver and Baz how it's done!

At least he'd stayed strong when Charlie had begged him not to show the video. That had been terrible – the look of desperation in those eyes was awful, as if that tape would destroy his life. Which, Nate guessed, it might.

'Want to go for a drink?' Nate asked Baz as they put away the last of the equipment. 'We've got some time between now and the studio segment.' He could really use a beer. Plus it was a chance to learn just what Baz had in mind for the next guy.

Baz stared. 'Are you joking? We've got to track down a cameraman and journo in Ibiza to secure that exclusive with Charlie's partner. Not to mention getting the PR department onto a press release.'

'Oh yeah. Of course.' *Idiot,* Nate silently berated himself. He really needed to pull himself together, get with the game.

Or executive producer or not, he wouldn't be in it much longer.

CHAPTER THIRTEEN

Two in three men say they are intimidated by strong women.
The same number fantasise about sleeping with strong women.

MATTIE CLOSED HER EYES as the car dodged traffic on the M4 back towards London. If she had her way, she'd never return to Staines again. Everything there reminded her of her father – of their life together, of him leaving, of having to move out of their family house and into a small studio flat under the pitying gaze of their neighbours.

It was probably the last time Charlie would go back, too, she thought wryly. She still couldn't believe the whole thing had been engineered by Nate and Baz – she hadn't thought them anywhere near clever enough. Suddenly a thought entered her head. What if the next ex *was* Kyle? What horrors would they try to pull then?

'We're here, Miss.' The car stopped in front of the TV studios.

'Okay.' She sighed and tugged up her low-cut top. 'Mattie Johns,' she said tiredly to the receptionist inside.

'Oh yeah!' The blonde behind the desk chomped her gum. 'You're that one on the new show, innit? The one with the exes! Ha ha, if I met up with any of my exes, I'd stick 'em with a knife or somethink. Stay strong, girl!'

'Um, thanks. I will.'

The girl checked her computer. 'You're to go over to Studio Two. Can't wait to watch you tonight, girlfriend! Good luck!'

That was different, Mattie thought as she followed the signs through the labyrinth of corridors. Usually, women shied away from her rather than support her – something Mattie had always chalked up to her strong personality. It was kind of nice to have another woman on side.

She entered the studio from the back, looking down over the rows of stadium seating towards the lowered stage at the front. This studio was much smaller than the one they'd held the live show in the night before – was it only last night? – and devoid of the audience and bright lights there was something a bit creepy about it.

Onstage the same metal pods glistened, but only three this time. She crept down the stairs, curious to see what they looked like inside. Walking on her tiptoes to avoid the annoying clack of her stilettos, she crossed the stage and heaved open the door of the first pod.

Jesus, she'd hate to be confined in there for any length of time. A folding chair took up most of the space and the walls were padded with cheap imitation black velvet. She sagged into the seat and pulled the door semi-closed. It was stuffy and dim, a cross between an airplane toilet and prison cell.

'Everything ready for tonight?' A woman's sharp voice pierced the silence of the studio.

Mattie held her breath and nudged the door open a fraction of an inch more so she could hear better.

'Yes, it's all set. Seamus is in make-up and Mattie should be here any minute now. The driver said he just dropped her off.' Nate sounded even more timid than usual.

'And the men are here?' Mattie's ears cocked at the sound of the men.

'They're all out back, ready to get into the pods. All except Charlie, of course.' Mattie could hear the note of pride in Nate's voice. She still couldn't believe the idiots had pushed Charlie out.

'Baz briefed you on the storylines he's worked up for the remainder of the dates, didn't he?' The woman's voice was like ice.

Mattie heard Nate gulp. 'Of course.'

'Remember, we need excitement, conflict. I don't give a fuck what you do to get it. We just can't afford to have the ratings drop.' Her voice grew fainter as they strode off the stage.

Mattie poked her head out to make sure they were gone then scurried from the pod and onto the stage. Was that the woman behind this whole thing? She sounded scarier than Mum, and that was saying something. Mattie swallowed. She could deal with Tweedledee and Tweedledum, but that woman would definitely be a more difficult adversary. Just how far would she go to get ratings?

'Oh, there you are!' Nate appeared from the wings again. 'Let me take you to the green room and run you through the rest of the day.' Mattie followed him backstage through another maze of narrow hallways to a small room with scattered sofas and chairs. She plunked down on a chair. Nate squeezed into one facing her.

'So, in this segment, you choose your date for tomorrow,' he said.

'You've told me that a zillion times,' Mattie snapped. She felt so tired.

'Here's what will happen.' Nate tried to shift in the chair but the armrests dug into his sides, moving the chair with him. 'Seamus will introduce you, and you'll come onstage. Then, you can ask the men one question – the same question for each ex. This allows the audience to compare and contrast your past dating choices, as well as try to identify any dating patterns. Cool, huh?' Nate puffed out his chest proudly, as if he'd just discovered the cure for cancer.

Mattie shook her head. What kind of idiot audience cared about her dating patterns? As if she even had any . . . unless you considered dating loser after loser a pattern. More like an inevitable consequence of being heterosexual.

Nate handed her a stack of cards. 'Here. Choose one of these. Please don't change the questions this time.' He gave her a stern look and Mattie sniggered. Like she was going to listen to him! And now that she knew those men were her exes . . . watch out!

'You'll choose your date for tomorrow, then Seamus will close out the show. It's not live, so we might retake things a few times.'

'Great.' Mattie gritted her teeth. She just wanted this to be over.

Mattie stared at the wall, trying to think of a question that would tell her exactly who these men were. One of them had a foreign-sounding voice but that didn't exactly narrow it down – she'd dated loads of men from Italians to Lebanese. No one could say she discriminated, she thought, plucking at a loose thread on the sofa.

What if one of the men was Kyle? What could she ask that might reveal it was him? *Did you ever love me?* Mattie shook her head to dislodge the thought. What a stupid question – and anyway, the answer was pretty bloody clear. Kyle had *told* her he loved her, but if you loved someone, you didn't go off and cheat, then steal their business. No, that question wouldn't separate him from the others.

What was one thing he knew about her no one else did? He knew about her prawn cocktail crisp addiction, something she generally tried to keep hidden (over-consumption of prawn cocktail crisps was hardly an activity a hard-hitting businesswoman should indulge in). He knew she hated oysters – like eating mucous, she'd told him on numerous occasions. And he knew she sometimes snored when she was really tired, that she loved sleeping with his arm curled around her side . . . and that sometimes, in the middle of the night, she'd wake up sweaty and shaky from bad dreams. Mattie's cheeks flushed at just how much he did know about her.

Did she really want to ask a question that would give away something so personal to the audience *and* show Kyle she was wondering if he was there? Even if he wasn't, he'd probably be watching the whole thing on TV with glee. She shifted through the boring questions on the cards. Probably better to stick with one of these for now.

'We're ready for you.' Headset waved her from the green room. Mattie stood and followed her into the wings. Onstage, she could see Seamus gripping the podium as if it was the last bottle of gin on Earth.

'Let's say hello to our luscious single lady, Mattie Johns!' Seamus slurred, nearly falling over as he waved his arms in her direction.

Mattie waited a moment, sure they would do a retake. But Headset gave her a push onto the stage and Mattie went flying forward, almost landing on Seamus's lap. Grimacing, she settled onto the stool near the podium, trying not to look at the pods. The studio was eerily quiet without the live audience.

Seamus leaned in close to her and nearly knocked Mattie out with the sweet smell of gin. His suit was shot through with some kind of hideous thread so that every time he moved it looked like sparks were coming off of him. It hurt her eyes. 'So, Mattie. An interesting date with Charlie, yes? Now it's time to choose tomorrow's lucky fellow.' He pronounced the last two words 'feel-low' and Mattie couldn't have agreed more.

Mattie smiled. 'Yes, I can't wait.' The less said about her last date with Charlie, the better.

But Seamus had other ideas. 'Did you know Charlie was *gay*?' He spit the word out, covering Mattie in a drizzle of saliva.

Mattie resisted the urge to wipe her face and/or throw up. 'Well, I suspected, but I wasn't sure.' No way was she going into all the details of her prom disaster on national television.

'How humiliating for you, my poor single lady.' Seamus patted her shoulder and Mattie tried not to grimace. 'Dating is tough, isn't it? So hard to make good choices!'

Mattie nodded along. At least she wasn't coming off as the baddie. Playing the victim was certainly a new role for her.

'Let's see if you have better luck next time around!' Seamus said. He leaned down and the overpowering odour of alcohol nearly made her faint. 'Who are the men in those pods, Mattie Johns? Is it someone you chucked, here for vengeance? Or the love of your life, back to try again?'

'I don't know,' Mattie said, trying to smile as best she could with her teeth clamped together. If only she *did* know just who those men were!

'Well, let's find out! It's time to ask our exes one more question. What will it be, Mattie?'

Mattie shuffled through the cards, trying not to think about whether Kyle was one of the men.

She grabbed a card at random.

'What do you do to stay in shape?' Stupid question.

'Ex Number Two?' Seamus said. 'I'll direct that to you first.'

The lights on the pod started flashing. There was a pause then the robotic voice said: 'I do many many exercises.'

Mattie rolled her eyes. Who *was* that? Had she dated a brain-dead cretin at some point? (Well, yes. Quite a number of them.)

'Ex Number Three?'

'I do four hours of exercise each day. Two hours of free-weights in the morning, then two hours of cardio each evening. Keeping in shape is extremely important to me.'

Mattie raised her eyebrows. Jesus, four hours a day? What kind of loser had that amount of time on their hands? The guy must be some sort of fanatic. A super-cut fanatic, but still.

'Ex Number Four?'

'I like to run.'

Mattie froze. Kyle used to go running. Could that be him? He'd dragged her along with him a few times and although she protested, secretly she loved the empty morning streets before the city awakened. They'd always gone for a big fry-up afterwards. Breakfast had never tasted so good.

Get real, she told herself. That could be anyone – millions of fitness-obsessed people run. Maybe she should have asked the prawn crisp question after all?

'So there you have it. Three men, three answers. Who will it be, Mattie?' Seamus bent down close to her again. 'Who will be up next on *The Hating Game*?' His over-the-top delivery seemed even more ridiculous without the audience reactions.

The real question was: which social reject was she

about to let out of the cage now? Well, she had to date all of them, so what difference did it make?

'Number Two, please, Seamus.' Might as well deal with the brain-dead cretin first. After today's drama, she could do with an easy ride tomorrow.

'Ex Number Two, come meet Mattie Johns . . . again!'

Mattie pasted a smile on her face as she waited for the simpleton to emerge. Who would it be?

A dark curly head appeared and its owner swung around to face her, offering the same bouquet of poisonous purple flowers Charlie had given her the night before. *'Ciao, bella!'*

It was . . . Mattie strained to remember: *was* it Giovanni or Giancarlo? She hadn't been able to get it straight even when they were together. Right now, all she could recall was meeting him last year when she'd escaped to Italy. She'd packed up Kyle's things, left his boxes in the stairwell, then took off to the Cinque Terre. She hadn't even told Jess where she was going or how long she'd be. She just wanted to get away.

Whatever his name, he'd been the manager of the hotel where she'd stayed. It was *so* clichéd: English woman, alone on holiday, wooed by the foreign man. Despite his tenuous grasp on English – or maybe because of it – she'd let herself just go with it. The fling was a welcome distraction from the hand that tore at her heart every time she thought of Kyle.

He crossed the stage and leaned down to kiss her on both cheeks, his spicy cologne burning her nose.

'Hello, um . . . Giancarlo?' she said tentatively. They *had* only been together for two weeks. Hardly long enough to remember a name, was it?

'Giovanni.' His face clouded but quickly morphed into a huge grin, which he dealt straight at the camera. Mattie remembered he'd once told her he wanted to be a model. Or an actor. Or a politician, because they got all the hot women.

'Yes, of course! Giovanni!' She nodded as if she'd known all along.

How exactly had they left things? Oh yes. Dinner at the hotel the last night of her trip. After watching Giovanni's mother boss his dad around in the small open kitchen, Mattie had remarked how his mum clearly wore the trousers – very unattractive polyester ones that really needed to be about four sizes larger, but Mattie had kept that bit to herself – in the relationship. Giovanni had got all puffed up and red in face and stormed out, and that was the last she'd seen of him. What a wuss, she thought. She'd meant it as a compliment but clearly it was too much for his ego to handle.

'So our single lady has chosen Ex Number Two, Giovanni Costa. Tune in tomorrow at eight to watch Mattie and Giovanni's date, then make your Date Rate! And see which lucky guy Mattie chooses for the next date!'

Seamus leered at the camera and swayed. 'There is no Date Rate tonight, due to Charlie's hasty departure. But stay tuned after this show for our live exclusive with Charlie's *former* partner Alistair Perry, as he reveals how he feels about today's earlier dramatic events. Get the real story, right here on X-ACT!'

The second the camera swung away from him, Seamus slumped to the floor, head lolling. A loud voice from the control room reminded him he needed to close, and he lifted his chin slightly but remained horizontal.

'So join us tomorrow for another edition of . . . *The Hating Game*!' The lights lowered and *The Hating Game*'s purple logo flashed up on the screen behind them, casting an eerie pastel glow on their faces.

'And we're out!' the voice boomed. And before Mattie could speak to Giovanni, she was ushered offstage, into the waiting car and away from the studio.

*

'Let me in! I've got your favourite!' Jess held up the king-sized bag of prawn cocktail crisps to the intercom and jiggled it around. She wrinkled her nose. How Mattie could eat these things was beyond her. They were downright foul.

'Hurry!' Mattie's voice sounded through the speaker. 'It's just about to start!'

Jess ran up the stairs to the first-floor flat, glancing at her watch. Five minutes until *The Hating Game* broadcast. Mattie wouldn't tell her what had gone down earlier that day – she'd only said Jess wouldn't believe it. Jess prayed whatever it was, it didn't involve poor Adam. He wasn't returning her phone calls or messages and she was starting to get worried.

Mattie swung open the door, holding a glass of wine, and Jess blinked. She still couldn't get used to Mattie's flaming red hair, although she had to admit it was growing on her. Anything was better than the boring black bob Mattie had since, well, forever.

'Have a seat.' Her friend immediately liberated the crisps from Jess's hands and plonking her glass on a bureau, opened the bag and popped a handful in her mouth.

'Come on, fill me in!' Jess took a gulp of the wine Mattie handed her. 'What happened? Who will it be tomorrow?' Please let it not be Adam, she chanted inside her head.

Mattie shook her head. 'Nope. I want to see your reaction. Honestly, the whole thing is just crazy.'

Jess nodded slowly, turning up the telly a few notches as the demented song by the *Jackson 5* blasted out. She normally liked the energetic bopping of *I Want You Back*, but someone had changed the tune so that the notes slid up and down like a camera going in and out of focus. It was just . . . weird. Jess rubbed her arms to erase the goose pimples.

'Tonight,' Seamus Leary's voice boomed from the set, 'Mattie Johns and her high-school sweetheart Charlie Robbins give love – and hate – another try. Has romance triumphed over revenge? Watch and see on . . . *The Hating Game*!'

'Jesus,' Mattie swore, stuffing more crisps into her mouth.

'Oh my God! Is that our secondary school?' Jess asked as they watched a limo pull up in front of the building and Mattie climb out. The camera cut to a shot of a man in a purple jumpsuit instructing them to relax and shake it off. Jess couldn't help giggling at the expression on Mattie's face on screen. 'You're dancing?'

'I know,' Mattie said grimly. They watched her and Charlie crash into each other. 'Pure torture. But keep watching. It gets worse.'

The camera cut to a shot of Mattie leaving the gym, then ballroom music was replaced by the blaring sounds of tango. All of a sudden, the man in the purple jumpsuit grabbed Charlie and pressed his body against him.

'What the . . .?' Jess's mouth fell open as she stared at the shots filling the screen: hands were sliding over body parts, purple jumpsuit man was nuzzling Charlie's neck and then a quick shot of Charlie's parted, panting lips.

'Oh my God,' Jess breathed. She glanced at Mattie. It was like prom night all over again! Minus the hideous outfits, hairdos and teachers. She took another look at the screen. Okay, minus the teachers.

Mattie nodded. 'I know. And the way they're cutting it makes it a million times worse. The guy was pretty much just dragging Charlie around.'

'Doesn't seem like it!' Jess said, motioning towards the screen where what looked to be Charlie's leg was pressed up against the purple bloke's crotch.

Together they watched as Charlie ripped off his mic and stormed out of the gym. Tears streamed down his face and Jess's heart ached for him. Imagine; your whole life destroyed in front of the nation.

'Mattie, you sure about all this?' she asked suddenly. 'I mean, the producers did surprise you with the ex thing. And look what they did to Charlie! Is being on this show really worth it?' As soon as the words left her mouth she knew they were futile. If the show could help Mattie save her business, she would sacrifice anything. It was all Mattie cared about – especially after Kyle had left, striking a major blow. Her focus and drive were downright scary.

Mattie stared at Jess as if she'd just announced she was pregnant with Hannibal Lector's love child. 'Of course the show's worth it! It's the only way to get back on track, finance-wise. You know that.' Mattie grabbed a handful of crisps.

Jess watched her best friend chomp as she tried to think of a response. But what was the point? Mattie wouldn't listen to her anyway.

'In a surprise move, Charlie has left *The Hating Game*,' Seamus's voice blared from the telly. 'There is no Date Rate tonight, due to Charlie's hasty departure. But stay tuned after this show for our live exclusive with Charlie's *former* partner Alistair Perry, as he reveals how he feels about today's earlier dramatic events. Get the real story, right here on X-ACT!'

Jess shook her head as the camera cut to a suave older man with a goatee. He was wearing leggings and a tank top and, like Charlie, sported a full head of highlights.

'I've been with Charlie since he first came here after secondary school,' the man was saying. He turned and blew his nose delicately on a silk handkerchief as the camera zoomed in. 'Excuse me, this is very difficult.'

'Also coming up on *The Hating Game*, our sexy single lady chooses a date for tomorrow!' Seamus's voice interrupted.

Mattie snapped off the TV. 'God, this is dumb.'

Jess grabbed the remote and flipped it back on. 'Wait! I want to see who you're dating tomorrow!'

Mattie rolled her eyes. 'Some idiot who can barely speak English. I don't know what I was thinking when I shagged him.'

A few minutes later, Jess's heart leapt as she watched a foreign man emerge from the pod. Thank God it wasn't Adam – he was safe for another day, anyway. She'd keep calling, keep trying to reach him. He had to pick up sometime, right? If he *was* on the show, maybe she could convince him it wasn't too late to back out.

'I'd better go,' Jess said, shrugging on her coat.

'Want to stay? I can make up the sofa again.'

Jess shook her head. She had to get home and attempt to get through to Adam again. Mattie was tough enough to handle whatever *The Hating Game* threw her way – but Adam . . .

She'd let him down once. She wasn't going to fail him again.

*

As the grating chords of *I Want You Back* filled his living room and the credits rolled across the TV screen, Adam switched off *The Hating Game* and turned on the latest version of Snake Software's interactive video game for his late-night workout. Every fibre of his being craved Jaffa Cakes, but he hadn't been working out like a fiend every day to ruin it all for some calorific treats.

No, he thought as he furiously beat the on-screen opponent by slicing off an arm with a sword, all his efforts wouldn't go to waste. He'd look like a suave hero if it killed him.

He held out the waistband of his trousers and smiled. Already he'd lost at least a stone, and by keeping to the protein shake and exercise regimen, he'd be sure to drop at least that much next week. The weight loss was visible in his face, too: cheekbones were emerging and his jaw looked firmer, more defined. Adam smoothed down his hair then ran a hand over newly polished skin. Yes, he was getting there.

After what had happened on the show tonight, he had even more of a chance to woo Mattie. Seeing Charlie had shocked him – any competition from secondary school was certainly unexpected. Still, Charlie got what he deserved, treating Mattie the way he had. Adam puffed hard, jogging on the spot as the game reloaded. He hadn't gone to the prom – if he couldn't go with Mattie, he didn't want to go – but he'd heard of the Kwong fiasco from Jess.

He watched the game's closing sequence; his favourite bit, where the hero sweeps away his opponent then climbs over the castle wall to rescue the damsel in distress. The hero clutches the damsel close, the music swells . . .

Game ready! flashed the screen. Adam took a deep breath and got ready for battle again.

CHAPTER FOURTEEN

*Eighty per cent of women consider Italian men the sexiest.
Only point five per cent of women would date a Scouser.*

'MISS? MISS! OPEN UP!'

Mattie groaned and opened her eyes. Whoever was at her door deserved a good beating. It wasn't even seven yet and there was still an hour left before she had to get up for Giovanni's date. Who the hell could it be?

'For Christ's sake, I'm coming!' she yelled, pulling on her robe. She swung open the door to be faced with a burly woman sporting a very unattractive brown uniform and the beginnings of a matching moustache. By the sound of the voice, Mattie had thought it was a man outside.

'Yes?' Mattie said, scowling.

'Bailiff from Eastwood Collection Services,' the woman said in a low raspy voice.

'Bailiff?' Mattie rubbed her eyes. The woman looked more like a zookeeper than a bailiff. 'You've got the wrong address.' She tried to close the door but the woman stuck her black-booted foot in the way. 'What the–?'

'I have a warrant from Westminster City Council to recover one hundred and twenty pounds.' The bailiff handed Mattie an official-looking document.

Mattie blinked as the small print swam beneath her eyes.

'What? One hundred and twenty pounds? For what?'

The bailiff snorted and grabbed the paper back again. 'Look, there's a record here of all the letters they've sent you. Original offence was six months back, a parking penalty charge notice for this vehicle registration number.' She waved the sheet in Mattie's face. 'Is that your car?'

'It was,' Mattie said. 'I sold it last month.' God, she missed that car.

'Well, it was registered under your name at the time of the offence. Now do you have the one hundred and twenty pounds, or should I start removing some of your goods?'

'But wait!' Mattie cried as the woman pushed past her and started eyeing her flat. 'I never received those warnings!'

'Yeah, right. That's what they all say.' The bailiff whipped her thick braid over her shoulder. 'Is this your address?' She shoved another white paper under Mattie's nose.

'Er, yes, but I don't remember seeing them . . .' Mattie's voice trailed off as something in her mind's eye recognized the Westminster City logo. She'd just thought they were more reminders of her overdue council tax bill. Her brain had completely blocked out the ticket she'd got by returning to her car just one minute after the parking meter had run out. Despite threatening and insulting the parking attendant until he'd started snivelling, he still hadn't let her off. Wanker.

'So what will it be? Cash or goods?' The bailiff was tapping her foot briskly and smirking at Mattie.

Mattie stared back, her mind running through her bank accounts. She was already *over* her overdraft in her business account; she'd be lucky if she had enough to cover the mortgage in her personal one; and her credit cards . . . forget it. She'd used every bit of her personal credit and equity to keep the business afloat. Nothing remained.

She scanned the room, unable to believe it had really come to giving a bailiff her possessions to pay a bill for such a paltry sum. One hundred and twenty pounds had never seemed such a big deal before. Mattie could remember when she'd blown that sum in one night with some pricey takeaway Thai food.

'Goods, I guess,' Mattie mumbled.

The bailiff cracked her fingers and Mattie winced. 'One hundred and twenty pounds . . .' the bailiff said as she circled the room. 'Do you have an old laptop or something? That might do it.'

'There's no way you're taking my computer!' Mattie scooped it up and held it against her chest.

The bailiff shrugged. 'Hurry up and give me something, then.'

'What, do you have an appointment at the barber?' Mattie asked. But the woman remained stony faced.

Mattie went into her bedroom and over to her jewellery box. She'd never been one for jewellery, so most of what she'd accumulated had been from Kyle. As soon as they'd split, she gathered it all up, shoved it in a sandwich bag and put it into her safety deposit box at the bank. Out of sight, out of mind. She pushed aside a jumble of old tangled necklaces. What was that? Light flashed on a creamy white stone set in a slightly tarnished silver band.

Mattie swallowed. It was the ring her father had given her on her seventh birthday. Mattie remembered rubbing her thumb across the opal, fascinated by the feel of the stone. The ring had been too big for her skinny fingers back then, but now . . . Mattie grabbed it and tried it on. It fit perfectly, and the cream of the stone set off her colouring. She turned her fingers back and forth, admiring the way the light reflected off the opal.

Would it be worth one hundred and twenty pounds? She slipped it off and looked at the band. There was a kind of mark on the inside; it must be real silver. But something caught in her heart when she thought of handing it over to the bailiff. Mattie slammed the jewellery box closed and went back out to the lounge. 'Take the television,' she said to the bailiff, who was pacing back and forth.

The bailiff shrugged and eyed the plasma screen. 'Fine. But it's probably worth more than what I need.'

Mattie waved a hand. 'I don't care. Just take it and get out.' Kyle had bought it when he'd first moved in, insisting he wouldn't watch anything on Mattie's tiny aging set.

The bailiff pulled the plug and heaved it onto her shoulder. 'Here, sign this.' She shoved a form at Mattie, who scrawled her name on it.

How ironic, Mattie thought as she sank down onto the sofa, staring at the blank spot where the television had once been. A reality TV star without a TV. She shook her head. God, this was the pits. How could Jess even ask if she *really* needed to do the show?

She had no choice – it was *The Hating Game* or broke.

*

A few hours later, Mattie rode in the car on her way to whatever delights awaited with Giovanni. She looked out the window, turning from Nate and Ram. After the earlier episode with the bailiff, she was in no mood to deal with Tweedledee, Tweedledum or a stupid idiot whose only aspiration was to appear on TV. Being forced into a too-tight corset and another miniscule skirt – despite her protests and empty threats – didn't help matters, either.

She looked over at Nate who was busily examining the production schedule on a clipboard as if his life depended on it. 'Tell me what's happening today,' she snapped.

Nate looked up at her, a hangdog expression of fear on his pie-like face. God, she could just slap him! Anger flashed through her and she gripped itchy fingers in clenched fists.

Nate cleared his throat. 'Um, you'll find out in a second. Right now we should probably do a few questions about your relationship with Giovanni.' He nudged Ram who was snoring beside him, softly despite his sizeable bulk. 'Ready?'

Ram jumped and jerked the camera to his shoulder. 'Ready.' He focused in on Mattie.

'There's really nothing to tell,' Mattie said. 'I went to Italy, we met, we fucked, I came home.'

Ram snorted and Nate's cheeks flushed. 'We can't use profanity before nine p.m. and this will air at eight. Do you think you could say that again, um, without fuck?' He slid away from her as if she might hit him.

'Oh, for God's sake,' Mattie huffed. Wet men like Nate probably preferred *making love* to fuck, but the reality was that she and Giovanni had fucked. There'd been no love involved. The only real time she could say she made love had been with . . . No, she wouldn't think about that.

Thankfully she was saved from repeating her answer by their arrival at a battered building just off Whitechapel.

'We'll get the clips later,' Nate said to Ram as they got out of the car.

'Where are we?' she asked. There was no sign and

the rusted aluminium facade of the building gave nothing away.

'Just hang out here a sec,' Nate said. 'I'm going to check and make sure everything's set then we'll bring you through. Giovanni will explain what you'll be doing today.' An expression Mattie couldn't quite read flashed across Nate's face. 'Ram, stay here. I'll give you the signal when we're ready.'

Ram nodded and lit a cigarette as Nate disappeared inside.

Mattie turned towards him. 'Is this all you do? Just follow instructions? Can't you think for yourself?'

Ram took a drag of his cigarette. 'Look, lady, just 'coz you're angry about sommat or other don't mean you can take it out on me. If you want to get your teeth into something, get a bone and chew on it.'

She opened her mouth to let loose a stream of words but Ram turned on the camera and focused in on her. 'They're ready for us.'

Mattie smoothed her corset and tried to tug down the skirt to at least a level where it covered one full butt cheek. She pulled open the door and entered the fluorescent-lighted foyer, which reeked of sweat and rotten eggs.

Giovanni was leaning against the wall, jutting his hipbones out underwear-model style. *'Ciao, bella. Va bene?'*

Despite the anger curling through her, she couldn't help grinning at the cheesy greeting. It was the first thing he'd said to her when they met, back when she'd been feeling anything but *bella*. Giovanni's words that night in Italy had made her smile then, too.

He leaned down and gave her a kiss, his stubble scraping against her cheek.

'So, what do you have planned?' She tried to sound excited for the camera.

Giovanni grinned. 'You gonna love it. We gonna do the . . .' He paused for dramatic effect and Ram brought the camera in even closer. 'Mudwrestle!'

Giovanni slid an arm around her waist and tugged her up against him.

Mattie extricated herself from the bear grip. 'You must be joking. Who *mudwrestles*, anyway? Other than demented women trying to turn on equally demented men who actually get off on that sort of thing.'

Giovanni shrugged. 'De-mented? I donna understand thatta word.'

'Oh, forget it. Nate!' she bellowed. Magically Nate seemed to have disappeared, but Spaz was sitting nearby, whispering something into a mobile phone.

'BAZ!'

He sighed and snapped the phone shut. 'Oh, hello, Mattie. You made it.' He leered at her corset and skirt combo. 'Nice.'

'Nice for a prostitute,' Mattie spat. 'You do realise I'm not going to mudwrestle, don't you?'

Baz cocked his head. 'Actually, no. No, I don't realise that, at all. You'll do what we tell you to do. Know why? Because, remember, we have a stand-in ready to go the instant you refuse to do something we ask. Don't think we won't drop you.'

'You wouldn't dare throw away everything you've spent so far,' Mattie said, staring into his beady eyes. Even a network as big as X-ACT couldn't chuck out three days' worth of production costs, could they?

'Wanna bet?' Baz jerked his chin upwards, smiling gleefully.

Mattie let out a puff of air in disgust, then turned away. Bloody hell! He was bluffing, she was sure – almost. Gritting her teeth, she reasoned that at least mudwrestling wasn't pole dancing, although it wasn't that far off.

Nate reappeared from whatever hole he'd squirmed into. 'Mattie, we need you to put this on.' He threw her a bikini that looked better suited for a belly dancer than a mudwrestler. It jangled like a tambourine in her arms.

Mattie prodded it with one finger, shaking her head as it jingled in response. 'Nate, seriously.'

'What?' Nate's face was open. Given his looks, shaking a tambourine was probably the most action he'd get all year, Mattie thought. God knows he wouldn't be shaking his booty.

Baz elbowed his way between them. 'We don't have time for this. Ram, follow Mattie into the changing room to get a few interior shots. We'll meet you in the main ring in ten.'

'Righto,' Ram said, chomping on his gum and eyeing Mattie's barely covered rear.

'Back off, Ram,' Mattie said as she swung around to face Baz. The ratings-hungry producer mightn't give a toss about her, but maybe he'd care about the reaction of the female audience segment when they saw her kitted out like a stripper. She shook the costume in the air, grimacing at the noise it made. 'You know, any female watching this will be up in arms! You can't just expect a woman in this day and age to strip off and exploit her sexuality on live telly.'

Baz rolled his eyes. 'Don't worry, Mattie, it's not live, and Giovanni's stripping too.' He took her shoulders and swivelled her in the direction of the changing room. 'You really don't get it, do you? People *love* to watch this kind of stuff. They lap it up!'

Mattie opened her mouth to respond but a memory stopped her: Jess, laughing over an episode of last year's hit reality show, *Rockin' Royals*. The show took a group of B-list royals and tried to make them into a rock group. In one episode, Lord Gerrard of somewhere-

or-other was made to dress up like a condom and serenade a Soho street just as the bars were letting out. He'd been set upon by the crowds and one over-enthusiastic drunk bloke even tried to snog him! The normally sympathetic Jess had chortled with delight as she recounted the event. Baz was right. People did love this stuff.

Mattie sighed and walked into the tiny ladies' changing area. The tiles were cracked and it was freezing. 'Don't get too excited,' she said to Ram, still following her. 'You're not going to see anything.'

Ram sniggered. 'I've seen it all a million times. Anyway, don't worry. I like mine of the put-up-and-shut-up variety.'

'If they're with you they probably don't have enough brainpower to form thoughts, anyway,' Mattie said, shuffling into a narrow cubicle where she knew Ram couldn't follow.

She pulled on the belly-dancer outfit, creating a symphony of noise. Jesus Christ, she thought, unable to keep the smile off her face at the ridiculousness of it all. She jiggled back and forth, covering her ears as the noise of the bells echoed off the cubicle's bare walls.

'What the hell are you doing? Come on!' Ram shouted.

Not daring to look in the mirror, Mattie left the small cubicle, toes curling at the feel of cold grimy tiles. She'd need a tetanus shot after this, for sure.

Ram guffawed at the sight of her. 'You certainly pulled out all the bells and whistles.' He hoisted the camera to his shoulder as she jangled her way towards him.

Mattie pasted on a smile. Remember, be nice while the camera is rolling, she told herself. The audience was on her side now, no point in losing that advantage.

Inside the large gym it was even cooler. She rubbed

her arms as she walked over to the centre of the room, where a boxing-style ring was set up. Its high sides prevented her from seeing what was inside – not that she was eager to find out.

'You and Giovanni will have three rounds,' Nate explained as she and Ram walked over. Giovanni was slowly jogging laps around the perimeter of the room, wearing a pair of silk shorts and throwing Rocky-like punches in the air. Idiotic, yes, but Mattie had to concede he had a killer body. 'Five minutes in the ring, then a five minute break.'

'No other rules?' She glanced nervously at Giovanni. It was all fun and games, right? Surely he wouldn't *hurt* her; that wouldn't make him look very good to the public. Not that Giovanni had the smarts to think strategically – he'd once asked her if the Queen was a man or woman! But if he was here to show off his muscles, well . . . it wasn't like she could count on Baz or Nate to protect her.

Mattie drew herself up to her full height and tried to remember the defensive moves Miss Pedlar had demonstrated in secondary school PE. She'd never had to use them – she prided herself in taking care of any situation without so much as raising her voice. A group of chavs once tried to tear her BlackBerry from her hand in Kilburn, but she'd just stared at the four skinny losers, asked them if they were on medication for their skin conditions and told them they'd better hit the gym to bulk up if they ever wanted to get laid. They'd slunk off down the street without a backward glance.

Nate clapped his hands. 'Let's get going.' Giovanni jogged over, sweat glistening on his hardened pecs. Two giant spotlights flicked onto the ring and the fluorescent lights dimmed so the rest of the place was almost dark. 'All right, Mattie and Giovanni, into the ring. When I say action, I want you to shake hands and wait for the horn. Then you can start.'

Mattie walked over to the raised platform and swung herself up through the ropes. Her bare foot plunged into a layer of slime reaching up to her shins. Don't look down, she told herself as she manoeuvred into the corner of the ring. Don't even think about what might be in that slime. Whatever it was, it pulled at her feet with each step she took. And – she wrinkled her nose – it smelled terrible; a combination of damp socks and decaying meat. Her stomach roiled with nausea and she tilted her head upwards to gulp in fresh air.

'Ready?' Nate yelled, his voice echoing around the empty space. 'Action!'

Mattie let go of the ropes and took a tentative step towards the centre, trying to read the expression on Giovanni's face as he came towards her. They shook hands quickly and Mattie retreated slowly to the corner, breathing deeply. She'd be fine. She was just cold. Once she got moving she was sure everything would be all right.

BEEP!

The klaxon sounded and the spotlights got even brighter. Mattie could only just make out Giovanni's silhouette against the blinding light. She raised a hand to cover her eyes, squinting, trying to move towards his shape.

'Ouf!' Giovanni put his arms around her waist and levered her off her feet before slamming her down into the mess below. Mattie spit out the brown goo sliding down her face and slicked back her hair before grabbing Giovanni's feet and pulling. Before she knew it, he'd toppled over into the mud, too. She grabbed a handful of slop and slung it in his direction. It landed with a satisfying plop on his perfectly tanned face.

She couldn't help giggling as Giovanni tried to wipe

off the sludge, spreading it even more around his face. She threw another glop. To her surprise, Giovanni smiled back, then lobbed a chunk in her direction.

Soon, they were laughing and sliding around the pit. The klaxon sounded and they retreated to opposite corners, sagging against the ropes, breathless with mirth.

'Cut!' Nate yelled. Mattie looked over at him with surprise. Baz was furiously whispering in his ear, the look on his face anything but pleased. What were those two clowns up to? She ran a tentative foot along the bottom of the slime. Could Kyle be hiding there in scuba gear? After what she'd seen the TweedleDuo do to Charlie, she wouldn't put anything past them. Or maybe they were just annoyed because she and Giovanni were having fun.

Whoa! Mattie stole a glance at Giovanni as he wiped his face with a towel. They *were* having fun. She couldn't remember the last time she'd actually had a good time with a guy on a date. Usually, she was so concerned with making sure he knew who was boss she couldn't relax. It'd been different with Kyle. She already *was* his boss. And when they were together, she could just let herself go without worrying.

But this isn't a real scenario, she reminded herself. We're in a mudwrestling ring, for God's sake. In the boardroom, I'd have him begging for mercy in a heartbeat.

'Right, guys, that's fine for now. You can come out of there,' Nate called. The giant spotlights switched off with a pop.

Thank God, Mattie thought, trying not to slip as she stepped out of the ring. It'd been fun for a few minutes but she wasn't about to stick around in the stinky slime for more. She headed for the changing room, fantasising about a lovely hot shower. Now that she wasn't moving, the gunk on her skin had become hardened and cold. She wrapped her arms around her body to keep warm.

'Wait a sec,' Nate called. 'Just give yourself a quick wipe down, then we're going to a café. You and Giovanni will make pizza.'

'I do notta cook,' Giovanni shouted from where he was still standing in the ring. 'Cooking is for da ladies. I am not da lady!'

What a chauvinistic pig. Mattie smirked as he tried to climb out of the ring but fell back into the mud with a sploshy thud. 'Doesn't your father cook?' she asked, knowing full well he did. Her mind flashed back to the image of Giovanni's mother screaming at his father that the pasta needed another *minuto stupido!* 'Surely he taught you how to make pizza, at least!'

Giovanni slapped the slime from his face and struggled to his feet. 'No! I do notta do da cook!' His voice rose with every syllable.

'I'll see you in the kitchen!' Mattie smiled sweetly, pulling the towel around her shoulders. She padded back over to the changing room, tingling feet leaving a trail of muddy footprints.

An hour later, Mattie and Giovanni were in Peace of Pizza, a grimy little café just outside Liverpool Street Station – one of those holes-in-the-wall that Mattie avoided like the plague. There was barely enough room for Mattie, Giovanni and the Iraqi owner to fit in the kitchen, and with Ram jammed up in the corner it was downright claustrophobic.

You'd think they'd at least plump for Pizza Express, Mattie thought as she looked around at the stained walls and peeling paint. But this? She shuddered, nearly stepping into a stream of unidentifiable liquid leaching from the back wall. Christ, what if she caught dengue fever or something? The whole thing seemed very poorly organized. Nate and Baz had rushed in from the car to check out the premises; obviously they hadn't even been here before!

If they were working for her, she would have fired them.

'Can we just get this started?' Mattie interrupted Giovanni and Ali the owner, who were arguing furiously about the best pizza toppings. Her skin was crawling from the mud-pit slime and her face burned with the heat coming from the large oven in the corner of the room. And the day was far from over – after this, she still had to go back to the studio to choose the next loser for tomorrow's date. She'd certainly have earned her two hundred thousand pounds when this whole thing was finally finished.

'Ali, when Ram gives you the signal, you demonstrate how to roll the base,' Nate said, sticking his head in from the minute eating area out front. 'Then Mattie and Giovanni will roll their bases. Ali will show you the toppings to make the rest of your pizza. Pop it in the oven, then we'll cut to you eating.'

'Sounds great!' Ali rubbed his hands. 'Pizza is peace,' he said, smiling straight into Ram's camera – which wasn't even on. 'I welcome you very much to my café.'

'Another nutter,' Mattie muttered as she surveyed the cooking implements before her. She couldn't remember the last time she'd cooked something besides ready meals from Waitrose. Her mum had banished her from the kitchen at an early age, saying no daughter of hers was going to be a slave to domesticity. Luckily Jess had been on hand to show Mattie the basics, like making toast.

The one time Mattie *had* attempted to cook

something from scratch had been a disaster: a birthday cake for Kyle that had turned out more pancake than cake (who knew there were two kinds of flour?). Kyle had made a valiant effort to eat it anyway.

'Rolling!' Ram pointed the camera in their direction.

Ali smiled and laid his hands on his heart. 'I welcome you to Peace of Pizza. I believe we can make peace one pizza at a time.'

Mattie coughed loudly to cover bubbling laughter. Baz glared warningly at her.

'Now, I show Mattie and Giovanni how to bake their own peace-a!' With a flourish, Ali put a roll of dough in front of her before throwing one rather unceremoniously at Giovanni. 'First thing you must do is take your rolling pin' – he held his up in the air and nearly clocked Ram's camera – 'and smooth it out like so.' He deftly flattened his dough.

Giovanni shook his head, scowling like a toddler. 'I told you, I do notta cook.'

Mattie almost expected him to stamp his foot, too. 'Come on, Giovanni. I don't cook either!' She lowered her voice and covered her mic. 'Just do it,' she hissed. 'The sooner you do it, the sooner we get out of here.'

Giovanni jerked away, nearly knocking her and Ali over. 'You notta my mama! You do notta tell me whatta do!' He took the lump of dough in front of him and heaved it against the wall. 'I DO NOTTA COOK!'

Ali grabbed him by the neck. 'No violence in my kitchen! Pizza is peace!' He shook Giovanni with every word. 'You stay, you cook. You fight, you go.' He let go of Giovanni who stared at him, wild-eyed.

Giovanni and Ali squared off.

Mattie looked at them and wondered who would actually win if it did come to blows. Ali was an Arabic version of Danny DeVito, and even though he was half

Giovanni's size he was built like a bulldog. Her money was on the Iraqi.

'Okay, I stay,' Giovanni said, quickly recovering his composure and smiling into the camera. 'I stay.'

Mattie rolled her eyes. He'd obviously weighed up the options and figured being on television was worth a little ego bruising.

Ali stepped back over to where his dough was. 'Right.' He grinned into the camera. 'Let's make peace with pizza.'

CHAPTER FIFTEEN

*Thirty per cent of women admit to shopping for
a wedding dress, pre-proposal.
Seventeen per cent of wedding dresses purchased never get used.*

BACK AT LONDON STUDIOS, MATTIE slumped into a chair in the green room as she waited to go on set. She'd been so busy all day she hadn't had the chance to think about the two losers who were left.

Imagine if one was Stuart. She thought of his car blowing by her at the bus stop as she stood dripping and cold from the silly dunk tank incident, and anger shot through her. If it *was* him, she'd certainly do everything she could to exact revenge – including telling the whole nation about his toe-nail clipping habit and miniscule appendage. The women of Britain deserved to know. Maybe she could use her one question tonight to focus on pre-sex rituals?

And what if – no! She stopped herself from continuing that thought and picked up a copy of the *Daily News* on the table, leafing through the pages to distract herself from thinking about Kyle.

Jesus Christ! She nearly jumped out of her chair. There she was in black and white, smiling out of a massive photo with the headline 'Re-Match!' splattered across her forehead. She brought the paper closer to read the article by reporter Deniz Grady.

In the battle of the exes – and the sexes – single woman Mattie Johns faces off against four of her former boyfriends in The Hating Game, *a new reality show on X-ACT. With last night seeing off Charlie after he groped a male dance instructor, three exes remain.*

Blah, blah, blah, Mattie thought as she scanned the rest of the article, which explained the public vote and how she had to spend two weeks alone with one of the exes. She was just about to close the paper when the last paragraph caught her eye.

Psychologist Dr Willie Wheestle says this type of serial dating behaviour is very common among women whose fathers have abandoned them.

'Mattie Johns' father left the family when she was quite young,' Dr Wheestle said at his Harley Street clinic yesterday. 'So Matilda is leaving her men first, before they can leave her.'

Mattie snapped the paper shut as if the words burned her eyes. Fathers who abandoned them? Serial dating? And *Matilda*?! She was going to find this Deniz Grady reporter and *kill* her! After she cut off Weasel's balls – if he had any.

Mattie rested her head in her hands. Everyone would know about her father now. Even the horrible truth about her real name being Matilda – as bad as it was – paled in comparison to that. People would pity her; see her as a victim of a bad childhood and a woman who wasn't tough enough to escape the negative influences of her past.

She straightened and threw back her shoulders. Well, she'd show them how strong she could be. She wasn't going to let this affect her, not at all. She'd stride onto that stage, ask the men any question she bloody well pleased, and she'd show the nation who she really was. No more nice, smile-into-the-camera, do-as-she-was-told Mattie.

'We're ready for you!' chirped Headset, poking her head into the room.

Mattie glared, pleased to see her recoil. She followed

the girl through the corridors towards the studio. As usual, Seamus looked like he was about to keel over, and was holding tightly to the metal podium.

'It's been another day of exciting events here on *The Hating Game*. So let's say hello to our sexy single lady, Mattie Johns!'

Mattie marched onstage and settled onto her stool. Only two pods stood to her right. She couldn't wait to have a go at whatever idiots were left in there.

Seamus patted down his greasy hair and worked his upper lip into a wide smile. 'Well, well! Two dates behind you, Mattie, and two remaining. And I want to know' – he leaned in closer and Mattie instinctively jerked back from the stench – 'is it true?' He circled her, nearly knocking her out with the putrid mix of cologne and gin.

'Is what true?' Mattie asked, regretting the words as soon as they were out of her mouth.

'About your father.' Seamus put on a serious look so fake it was comical. He shook his head. 'I'm so sorry to hear how he left your family. Dreadful, dreadful stuff.'

What was this, *The Jerry Springer Show* or something?

Mattie gritted her teeth. 'No more dreadful than having to sit here being sprayed by your spit,' she said quietly, wiping her face.

Seamus ignored her and narrowed his eyes. 'And all those debts he left you with, too. Your mother struggled for years, didn't she? How could a father do that? Terrible, terrible.'

'Yup, he was a bastard all right.' Mattie tried to sound flippant.

'But he scarred you. He tainted your relationship with men, didn't he? Forever.'

'You need to go back to rehab if you believe that

rubbish,' Mattie snapped. 'You're obviously still drunk.'

Someone yelled loudly in Seamus's ear and he blinked as he tottered towards the podium. 'Okay, let's get back to the show. The time has come for you to choose your next date!'

Mattie nodded. 'Let's get this over with.' She was shaking with anger now. Bloody, bloody Seamus, analysing her like she was damaged goods. It wasn't enough that the whole nation had to read about it. No, they had to watch it, too, on national TV! She cringed as she pictured Kyle just lapping it up. Of course their relationship didn't fail because of his cheating. No, it failed because she was *scarred* by her father!

Seamus handed her the stack of laminated cards. 'It's time to ask your prospective lovers one more question. What will it be, Mattie?'

Mattie's heart pounded as she gripped the cards. 'My question for the two remaining exes is this.' She turned towards the pods.

'Who the fuck *are* you? What pathetic reason do you have for being here?' she shouted. They'd cut that for sure, but at least she'd show the TweedleDuo and whoever was in those pods she wasn't a victim of her past.

'Cut!' a voice squealed through the feedback on the system.

Nate burst onto the set, spraying sweat as he ran over to her. 'Mattie! Just stick to the questions. Please,' he added when he saw her face. 'And remember, this is airing before nine, so no profanity.'

'Yes, Nate. No, Nate,' Mattie parroted, wishing she could haul him off and punch his blobby big face until she felt better.

'Great, thank you!' he said, obviously not clocking she was making fun of him. He rushed off the stage.

Two hundred thousand pounds, Mattie repeated. *Two hundred thousand bloody pounds.* She remembered the humiliation of the earlier scene with the bailiff and took a deep breath. She had no choice. She had to do this.

'Mattie, we'll start again with your question,' Nate's voice boomed through the set.

Mattie flipped through the cards. 'All right, Ex Number Three. What do you do in your spare time?' Spare time was for rejects, Mattie thought. Rejects who weren't good at their jobs.

'I don't have spare time,' the robotic voice from the pod nearest Mattie came. 'I'm really engrossed in my job at the moment.'

Mattie cocked her head to the side. Hmm, could that be Stuart? He had been pretty work obsessed. 'And Ex Number Four?' she asked.

'I like to play video games,' the voice came.

Of course you do, Mattie said inside her head. Big loser. Had she really dated someone so lame? 'Seamus, I'll go with Ex Number Three.' After Charlie and Giovanni, maybe she would actually have *something* in common with this ex. She'd leave the computer geek until last.

Ex Number Three, come and meet Mattie Johns . . . again!'

Mattie fidgeted as the door opened and a blond head emerged. He turned and Mattie's heart clutched as she took in the familiar features.

It was him.

The man she never wanted to see again, as long as she lived.

The man who'd taken her heart and stomped on it.

Kyle.

He was walking across the stage in a dark suit with paisley tie – the paisley tie she'd bought him, what a nerve! – and carrying the same bunch of poisonous purple flowers the other men had. He strode with confidence, but his normally relaxed face looked tense.

Mattie stared as he got closer and closer. Kyle leaned down to kiss her and she jerked away when his designer stubble grazed her face.

'Don't touch me,' she hissed.

Kyle moved to her side and Mattie tried to breathe. She couldn't believe it was him. He had come on the show . . . for what? To mock her, to make the audience believe she really *was* scarred? Hadn't he tortured her enough already?

'So Mattie has chosen Ex Number Three, Kyle, the former love of her life! Tune in tomorrow at eight, to watch Mattie and Kyle's date, then make your Date Rate! And see who the last ex is!'

Seamus grinned at the camera. 'The lines are open now for your Date Rate of Mattie and Giovanni! Call the number on your screen and key in your vote from one to ten. See you tomorrow on . . . *The Hating Game*!' The lights went dim and *The Hating Game*'s logo flashed up behind them.

'We're out!' a voice boomed. Mattie turned to leave the stage as fast as she could, far from Kyle and the scent of his cologne. But Kyle caught her elbow.

'Mattie, wait.'

She spun around and met the familiar blue eyes. A slight beard poked out of his chiselled jaw – the jaw that made him look like one of those hunky romance heroes she always used to tease him about – and she noticed he needed a haircut.

'What? You want to humiliate me some more?' She tore her gaze away and looked over his shoulder to where *The Hating Game* logo was flashing like it was a strobe light at a dance club.

'I just want to answer your question. The reason I'm here.'

A giant hand pressed down on her chest; was this what a heart attack felt like? 'And?' She wanted to run, to pretend she didn't care, but her legs were numb.

Kyle moved his head so their eyes met again. 'I want you to know what *really* happened that day in the office. I want–'

'Save it, Kyle,' Mattie burst out, unable to keep her emotions checked any longer. 'You don't go on a show called *The Hating Game* to try to clear your conscience. I was an idiot to trust you the first time around. I'm not so stupid as to trust you now.'

'I didn't know this would be called *The Hating Game*!' Kyle replied in a rush. 'Nate told me it would be *Second Chance for Romance*! I'm not here to make your life more difficult, or to get revenge, or whatever they've told you. I just wanted a chance to really explain what happened, and maybe–'

'Maybe nothing, Kyle!' What the hell was he thinking? Had he been swigging Seamus's gin? She lowered her voice. 'I know *exactly* what happened with you and Chloe. So don't you worry about filling me in. I've got more than enough details to keep me away from you. Forever!'

Confusion covered Kyle's face. Mattie turned and forced herself to walk calmly from the set.

*

Silver swivelled her chair back and forth up in the control room, then grabbed a cocktail sausage and swallowed it in one gulp. Nate had seen her do that so many times it didn't even faze him now. The control room was hot and stuffy and he stifled a yawn. It had been a long day, and they still had to finalise the storyline for tomorrow. Thank God they'd been able to pull something out of the bag for Giovanni's date. Baz had suggested mudwrestling, thinking Mattie would tear Giovanni to shreds. When they'd seen how much fun Mattie and Giovanni were having, Baz had freaked and immediately pulled the plug. Luckily Nate had come up with the pizza, he thought proudly.

'Mattie will refuse to cook since she's a feminist or Giovanni will play the macho Italian. Either way, we have a guaranteed conflict on our hands,' he'd said to Baz. And Baz had to agree.

Baz bustled in. 'Sorry I'm late,' he huffed. 'I was just going through some lighting changes on set.'

Nate shifted in his chair. Baz always managed to look as if he'd been doing something important, but Nate happened to know Baz had actually been in the toilet re-gelling his product-packed hair.

Silver swallowed another sausage whole. 'We've got our first ratings, boys.'

Nate and Baz sat up straight in their chairs.

Silver let the silence stretch. 'Congratulations,' she said finally. '*The Hating Game* was the most watched programme in its time slot last night.'

'Yes!' Nate pumped a fist in the air and turned to high-five Baz, only to see both him and Silver watching with raised eyebrows. He quickly lowered his hand.

'That's great,' Baz said calmly. 'Now we need to think how we can keep this going.'

'My thoughts exactly,' Silver said. She turned towards Nate. 'So, Nate. What do you have planned for Kyle tomorrow?' Her laser eyes pinned him to the chair.

Nate swallowed. With everything that was going on, he hadn't had a chance to talk through tomorrow's storyline with Baz. All he knew was Kyle would take Mattie to Castle Combe, the small village in Wiltshire where they'd gone on their first date. Baz had thought heading back would surely cause some tension and a few arguments, too.

'Well, Kyle and Mattie will return to the village where they first got together,' Nate said quickly before Baz could beat him to the punch. He needed more, he thought frantically. Something guaranteed to shock. Desperate, Nate's mind flipped to the worst thing he could do. Suddenly a plan formed in his head.

He sat up in the chair and outlined the idea, watching Silver's face come alive.

'Yes.' She nodded slowly. 'Yes. It might be spectacular. *If* you can pull everything together in time. Baz will help you out.'

'But I already have something–' Baz whined.

Silver shot him a look. 'Help Nate.'

Nate tried to hide his grin. Ha! For once he'd one-upped Baz! Surely Nate would be Silver's pet now.

'Get the private investigator involved if you need to. And tell me when you have it all set up. I want to let the network's sales and marketing team know what we have planned. They can run some extra promos to pull in even more viewers.' Silver looked at her watch. 'Meet me back here at seven with updates.' She walked out.

Nate turned to Baz and rubbed his hands together. 'Let's get started. We have a lot of work to do.'

*

Back at her flat, Mattie gulped some whisky, noticing the glass shaking in her hand. She had to calm down! It had been hours since her confrontation with Kyle earlier that day but she could still feel the anger curling around her stomach.

It wasn't like she cared. Kyle could do whatever he

wanted, and if he wanted to do Chloe that was fine by her. Mattie squeezed a pillow tightly as his confused face flashed before her. What could he possibly want to explain? Did he think she didn't know? Even if she had an ounce of doubt about what had happened in the office that day, the first-hand account straight from the sly bitch's mouth had set her straight.

Mattie shuddered as she remembered running into Chloe at one of those insufferable media dinners she'd had to start going to after returning from Italy to find that Kyle had killed her business.

'So Kyle got me a great position,' Chloe had said during the pre-dinner cocktails, shaking back her long blonde hair and arranging a ruffled dress that barely covered her nipples.

'Probably underneath someone. I'm sure you're good at that.' Mattie smiled, grabbing a drink off a tray from a circulating waiter.

Chloe narrowed her eyes. 'Oh, I am, I am. Better than you, according to Kyle.'

Mattie flinched but kept her gaze steady, taking a sip to cover the flare of anger inside. It wasn't enough to cheat on her? He had to blab to Chloe about their sex life too? Clenching her jaw, Mattie scanned the room. Was he here? When she got her hands on him she'd twist his balls off. One by one.

Chloe shook her head. 'Poor Kyle. You know, I've never really understood what *frigid* actually is. Is it when he can't get it in because you're, like, frozen? Or is it just that you don't like sex?'

Mattie stared. Kyle never would have told Chloe that, would he? In the few months before their break up, their sex life had fizzled out a bit. But when they did make love, it was as good as it always had been. She was far from frigid!

Chloe swigged her champagne and burped. 'What,

you don't believe he said that?' She looked at her watch. 'He's going to be here in, like, fifteen minutes. Ask him yourself.' Chloe shook her head. 'Poor man. No wonder he practically attacked me in the office that day.'

Mattie was itching to smack her. 'Why I would want to be anywhere near that snake is beyond me. You two deserve each other.' She turned her back on Chloe's victorious smile and walked out of the packed room as quickly as possible. Her face was hot and her mouth dry despite the drink she'd gulped. Her heart ached like it had been impaled on her ribs and left there to cure.

Since she'd been back from Italy, she'd wondered if she'd been too quick to jump to conclusions about the incident in the office that day. It had all happened so fast, and she had to admit her anger might have blurred the reality. Had Kyle put his arms around Chloe, or had it been the other way? Part of her had hoped Kyle *had* been telling the truth. He'd never lied before – at least not that she'd known about.

But after her run-in with Chloe, she'd had no illusions. Kyle was a wanker, a *cheating* lying wanker of the top order, and she would *never* ever forgive him.

So why couldn't she get his face out of her head?

The psychotic version of *I Want You Back* blasted through her laptop's tiny speakers and Mattie sat back, banging the machine against the coffee table as it froze. She'd been hoping to watch that night's instalment of *The Hating Game* over at Jess's place in Clapham – although Jess's ancient television was almost as bad as trying to watch it on her stupid laptop.

She'd called Jess and left a few messages – between the bailiff, the mudwrestling with Giovanni, the *Daily News* and Kyle, there was so much to tell her. But, today of all days, Jess hadn't rung back. Where on Earth was she?

Oh, dear God. She cringed as she spotted Mattie-the-hooker on the screen. And just look at her covered in that mud! The edits quickly cut to her and Giovanni in the café, then Giovanni chucking the pizza dough and his confrontation with Ali – all set to dramatic music, of course. Was that really her? She squinted at the small laptop screen as she and Giovanni threw pizza ingredients willy-nilly on their wonky dough base. With her red curls and high-street gear, she hardly recognized herself.

That pizza *had* been delicious and she'd rather enjoyed cooking it. Once Giovanni calmed down, she'd chucked a bit of flour at him. He'd dumped a cup over her head – and the whole thing had escalated into a full on flour fight. It wouldn't be the worst thing in the world if she ended up with Giovanni for those two weeks.

'Meanwhile, back in the studio . . .' Seamus's voice intoned as the video cut to Kyle emerging from the pod. In a close-up of her face, she looked stunned – and angry. Mattie took a giant swig of whisky, staring at the screen as she jerked away from Kyle when he bent down to kiss her. She looked every inch the woman scorned – and scarred, as Seamus said. Why hadn't she just smiled blandly, kissed him, and acted like she didn't care? Because she didn't!

She grabbed the phone and dialled Jess's number, listening to the tinny ring. Where *was* she? If ever Mattie needed support, it was now, the night before facing off with her cheating ex.

'Lines are now open for your Date Rate! Let us know how you feel about Mattie and Giovanni. And tune in tomorrow . . . when Mattie faces the only man she's ever had a serious relationship with . . . and gets the shock of her life!' The music blared again and Mattie switched off her laptop.

The shock of her life?

Hardly, she snorted. Been there, done that.

*

'You going to get that?' Deniz Grady from the *Daily News* asked after Jess's phone rang for the millionth time. Mattie's name flashed up on the screen.

'No, it's fine.' Jess angled the mobile away from her, as if Mattie could see through the phone. 'What was the question again?' She tried to focus back on Deniz, feeling a bit nauseous.

She never should have let the reporter through the door in the first place, but Deniz had said she just wanted to ask a few questions about Mattie, then barged right in. After all that awful stuff about Mattie's father in the paper today, Jess had thought maybe she could set the reporter straight. But Deniz only seemed interested in asking questions about her relationship with Kyle.

When she got Mattie's message she'd be dating Kyle tomorrow, Jess could barely believe it. She'd been so sure Kyle wouldn't want to hurt Mattie any more than he already had. Maybe he *did* want to get back together. And if so, this article could help smooth things over before tomorrow's date.

Deniz crossed her long legs and brushed the lapels of her tightly fitting blazer. With her sleek dark hair and perfectly made-up face, she was a dead ringer for Courtney Cox. Jess felt like a country bumpkin beside her.

'I said, how did they meet?' Deniz repeated loudly and slowly, as if Jess *was* a country bumpkin with hearing problems.

'I think it was some kind of networking event for recruitment people,' Jess said.

Deniz huffed. 'Can you make it a bit more exciting? What was the name? When was it? Come on, give me the nitty-gritty.'

'I'm not sure I remember,' Jess said, worried now she might not be able to give Deniz what she wanted and slightly terrified of the impatient woman in front of her.

'Look, it doesn't matter if it's not one-hundred per cent accurate.' Deniz tapped her pen against her voice recorder and flipped open a notebook. 'Just do the best you can.'

'All right,' Jess said slowly. 'Well, it was the UK Recruitment Society, or something like that. A power breakfast at The Wolseley.' Jess surprised herself; she didn't even know if that's where it had been held. But it sounded good. 'Kyle approached Mattie to congratulate her on winning a contract his company had bid for. And he asked her if she had any positions opening up in her agency.' That much, at least, was true. Jess remembered Mattie being impressed that Kyle wanted to work for her. When it came to business, most men ran in the opposite direction when they saw her coming.

Deniz looked up from her notes. 'And then?'

'She needed someone since the business was expanding quickly, so she took him on. At first she was really paranoid he was a spy for his old agency. But Kyle worked hard – harder than Mattie, which is almost impossible – and the business grew and grew.'

'And their relationship?'

'Mattie hadn't had a long-term relationship since, well, forever. She couldn't find a man who would live up to her expectations. Actually, I'm not really sure she wanted to.' Much as Mattie said she wanted a boyfriend, Jess always thought Mattie was too scared to trust someone. Until Kyle.

'Anyway, Kyle surprised her one day and took her off for the weekend – out to the Cotswolds to some small village where he'd booked a cottage.'

Deniz raised an eyebrow. 'Gutsy man.'

'Yeah, he's a pretty cool guy,' Jess said. 'I didn't think they'd last long. Kyle was just as strong-willed as Mattie; he wouldn't let her push him around like she did other men. He stood up to her, dragging her off to dinners even when she said she was too tired. She was really happy – although she never admitted it. They even moved in together.' Jess smiled, remembering the day Mattie sheepishly told her Kyle had transferred his things to her flat.

'Ah hmm.' Deniz kicked off a high heel as she scribbled. 'So why did they break up, then?'

'Well, Mattie thought Kyle cheated on her.' The words were out of Jess's mouth before she realised what she was saying. She bit her lip, wondering if she should reveal more. She was supposed to be smoothing things over, not stirring them up. But now that she started, she'd have to explain.

'Go on.' Deniz's eyes lit up.

'Mattie came into the office one day when she was meant to be at a client meeting. And she saw Kyle snogging a woman he was supposed to be placing with one of their biggest clients.'

Even now, Jess still wasn't sure exactly what had happened that day.

Mattie claimed she'd caught Kyle red-handed. But when Mattie was away in Italy, Kyle had rung up Jess and told her his side of the story: the woman had thrown herself at him. He'd begged Jess to explain to Mattie what had happened, since Mattie wouldn't even answer his phone calls. Jess had made a few tentative attempts but quickly backed off under the power of Mattie's fury.

'Cool,' Deniz said, her pencil scrawling across the notepad. 'What else?'

'Well, Mattie fired Kyle on the spot – both from her life and the business. She took off to Italy without even giving him the chance to explain. And when she got back, half her clients had gone to Kyle. He'd set up his own recruitment agency.'

Deniz let out a low whistle. 'Wow! He cheated on her *and* stole her clients?'

Jess swallowed. This wasn't exactly going the way she planned. She didn't want to make Kyle look bad. 'Well, I don't think he really stole the clients. When they heard he was starting up on his own, they wanted to go with him.' That's what Kyle had told Jess, and she believed him. She couldn't picture him stealing clients anyway, particularly as he'd been so desperate to get back with Mattie.

Deniz rolled her eyes. 'Sure, sure. That's what they all say. Sounds like quite the tosser.'

'He's really nice,' Jess said desperately. 'He treated Mattie well, you know. She was happy.'

Deniz gave her an odd look. 'I thought you were her best friend? Why would you want her to get back together with a bloke who cheated on her?'

'I thought they were good together. Really good.'

Deniz rolled her eyes again and started to close her notebook.

'They were going to get married!' The words shot of Jess's mouth. She hadn't meant to let it slip, but she couldn't let Deniz go away and cast Kyle as the villain.

Deniz's head snapped up and she opened her notebook again. 'I'm listening.'

'Well, okay, they weren't engaged or anything. Kyle hadn't proposed. But Mattie had the dress.' Jess slapped a hand over her mouth. She couldn't believe she'd just said that! Mattie had sworn her to secrecy, saying if anyone found out she'd look like one of those psycho women desperate to get hitched.

'Really?' Deniz looked up with glee. 'Tell me more.'

Jess bit her lip again. It was out now. She might as well explain how it all happened and minimise the damage as much as she could. 'Well, after Kyle moved in, Mattie and I met up for some shopping, just the two of us. It had been ages – Mattie was usually busy with work and Kyle.'

Jess remembered how much fun they'd had together that afternoon. Mattie had been optimistic about the future with Kyle and the more drinks she'd had, the more she babbled on and on about how much she loved him. Jess had fallen in line with her fantasies and together they constructed an elaborate vision of Mattie and Kyle as the lords of Surrey, living in a mansion with their 2.4 kids and the prerequisite golden retriever. And an army of maids, of course, since Mattie wasn't exactly domestic.

They'd stumbled out of the champagne bar at Selfridges, supporting each other down the stairs. Jess had never seen Mattie so sloshed, but whether she was actually drunk or just high on life it was hard to tell.

'Let's go look at wedding dresses!' Jess had said, still caught up in the fantasy they'd created. Even in her inebriated state, she fully expected a firm refusal from Mattie, but to her surprise Mattie just burped and said 'Great idea!' and they headed over to the frothy selection of Vera Wang wedding dresses.

The two of them gulped their way through the department's champagne supply as Mattie pulled on dress after dress. Jess hadn't actually thought there could be so many styles. Puffy, sleek, silk, satin . . .

'What do you think of this one?' Mattie breathed as she pivoted in strapless satin. The bodice was tight and rather plain, but the way it hugged Mattie's small frame and fell to the floor in a soft flare made her look more feminine than Jess could have imagined. Her normally neat black bob was messy from trying on the dresses and her cheeks were flushed from the drink. Jess thought she'd never looked so beautiful.

'It's gorgeous.' Jess could barely get the words through the lump in her throat. Her eyes misted over as she pictured Mattie walking down the aisle towards Kyle, handsome in a dark grey morning suit . . .

'Don't cry!' Mattie put her arms around Jess in a rare show of affection. 'This is it! Can you unzip me?' She turned her back towards Jess.

'What do you mean, this is it?' Jess stared. 'You're not going to buy it, are you?'

'Yup!' Mattie said. 'Why not? I like it, we're here, and it'll save me time when I am ready to get married.' She fixed her unsteady eyes on Jess. 'Just don't say anything to anyone. I mean it. Least of all Kyle. I don't want him to think I'm dying to tie the knot or anything.'

'I promise,' Jess had said, holding onto Mattie's arm as she teetered out of the dress. She couldn't believe Mattie was buying it now. Wasn't that bad luck or something? But Mattie was adamant – she'd found it, she loved it and who cared about silly superstition. She plunked down her black Amex and the gown was hers.

Mattie had dropped off the dress at Jess's flat, telling her there was no way she could risk Kyle finding it.

And that was the last they'd ever talked about it.

Now with Kyle out of the picture, Jess was afraid to

bring it up – why risk Mattie biting her head off?

Deniz made an impatient noise and Jess realised she was waiting for her to continue. 'Well, Mattie saw a wedding dress she liked. She tried it on and bought it. Then, of course, she and Kyle broke up.'

Deniz's eyes glinted. 'So where's the dress now?'

'Oh, just hanging in my closet,' Jess said casually.

'It's here? In this flat?' Deniz scanned the walls as if she was hunting down a lost treasure. 'Can I see it?'

'Sure,' Jess said hesitantly, wondering why Deniz was so excited. She led the reporter over to the narrow broom closet and unzipped a garment bag, revealing the dress inside.

'If you could just step out of the way. . .'

Jess moved to one side and before she knew what was happening, Deniz had taken a camera out of her bag and snapped a photo of the gown.

'What are you going to use that for?' Jess asked nervously. It was bad enough Jess had let slip about the dress, but if Deniz put a photo of it in the paper, her friendship with Mattie would be over.

'Oh, just background research. Don't worry,' Deniz said airily. 'I think I've got all I need here. Thanks for your time.'

'Wait!' Jess cried. 'When will the article come out?'

Deniz looked at her watch. 'There's still enough time to file tonight. So it'll come out in the morning edition. I've got to run. Thanks again.'

Jess closed the door and sagged against it.

There was only one thing to do.

She had to call Mattie and tell her what she'd done.

CHAPTER SIXTEEN

*Three per cent of women prefer to make the first move.
Seven per cent of women actually do.*

MATTIE AWOKE TO THE ANNOYING ring of her mobile – again. She glanced at the screen then chucked it under the pillow to muffle the sound. Jess, for the millionth time. God, that girl was really persistent. She'd rung all through the night, stopping briefly then starting up at – Mattie looked at the clock and let out an exasperated sigh – five thirty a.m.

She hauled herself out of bed, trying to ignore her aching head. In the mirror, her eyes were red and bags hung underneath like soggy water balloons. She hadn't slept properly since *The Hating Game* had begun. No, strike that: since Kyle had left. Funny, she was such a light sleeper that she usually dreaded sharing her bed. But she'd never had problems sleeping with Kyle beside her.

Last night she'd fought with her pillow for half the night, trying to get comfortable and find some position – any position – to keep Kyle out of her head. But try as she might, nothing could banish that look in his eyes when he'd told her he just wanted to explain; the confusion on his face when she said she already knew. What the hell could he be so confused about? Was he just surprised she'd talked to Chloe?

It really didn't matter, did it? Chloe aside, there was still the whole stealing-of-her-clients thing.

There was nothing to wonder about when it came to Kyle. Mattie just needed to get her subconscious in line and all would be fine.

Thank God for the thick game show make-up they plaster on me, she thought as she pulled on her Juicy tracksuit and headed out to the kitchen. Stomach rumbling, she scanned the shelves, but there was nothing even worth trying to fashion into an edible bite. Her eyes fell on the empty prawn cocktail crisps bag and she licked her lips. She could really go for some saltiness right about now. She'd just nip to the 24-hour off-licence around the corner.

Outside, the streets were deserted except for a glum street cleaner and a group of what looked to be builders gathering on the corner, thumbing through the tabloids. A few were swigging beer from giant metal cans. One took a long look at her and whistled. Jesus Christ, Mattie thought, if they think this tracksuit is sexy they really *have* had too much to drink.

'Hey! Darlin'!' the builder called. Mattie's head swung in his direction. 'I'll marry you!'

The men laughed and started trumpeting the wedding march in time to Mattie's steps as she neared the off-licence. She shook her head. They were clearly mental.

She hunted through the aisles but there were no prawn cocktail crisps to be found anywhere. Desperate now, she walked up to the wizened man behind the counter. He was so busy watching a *Coronation Street* episode from what looked to be the 1970s that he didn't even notice her.

'Excuse me!' He didn't turn a head. No chance of hearing her with that bush of hair growing out of his ears, Mattie sniffed. 'Hello!' she said again, more loudly. As she waited for her voice to penetrate his furry ears, she glanced at the papers in front of her, absently picking up the *Daily News*. What rubbish did they have in there today?

Oh my God! She squinted and drew the paper closer, letting out a strangled gasp. Right there in vivid colour was a giant photo of her, next to a shot of a wedding dress. And not just any wedding dress: the dress she had bought on a drunken whim with Jess!

EXCLUSIVE! MATTIE'S GAL PAL SPILLS ALL! The ex who destroyed The Hating Game *star and the wedding dress wasted!*

Mattie tore her eyes away, slapped some change on the counter and dashed out of the shop, paper in hand. Gathering tears made the group of builders on the corner look like shapeless blobs. They started singing again as she passed, the notes ricocheting through her head.

How could Jess do this to her? *How?* She'd sworn Jess to secrecy once she realised how stupid she'd been to buy that bloody dress in the first place. And if there was anyone she trusted, it was Jess. Jess had never let her down, ever. Even when Mattie knew she'd acted, well, like a bit of a bitch, Jess had always supported her.

And Kyle. Oh Jesus, Kyle! Mattie's face burned as she pictured Kyle reading the paper, discovering she was one of those pathetic panting women who bought a dress before they even had a *proposal*. Would he laugh and shake his head? Or would he just roll his eyes at how silly she was? Mattie sank down onto the sofa and lowered her throbbing head against her palms, pushing at her eyes to stop the tears from falling.

Her mobile rang. She glanced at the screen – yes, it was the traitor, calling again, probably to beg for forgiveness.

Briefly, she considered answering it. Perhaps there was some reasonable explanation? But Mattie hardened her heart. Hidden wedding dresses didn't just materialise on their own.

Mattie pressed a few buttons and diverted any calls from Jess straight to voice mail. 'Bye, bye, Jess.'

*

'Well!' Silver lowered herself into a chair between Nate and Baz's cubicles. 'I never thought I'd say this, but you two have actually exceeded my expectations.'

Nate tried to keep the surprised expression off his face. He had no idea what Silver was talking about, but if she was happy it could only be a good thing.

'An exclusive in the *Daily News*.' Silver nodded, throwing the paper on Nate's desk. 'Well done.'

'Thanks.' Baz leaned back in his chair smugly. 'Deniz and I go way back, so I just rang her up and told her we were planning something big for Mattie and Kyle's date. She thought it would be good to get some dirt beforehand. Deniz tracked that Jess down, no problem.' He grinned. 'Some best friend!'

Nate stared. When had Baz done all that? He hadn't said a word to Nate about it when he'd ducked out last night, leaving Nate to arrange practically everything for today with the private investigator.

'So is everything ready for the date with Kyle?' Silver asked.

Nate nodded. 'Yes. All set.' He was still feeling a bit, well, strange about today's plan. But it was a game show after all. Mattie and Kyle *had* willingly signed up to it.

'Good.' Silver ran a hand through her hair. 'I'll see you back here, later this afternoon.' She walked away, her perfume fogging the air behind her.

Nate turned to Baz. 'You didn't tell me anything about this article!' He pulled the paper closer and quickly scanned it. Jesus Christ, he thought, wincing. Mattie had a wedding dress? She actually wanted to marry Kyle? He felt a bit lightheaded thinking about how she'd respond to the events planned for later.

Baz shrugged. 'I didn't know if Deniz'd even talk to me. I banged her once in the loo at China White and never bothered ringing her – she was pretty rubbish. Thank God I saved her number.'

Nate shook his head. He'd never even been to China White, let alone made love to someone in a toilet.

'I just told her what we had planned and she did the rest, tracking down Mattie's friend, et cetera, et cetera. Plus I got another shag out of it after we hooked up last night.' He nudged Nate with his shoulder. 'Better rubbish than nothing, eh, mate?'

'Yeah,' Nate responded weakly. *Nothing* was the best description of his love life right about now.

'All ready to go get Mattie and Kyle then?' Baz stood up, smoothing down his perfectly pressed shirt.

Nate lumbered to his feet. 'Ready.'

*

Mattie watched the blocks of flats give way to trees and fields as the limo left London. Bloody Kyle, taking her to the middle of nowhere for their date! If he wanted her to believe he'd signed up for *Second Chance for Romance* and not *The Hating Game*, then he shouldn't be subjecting her to smelly animals and soggy fields. Still, navigating cow patties was nothing compared to the shit Jess had dropped her into, telling that reporter about the blasted dress.

Mattie took a deep breath and tried to push Jess's traitorous behaviour from her mind. Now, more than ever, she had to remain calm; act as if nothing was wrong. Luckily, she'd spent years perfecting that performance after her father left. Keep the face neutral, the voice even and smooth. No one would ever know the difference.

'Where are Baz and Ram?' Mattie asked. The car was blissfully silent without them.

'Riding in the other car with Kyle,' Nate said.

'Great.' Mattie slumped further into the leather seat. She could only imagine the kinds of questions Spaz and his gorilla cameraman would be throwing at Kyle. *Did you know she had a dress? Had you even proposed? Guess she was desperate to tie you down, mate. Hah hah hah.*

Mattie didn't know what was worse, pity or mockery. At the studio earlier, Fabio and Cyndi had practically smothered her with kindness, clucking around her affectionately instead of commenting how she should take better care of herself. Mattie just sat there and let them fuss. She should have acted even ruder than usual to show she didn't care. But she didn't have the energy. The tabloid article had sucked it all right out of her.

At least she wouldn't have to face Kyle looking like she was about to deal crack in Kings Cross. No, wardrobe had dressed her in a pair of skinny jeans (tight, yes, but at least they covered her legs) and a white and blue checked shirt, the likes of which she'd seen recently in TopShop, but was so far from her normal style she'd never tried it on. The shirt had a hideous ruffle down the front, but at least it wasn't lamb dressed as embryo, as with the previous outfits.

The sign for Chippenham came into view. Hmm. Something about this route seemed familiar . . . oh God. A strange pain grinded her stomach – nerves mixed with a flutter of fear – as she figured out their destination. They were going to Castle Combe, a tiny village with a fairy-tale allure even Mattie couldn't resist. She'd fallen in love with it. And it was where she'd fallen in love with Kyle, too.

Memories flooded back as the limo wended its way down a narrow track towards the village, the light dimming as the dense trees overhead formed a tunnel. It had been a Friday, a few months after Kyle had started working for her. Her business was going full steam ahead: clients loved his easy-going approach, the perfect foil to Mattie's more direct style.

Out of convenience, they'd started having lunch together. Although they always started out discussing what needed to be done, they usually ended up in fits of laughter at Kyle's hilarious client impersonations. Despite his successful business-like exterior, Kyle was warm and friendly, with a killer sense of humour that made Mattie laugh despite herself. Sure, their eyes had met a few times and Mattie had felt a frisson of something between them, but she'd dismissed it as too much hot chilli sauce.

They'd been finishing up a pitch presentation one day when Kyle snapped the laptop closed. 'Enough of this. I'm taking you away for a corporate bonding weekend.'

Mattie's mouth dropped open. 'What?' she sputtered. 'You didn't run this by me! Anyway, I'm busy this weekend.' That was a lie – she'd planned to work – but she didn't want Kyle thinking she could drop everything at the last second.

Kyle shook his head. 'You're coming with me. It's in our professional interest. You work too hard and you need some time away.' He started packing up their things. 'Come on, we'll go to your flat and get your case, then we're off.'

Mattie couldn't help responding to his forcefulness. And she couldn't deny that it would be good to get out of the office. And with Kyle, a small voice inside piped up. She snuck a quick look at him as he neatly wound the laptop cord. He was gorgeous, with blond hair curling over his collar and five o'clock stubble poking through. She tore her thoughts away. This would be a *professional* weekend.

At her flat, Mattie had thrown her only pair of jeans and a few jumpers into a case as Kyle commented how he'd never known a woman to get ready so quickly. They jumped in his car and hurtled down the motorway – Mattie admiring Kyle's propensity to speed just like her – singing along to his surprisingly thorough collection of Bon Jovi tapes. With every mile they drove from London, Mattie felt more and more relaxed. She couldn't remember the last time she'd been out of the city.

Just as dusk was falling, Kyle pulled off the motorway and onto a small country road. Mattie cranked open the window, breathing in the soft air of a June night. Small stone cottages flanked the road and in the distance, across a rolling green field, the peaks of an elegant manor house rose. Normally she wasn't one for twee countryside villages, but this place – Castle Combe, Kyle told her – wasn't twee. In the dim light, with the glow of street lanterns and the sound of a brook bubbling through the open car windows . . . it was magical.

Kyle pulled up before a small bridge. 'I've booked us in here.' He gestured towards a cottage perched on the banks of the brook. 'Hope this is all right.'

Mattie nodded slowly. She'd been thinking more along the lines of the sterile comfort of a large hotel – something like the manor house she'd seen – where they'd eat in a large open dining room and sleep separated by hotel corridors. She wasn't good at sharing space and this was a little too close for comfort.

But Kyle made everything easy, ignoring her

prickliness and making her laugh. He cooked a simple dinner of spaghetti Bolognese and laughingly forced her to do the washing up by hand (the first time ever – no dishwasher in the archaic cottage!). She'd flicked some dishwater at him and he'd encircled her, trapping her arms by her sides. She'd laughed and struggled, but she had to admit the feel of his body against hers made her tingle.

Finally, she stopped trying to get away. She looked up into his eyes, and he'd leaned down and kissed her. It wasn't one of those wet, mushy kisses, where Mattie had to direct everything from lip pressure to tongue movement to head tilt. It was a kiss where her head actually went blank, and all she could think about was wanting more.

She couldn't remember who had led the other up the narrow staircase and into the timber-framed bedroom. Once they stood there, facing each other in the dark, she suddenly felt nervous. She never felt nervous – usually because she was so busy undressing the bloke she didn't really have a chance to think. As she watched Kyle peel off his shirt and move to undo her buttons, butterflies swarmed in her belly. She'd taken a step back, but Kyle had just smiled and pulled her against him.

Having sex with Kyle had been like his kiss – just *easy*. She found herself enjoying it, rather than rushing things through to the end like she usually did. This will only happen once, was the last coherent thought she'd had as she leaned into him.

But oddly, her infamous willpower deserted her and she couldn't stop sleeping with Kyle. Soon, they were together all the time, their lives meshing in a way that took Mattie by surprise.

Things got a bit difficult in the last few months before their break-up. Kyle had nagged at her to go out more, and then there'd been that incident when he'd tried to drag her off to a late-night picnic in Soho Square, complete with strawberries, champagne and the prerequisite drugged-up hookers (it *was* Soho, after all). She'd pushed him away, angry he couldn't see how busy she was trying to find just the right producer for their biggest client. She couldn't drop everything because he said so!

Well, if he wanted a woman who'd jump at his every command, it hadn't taken him long to find one. The week after their two-year anniversary, Kyle threw himself at Chloe. Mattie still couldn't get her head around how a man could go from celebrating a two-year landmark one week to shagging another woman the next.

Don't try to understand, her mum had said. Men go for two things: easy money and easy lays. And while that sentiment hadn't exactly provided the comfort she'd been looking for, she had to admit Mum was right.

The car stopped next to an old stone market cross in the centre of the village. Nate undid his seatbelt and put his hand on the door.

'Wait,' Mattie said. 'You haven't asked me any questions about my history with Kyle! Don't we need to do that first?' She really wanted to get in her side of the story.

Nate just waved his hand. 'No, that's fine. We're going to get Seamus to do it all by voice-over later.'

'But Nate—' Mattie huffed as Nate slammed the door. How would she show people she wasn't the idiotic love-sick woman splashed across the *Daily News*? She drew in a few deep breaths. If she acted all cold and distant, people would think she still cared. If she was a bitch . . . even worse.

No, the only thing for it was to be as smiley and

bland as possible. That would set Kyle on edge, if nothing else.

Mattie noticed another black limo pull up. She strained to see inside but she couldn't make out anything through the smoky windows. It's like we're Hollywood stars or something, she thought, watching curious villagers milling about, trying to sneak a peek.

Finally the car door opposite opened and jean-clad legs with Converse trainers appeared. She gulped. She recognized those trainers – she'd bought them for Kyle in a desperate bid to rid him of the manky old sneakers he'd had since secondary school.

Kyle followed Baz to a stone pedestal right beside the market cross where three narrow streets converged. Her mind flashed back to that first night when Kyle had pulled her up onto the pedestal, wrapping his arms around her waist to steady her.

Stop it! she screamed inside her head. She needed to forget the past – or at the very least, pretend to have forgotten it. She got out of the car, striding over to where Nate had now joined Kyle and Baz.

'Hello, Kyle,' she said, extending her hand with a giant unnatural smile. Her cheeks actually hurt, she was grinning so hard.

Kyle raised his eyebrows at her friendliness. 'Hi, Mattie.' For a second he looked like he was going to lean down for a kiss, but he remained standing on the platform above her.

'Get back in the car!' Baz said, clambering down. 'We need Ram to film your first meeting.'

'No problem,' Mattie said as Nate ushered her away. She turned back to smile at Kyle again. 'See you soon.' His baffled expression made her smirk to herself.

That would show him! She was *so* over Kyle. Sure, she might have bought a wedding dress. Sure, the whole nation might know about it – bloody, *bloody* Jess! – but if she acted as if everything was all right, people would believe it. And everything *was* all right. She didn't need Kyle. She didn't need Jess.

She didn't need anyone.

CHAPTER SEVENTEEN

*Sixty per cent of people rate trust as the most
important thing in a relationship.
Seventy-three per cent think white lies are necessary
to maintain a healthy relationship.*

AN HOUR OR SO LATER, Mattie and Kyle strolled down the main track through the village, followed by Ram, his camera and the curious villagers. A soft filmy drizzle hung in the air, and Mattie could already feel her make-up melting. Although the manic smile was still glued to her face, she just couldn't form words and the silence lay heavily between them.

'Talk! Talk!' Baz hissed at them as he trailed behind Ram. 'For God's sake! Do something!'

Kyle cleared his throat. 'So I thought I'd bring you back to where we first got together.'

Duh, Mattie thought as she nodded and smiled. He certainly hadn't got any smarter since they'd broken up.

'We'll take a walk through the woods,' he continued. 'Then we'll have dinner up at Manor House Hotel.'

Mattie sighed and some of the tension drained out of her body. Thank God they weren't going back to the cottage where they'd first made love – slept – together. It would be too awkward for words. As practised as she was at hiding her feelings, she didn't think even she could keep up the facade inside the tiny space.

They crossed the bridge over the brook below. At least Kyle wasn't going to torture her by trying to get her to take a small row boat on the water, as he had that first weekend. She'd made plenty of excuses before finally admitting she'd never learned to swim. Kyle was one of the few people she'd actually told. It seemed like something from Victorian times, not being able to swim, but her mother just hadn't had time. She did manage to find the time, though, to show Mattie how to file a tax return at the age of ten.

Financial independence is the key to happiness, her mum had said as Mattie struggled with the form, not even understanding what 'financial independence' meant. But if it made her mother happy, it must be a good thing. Mattie had heard her mum crying late at night and the sound always terrified her.

Inside the wood, the air was even denser and the forest's cloying scent invaded her nostrils. Mattie wrinkled her nose at the mouldy smell of damp earth. *This* was the reason she never came to the country in the winter: the whole thing was just foul. When she and Kyle were last here, blossoms and green had perfumed the air and wild flowers lined the path. Now – Mattie raised a squelching foot – it was like walking through the mudwrestling pit again.

Kyle grabbed her hand. 'Come on!' He tugged her off the path and dragged her through the low undergrowth of the forest, wet leaves slapping her in the face.

'What are you doing?' Mattie yelled as she tried to break free. But Kyle had an iron grip on her wrist. 'Let go of me!' She swivelled her head and tried to make out where Nate and Baz were but she couldn't see them through the dense foliage.

Kyle pulled up next to a swollen stream and wiped his face. A bit of leaf still clung to his eyebrow but Mattie wasn't about to tell him.

'What do you think you're doing?' she managed to get out between breaths. It had been a while since she'd run like that. Kyle didn't even seem winded.

'Look, Mattie.' Kyle paused. In the silence, they could hear the crash of Ram, Nate and Baz approaching through the trees.

'What?' Mattie said impatiently. The drizzle was turning into rain now, with fat drops splattering off leaves onto her cheeks.

'Look,' Kyle said again. 'I didn't know you had a dress.'

'Oh, Jesus,' Mattie muttered. She looked him straight in the eye. 'Don't flatter yourself, Kyle. I was drunk, I liked the dress. That's it. End of story.'

Kyle glanced over his shoulder. The crashing was getting closer. He tried to touch her arm, but Mattie jumped back. No way was he getting his mitts on her again.

'After last night, well, I was about to give up. But when I read about the wedding dress – Mattie.' He reached out to take her hand and she stared down, numbly watching as his fingers closed around hers. How she'd loved his hands – his fingers were the perfect width and his knuckles had just the right sprinkling of hair.

'It made me realise that you really did care. And now more than ever we need to clear things up,' he said.

Mattie forced her hand out of his grip and looked up into his eyes. 'Kyle, there's nothing to clear up. I told you, I heard it all from Chloe.' Suddenly she felt so tired.

'Mattie! Kyle!' Nate's voice ricocheted off the tree trunks around them.

Kyle's browed furrowed. 'What do you mean, you heard it from Chloe? I haven't seen her since that day in the office!' Anger shot across his face. 'Nothing happened there, Mattie. You *must* know I would never do that do you. If you'd just given me a chance to explain–'

'There you are!' Nate's hair was plastered to his face and his clothes were so sodden it looked like he'd taken a bath in them. But Mattie couldn't care less about Nate. Kyle's words were hammering her head. What did he mean, he hadn't seen Chloe since the office? According to Chloe, they'd still been hot and heavy a month later.

Kyle cursed and turned to face him. 'Yeah, sorry, mate. Just wanted to talk to Mattie about something.'

Baz poked his head out from behind a bush. 'You're supposed to talk *on camera*. That's the whole point of a *reality show*.'

Mattie itched to slap him.

'Um, guys?' Nate stepped forward. 'Do you think you could repeat the conversation for us?' He looked around. 'Where's Ram?' Nate backed off into the woods and bellowed for the cameraman.

Mattie darted a quick look at Kyle, jerking away as she met his still-puzzled gaze. *Was* he telling the truth? Sure, Chloe was a big enough bitch to make it all up, but why would she bother?

Mattie shook her head. It doesn't matter, she told herself. Remember, you're about to go bankrupt because of him. Bankrupt. Bankrupt. *Bankrupt*.

'Here he is!' Nate reappeared with a mud-splattered Ram.

'I lost a wellie,' Ram grumbled, lumbering over to them with a face like a giant toddler's.

'Nice sock,' Baz smirked as the group took in the fluffy white sheep printed on Ram's foot.

'Bugger off.' Ram swung the camera back over his shoulder. 'Let's get this over with before I kill someone.'

If the look on his face was anything to go by, Mattie

didn't doubt he was about to commit murder. She hoped Baz would be the first to go.

Nate nodded. 'Ready, guys?'

Please don't bring up Chloe, Mattie pleaded with her eyes as she stared at Kyle. After the whole wedding dress fiasco, the last thing she needed was any further humiliations. She hoped the message in her eyes would bore into his brain.

'Can you trust me, Mattie?' Kyle asked. His question took her by surprise and she stepped back, almost falling over a branch. Kyle reached out to steady her. 'I want to start again.'

'Before or after I go bankrupt?' The words slipped out of Mattie's mouth and she cringed as she saw Baz's face light up. Shit. She hadn't meant to let Kyle know business was so dire. She'd just wanted to harden herself against him, not tell the whole nation.

Kyle's brow furrowed. 'Bankrupt? What do you mean?'

Mattie tossed her head and stayed silent. She could tell everyone he'd destroyed her business but she already looked like a sad loser. She wasn't about to fill him in on all the gory details.

Kyle reached out to touch her shoulder but she moved away. 'Mattie?'

She focused on a tree behind him, refusing to meet his gaze.

'Mattie, you going to answer that?' Nate asked as the silence stretched. Mattie shook her head.

'Jesus Christ. We're not going to win any awards with this dialogue. Silver's going to kill us,' Baz muttered when the silence had gone on too long. 'Cut!'

Mattie darted away from Kyle and over to where Ram was wringing out his sheep sock. She forced a calm look onto her face but inside her head was whirling. How could he not know her business was on the rocks? He'd taken half her clients! And what if she *had* been wrong about Chloe?

Mattie tilted her face up to the grey sky and let the rain pound her cheeks, hoping it would make her head clearer. Kyle wanted her to trust him. He wanted to start again. He made it all sound so clear, so easy. He hadn't been with Chloe. He hadn't destroyed her business. He hadn't even known she was going bankrupt.

Or so he said. Mattie wiped the rain from her face. Could she even entertain the thought of believing him? For a second, images of them together flashed through her mind: the softness on his face when he looked at her in the morning after waking up; the two of them celebrating after scoring a major account . . . He'd been such a big part of her life.

She'd said she could never forgive him. But what if she'd been wrong?

Nate herded Mattie and Kyle back down the forest track and across yet another endless field towards the Manor House Hotel. Mattie walked a few steps behind Kyle, her mind still a swirl of confusion. No matter how many times she tried to corral her thoughts into the 'Kyle's a cheating loser who stole your clients' pen, a million questions darted out again, bleating until she had no choice but to pay attention.

Thankfully, Kyle let her be, turning only occasionally to throw her a look. She could feel his eyes on her and it took every last bit of willpower not to look at him.

Mattie collapsed at a table inside the Bybrook Restaurant at the Manor House. Dim light filtered through the leaded windows, matching the gloominess that had settled on her. She grimaced as she wiggled her toes in a vain effort to dry them faster. Sodden shoes didn't exactly help her mood.

'Kyle?' Nate beckoned Kyle to join Mattie at the table. 'So, this is just a dinner scene,' he said when Kyle sat down. 'Just chat, act natural and ignore the camera. The usual.'

Mattie rolled her eyes at Ram who even as Nate spoke was jamming the lens in her face. He still hadn't found his errant boot and judging by the look on his face, he was far from happy about it.

'And . . . action!' Nate yelled.

Waiters buzzed over to the table, pouring wine and setting some sort of poncy green creation in front of them.

Mattie grabbed the glass of what looked to be kir and drained it in one go. She could really use a whisky right about now.

'Could we get two whiskies, please? Famous Grouse?' Kyle asked the hovering waiter before she could open her mouth. Mattie met his eyes. She'd forgotten he liked Famous Grouse, too.

In the candlelight, his eyes glowed darkly and a strange feeling squeezed her gut. She grabbed the newly offered glass and took a gulp.

'I didn't know your business was having trouble. I've been so busy, I've barely had time to lift up my head these past few months,' Kyle whispered, sliding his hand over his mic.

'Sure, rub it in!' Mattie hissed, trying to replace the odd feeling with anger. 'But you must have known. All *your* clients used to be ours!'

'You're so good at getting new business I never thought it would be a problem,' Kyle countered. 'And they're not all ours, you know. Only five or six accounts came over to me.'

Mattie stared, the wheels turning in her head. Only

five or six accounts? She'd lost a good twenty – at least – since he'd opened up shop.

'What about Cerillion Productions?' she asked, naming one of their biggest. She'd come home from Italy to find them off her books. 'And Belamy?'

Kyle shrugged. 'I don't know. I heard something about Cerillion taking all their recruitment back in-house. And Belamy had financial difficulties, I think. They've implemented a hiring freeze.'

Mattie stared. She'd been so convinced he'd poached all of them, she hadn't even bothered checking. Still, he *had* taken five accounts – whether they'd gone voluntarily or not didn't matter.

'Can you two hurry up with the salad? We need to move on to mains,' Nate shouted, gesturing for the waiter to clear their plates. Mattie watched as the waiter carried their dishes back to the kitchen, squinting in the dim light as someone ducked out and waved at Nate.

Was that Baz? He'd been AWOL since the forest. Mattie just assumed he was redoing his hair, which had wilted sideways under the force of the rain. Why was he hiding out in the kitchen?

Kyle turned, following Mattie's gaze. Another cameraman crept into the room, positioning himself in the corner and training his lens on the kitchen door. And Nate was doing that twitchy-toilet thing again. Something was definitely going on.

The kitchen door swung open.

And out walked the woman Mattie had hoped never to lay eyes on again.

Chloe Collins.

Chloe swayed her hips and high-stepped over to the table. Her long blonde hair was perfectly groomed and her make-up was tasteful instead of appearing to be applied with a trowel like the last time Mattie had seen her. Her wrap dress – definitely Diane von Furstenberg – hung on her curves as if it had been moulded onto her body. She'd fit right in on any Milan runway.

Painfully, Mattie pictured what she looked like just now – no make-up, wet hair, and dressed in a bloody checked shirt. For God's sake, she was even wearing *trainers*!

'Jesus.' Kyle voice was tight and angry. 'What the hell is she doing here?'

Chloe reached the table and put a hand on Kyle's arm.

'Hi, lover,' she purred in a silky voice. 'I missed you. You left so early this morning, I didn't even get a chance to kiss you goodbye.' She pulled his chin towards her and planted her painted lips on his. The extra cameraman zoomed in and Mattie could hear the whir as the lenses caught the expression on her face.

Keep your face still, she told herself. Don't show the camera or Chloe any sign of emotion. She bit down hard on her lower lip and looked over at Kyle. Was he really surprised? Or was everything he'd been telling her complete rubbish? Maybe he was in on this; maybe he'd been trying to really play her, to destroy her for good.

'Cut!' Nate yelled, coming towards them. Kyle jerked away from Chloe and wiped his mouth, leaving a big smear of red lipstick across his cheek.

'What the–?' Kyle swivelled towards Nate and Chloe, his eyes flashing. 'Chloe, what the hell are you doing?'

Chloe just smiled and waved her fingers in the air. 'Bye, Kyle. See you back home!' She disappeared through the swinging doors into the kitchen.

Kyle turned to Mattie, his eyes wild.

'I'm not with her! I never have been! She's just

angry because I told her I only wanted to be with you. I had nothing to do with this whole thing. Tell her, Nate. Baz! Tell her!'

But Nate just stayed silent.

Baz thumped Kyle on the back. 'Relax, mate – and thanks again for helping us set this whole thing up.'

Kyle shoved away Baz as if he was diseased. 'Mattie, please. I wasn't involved in any of this.' He tried to grab her hand but she pulled it out of reach just in time.

'Fuck it,' Kyle said angrily as he pushed his chair out.

Mattie looked up at him in surprise. She'd rarely heard him swear – or seen him so angry. His face was red and sweat beaded on his brow.

'You can't seriously think I was part of this,' he said, looking down at her. 'You can't. I only came on here because you wouldn't talk to me any other way.'

Mattie stared. The Kyle she'd known wouldn't be involved in something like this. But she'd never thought her father would leave her, either. She tried to shove the thought away. How had that worked its way in there?

Kyle reached out with his other hand and a gentle expression slid over his face. 'Come on. We don't need this circus. Let's just leave. We can start our own business together – equal partners this time. I'll help you pay off whatever debts you have, and we can start again.'

Was he serious? Mattie dragged her eyes away and pressed her fingers to her throbbing temples. Confusion swirled inside. She might have been wrong about Chloe and the clients. Maybe – she needed more time to really think about it. But did Kyle expect her to abandon two hundred thousand pounds? To trust him again, just like that?

'Come on,' he said, moving towards her again. 'Let's go.' His hand closed around hers but she pulled out of his grasp, shaking her head.

'No. No, Kyle.' Seeing Chloe reminded her how painful that whole post-Kyle episode had been. Whether he'd been telling the truth or not, just knowing how much he could hurt her was terrifying. She couldn't put herself at risk again. Emotionally or financially.

Her mum was right. Financial independence *was* critical, the key to happiness. All Mattie had left now was her business. And she'd do everything she could to keep it going, to keep *her* going. On her own, without help from anyone. It was safer that way.

Mattie pushed out her chair and stood up. Heart pounding, she elbowed Nate and Baz out of the way and headed towards the door.

'Mattie!' she could hear Kyle calling. 'Mattie!'

But she ignored him, walking out into the still-pouring rain, climbing inside the car and slamming the door behind her.

'Just go,' she said to the driver, desperate to get away. 'Go!'

He started the engine and Mattie watched the Manor House fade away into the February gloom. She'd made the right decision, of that she was sure. She'd protected herself and her business.

So why did she feel so sad?

At the studio a couple hours later, Mattie took some deep breaths and told herself she'd feel better soon. She had to, anyway – in a few minutes she'd be on set, ready to meet the man for her final date.

She walked over to the mirror in the green room. Even though she'd had a lengthy session of hair and make-up, her face still looked pale and drawn and her eyes . . . She tore her gaze away and plopped down on the sofa.

Stop being an idiot, she told herself. There's no way you could walk away from the show, away from your business. You made the right choice. There wasn't even a choice to make!

'Um, you okay?' Nate poked his head into the room, hiding his body behind the door.

'Fine.' She didn't even have the energy to snap at him.

'All right.' Nate looked at her as if assessing the possibility of an implosion. 'Well, this will be quick. Seamus will go through a brief introduction and then the final man will come out of the pod.'

'Great.' Mattie stared at the wall, his words washing over her.

'So, come with me, then.'

Mattie got to her feet and followed Nate through the now-familiar passageways towards the studio.

'And here she is, our luscious single lady, Mattie Johns!' Seamus was crowing out onstage.

God, she was sick of him. She was sick of all of this. Mattie put up her hands to cover her eyes from the glare of the lights as she walked out and settled onto her stool.

'First your father lets you down, then your ex – or should I say former fiancé, ha ha! – spurns you for another sexy single lady.' Seamus leered at her. 'It hasn't exactly been a good day for you, has it, Mattie?' He paused and looked at her expectantly.

'So?' Mattie shrugged and clenched her jaw, focusing on a light near the studio door. He wasn't going to get the better of her.

Seamus was shaking his head. 'Well, tomorrow's a new day! And a new chance for romance . . . or not!'

The lights dimmed and the sickly purple logo flashed up. 'So . . . let's play *The Hating Game!*'

Anger filled her as she stared at the purple hearts and sparkles. Bloody *Hating Game*! Just focus on the business, she told herself. That's what's important.

'Now, Mattie. There's one man remaining in that pod over there.' Seamus gestured towards the oval structure onstage. 'Any idea who it might be?'

Mattie shrugged. 'No.' *And I really don't care.*

'Well, let's find out, shall we? Ex Number Four, come meet Mattie Johns . . . again!'

That line was getting really tired, Mattie thought, as she continued gazing straight ahead. What did it matter which loser it was? Now that Kyle was out of the way, one ex was just as bad as another.

She squinted as a well-built man crossed her line of vision. Who *was* that? Underneath his perfectly styled jet-black hair, something about the pale face was recognisable but she couldn't quite place him.

'Hello, Mattie,' the man said, handing her the usual bouquet of purple flowers. 'It's so good to see you again.'

Mattie took them automatically, her mind still working. There was something about the voice . . . slightly robotic sounding, even out of the pod. Her memory stirred.

Wait a second. Could that be *Adam*? The geek she'd dumped back in secondary school?

Her mouth dropped open as she took in his tailored black suit and smooth skin. Whoa. He'd sure cleaned up nicely – the last time she'd seen him he could have done with a year-long stay in a fat camp and his face had looked like a pizza. Shame nothing could be done about those squidgy eyes, though. There was something about the way his eyes crowded his nose that made him look downright creepy.

'Hi, Adam,' she said, meeting his intense stare. Something else was different, Mattie thought, scanning his face. Oh – he waxed his unibrow! Her mouth twitched. Don't laugh. *Don't!*

'So one date remains for our single lady,' Seamus said. 'One date, to find love – or hate. Tune in tomorrow at eight to see what it will be, and then make your Date Rate!'

Seamus turned to the camera. 'I'll be back tomorrow night with all the action from Mattie and Adam's intimate get-together! And make sure to watch next Sunday night, when we reveal the winner and the answer to the question you've all been asking: which lucky ex gets to spend two weeks alone with Mattie Johns? See you next time on . . . *The Hating Game!*'

'We're out!' a voice boomed.

Adam turned to Mattie. 'I'm looking forward to our date tomorrow.' The corners of his mouth lifted in a mechanical grin, and his voice was so flat it sounded like he was reading off a cue card.

'Yeah.' Mattie couldn't muster the energy to bother looking him in the eyes right now.

She walked off the stage, through the corridors and out the back door of the studio onto the South Bank. It had stopped raining and a giant moon hung in the sky, reflected in the Thames. She moved over to the railing at the side of the river and leaned against it, drawing in a big breath.

Forget Kyle. Just forget him and move on. Whatever happened with Chloe, if he stole your clients or not . . . it doesn't matter.

Once you shut the door on a man, never re-open it. That's what her mum always told her, usually after her father had turned up asking for Mattie. Back then, Mattie had jammed on her headphones and cranked up the music to escape the sound of her father's pleas through the front door, trying to ignore the fact that she was longing to see him too.

She didn't have any headphones now, but she'd just file today in the depths of her brain, in the place she never visited. All the hard work was already done – kicking him out, getting over him. No way could she go through that again. Her mum was right: never go back.

One more date, then all this would be finished. She could resume her normal life again, rebuild the business, and all these mixed-up emotions would disappear. Sure, she still had to spend two weeks with whatever loser the audience chose. But after the Chloe fiasco today, it definitely wouldn't be Kyle, and the two weeks would be a much-needed break. Mattie was already picturing palm trees, pina coladas and sun – these kinds of shows always ended up in the tropics, didn't they? And she could deal with Giovanni or Adam hands down.

She breathed in again. Everything would be fine. Just fine.

CHAPTER EIGHTEEN

*Twenty-two per cent of people confess to secretly
fancying their best friend's partner;
eight point five per cent act on it.*

JESS DROPPED HER HEAD INTO her hands as she watched Chloe Collins burst through the kitchen doors on *The Hating Game*.

'I can't bear to watch,' she muttered, curling up on the sofa. Peeking through her fingers, she saw the stricken expression on Mattie's face as Chloe bent to kiss Kyle. Watching Mattie reject Kyle's plea for a second chance – and then Mattie accusing him of almost bankrupting her business – had been bad enough. But this . . . Jess shook her head.

How had they managed to track down Chloe? Jess's heart quickened – it hadn't been something she'd said to that reporter, had it? She ran through her conversation with Deniz. No, whatever other damage she'd done, at least she hadn't said anything about Chloe.

Jess looked over at the wardrobe where the wedding dress hung under lock and key. The whole nation knew about it thanks to Deniz, but Jess just felt safer with it locked away. She couldn't believe how stupid she'd been.

She picked up the phone to call Mattie for the thousandth time, but the call went straight to voice mail. She wasn't surprised. Whenever Mattie was angry or hurt, she'd completely blank people. It was what she'd done to Kyle – and her father, who Jess knew had tried to contact her a few times over the years.

Jess picked up a furry cushion and held it against her, waiting to see the remaining ex revealed. With all her might, she prayed it wouldn't be Adam.

'Ex Number Four, come meet Mattie Johns... *again*!' Seamus Leary yelled.

Jess stared at the television as the pod slowly opened and out came...

Oh my God! It was Adam! She let go of the cushion and leaned closer to the telly.

He looked like a totally different man! Jess smiled, pleased to see he'd finally pulled himself together. So there *was* a hot guy lingering inside the chubby one – she'd thought as much. After his disastrous Mattie episode, Jess had even tried to do a mini-makeover on him but he'd refused to wear the cool leather jacket and the perfectly worn-in jeans she'd got at a second-hand store. Jess's mum had shaken her head when Jess had to explain what she'd done with her month's allowance, saying Jess needed to stop making people into projects.

But she'd been right, Jess thought triumphantly. Adam had just needed a new wardrobe – she peered at the TV – and maybe some kind of skin therapy and a weight-loss programme, too. He looked great! Was it possible he'd toughened up on the inside, as well?

Without thinking, she picked up the phone and dialled Mattie to see what she thought of Adam's new look – it clicked through to voice mail again. Jess sighed and hung up. She couldn't stand it when Mattie was upset with her – not that it happened often. They rarely fought; Jess was usually happy enough to go along with whatever her friend wanted.

Jess called Adam next, eager to praise his new

style. The phone went through to voice mail there, too. Frustrated, she threw the mobile onto the sofa and looked around her small flat. She didn't feel like watching telly any longer. She'd love to go out for a drink and a gossip. But now that Mattie wasn't talking to her, she didn't really know who to ask. It was usually just the two of them. Anyone else who'd come along had been Mattie's doing.

Jess bit her lip. Without Mattie, she felt kind of . . . lost. Mattie would come around, right? Jess just hoped it would be sooner rather than later.

*

Adam couldn't believe his chance had finally, *finally* come. He'd waited and waited, shoved inside the stuffy pod, while Mattie chose everyone but him. Every rejection had sent a jet of anger through him, but he'd managed to control it thanks to thousands of press-ups each night.

Those and countless drive-bys of Mattie's flat to keep an eye on what she was up to.

If nothing else, being the last date meant he'd had time to shift any extra weight and make his newly formed muscles even more defined. Physically, he decided, he was almost exactly like the video-game hero he created. Now he just had to make sure to act that way, too: hard and in control. That's what women like Mattie really wanted.

Adam cut the queue and ducked into a cab at the rank just outside Waterloo Station, ignoring the shouts of the irate people left standing in line. The old Adam would have slouched around, waiting for hours. The new Adam waited for no one.

He smiled as he thought over the past few hours, some of the best in his life. The look of admiration in

Mattie's eyes as she ran her eyes over his hard body; all the new friends he'd made down the pub . . .

He'd never been good at socialising but after the taping he'd decided to duck into a nearby pub, the Founders Arms. As soon as eight o'clock rolled around, he demanded the incessant white noise of a football replay be changed to the channel featuring *The Hating Game*. It had taken some doing – greasing the sweaty palms of the bartender and ignoring some stick from the punters – but no way would he let his television debut go unremarked. Once he'd moved in on a few of the dissenters and got up in their face, they'd backed down surprisingly fast. That certainly hadn't happened when he was a fat arse.

Then they saw he was on TV and a few drunkenly cheered. Adam bought everyone a round of drinks to celebrate and good humour was restored. From that moment on, things had been brilliant. The night went a long way in relieving the fury he'd felt from the rejections of the past week.

Adam rubbed his eyes as the taxi crossed Waterloo Bridge. His vision was a bit blurry – he wasn't really used to alcohol. Drinking always made his bad memories of secondary school resurface, stirring up the well of resentment inside of him. But now he was actually . . . happy. And he'd be even happier soon, once he had Mattie.

He'd do another thousand press-ups when he got home. Come tomorrow, Mattie wouldn't be able to keep her hands off him.

*

'Sorry, I was just going over tomorrow's shooting schedule with Ram,' Nate said as he burst into the control room for the nightly meeting with Baz and

Silver. He'd been hiding in the loo for the past ten minutes, determined to be the one to look busy. Baz wouldn't one-up him this time.

But Silver and Baz didn't even seem to notice. Nate slumped onto a chair, nearly knocking it over.

'Nate,' Silver said, finally looking up from the papers in her lap. 'We've just been going through the ratings.'

'And?' Nate held his breath.

'Still good. Lucky for you, you were able to track down that blonde bimbo.'

Nate puffed out his chest. 'Chloe? Yeah, thanks.' It had been easier than he'd thought – the PI Harry Horne had Mattie on tape, from when he'd first met her back in the bar, saying Chloe's name. Once they'd found her, she'd practically jumped at the chance to get back at both Mattie and Kyle. Something about how 'no one rejected the Chloe-meister', Nate remembered her screeching.

'So, I have a great plan for Adam's date with Mattie tomorrow,' Nate said eagerly, keen to stay on Silver's good side. He'd been thinking about it all afternoon. Baz had arranged for a hot-air balloon ride – pretty tame stuff; no drama there. Nate would plan for the balloon to go off course, and then–

Silver was shaking her head. 'No, no, that's fine. With all the drama that's happened, X-ACT wants *one* date with a bit of romance. So try to pump it up, you know? Hire one of those luxury hot-air balloons. And get a waiter in a tux. Not too hot, in case Mattie goes for him instead.'

Baz nodded. 'Great idea! Nate and I will get on it right away.' He clapped Nate on the back. 'Right, Nate?'

Nate nodded as Silver strode out of the room.

'You'd better get busy booking that balloon,' Baz

said, checking his teeth in the reflective glass of the darkened monitor. 'I've got a big date with Chloe.'

'Blonde slapper Chloe?' Nate shook his head in disbelief.

'Yeah, man. I told her I could get her on the next reality show no problem – if she invited me over tonight.' He winked at Nate. 'I know, I know, I'm a dirty dog.' He flipped up his collar. 'Wish me luck!' he said as he walked out.

'Wait, Baz! Can you help me . . .' Nate's voice trailed off as he heard the whir of the lift. Bloody Baz! Well, at least it was a chance to get stuck in; to show he could organize something without Baz project managing the whole event.

Better get started, Nate sighed, grabbing the phone book. Should he look under B for balloons or H for hot-air balloons? Actually, he was glad tomorrow's date would go off without any scheming on the production team's part. When he thought about the look on Kyle's and Mattie's faces earlier today as Chloe made her entrance . . . well, he hadn't felt so good about that. He didn't care so much about Mattie – she dished it out, she could take it – but Kyle was a decent bloke.

Ah, here it was. H. Nate picked up the phone and dialled the number.

CHAPTER NINETEEN

*Four in five men believe a date will end in sex,
compared with one in five women.
In reality, forty-one per cent of first dates end up in bed.*

THANK GOD THIS WAS THE LAST date, Mattie thought as she climbed out of the limo early the next morning. She didn't know how much more supposed romance she could take. The impending two weeks in the sun were definitely well deserved.

Mattie shivered and rubbed her bare arms as she looked at the limp balloon in front of her. Lying on the ground all deflated like that, it reminded her of the time when – what *was* his name? – couldn't get it up. You're kind of intimidating, he'd said, as Mattie had snorted in disgust and pulled on her clothes.

'Are you cold?' Beside her, Adam was wearing a smart black wool coat, some crisp jeans and a pair of shiny black loafers. It was the kind of corporate-cool outfit Kyle used to wear – not that she was thinking of Kyle.

She gestured to her bare legs and arms, feeling Ram zooming in with the camera as she did so. 'Um, yes.' Idiot! she added in her head. I'm only wearing a bloody miniskirt and bustier! Hardly appropriate clothing for February, but Baz the Spaz wouldn't know appropriate if it bit him in the arse. Mattie had let out a stream of protest when she saw today's skanky outfit, but one mention of the phantom single lady waiting in the wings and Mattie had snapped her mouth closed.

Ruse or not, she hadn't come this far to lose the prize money now.

Adam shrugged off his wool coat and draped it around her shoulders. 'Here, take this.'

Mattie drew the scratchy fabric around her. 'Thanks,' she grunted in his direction.

Adam wouldn't be a bad candidate to spend those two weeks with – she could easily make it through to the end with someone as dull as him. Sure, there was something slightly disturbing about those deep-set hedgehogy eyes and the way he kind of . . . fixed them on her. But holidaying with a robot was preferable to dealing with any kind of emotion right now.

She shivered again despite the warmth of Adam's coat. She'd tried all night to hang onto the feeling of control she'd conjured up after leaving the studio. But when she got home and watched the recap of her date with Kyle on the laptop, she'd felt her restraint slipping away.

Kyle had looked so angry and confused when Chloe showed up. The only other time she'd seen Kyle so shaken was when she'd packed his things and told him to get out. And the hopeful expression on his face when he'd asked her to trust him . . . She kicked at a tuft of grass with her stiletto.

'You ready?' Baz yelled, charging across the field towards them. The balloon was slowly beginning to fill with hot air.

Mattie and Adam walked over to it, the whoosh of the burners filling their ears. Adam scurried over the high side of the wicker basket as Mattie stood, contemplating how to navigate a balloon basket wearing a miniskirt.

'Aren't you getting in?' Ram sneered from behind her, camera poised.

Mattie kicked off her stilettos and grabbed the side

of the basket, neatly flipping herself over the edge and landing in a heap in front of Adam and a posh-looking bloke in a tux who was controlling the hot air.

'Oopsie!' The man helped Mattie to her feet as Adam watched with a blank expression. 'All aboard?'

'Ram, you need to get in, too,' Nate said.

Mattie looked around inside the basket. There were already three of them in there and they could barely move. Where would Ram fit?

Ram was shaking his head. 'Uh-uh. No way. You never told me I was shooting a bloody balloon from *inside* the balloon. '

Nate stared. 'Well, how did you think you'd be filming it?'

Ram pointed to his feet. 'I stay on the ground. Always. I ain't going up there.' He pointed at the sky as if it was a building on fire.

'Excuse me, chaps, we do need to get this show on the road,' the posh man interrupted. Mattie followed his gaze upwards, where the balloon was almost fully inflated. She looked back to the Mexican stand off between Nate and Ram.

'I need those shots.' Nate looked desperate, all quivery and scared. Mattie glanced away. There was nothing more disgusting than a man who begged. She should know! But when she turned back again, Nate's chubby face was strangely serious.

'You get those shots or you're fired.' His voice trembled but his expression remained fierce.

That man needed a good session of assertiveness training – or a kick up the rear, Mattie thought as the two men squared off. Finally, Ram shrugged and walked over to the balloon, handed his camera to Adam and puffed and heaved his way inside.

The balloon began to rise from the ground and the figures of Nate and Baz grew smaller and smaller.

'Jesus Christ,' Ram said as the basket swayed slightly in the wind. 'I think I'm going to be sick.'

Mattie moved as far away from him as she could in the tight confines. 'Just don't do it on me.' She glanced over at Adam, who was staring with a detached gaze across the misty countryside. Did he ever show emotion?

'Look, if you try focusing on your work, maybe you'll forget you feel sick,' Mattie said. She couldn't cope with vomit right now. 'Just start shooting the view or something.'

'It is beautiful, isn't it?' the posh balloon operator said, gunning the hot air so they rose even higher. The balloon swung over the green patches below them and Mattie could see the sprawl of London in the distance. Even squished as she was – with the threat of Ram's stomach contents – it was nice floating over England like this. If only she could stay up here for good, away from the thought of bankruptcy, Jess's betrayal . . . and Kyle.

'Cheers!' The operator opened a bottle of champagne and topped up two glasses, handing one to Mattie and one to Adam. Mattie drained hers straight away. If nothing else, it might make her feel a bit warmer – and maybe help make yesterday fuzzy.

She grabbed the bottle and refilled her glass, trying not to burp as the bubbles hit the back of her throat. Bloody poncy champagne – that's why whisky was such a great drink. No burping, just burning. She noticed Ram focusing on her cleavage.

'Feeling better?' she said sarcastically.

He laughed. 'Much. Thanks.' He zoomed in closer.

Mattie took another gulp of her drink, pulling Adam's jacket tighter around her shoulders.

'It is cold up here, isn't it,' Adam said, watching her do up a few of the buttons.

She nodded. God, he was as boring as ever.

'So, what have you been up to since secondary school?' he asked.

'Oh, you know. This and that.' No way was she going to give him a blow-by-blow account of her life in the past ten years. Although he could read most of it courtesy of the *Daily News Online* if he wished. She drained her glass and held it out. 'Top me up.'

Adam handed her his. 'Just have mine. I don't drink very often.'

What kind of loser didn't drink? Still, if it meant more for her. She needed all the alcohol she could get her hands on right now; yesterday was still too sharp in her memory. She took a few more big gulps from his glass.

They both watched in silence as hills and scattered houses flowed beneath them. The first rays of a weak sun were beginning to penetrate the clouds, forming patterns of dark and light patches on the land underneath. Mattie put her hands to her head, suddenly feeling dizzy. That champagne had more kick to it than she'd thought. Then again, she'd hardly eaten anything since yesterday.

'You okay?' Adam laid a hand on her shoulder. Mattie wanted to shrug it off but she couldn't move. Suddenly the ground underneath them was swirling like a kaleidoscope and she sank onto the cushions at the bottom of the basket, desperate for something to anchor her. Adam sat down too, snaking an arm around her.

'You'll be all right. Just breathe.' He patted her back. She tried to move away but even an inch made her dizzy. She breathed in, conscious now of Adam weaselling his way even closer. Before she knew it, he was right up against her and pulling her head down to his shoulder.

Mattie heard the whir of Ram's lens zooming in but she was beyond caring. The only thing her foggy brain could think of now was Kyle. She wanted – needed – to put something between him and his words last night, something that would close the door for good. Right now, that something was Adam.

She lifted her numb lips in a smile for Ram. Everyone would see she was just fine after what had happened yesterday.

And she was.

Really.

*

Jess clicked off the telly and grabbed a cushion, hugging it tightly as she tried to absorb what she'd just seen. What the hell? Had Mattie really been snuggling with *Adam*?

She shook her head. What was Mattie playing at? Jess would never believe Mattie had let Adam come within an arm's length of her, let alone cuddle with her. Since when did Mattie *cuddle*, anyway?

And Adam! She didn't even recognize the chubby shy man in this new bold bloke who'd been brave enough to make a move on Mattie.

The whole thing had looked so romantic, a hot-air balloon ride drifting over the English countryside, champagne . . . Jess had kept waiting for something horrible to happen, like it had with Charlie and Kyle, but the date went off without a hitch.

A strange feeling snaked into her as she pictured Mattie and Adam together. She knew there was no way they were *really* together, but it was just weird. She was the one who had listened to them when they needed her; cheered them up when they were down. But for the past few days – despite her endless phone calls – neither of them had bothered to ring her back. They'd cut her out of the loop; she was no longer needed.

She grabbed her mobile and tried to call Mattie. But yet again it went straight to voice mail. Jess sighed. She'd gone by last night and she *knew* Mattie was home – the lights were on – but Mattie had refused to answer the buzzer. And after tomorrow, Mattie would be gone for two weeks with whoever the audience chose.

Jess gulped as she pictured Mattie and Adam together in a romantic tropical location, sipping cocktails and lounging on the beach. When they got back they'd have loads of inside jokes she wouldn't understand . . . if they even managed to keep in touch with her.

Maybe it wouldn't be Adam. It could still be Kyle or even that Italian man. Anyway, it would be better for Adam if it *wasn't* him – he needed to move on. She'd be the first to tell him everything was okay if he didn't get chosen.

Stroking the furry pillow, Jess reassured herself that it would all work out. Mattie might be out of the picture for the next two weeks. But Adam would still need her if things didn't go how he wanted – now more than ever before.

CHAPTER TWENTY

Ninety per cent of people believe their partners aren't completely truthful; seventy-five per cent admit to regularly lying to their husband or wife.

MATTIE AWOKE THE NEXT MORNING with a throbbing head and a queasy feeling in her stomach. Her mouth was like the Sahara, and as she slowly raised herself up on one elbow, the room swung around her.

'Oh God,' she croaked, as memories of yesterday's balloon ride flooded back. She'd had all that champagne, and then Adam . . . she shuddered as she remembered him putting his pale arms around her and pulling her against him. *Jesus.*

Strange that there'd been no drama, no conflict; just her and the robot, huddled together in the basket. From Charlie to Kyle, every other date had included some sort of clash. Did the show *want* the audience to vote for Adam?

Maybe they'd edited in a bit of excitement, somehow. She'd passed out as soon as she got home from the date and hadn't watched it on her laptop. Well, however Tweedledee and Tweedledum had made her come across, at least the great British public would see she wasn't scarred by Kyle – that she had moved on. Even if it was with a zombie like Adam.

And Kyle would know things were definitely over between them. Maybe he wouldn't even turn up for the show tonight. He'd threatened to quit after their date; it was possible he'd pulled out. Relief mixed with the heaviness in the pit of her stomach when she thought about not seeing him again.

It would be for the best, she told herself as she threw on old jeans and a tatty T-shirt sporting a faded logo of The Stones. They had nothing more to say to each other, anyway.

Might as well see what drivel was in the *Daily News* today, she thought as she headed out into the grey February morning. No way was she going to let herself be surprised like she had been in the past. Sighing, she forced herself to think positively. One more show tonight and then she could relax for two whole weeks. She couldn't wait.

She grabbed a copy of the *Daily News* and some prawn cocktail crisps, nodding to the hairy-eared man behind the till who was blasting last night's *Coronation Street* as usual.

Mattie flipped to Entertainment. Some girl singer appeared to have gone onstage looking like a giant tampon . . . Seamus Leary had been found passed out on a bench in Hyde Park . . . Mattie smirked. Should be fun to see what state he was in tonight, then.

Ah, here was something, she thought as she spotted Deniz's by-line. Her hand trembled as she held up the paper and quickly read the piece. Whew. Just a teaser for tonight's live show and a lame shot from last night's episode of her leaning against Adam's chest with her eyes closed. Christ, she looked completely smashed. Unfortunately, there was nothing about Kyle leaving the show.

Mattie slammed back into her flat and started making an espresso. She'd need all the caffeine she could jam into her veins to fortify herself for whatever happened tonight.

Just keep going forward, moving ahead, she told

herself as she gulped the strong black sludge. That was the only way to get through.

*

Adam pivoted in front of the large new mirror he'd bought, smiling at his reflection. Tonight was the night – the night when he would win the two weeks alone with Mattie, and the chance to show her what kind of man he really was. No more snivelling, overweight loser. No, he was a hard hero now, inside and out, the kind of bloke who never cracked; always in control no matter what. Exactly the sort of man Mattie wanted.

Surprisingly, he wasn't even nervous. After the disaster dates of Charlie, Giovanni and Kyle, Adam reckoned he'd win hands down. A romantic balloon ride, champagne . . . and Mattie had let him put his arms around her! He could barely believe his luck when she hadn't moved away, even leaning her head against his chest. All that effort in creating the new him was really paying off!

Just in case, though, Adam had instructed each and every one of his employees to stop working on their next video-game release and dial around the clock, making sure to give him the highest Date Rate of any of the men. Plus he'd drafted in several lowly interns to make up the audience tonight, promising them all jobs if they made their support loud and clear. People were like sheep, and if those watching at home saw the majority in the audience supported Adam then they might just ring up and vote for him, too.

Adam stuck his newly muscular chest out and curved his arm into an arc, picturing Mattie beside him. They'd make a great couple. Adam and Mattie, together forever.

He couldn't wait.

*

'How you feelin'?' Fabio asked as he tugged at Mattie's extensions an hour or so before the live show. 'It's the big night. You gonna spend two weeks alone with one of them.' He waved his hand in the general direction of the green room.

Mattie watched him untangle her red curls. They didn't seem so strange any more – funny, she was getting kind of used to them.

'I'm fine,' she said firmly. The week had been a whirlwind of emotions, from the disaster that was Charlie, the tabloid articles about her father and the bloody wedding dress . . . and, of course, Kyle. But she'd had all morning to get her feelings in order and everything was nailed in place now. She was ready to move on with her life.

'So who you want to be with?' Fabio asked. 'I been watchin' each night down the pub. Everyone says Kyle's the one that should win those two weeks.'

Mattie jerked her eyes away from her reflection to meet Fabio's. '*Kyle*? Are you insane?' She shook her head. 'Didn't you see what happened? Some things are better left in the past,' she mumbled to herself.

The hairdresser wagged his finger. 'Uh-uh. Not if they're good things. Good things are worth fighting for. And that blonde bird?' Fabio's Liverpool accent crept in. 'No way that was for real. Did you see the look on Kyle's face?'

Mattie shrugged. 'Whatever, Fabio.' She was done thinking about it. Chloe didn't matter, either then or now. The only important thing was getting on with the game and saving her business.

'It's just a show, anyway.' Mattie tried to make her voice calm but instead it sounded like a hiss.

'Okay, okay.' Fabio put his hands up. 'Jesus,' he muttered under his breath as he played around with her curls, piling them on top of her head so a few tendrils hung loose on her cheeks. 'Whoever it is, I hope he brings his pepper spray along. Here.' Fabio handed her a zipped garment bag. 'Wardrobe left this for you.'

Mattie unzipped the bag, wondering what monstrosity they would force her into this time. The dress inside was shiny and slinky, a stretchy jade-green material covered in millions of sequins. Mattie held her breath and shimmied into it, tugging the fabric down into place. Hmm. Not too bad. In fact, she looked half-way decent. Sexy, yes, but not the prostitute-gone-wild look she'd been forced to sport in the past. Or maybe she was just getting used to revealing a little skin?

Nate appeared at the door. 'Ready to go?'

Mattie nodded, eyes bulging at Nate's gelled-up hair and tight-fitting shirt that accentuated his rolls of fat.

He looked like a blow-up version of Baz with specs.

'So here's what will happen,' Nate said, pulling at his top. 'You'll be on the set next to Seamus, as usual. The men will be on chairs to your right.'

'Is Charlie coming back?' Mattie interrupted. She wouldn't be surprised if he'd offed himself after what had happened.

Nate squirmed. 'Um, no. We couldn't get in touch with him. His ex told us Charlie's gone to some Buddhist retreat in Indonesia.'

Mattie rolled her eyes. Typical. Well, at least he was still alive.

'So we'll show some clips and highlights from the show. Then the voting lines will close, and there'll be a brief commercial break while the final scores are tallied. Seamus will announce the winner of the two weeks with you, and we're out.'

Mattie shrugged, trying to make it look like she didn't care. But inside her heart pounded. What if more people thought like Fabio and Kyle won those two weeks? Could she keep a steady grip on her feelings with him beside her all that time? Even knowing he was somewhere in the building right now made her crave a whisky like never before.

'Break a leg!' Nate said as he shoved his specs up his nose and did his usual hamster-run from the room to the studio.

Mattie swallowed and smoothed out her dress. Everything would be all right. She could endure anything – even Kyle – for her business. Financial independence, her mother's voice echoed in her head. The key to happiness.

'Let's go!' Headset motioned her to follow. Mattie wound her way through the corridors and towards the wings of the same big studio where the kick-off show had been filmed. As she stood next to the grey swinging door that blocked the stage from view, she wondered if Jess was here. Mattie had to admit, as angry as she was, she kind of hoped there was some support in the audience.

'And now, let's bring out our sexy single lady. Please welcome back . . . Mattie Johns!' she heard Seamus shout.

Cheers and whoops broke out from the audience, getting even louder when Mattie walked onstage. Mattie couldn't help smiling. Having people cheer for her actually felt comforting.

She glanced to her right as she perched on the stool. No men yet.

She tried to keep her face neutral as the *Jackson 5*

music swirled through the studio and the on-air sign lit up again. Last show, she said to herself. Think about the money. The money!

'So Mattie!' Seamus bent down close, a bit of dribble oozing its way down his chin. Mattie leaned back, trying to get out of the firing line. He smelled even more like a brewery than usual and his swirly pink tie was so bright it hurt her eyes.

'You've had quite the week, haven't you? Tell us, which one of the men do *you* think deserves a second chance for romance? Not that you get a choice,' Seamus sniggered.

The studio went quiet and Mattie could hear the audience rustle as they awaited her answer. Who to say? Giovanni would probably try to seduce her every ten seconds; Kyle . . . not even an option.

That left Adam.

Yes, she could deal with Adam for two weeks – a robotic nerd was better than an underwear-model wannabe.

But if she said Adam, would the audience vote for someone else just for fun, to go against her? Maybe vote for Kyle, to mix things up? Maybe she should say Kyle, so they'd go for another man. But then Kyle would think she wanted to be with him, and . . . no, she couldn't face going through that again. Anyway, these were lame people who watched game shows, not corporate strategists. She was over-thinking the whole thing.

'I think Adam deserves a second chance,' Mattie said finally.

The audience erupted. 'AD-AM! AD-AM!'

Clearly there was no accounting for taste, Mattie thought. How anyone could root for the robot was beyond her.

'Well, let's get our men out here and see what they

have to say!' Seamus crowed. 'Welcome back to the stage . . . Giovanni!'

Mattie swivelled as Giovanni trotted on, resplendent in cowboy boots with heels and a tight-fitting shirt *à la* Baz tucked into a pair of leather trousers. Good Lord, did he plan to hit Pimps R Us after the show? There was a smattering of applause and he bowed with a flourish before settling onto his stool, legs wide part to ensure maximum exposure of his goods.

'And . . . welcome Adam!'

The audience burst into cheers as Adam appeared, moving forward with jerky strides, looking polished in yet another tailored black suit. Everything – from his shiny shoes to his crisp white shirt and lacquered hair – was perfect, as if it'd been pinned into place.

'And finally, welcome back Kyle!'

Mattie studied the audience, anxious to gauge their response. A few boos – but surprisingly, plenty of cheers – rang out in the studio.

What if Fabio *did* reflect the thoughts of the nation? Sweat broke out on her upper lip and she quickly wiped it away.

Suddenly the studio lights felt a million degrees hotter. It didn't matter if Kyle won. It didn't! She'd deal with it.

Seamus pushed back from the podium and sleazed over to the men.

'Let's talk to Giovanni first. Giovanni, voting lines close in fifteen minutes. Tell me, why should people vote for you to be with Mattie?'

Giovanni grinned into the camera. 'I amma cool. I amma fit.' He looked over towards Mattie. 'We have da fun, yes? I fun!'

Mattie couldn't help but nod mutely. He *had* been fun, she thought, remembering their flour fight in Ali's small, dingy kitchen.

'And now over to Adam. Adam, same question. Why should people vote for you?'

'People should vote for me because Mattie and I have chemistry. If you watched our date, you must have seen it. We belong together.'

'Awwwww!' the audience sighed. Mattie only just stopped herself from snorting. Chemistry? They barely had enough spark to light a match! There was something so dead about Adam the only chemistry would be decomposition.

'And finally, Kyle. Kyle, why should you be the one to win those two weeks with Mattie?'

Mattie held her breath and stared straight ahead even though every inch of her strained to turn in Kyle's direction. She steeled herself against his coming words.

There was a pause, then she heard Kyle say: 'I shouldn't.'

What? That was the last thing she'd expected – she'd been psyching herself up to ignore another plea. She swung around to face him, trying to read his thoughts. Was this some kind of game? But his pale face and the tense expression made it clear it wasn't. Mattie had never seen him so exhausted.

'Mattie's made it clear she doesn't trust me, that she doesn't want a second chance,' he said, staring straight at her. 'I have to respect that.'

Mattie wrestled her eyes away from his, struggling not to show her surprise. Kyle had tried hard to talk to her after their break-up, begging for a second chance. He'd even come on this show, for God's sake! Had he finally given up on them? A strange feeling fluttered in her gut and she forced herself to smile. She should be happy. He was finally leaving her alone. Yes. She *was* happy. The way forward would be much easier now.

'Yeah, you've got someone waiting at home anyway, eh Kyle?' Seamus sneered. The audience laughed as he walked back over to Mattie and put a hand on her shoulder. She could feel the heat and sweat seeping through the sequins of her dress. 'But it's not up to you or Mattie. It's up to our audience.' He leered at them. 'With five minutes remaining, let's see a few highlights from the four dates.'

The big screen behind them lit up and the *Jackson 5* theme tune rocketed through the speakers. Mattie spun around to see images of the ballroom dance instructor dry-humping Charlie and Charlie leaving in tears. Poor idiot. Then she and Giovanni were laughing in the mud pit, Ali grabbing Giovanni by the throat . . . and she and Kyle in Castle Combe, and him telling her he wanted to start over.

Her throat tightened as the video cut to the angry look on Kyle's face when Chloe came in the restaurant. Mattie shook her head. No matter what else Kyle had or hadn't done, she couldn't *really* believe he'd been involved in the set-up – he wasn't that good an actor. A few horrific shots of her and Adam snuggling in the hot-air balloon came on and then the video ended. The lights flashed on and off again and the giant purple *Hating Game* logo came up.

'And lines for your Date Rate are now closed.' Seamus paused and looked meaningfully into the camera. 'Join us after the commercial break when we reveal which sexy ex gets to spend two weeks alone with our single lady to repair their relationship or destroy it – forever!'

'We're out! Five minutes,' a voice off-stage boomed.

Fabio breezed out from the wings and gave Seamus's greasy hair a quick comb, then minced over to Mattie's stool. 'You saw Kyle's face, right? In the video?' he whispered as he tugged a curl. 'I told you! It was a set up!'

'Are you deaf as well as dumb?' Mattie dodged a brush. 'Didn't you hear what he said? It's over between us. For good.' Even though she'd been saying that ever since their break up, a surprising heaviness pushed at her heart as she heard herself speak the words.

Fabio shrugged. 'Of course he's saying it's over – didn't you run out on him last night? You haven't given him much choice. Come on, girl. Get some guts and go for it.'

'Thanks, Dr Phil-io,' Mattie muttered. She opened her mouth to say more, but was cut off by Nate running around the stage like a rodent on speed trying to get everyone back into place.

'Thirty seconds!' he sang out, clearly trying to appear authoritative but sounding more like an adolescent whose voice was changing. 'Thirty seconds!'

Mattie settled onto the stool and tried not to look in Kyle's direction as Fabio's words swarmed through her head. She *was* being gutsy! Saving her business was the smart choice; the choice a modern, independent woman would make. It wasn't the 1950s for God's sake. She didn't need a man to come rescue her. If Kyle couldn't accept that – which clearly he couldn't – it was his problem.

'Back on in three! Two! One!' The floor manager cued Seamus.

'Welcome back to *The Hating Game*.' Seamus grinned into the camera. 'It's now time to reveal . . . which one of these men will spend two weeks with our lo-ve-ly single lady?' He paused, swaying dangerously. 'Can I have the envelope please?'

Mattie's heart thumped as a runner darted onto the stage and handed Seamus an envelope.

'And the winner of the two week holiday . . . with

gorgeous single Mattie Johns . . . the ex with the highest Date Rate is . . .' Seamus struggled to open the envelope with his sausage-like fingers.

Hurry up! Mattie's head was about to explode.

The pissed host peered closely at the card, his hand visibly shaking.

Oh come on! Couldn't they just tell him through the earpiece? He couldn't even walk straight, let alone see straight.

Another dramatic pause, then Seamus opened his mouth.

'Adam!' he yelled.

The *Jackson 5* song started up again and the audience burst into applause. Mattie arranged her face into a smile over the chorus of their chants and cheers, willing her eyes away from Kyle. Adam had won. That was okay then.

'No! There's something wrong!' Giovanni got up off his stool. 'It shouldda have been *me*!' He swung his cowboy-booted foot back and kicked the flimsy metal chair, sending it flying off-stage and into the crowd. Two burly security men grabbed him and dragged him into the wings as he accused the production team of a 'stitchha up'.

'Adam, come on over.' Seamus waved his arm.

Adam got off his stool, his muscles looking even more defined underneath his fitted white shirt. He was grinning but the smile didn't quite reach his eyes.

He put his hand on Mattie's shoulder and squeezed. 'I can't wait to spend those two weeks alone with you, to get to know you better. To see if we can rekindle what we had all those years ago.'

'Um, yeah,' Mattie said, trying to ignore the fact that his hand felt like a pincer. Was he for real? Rekindle *what*? Him pasting her head on a Page Three model like he'd done back in secondary school?

That was about as close as they'd got to a relationship.

Seamus turned to the camera and smiled. 'Tune in tomorrow at eight when we'll reveal the secret location of the next two weeks and see if Mattie and Adam can heal past rifts on . . .'

'*The Hating Game!*' the audience roared.

'And we're out! Good show, everyone,' the floor manager yelled.

Adam gave her shoulder another squeeze. 'So I'll see you tomorrow,' he said, still staring into her eyes. Mattie repressed a shudder.

'Yup, see you then!' she said flippantly. She watched Adam walk off the stage, then turned slowly towards the men's stools. Knowing Kyle, he'd be waiting there, wanting to say good-bye so they left things on a good note.

The stool was empty.

Mattie took a deep breath. His loss.

Well, that was it, then. Soon she'd be far, far away from here and all of this would be behind her.

Tomorrow couldn't come soon enough.

*

Nate, Silver and Baz sat in the control room as the monitor faded away to black.

'That's it, boys.' Silver swung around in her chair. 'The network will be happy Adam's won. Very happy indeed.' She cracked open a bottle of vodka resting at her side and poured them each a large neat shot.

'Cheers!' She downed hers and Nate and Baz followed suit, Nate grimacing as the liquid slid down his throat. He'd always been more of a beer bloke. Still, he deserved a little celebratory drink, right? The show's ratings were through the roof and the network was happy. And he, as EP, had a big hit on his hands! His future looked exceedingly bright.

'Why did X-ACT want Adam?' Nate wondered, holding out his glass for more. 'Yeah, he had a good date with Mattie, but only because we didn't make anything happen. Wouldn't it have been better to have someone Mattie actually connects with? I mean, I know it's *The Hating Game* and all, but still . . .' His voice trailed off as he realised in horror he was spewing his thoughts aloud. That vodka was going straight to his head.

Baz just rolled his eyes but Silver actually snorted.

'Nate, Nate.' She took another shot, licked her lips, and did another. 'How many times do I need to say it? It's not about romance; it's about ratings – and getting the maximum with minimal output.'

Nate darted a look at Baz to see if Baz was confused, too. But Baz was nodding along as if he understood.

'What do you mean, minimal output?' Nate asked with numb lips. His head was fuzzy and everything was taking on a second outline.

'The network doesn't want to shell out the two hundred thousand pound prize money. They promised us all a bonus – and first rights refusal to produce the next reality-show concept – *if* Mattie drops out before the end.' Silver's eyes gleamed.

Nate stared at Silver's two heads. 'But that's fraud,' he slurred. Not pay the prize money? He couldn't believe even Silver would go that far.

'No, it's not. They only pay if Mattie makes it to the end; it's all in her contract. And I can guarantee you, with Adam and what we're going to pull, there's *no way* she will.'

Silver unearthed a cocktail sausage from her suit pocket and bit into it. 'Timing is everything, though: X-ACT only has space in its schedule to broadcast one week max of Relationship Repair. They've already sold the advertising slots for the first five days, so we need to think strategically. The network can lose out on their advertising revenue if Mattie goes too soon.'

'What do you mean, with Adam and what we're going to pull?' Nate rubbed his eyes but his double-vision remained. He blinked, trying to focus on Silver's words.

Silver shrugged. 'One thing at a time, Nate. Let's just make sure we're set for tomorrow first, hmm?' She turned to Baz. 'Got the cars all ready? Everything sorted at the site?'

Baz nodded. 'Of course. And we have Nate's relationship activities all lined up, one for each of the five days.' He smirked.

Nate lurched unsteadily to his feet. 'But wait. Mattie's not going to get anything?'

Silver made an impatient noise. 'Sit down, Nate. I told you, it's in all our best interests – *your* best interest if you want to continue here – to get her out before the end.' She fixed her laser eyes on him. 'If you can't help us do that, there's the door.'

Nate stared at her blurry two-headed form as visions of the past week waved through his head. He'd thought that had been bad enough – he'd manipulated and lied, and destroyed any chance of a future for Mattie and Kyle. But he'd done it thinking that would be all; that the next two weeks would be a breeze – enjoyable, even. And now Silver wanted to push Mattie out? How would they accomplish that?

Nate swayed back and forth in the doorway as the faces of Baz and Silver swam beneath him. He collapsed heavily into a chair.

There was no choice, was there?

He'd come this far.

He wasn't about to back out now.

Jess sat on her sofa, frozen. She put her hands to her ears to block out the eerie theme tune as *The Hating Game* credits rolled across the screen. So that was it, then. Mattie and Adam would be off together somewhere, while she was stuck here in London. Alone.

A rare flash of anger shot through her. She'd always been there for them, listening to Mattie's tirades and answering Adam's endless questions about her best friend. And now they were ignoring her calls and messages – she was no longer any use to either of them. Yes, she'd messed up with that wedding dress fiasco, but surely she deserved a chance to explain instead of being completely blanked?

And what about Adam? All she'd ever done was provide a shoulder to cry on; his only friend when the world rejected him.

Jess switched off the telly. She'd had it with *The Hating Game* and Mattie and Adam. The two of them could do whatever they wanted in their secret location – she wouldn't watch any longer.

The time had come to do something for herself.

CHAPTER TWENTY-ONE

Three in five take beach holidays to help mend broken hearts.
Of those, thirty per cent get their hearts broken again on holiday.

THE NEXT MORNING THE NOISE OF BIG fat raindrops splattering across the window woke Mattie from a troubled sleep. Thank God she'd be out of London soon. Last night the BBC had declared that today the UK would see its biggest rainstorm in years. Lying in bed trying to block out the never-ending loop of Kyle asking her for another chance, Mattie had mentally packed her suitcase at least fifty times: green bikini; white linen trousers; little Monsoon sundress. Thank God she no longer had to sport stripper gear.

Crawling out of the covers, she started removing those items from her wardrobe now. Not that Tweedledee or Tweedledum had given her any indication of where she and Adam might be going, but she was familiar enough with these lame shows to know the formula dictated somewhere hot and humid. Despite a thorough grilling, Nate refused to provide any clues, simply telling her the car would be there at eight.

Mattie threw on jeans and a thin baby-blue linen shirt, shoving her feet in the one pair of flat sandals she owned. She hoped the ensemble was a good Britain-meets-the-tropics compromise. Soon she'd be miles away from all of this, lounging in the sun with a cocktail. Two weeks later she'd be back, two hundred thousand in hand, ready to rebuild her life. A life blissfully free of men.

A horn hooted from below. Peering out the window through the translucent grey slant of rain, she could only just see the ominous black car from the studio. Throwing a few more items into her rather empty case she ran downstairs and launched herself into the car, finding herself sitting in Adam's lap.

'Sorry!' she said, moving quickly away. Dressed in an Englishman Abroad outfit of white cotton trousers, crisp white collarless shirt and tan boat shoes, Adam obviously assumed they'd be heading somewhere tropical, too.

'Morning, Mattie,' Adam said in his flat voice. Reaching out his arm robotically, he lowered it onto her knee. Mattie stared, then calmly placed it back on his own leg, ignoring the angry look that flashed across his face. As if!

'Hey, Ram.' She dodged the camera shoved in her face, knowing the cameraman hated it when people talked to him during shooting. He grunted in response.

'So any idea where we're off to?' she said to Adam.

He shook his head. 'No. I asked Nate last night but he wouldn't tell me anything.'

'Yeah, he didn't tell me, either.' Mattie leaned forward and knocked on the shadowed glass partition. 'Hello! Anybody home? Where are we going?' You'd think it was a national secret or something.

And like the lame producers they were, of course there was no answer.

The car wound its way through the city and Mattie watched as the West London suburbs flashed by. They must be on their way to Heathrow, naturally. It would feel so good to relax, to chill out on the white sand . . . when was the last time she'd had a holiday, anyway?

The partition lowered and Nate's potato head appeared.

'Here, guys. Can you put these on?' He handed them two blindfolds.

He sounded even whinier than usual, Mattie thought. And looked more wretched, too. Big circles ringed his bloodshot eyes and his 'fro would have Bob Marley looking for the nearest barber in horror. Plus, the usually smooth baby-face was littered with gingery stubble.

'What happened to you?' Mattie asked. 'You look like shit.'

'Yeah, just a bit too much to drink,' Nate mumbled, not meeting her eyes. 'Can you please just put on the blindfold?'

'You're joking,' Mattie said, eyeing the black velvet band. 'Blindfolds?' Actually, a blindfold might not be a bad idea – at least she wouldn't have to look at Adam and she could get some sleep – but she wasn't about to follow orders from a man who couldn't even comb his hair properly. Or from a man, full stop.

'It was Baz's idea,' Nate muttered. 'It's just until we get to our departure point.' He looked at his watch. 'Should be another hour and a bit. Please, just put it on. Please?'

Ugh, she'd do anything to block out his baleful, blobby face. 'You're lucky I want to sleep,' Mattie said, fitting the blindfold over her eyes and savouring the darkness. So they weren't going to Heathrow, after all. What departure point was only an hour or so away? Was it a private airport?

Leaning back against the seat, the exhaustion of the past weeks overwhelmed her, and Mattie fell into a deep slumber.

'We're here!' Mattie's eyes flew open as the car came to a halt. Everything was black and she clawed at the blindfold.

'Just leave it on for five more minutes, okay?' Nate said. 'We'll grab your luggage and lead you onto the next stage of transportation. Ram, if you could film this . . .'

Mattie listened as the car doors opened and slammed shut again. Then someone took her arm and led her out of the car. She inhaled, expecting to smell the petrol of an airfield. Instead, it smelled like – she sniffed again – dead sea creatures? Where the hell were they? At least the rain had stopped, although the air was heavy and damp.

'So where are we going?' she asked whoever was manoeuvring her down some sort of wooden contraption. She could hear the thump of her feet echoing on the boards.

'You'll find out,' a smug voice said. Was that Baz? She could tell he was enjoying this. She was wondering where the slimy little cretin had got to. As sad as Nate was, Mr Blobby was preferable to Baz the Spaz.

'Take her arm,' Baz said to someone who reeked of fish. Mattie felt herself being pulled in one direction, then plopped down onto a hard cold surface. She heard Adam being brought over and plunked next to her.

'Right, guys.' The annoying authoritarian voice was really beginning to grate now. 'When I count to three, remove the blindfold. Ram, make sure you get this.'

Mattie smiled at Ram's huff of frustration. One day she'd really like to see him haul off and punch Baz right in his smug mouth.

'Okay. One, two . . .' Baz paused for dramatic effect and if Mattie had been able to see she wouldn't be able to refrain from hitting him. 'Three!'

Mattie fumbled with the blindfold's strings. Somehow they'd managed to work themselves into a knot, and the fake nails Cyndi had insisted on weren't helping.

'What the–?' Adam said. She could hear the boards creak as he stomped around.

There was a rumble underneath her and she felt whatever she was in moving. Finally the blindfold gave way and she blinked against the light filtering though the heavy clouds.

Mattie glanced around, heart sinking. They were on a boat – a fishing boat, judging by the overpowering smell and the nets heaped in one corner – pulling away from the coastline. The wind bit into her bare arms and the sky looked like it was about to bring on a flood of Old Testament proportions.

'Jesus Christ,' she said as she took it all in. 'Nate! NATE!' But both Nate and Baz had conveniently disappeared.

'Where do you think we're going?' she asked, joining Adam at the railing and looking down into the choppy grey water. Her teeth started chattering and she rubbed her arms to keep warm.

Adam's blue lips made him look even more corpse-like. 'I don't know. Calais?'

'God, I hope not,' Mattie said. Surely there was no way the producers could eke out two weeks in Calais. Apart from cheap booze and illegal immigrants, Mattie couldn't think of anything else interesting about the coastal French town.

Over in the corner, Ram was struggling to balance against the sway of the boat as he filmed them. His face was slowly draining of its usual ruddy colour and turning green.

'Ram?' she shouted over the engine noise and wind. 'Do you know where we're going?'

But the cameraman's only response was to turn his head and heave over the side.

'Guess not,' Mattie muttered, crouching under the tarpaulin at the front of the boat to try to get warm.

She sighed. Did it really matter where, given they were still in bloody Britain and not on the way to an exotic location to lounge in the sun? Shaking her head, she reflected on the clothes she'd packed. She was going to freeze her arse off for the next two weeks. But maybe they'd booked a manor house hotel, like the one in Castle Combe? She wouldn't even need to go outside – she could just spend the whole time in the spa, the pool . . . it might not be so bad.

After what felt like an eternity, the boat bumped against a small wharf, nearly throwing her off her feet. Finally Baz and Nate appeared from the narrow space below, holding steaming cups of tea in their hands.

'Bastards,' Mattie mumbled.

Baz just smiled. 'We're here!'

'I'd love to get excited,' said Mattie, 'but you haven't exactly told us where "here" is.' She took in the large white cliffs looming above the shore and racked her limited geographical knowledge. They couldn't be in Dover, could they? It was the only place she could think of with white cliffs.

'Yeah, where are we?' Adam asked. A seagull swooped over them and a bullet of brown and green goo plopped on Adam's white shirt. 'For God's sake!' he grunted, holding the shirt out away from him. Mattie put a hand over her mouth to hide her grin. That was the most animated he'd been so far.

'Welcome, Mattie and Adam, to' – Baz swept a hand across the coastal landscape behind him – 'the wonderful Isle of Wight.'

'The Isle of *fucking* Wight?' Mattie followed his hand to the coastline, eyes frantically searching for a luxury five-star hotel. All she could see were more scavenging seagulls and a few isolated houses dotted here and there.

'It's really nice,' Nate said weakly. 'The biggest island in England! An area of outstanding beauty, lots of beaches, you know.'

'It might be nice in the summer,' Mattie said, taking a step towards the duo. 'But have you forgotten it's bloody February?'

As if on cue the sky opened and precipitation rained down on them.

'Come on, let's get in the car!' Baz yelled, pointing to a battered Land Rover waiting up ahead.

'Perfect,' Mattie said, climbing into the rusty car. 'Just perfect.'

Mattie and Adam were silent as the four-wheel drive – circa 1950, without its original or subsequent suspension – bounced away from the port and along a narrow side road. The view over the clifftops out to sea *was* spectacular, if you liked that kind of rugged, rough outdoorsy beauty. Mattie preferred the tamer environs of, say, Italy or France, where everything looked like it had been arranged for maximum sensory pleasure. The landscape here was untidy and wild, as if it was a painting in progress.

'You all right?' she asked Ram, who was jammed in the backseat with them. He was doing his best to film their journey to God knows where, and although the green pallor had subsided he still looked queasy. The last thing Mattie needed was *eau de vomit* mixed with the wonderful smell of oil and fish she was carrying from the boat.

'Yeah, I will be now that we're off that bloody death trap.'

He shot daggers at Baz who was bossily giving Nate directions from the passenger seat.

The Land Rover turned off the road onto an even narrower one, bumping over potholes the size of craters. Thick over-arching trees made it even darker and Ram switched on the camera light.

'Jesus,' Mattie swore, temporarily blinded. Adam smiled into the lens and put his hand on Mattie's leg again.

'I'm really looking forward to spending some time here with you,' he said, thumb pressing hard into her thigh.

Mattie shoved his hand off. Gross! Did he actually think he had a shot with her? She'd put an end to that soon enough.

The Land Rover jolted to a halt in front of a corroded gate and Mattie leaned forward to try to make out where they were. A faded sign with greying letters spelled out 'Cliff Top Holiday Park'. Scrawled underneath was a demented-looking happy face beside the words 'is shit'. Baz got out and opened the gate, waving the car forward.

'A holiday park?' Mattie said in horror. She leaned forward and poked Nate in the shoulder. 'We're not going to stay here, are we?'

But Nate just sat there like a lump. Baz got back in and the car rolled forward down a narrow paved track that ran between two rows of tightly packed caravans. No other cars or people were around and the whole place was dark.

What were these two idiots playing at?

It's like a bloody immigration camp for senile holidaymakers, Mattie thought, taking in the small, hunched caravans, some no bigger than the size of her lounge in London. She shuddered as she remembered the adverts on telly for holiday parks, where families with snot-nosed toddlers could let their kids run amok while they stuffed themselves with warm beer and every type of thrice-fried food under the sun. At least there didn't seem to be any kids, she thought, looking around the deserted field.

'Right, this is it!' Baz said as the car came to a halt. He and Nate opened the doors and got out, but nobody else moved. Rain continued to lash the car windows.

Mattie sighed. Surely this was just a ploy to shock them before they went off to a lavish, warm hotel where she could take a hot bath and wrap up in a cosy fluffy robe. So the sooner they got this joke segment over with, the sooner she could do just that.

Trying to ignore the pelting rain, she walked over to where Baz and Nate were huddled under a small drooping umbrella. They looked so comical, standing there practically on top of each other, that Mattie almost grinned. She glanced over at Adam. Rain was pouring down the furrow between his eyebrows and dripping off his nose. His blue eyes looked grey in the dull light and he was staring unseeingly into the distance.

'At least your shirt is clean again,' she remarked, but Adam didn't even respond. Jeez, talk about android. Somebody must have hit the off switch!

'Mattie and Adam, I'd like to welcome you to your new home for the next two weeks: Cliff Top Holiday Park!'

Baz turned to Ram who was busy zooming in on Mattie's horrified expression. 'Ram, make sure you get this.'

'For fuck's sake! I got it!' Ram backed up straight into him, nearly knocking Baz into the giant puddle forming beside one of the cement blocks the caravan was perched on.

Mattie walked over to the two producers. 'Ha ha,

very funny,' she said. 'Now show us where we're really staying.'

Baz smirked. 'What do you mean? This *is* where you're staying.' He threw out an arm with a flourish.

'If this is our new home for the next two weeks, how come Seamus Leary's not here to welcome us?' Mattie asked, tapping her foot. What bloody amateurs. If the TweedleDuo really wanted to fool them, they could have at least trotted out the host.

'Er, Seamus won't be joining us here. He'll just do a voice-over back in the studio,' Nate said. 'He had other contractual obligations.'

'Yeah, with a detox facility,' Mattie muttered, hoping they locked him away for good.

'I'm not staying here,' Adam said stiffly. He plucked at his sodden shirt. It made a sucking noise as it peeled away from his skin. 'I need access to an exercise facility, my special diet . . .'

Baz waved a hand in the air. 'Look around you. You can jog for miles if you want!'

Adam took a step forward, sinister eyes boring holes in Baz.

'It's not that bad,' Nate piped up quickly. 'Why don't you two go check out the inside?'

Mattie shot him a look, then climbed the rickety stairs and threw open a door covered with numerous dents. Ugh. The caravan reeked of stale cigarettes and bleach. It had a miniscule lounge with a battered sofa and a tiny galley kitchen. Down the narrow hall, a small single bed was squeezed into a broom closet cum bedroom.

Mattie took a breath. Okay, so it wasn't exactly Club Med – more like Club Dread. But she could do this. For two hundred thousand pounds, she could. She plopped her suitcase on the bed. 'So where's Adam's caravan?' she asked Nate.

Nate pushed up his specs. 'Um, actually, Adam's staying here, too.'

Mattie's mouth dropped open. 'What? You can't be serious!' she spluttered. 'There's only one single bed!'

Nate squirmed. 'I know. But it's only for two weeks, and I'm sure you guys can work it out.'

Baz squeezed into the room and sat down on the bed. 'Yeah. You can come to an *arrangement*.' He waggled his eyebrows. 'It'll be nice and coz-zy.'

Thank God Adam wasn't listening to this. He was still in the lounge trying to figure out where his 'on' switch was or something. 'Shut up, Baz,' Mattie said. 'You know nothing's going to happen between Adam and me.'

'You never know,' Baz said as he backed down the corridor. 'You just never know.'

Mattie rolled her eyes. It was just like Spaz to try to drum up drama where none existed.

'Come on, Nate. Let's leave them to get settled.' Nate raised a hand and he and Ram dutifully followed Baz out the door.

'Wait! Doesn't Ram need to stay?' No way did Mattie want to be left alone with the robot. But the door had already slammed shut, cutting off her words.

Mattie watched them race off between the caravans. Where were they going? And if they didn't need Ram to stay and film, did that mean there were cameras installed in here?

Mattie returned to the bedroom and looked up into the corners of the room. Sure enough, a glassy eye returned her gaze. She went into the tiny toilet. Those sickos wouldn't put a camera in here, would they? She didn't see one, but she really wouldn't put it past them. She jimmied the plastic sliding door, trying to close it. Stupid thing, she thought, struggling with the flimsy handle. It was stuck fast.

Mattie sank down onto the toilet and wrapped her arms around her torso to try to warm up. She couldn't believe her two-week luxury vacation had turned into this! Stuck on the Isle of Wight, in a deserted holiday park with an automaton as company – and the door to the loo didn't even close!

She took a deep breath and Kyle's face popped into her head. If he'd won the two weeks with her, he'd be making jokes right now, trying to cheer her up. Might even have snuck in some of that vintage whisky from Scotland he knew she loved . . .

No. She shook her head, dislodging the fantasy. What the hell was wrong with her? Why couldn't she stop thinking about *Kyle*? Sure, he might not have done those terrible things she thought he had. But that didn't take away from the fact that he expected her to give up the chance to save everything she'd worked for.

He didn't know her at all if he thought she'd just throw all that away.

CHAPTER TWENTY-TWO

*Four in five women refuse to eat garlic if they fancy their date,
but four in five men have no problem consuming it.*

ADAM AWOKE THE NEXT MORNING with a kink in his back. Without his special pillow-top mattress, he'd tossed and turned on the narrow sofa. He'd even got up and done an extra thousand press-ups but it had only made him even more alert. Still, it had helped relieve some of the residual anger he'd felt when Mattie had pushed his hand away in the car yesterday. Got to go slowly, mate, he reminded himself. Mattie wasn't like other women; girls desperate enough to fall at the first advance.

He stretched and looked out the grimy window. A dark grey sky hung over bare tree branches, dripping with the aftermath of yesterday's rain storm. But the weather didn't matter. All that mattered was staying in control, just like the hero in his video game. If he could do that, Mattie would be his.

*

Nate poured a cup of coffee for himself and Baz in the comfortable caravan they'd kitted out right next to the mobile production unit.

'So everything set for today's Relationship Repair?' he asked Baz, trying to reassert control. Baz might have been in on Silver's plan to knock Mattie out from the very start, but Nate was still EP. He was the one leading the whole concept – sort of – and it was time to step up. Yes, the whole no-prize-money thing made him queasy. But it was going to happen whether he stuck around or not. And no way was he voluntarily going back to blow-drying ferrets!

Nate couldn't wait to see his Relationship Repair plans in action. Today's activity encouraged selflessness. He'd arranged for Mattie and Adam to make their way through an obstacle course of garlic goodies, garlic being a speciality of Isle of Wight farmers. If they ate everything, they won a treat – and if one of them couldn't down something, they could pass it to the other to consume. Since garlic wasn't *too* terrible, it was a safe bet they'd work together to score the prize.

'Yeah, I've spoken to the garlic farm and everything's ready,' Baz said, taking a gulp of the coffee. He made a face and pushed it away. 'This tastes like rat piss. Look, Nate, as cute as your garlic idea is' – he smirked – 'I thought it might be good to have a few other foods. Just to see how selfless they *really* are.' His eyes shone.

Nate grimaced at the thought of his Relationship Repair activity turning into something else entirely. Now that Baz had added his own disgusting delights, the whole thing would likely end in about ten seconds.

The chance of Mattie swallowing something slimy was about as likely as Adam developing a personality.

'Did you organize the treat?' he asked Baz, just in case a miracle did happen and Mattie and Adam somehow morphed into caring, sharing beings.

Baz smirked. 'Oh yeah, I got the treat all right.' He rose and emptied his mug in the sink. 'I'm going to duck out and get some proper food. I'll drop you off at the garlic farm first, then come back for Mattie and Adam.'

Nate nodded in what he hoped was an authoritative way. 'Okay. Let's get this show on the road.'

*

Mattie's bed vibrated as the pipes beneath it clanked and clunked. She forced her eyes open. Adam must be having a shower or something – it was like an earthquake erupting below the bed. She closed her eyes again and waited for it to stop. No way was she going to get up now and risk a sighting of Adam's appendages.

'Hello!' An annoying tap was followed by a shaking of the caravan door. 'Hello!'

Bloody Baz. Mattie pushed aside the covers and sat up, wiping her face. Thank God she'd slept in her clothes last night – she wasn't going to let the nation get a look at her PJs. Not to mention she'd freeze to death.

'Everyone decent? I'm not interrupting anything, am I?' Baz poked his head around the corner, closely followed by Ram.

'You wish.' Mattie rubbed her eyes, conscious of Ram focusing in on her. She pulled on another T-shirt in a vain effort to keep warm. It was freezing and chilly draughts seeped through the thin insulation of the caravan.

'So what are we doing today?' She crossed her fingers the agenda would include something of the spa variety, although it was unlikely there was anything as civilised as a spa on this godforsaken island.

'Well, Mattie, as you know, you're here to see if your relationship with Adam really can be repaired. So every day, you'll participate in a Relationship Repair activity, designed to bring you together and remind you of important relationship values.'

Mattie groaned and saw Adam, who'd come into the doorway, stiffen at her response.

'Today's activity will encourage selflessness. You and Adam will head to a garlic farm and work as a team to consume culinary delights from around the world. If you eat everything we put in front of you, you both receive a treat.'

Mattie snorted; winning a 'treat' courtesy of the TweedleDuo wasn't exactly an incentive. And she could only imagine what kind of puke-worthy foods they'd dragged out from various rubbish bins around the globe. 'I'm not hungry,' she mumbled, despite the fact her stomach was painfully empty.

'Guess you'll really have to be selfless, then,' Baz said, familiar smirk on his face.

Selfless? Mattie stared at Baz's smug expression. Anyone who was selfless in a relationship was just encouraging the other person to walk all over them. Look at what had happened to her. She'd opened her heart – and business – to Kyle and he'd thrown it all back in her face. Or had he? She shook her head. It didn't matter now.

'Ram, film them getting ready. Be outside in ten minutes to leave for the farm. You'll have your breakfast there.' Baz banged out of the caravan, the walls shaking in response.

'I swear to God, if that tosser gives me any more film tips, I'm going to shove this fucking camera down his *fucking* throat,' Ram snarled.

'Oh, please do,' Mattie said, splashing cold water from the kitchen sink onto her face and trying to tie up her hair without a mirror. There was no way she was going to venture into the loo with Ram filming every move either of them made. No, she'd hold it until she got to the garlic farm.

She pulled on another T-shirt – that made three – and headed outside to the ancient Land Rover where Baz was already waiting, sipping fresh coffee and nibbling a warm croissant. God, she *was* starving.

They jolted down the mud track and onto the coastal road. Rain slashed into yellowed meadows and the grey ocean churned against the cliffs. If she'd had proper gear and a five-star hotel, it might be possible to appreciate the vista – from behind a nice double-glazed window.

The Land Rover pulled onto a road between two open fields and bounced towards a sprawling group of buildings. A large sign proclaimed 'Garlic Farm'.

Duh, Mattie thought. So much for originality.

Baz turned to face them. 'Hope you're hungry! There are bulbs and bulbs of roasted garlic and lots of other goodies just waiting for you!'

'Super,' Mattie said through gritted teeth. Adam was silently staring out the window, wearing his usual vacant expression.

'Everything ready?' Baz asked Nate, who was waiting for them in front of a small shop.

Nate nodded. 'Yup. Come on in, guys.'

Inside the shop, the pungent smell of garlic met Mattie's nose. It was so strong she could feel it winding its way down her throat. She coughed, trying hard to keep her face neutral.

'Hello!' A stooped man kitted out in mac and wellies joined the group. 'I'm Gordie. Welcome to the Garlic Farm.' He held out his hand to Mattie, small periwinkle eyes twinkling in his lined face. Mattie couldn't help smiling in return. He reminded her of a small, friendly elf. Gordie the Garlic Elf, she thought to herself.

'Wait!' Baz yelled, holding up his hands. 'You have to do that again. This time wait until we say we're ready!'

'Sorry, sorry.' Gordie backed away from Mattie.

They went through the whole scenario a few more times until Baz finally agreed it was passable.

'Phew,' Gordie said, leading them into a small restaurant off the shop. 'I'm not used to the camera, me. Don't know how you lot do it.' He wiped beads of sweat from his balding head.

Mattie put a hand on his arm, wanting to kill Baz for making the poor man stress. 'It's hard, but you get used to it. Just pretend it isn't there.' Easier said than done, she thought, when Ram was shoving the lens in your face.

'We're going to start you off with the finest garlic treat you've ever tasted!' Gordie said, rubbing his hands together. 'Our best roasted garlic bulbs. You can't imagine how delicious they are.'

'Great!' Mattie tried to sound enthusiastic. Poor old man, out here all alone with only garlic for company. She didn't want to hurt his feelings, but she was pretty sure that despite rabid hunger, her desire to enjoy a garlic bulb for breakfast was extremely lacking. Still, it was probably better than what was coming – not that she was going to even bother eating something foul for a so-called 'treat'. What a lame idea.

'So we need you and Adam to sit down there.' Nate pointed to a table with two small bowls of garlic heads. 'I'll count to three and then you'll start eating. Once you finish your dish, we'll bring you the next one. Remember, if you can't finish yours, you can pass it to your partner. Ready?'

Mattie and Adam nodded.

'One. Two. Three!'

Mattie slowly extended a hand and chose a garlic

bulb. Beside her, Adam already had one in his mouth and was swallowing, reaching out for another. Jesus! Either he really liked garlic, or he actually liked *her*.

Could that be true? she wondered, tearing the bulb apart slowly, delaying the moment when she'd have to put it in her mouth. Was he on this show because he actually thought he had a chance with her? Surely not – especially after what had happened back in Year Ten. A pang of guilt hit her as she remembered slating Adam in front of the whole class. She *might* have gone a bit overboard, yes. But that didn't mean he had a chance now.

She put a bulb in her mouth and crunched down hard, the overpowering flavour of garlic exploding in her mouth. Hmm. Actually, it wasn't too bad. She swallowed and reached for another. God, Adam's dish was almost empty!

'Umm, ummmmm,' she said, rubbing her stomach for extra emphasis and enjoying the look of dismay on Baz's face. 'This is delicious.'

'See?' Gordie looked as proud as if the garlic were his offspring. 'I told you.'

'Done!' Adam swallowed and held up his empty basket. 'Want some help?'

Christ, it might even be love, Mattie thought as she shoved her dish his way. Nobody could fancy garlic that much. Or blubber, or jellied blood, or some dirty-sock-smelling fruit called a durian . . . Mattie watched with a mix of horror and awe as Adam downed dish after dish, then reached for hers, too. Finally the food was finished, and Adam sat back, looking sick but victorious.

'Great! Now time for your treat!' Nate cleared away the stinking mess from the table. 'Baz?'

Baz stepped forward. 'Your treat for consuming all the culinary delights is . . .'

A stomach pump? Mattie finished in her head. Judging by the look on Adam's face, he'd need one any second now.

'A romantic massage lesson for two! We've laid on a therapist back at the caravan to teach you two how to make the other feel goo-od!' Baz drawled.

'Oh, gross. No *way* am I doing that! Forget it.' The words slipped out before Mattie could stop them, and she swung her eyes over to Adam. His face twisted with fury and he looked like he wanted to dismember her. Shuddering, she clamped her mouth closed. She hadn't meant to sound so harsh, but the thought of Adam's robo-mitts on her was just vile.

'Right, that's it here. Let's get packed up and move to the caravan,' Baz said. 'Ram, you can stop filming now.'

Ram grunted. He was already packing up the camera in the corner of the room.

Adam pushed back his chair and gripped his stomach, following Nate, Baz and Ram out the door to where the car was waiting.

'Thanks, Gordie,' Mattie said to the little man who was already sweeping up after them. She couldn't believe Baz and Nate had just left without even saying good-bye.

'Thanks for coming,' Gordie said gratefully. 'This farm means a lot to me.'

'Is it just you here?' Mattie asked. It was such a lonely place to be, for only one man.

Gordie stopped tidying and glanced at Mattie. 'It wasn't always. My wife didn't want to live out here no more, couldn't take the isolation. When she saw I wouldn't listen, she left.'

Mattie touched his arm. 'I'm sorry.' She wanted to say she knew what that felt like, being left behind. But her throat had closed.

Gordie shrugged. 'It was over twenty years ago now. You know, I was so hurt she wanted to leave everything I built here that I didn't even think about going with her. Wish I had now,' he sighed. 'I called a few years ago, said I'd changed my mind, but she'd remarried. Said she was happy.'

'She couldn't expect you to give up your business, surely,' Mattie said stiffly.

Gordie looked into her eyes. 'Tell you what. I'd rather be with her and the kids right now, without this' – he spread his arms out wide – 'than here and alone.'

Something shifted in Mattie's chest as she stared into Gordie's sad eyes. Would she feel that way back in London . . . company on track at last but all alone? The weight that had lodged itself in her chest since that day in Castle Combe got heavier.

'We're leaving!' Nate poked his head through the door.

Mattie surprised herself by giving Gordie a quick hug. 'Thanks, Gordie.' She followed Nate into the Land Rover and climbed into the back seat.

As the car pulled away, she waved to the small bereft man, standing alone in front of his precious garlic farm.

*

Jess caught herself humming the *Jackson 5* theme tune to *The Hating Game* as she pulled out of the school car park after the Staines Secondary School reunion.

The game show was all anyone at the reunion wanted to hear about.

She'd been thrilled so many people wanted to talk to her, but when all the questions focused on Mattie and Adam, the happiness gave way to annoyance.

Didn't anyone want to know how *she* was; what *she* was doing? Apparently not.

Thank goodness she'd stuck to her vow not to watch the daily update from wherever Mattie and Adam were stashed. She needed to forge her own life; to carve out a place besides being Mattie's sidekick and Adam's one-woman fan club. The class president had even pushed her onstage as a stand-in to accept Adam's award – Most Successful Entrepreneur – since obviously he hadn't been there to get it. Collecting awards for others, just as if *she* didn't exist.

With nothing to do back home, she decided to drop off Adam's award with the concierge at his block of flats in the town centre. She pulled into the covered car park of the modern glass and metal building and rang the buzzer. The door clicked open and Jess walked inside. She knocked on the concierge's door.

'Hello?' Her voice echoed in the foyer. The place was super cool, she thought, glancing at the reception area overlooking the river. Low metal tables and chunky chairs were scattered throughout the space, polished to within an inch of their lives. She could see the new Adam fitting in here perfectly.

She knocked again. No answer.

Shit, she thought, juggling the awkward plaque. What was she supposed to do now? Maybe knock on his neighbours' doors, see if they would hold it until he got back. She looked up Adam's flat number on the buzzer list by the door, then headed into the lift to the tenth floor. Loud techno music boomed down the corridor and she followed the sound to Adam's neighbour. At least someone was home! She rapped on the door.

'Yeah?' It swung open to reveal a guy about her age with a goatee and no shirt.

Jess flushed and held out the plaque, feeling slightly idiotic. 'Um, hi. I was just wondering if you could hang on to this until your neighbour, Adam, gets home?'

The man rubbed his beard. 'Adam? Oh, the bloke next door. Never actually met him, you know.'

'Yeah, well, he's shy,' Jess mumbled.

Rummaging in a metal box by the door, he passed her a key. 'Here. You can drop it off yourself. My mate used to live there before your guy moved in. I never got around to giving it back when he left. Take it, it's yours.'

'Oh, he's not my guy . . .' The door closed before she could finish the explanation. Well, at least she could leave the plaque. And it would be kind of cool to see what Adam's place was like.

She fitted the key in his lock, not sure what to expect. Usually she could picture what a person's home would look like but with this new Adam . . .

She swung open the door.

Wow! Everything was sharp edges and clean lines. Two black leather sofas formed a right angle overlooking a massive glass window. Strange red flowers spiralled from a futuristic vase on a table that resembled a cement block. In fact, the whole place was like the Tate Modern, and it couldn't have been further from her own comfy lived-in flat.

Jess tiptoed over to the cement block and carefully perched the plaque on it, backing away. Its cheap wood and engraved metal looked so naff. She picked it up again. Maybe it would look better in . . . the office? Did Adam even have one?

She headed down a corridor and looked into the first room. A giant king-sized bed with a black duvet took up most of the space, and the walls were bare. There was another door off the corridor. Maybe that was the office?

Ah, yes. Computers big and small lined one wall, while the other was covered with shelves holding what appeared to be video games. Jess peered at the spines and picked one at random.

She stared at the image on the front. The woman was a dead ringer for Mattie – albeit, with a bust inflated to about twice normal size. And the man looked almost exactly like Adam did now. Weird.

She selected another one. Same thing. And another, and another . . . Did all Adam's games have him as the hero and Mattie as the heroine? It was a bit strange, but not really surprising. Jess had always known Adam wasn't over Mattie.

Wait, what was this one? She drew out a CD with 'Mattie' scrawled across it. Curious, she booted up one of the computers and slipped it in, her mouth dropping open as the images loaded.

Thumbnails of hundreds – if not thousands – of photos of Mattie filled the screen. Jess clicked one open, then flicked through them.

Mattie outside her flat; Mattie having a drink; Mattie going into her office . . .

Fuck. Adam's plaque fell from her arms, landing with a thump on the floor, but Jess didn't even notice. This was more than not being over someone.

This was obsession.

CHAPTER TWENTY-THREE

Eight in ten men believe a show of strength impresses women.
Nine in ten women admit they are most impressed by wealth.

'DAY TWO,' MATTIE SIGHED AS SHE opened her eyes the next morning. She almost felt like scratching a marker in the scarred bed frame, counting off the days like they did in prison. Only twelve more left. It seemed like an eternity.

She'd had another brutal night, trying to thump the pillow into shape as Gordie's words floated back and forth across her consciousness. It would be grim to end up like Gordie. Or Mum, who always said she was happy alone, but Mattie had seen the sad look slide across her face when she thought no one was looking.

Mattie pulled the thin covers around her neck to try to get warm. What torturous event had Tweedledee and Tweedledum planned for today? Yesterday had been suspiciously tame – for her, anyway.

She heard Adam lurch into the loo for the countless time that morning and dragged the pillow over her head to block out any noise. The way he'd binged on all those horrible dishes yesterday, it wasn't surprising he was suffering digestive issues. Mattie didn't even want to recall the terrible sounds that had come from the toilet as soon as they'd returned from the farm yesterday. And with no door . . . At least Adam's stomach explosion and resulting stench had sent the waiting massage therapist scurrying for fresh air

– not that Mattie would *ever* let Adam massage her, anyway!

The caravan shook with an aggressive knock.

'Morning!' Baz burst in, followed by Nate and Ram. 'Ready to go? We've got a big day ahead!'

'Do I look ready?' Mattie grumbled as she threw aside the covers. Actually, she *was* pretty much ready, having gone to bed wearing almost every piece of clothing she'd brought in a bid to keep warm. She tidied her hair into a ponytail and brushed her teeth in the kitchen sink, conscious of Ram's ever-present camera.

'So what are we doing?' Mattie asked, slipping on mud-splattered shoes.

Baz motioned for Ram to train the camera on her. A muscle jumped in Ram's jaw, but he swung the lens as directed. 'Well, Mattie, today's Relationship Repair will focus on teamwork. I hope you like sports, because we're going to learn how to play rugby!'

'Are you two freaks serious?' Mattie said, forgetting Ram and his camera. She looked over at Nate. 'It's raining outside. And it's February.'

'A little rain never hurt anyone. And haven't you ever heard what doesn't kill you makes you stronger?' Baz bared his teeth at her. 'Ah, here he is! Morning, Adam.'

'Morning,' Adam said in a deep monotone.

'We need to get going.' Nate looked at his watch. 'Got to be at the field in twenty minutes. Adam, you might want to wear something more, er, suitable.'

Adam smoothed his neatly creased linen trousers – how had he kept them so perfectly pressed, Mattie wondered? – and his short-sleeved button-down. 'No,' he said stiffly. 'I want to wear this.'

Nate shrugged. 'Whatever. Let's go.'

*

Adam stared blankly out of the car window as sodden fields flashed by. He took deep breaths in and out – one of the calming techniques a therapist had recommended after his break-up with Mattie, back when he just couldn't live with the pain of rejection any longer. Right now what he really needed was a good thousand press-ups, but there hadn't been time this morning and the built-up anger over yesterday was threatening to overwhelm him.

When Mattie hadn't appreciated his efforts to win the treat yesterday, he'd nearly exploded. But he had managed to keep it together – until she'd rejected just the *notion* of a couple's massage class! Luckily he'd ducked out of the restaurant before she could see just how upset he was.

Gripping the armrest Mattie had tugged down between them, he vowed today was the day she'd see the real Adam. He wasn't a pathetic loser any longer. Not by a long shot. Sports had never been his forte, but now – thanks to all that training – he could show her just how much of a man he really was.

Once she saw that, there was no way she'd be able to resist him.

*

An hour later, Mattie was standing in the middle of a field, the wind whipping rain across her face so vigorously it stung. Thank God the Australian instructor had lent her a rugby jersey or she probably would have passed out from the cold. Her fingers were numb and she'd lost all feeling in her limbs.

'Right, I think you've got the ball chuckin' down now,' the Aussie said in a broad accent. 'Ready for a scrum?' He smiled and put a hand on her back. Normally she would have shrugged it off in a heartbeat but she was freezing and his hand was lovely and warm.

'A scrum? What's that?' Mattie had never watched rugby, let alone studied the terminology. She'd always thought rugby was for Neanderthals who had nothing better to do than grunt and act out homoerotic fantasies.

'You know, trying to get the ball from your opponent,' the Aussie said, grinning again and patting her shoulder. 'You remember the rules, right?'

'Sort of.' Mattie hadn't bothered to listen. It wasn't like she'd be doing this again anytime soon.

'Adam? Ready for a scrum?' the Aussie shouted.

Adam didn't even move. God, he looked angry, Mattie thought, taking in his laser eyes burning a hole through Aussie's hand on her shoulder. Adam's usual robotic facade was gone, replaced by the face of someone who looked like he was about to take up cannibalism.

The field suddenly flooded with huge, mountainous men. A whistle blew, and the men sprang into action. Unsure of exactly what to do, Mattie held her ground and watched as Adam streaked towards the far corner of the field, where she and Aussie stood.

He slammed into Aussie, tackling him to the ground. Interesting, Mattie never would have thought that Adam, of all people, would be good at rugby. She remembered back in Year Ten when he'd fallen over a hurdle and broken his front tooth.

But wait – surely pummelling someone in the face wasn't a part of the game?

'Jesus!' Mattie breathed as Adam pounded his fists into Aussie over and over.

The rugby instructor struggled and kicked then his

body went limp. But Adam kept punching.

'Adam! Stop!' Mattie screamed as a swarm of swarthy players stampeded across the field, making a beeline for Adam. Where the hell were Baz and Nate? She caught sight of Ram at the side of the field, filming.

'For God's sake, Ram!' she shouted. 'Help!' Ram hesitated then put down the camera and started towards Adam as well.

Finally Ram and the players managed to pull Adam away. Adam looked like a maniac: heaving chest, red cheeks and hair plastered by sweat to his head. Nevertheless, he appeared to be unscathed. The same couldn't be said for poor Aussie, who was just now coming around and trying to move his legs, moaning and groaning loudly. Blood gushed from his nose, one eye was starting to swell and – Mattie averted her gaze – a tooth was barely hanging onto his top gum.

'Let go of me,' Adam panted. 'I won't go near him.'

'You better not, mate,' the beefiest of Aussie's teammates said. 'Or you won't go near anyone, ever again. Because you won't be breathing.'

Adam shook them off and stepped back.

'Christ, what a nutter,' another muttered, moving away. He turned towards Baz and Nate who were sauntering over. 'What kind of television show is this? Your man nearly killed him!' He gestured towards Aussie who was lurching to his feet, blood pouring from his mouth.

'Shame,' Baz said, shaking his head, but unable to hide his gleeful expression. 'Good thing you all signed those forms. You know: *participation at your own risk . . .* ring any bells? Not my fault if you can't read.'

The man narrowed his eyes. 'I'm calling the police.'

Baz shrugged. 'Sure, go ahead. But your team won't

get its fee. And didn't I hear something about needing the money for next season, or you'll have to fold?'

Mattie watched as the group of men started advancing on Baz, baring their teeth. Baz backed away nervously. 'Come on, let's pack up.' He turned towards Adam. 'You all right?'

'Fine,' Adam spat through clenched teeth. His face had returned to its usual vacant expression. Beating the mud off his clothes, he trotted with Baz and Nate towards the Land Rover, the players angrily stomping after them.

'Thanks for your help back there,' Mattie said to Ram sarcastically, watching as the trio climbed into the Land Rover just before the players reached them. Mattie shook her head as the men swarmed the car and started banging on its doors.

Ram looked up from cleaning the lens of his camera. 'I helped!' he said.

'Yeah, after you got all the gory action.'

He shrugged. 'It's my job, innit?' He shook his head. 'This place is a fucking nuthouse. Thank God I only got three more days after today.'

Mattie stared. 'What do you mean, only three more days? Is someone coming in to replace you?'

Ram shrugged. 'I told you, they don't tell me nothin'. All I know is they got me contracted until Friday.'

'Shit.' Ram was hardly her favourite, but who knew what kind of idiot they could get for the last week of the show? It seemed kind of strange, switching the principal cameraman for the last week. Did Nate and Baz have something else up their silly faux-designer sleeves?

The Land Rover screeched into gear and bounced across the field towards them, the players trailing after it. It skidded to a halt, and Mattie yanked open the door and jumped in beside Adam, trying to keep as much distance between them as possible. As they pulled away, she saw Aussie hobbling towards the clubhouse. Imagine, Adam doing that to someone, she thought, sneaking a look at his frozen face.

And for a split second, she felt scared.

*

Jess parked her car in front of her flat and grabbed the keys, still trying to absorb what she'd seen. Stuck in traffic near the Chiswick roundabout, she'd tried over and over again to come up with a reason why Adam had those photos in his flat. But as she did, incriminating pieces of a sordid puzzle kept falling into place: Adam's questions about Mattie, her flat, where her office was . . . Jess had just blathered on, as usual, without thought for the consequences.

There was no logical explanation other than the obvious: Adam was dangerously obsessed with Mattie. For the first time since she'd sworn off the show, Jess felt her resolve waiver. Maybe she should check in and see what was happening. Just to make sure everything was okay.

She glanced at her watch – almost eight, and time for the show's daily recap. She turned on the telly.

The *Jackson 5* tune filled the room and Seamus's voice boomed out: 'Tonight, on *The Hating Game*. Mattie and Adam take to the rugby field . . . where you won't believe the dramatic turn of events.'

Jess crashed down onto the sofa, eyes glued to the dusty screen, heart caught in her throat. Dramatic turn of events? What had happened? She watched as some toothy Australian man sleazily patted Mattie's back and the camera cut to the expression on Adam's face. He didn't even look like the Adam she knew – his eyes seemed to burn holes through the television set.

All of a sudden, Adam was slamming into the Australian, landing a punch on his meaty face. Jesus Christ, Jess thought, hands flying to her mouth in horror. Who *was* this person? The man she knew wouldn't hurt a flea!

Jess's heart pounded as she envisioned Adam crouching behind rubbish bins and hiding around corners to take all those photos of Mattie. She shivered; definitely not the sign of someone normal. Nor was smashing some poor bloke in the head! No, this new Adam was scary.

What if the obsession got out of hand and he hurt Mattie? Tomorrow was Valentine's Day, and who knew what crazy kind of romantic rubbish those producers had planned! Her friend could be in serious trouble.

She had to warn Mattie. But how? Jess grabbed her mobile and dialled Mattie's number. Unsurprisingly there was no answer – wherever they were, phones probably weren't allowed. Besides, when Mattie saw who was calling she wasn't likely to answer anyway.

Jess sat back, staring as the rugby man finally struggled to his feet. If she couldn't warn Mattie, then she should warn the show. Once they found out just how obsessed Adam really was, surely they'd pull the plug on the whole thing?

The credits rolled across the screen and Jess caught the name of the executive producer, Nate Reilly, and the company that made the show, SiniStar Productions. She scribbled down the names, then Googled the company and quickly accessed their website, scrawling down the number from the Contact Us page.

Jess's heart beat faster as she punched in the digits then crossed her fingers someone – anyone – would pick up.

'Welcome to SiniStar Productions,' the recorded voice answered. 'Our offices are now closed . . .'

Jess hung up. She wasn't about to leave a message they could easily ignore. If she couldn't get in touch with the production company, she'd try reaching this Nate Reilly directly. But how? She tugged a strand of hair around a finger as her mind worked, then sat up straight as a flash of inspiration hit. Kyle might know the number; maybe the show gave contestants the producers' contact numbers in case of emergency. Mattie might have rejected Kyle – again – but Jess was sure Kyle wouldn't let any harm come to her. He'd help Jess get Mattie out safely.

She scrolled through 'Contacts' on her phone, hoping she still had Kyle's private details. They hadn't spoken since Kyle had rung, pleading with her to help convince Mattie to give him another chance. Jess hadn't exactly been successful . . . Oh good, she *did* have the number. She hit 'Call' and waited, listening to ring after ring.

'You've reached Kyle Cook. I'm currently unavailable until the twenty-fifth of February. For any client inquiries, please contact my office at . . .' Jess hung up, biting her lip. Poor Kyle, she couldn't blame him for taking off after what had just happened. But what was she going to do now?

Typing 'Nate Reilly London' into Google on the off chance she'd strike gold, her heart sunk as result after result filtered onto the screen. It would take forever to track him down that way. She grabbed the white pages and flipped to R, gulping at the long columns of 'N Reilly', then determinedly dialled the number at the top of the list. She'd call all night if she had to! And at the very worst, she'd just ring back SiniStar tomorrow and demand to speak to someone. Anyone.

After all, her best friend's safety was at stake.

CHAPTER TWENTY-FOUR

*Ninety per cent of women expect a romantic gesture
for Valentine's Day.
Twenty per cent of men plan one.*

'NOW, DON'T YOU WORRY,' Nate heard Baz saying to someone the next morning. Nate raised himself up on one elbow and tried to pat down his curls into some kind of order. Who was Baz talking to?

'No, no, I assure you, it's fine. Adam, like the rest of our contestants, is mentally fit. They all have to go through a psychological assessment, you see.'

Gosh, Baz was smooth, Nate thought. It was nine a.m. on Wednesday – finally a morning when Nate could have a lie-in – and already Baz sounded like he could be on Radio 1. Nate yawned. He'd had a terrible sleep, the mangled face of that poor rugby player plaguing him all night. He really should have intervened despite Baz's insistence otherwise.

'Look, whatever you found in Adam's flat, it's not really important. We keep a close watch on all our competitors and we wouldn't hesitate to remove them if we felt anyone was at risk. So thank you for calling and I hope you enjoy the rest of the show.'

Nate wandered into the lounge. Who *was* that on the phone? What could they have found in Adam's flat?

'Took the bullet for you on that one, mate,' Baz said, waving the phone. 'Some crazy woman wanted to talk to you but I managed to put her off.'

Nate pushed aside annoyance that Baz had taken his call. As EP, though, he did have to start learning to delegate. 'What did she want?' Nate asked, pouring himself some water.

Baz shrugged. 'Aw, I don't know. Some rubbish about how Adam's all fucked up.' He snorted. 'Tell me something I don't know.'

Once again Nate pictured Adam pummelling the rugby player. 'He's not really that fucked up, though, right?'

'Oh no, no. Of course not,' Baz said quickly. 'Look, I'm going to go wake up Mattie and Adam, get them ready for the big day. Everything's set for tonight, right?'

Nate nodded. 'Yeah, it's all set.' If Adam wanted to kill someone yesterday, just wait until things played out tonight. Today's Relationship Repair was focused on romance, it being Valentine's Day and all. Nate had organized a schmaltzy dinner but late last night Silver had rung with a whole new plan that would ensure romance was the last thing on the menu.

'Cool. Should be, like, *awesome*,' Baz said. 'I'll be back in ten.'

Nate watched as Baz banged out of the caravan. Was he telling the truth about Adam's mental state? Nate squinted, trying to remember if he'd actually read Adam's psychological assessment. He vaguely recalled the doctor saying he'd emailed the files and that was the last Nate had heard of it. Baz had come in, taken over all the paperwork stuff, and Nate had been more than happy to let it go. Was there something about Adam he didn't know?

He lumbered over to the computer and logged onto SiniStar's Intranet, then accessed the folder where they kept all the show's paperwork – contracts and such. Would the psychological assessments be in with the contracts? He snuck a peek outside the window to make sure Baz was definitely gone, then double-clicked the contracts folder, humming the theme to *The Hating Game*.

Nate scrolled down past the contract between Cliff Top Holiday Park and SiniStar Productions, Ram's filming contract, blah blah blah ... he stopped. Jackpot! Here were the psychological assessments. He clicked on Adam's and squinted at the screen.

Adam suffers from heightened rejection sensitivity.

What the hell was that? Trust the shrink to come up with some indecipherable mumbo-jumbo.

People with rejection sensitivity suffer from low self-esteem and often depression, usually as a result of bullying as a child. They experience deep anxiety and humiliation at even the slightest rebuff and may interpret any social signal as rejection, resulting in frustration, intense anger and aggression.

Nate rubbed the stubble on his chin. That certainly sounded like Adam's behaviour over the past few days, from what Nate had seen.

So according to the doctor, Adam *was* fucked up – and the ideal candidate to make sure Mattie wouldn't make it through to the end. It was a recipe for disaster: putting a man who'd explode at a hint of rejection together with the Rejection Queen herself. No wonder Silver had wanted Adam to win those two weeks with Mattie. He looked down at the final words in Adam's file.

To enable the patient to deal with the stress of the coming show and to stabilise behaviour, I prescribe a course of Prozac to be taken three times daily.

Prozac? Adam? Nate had never seen Adam taking any drugs – and unfortunately he'd had to watch pretty much everything the contestants did. Looked like Silver really was prepared to do whatever it took to stop Mattie and Adam from making it to the end. It was bad enough to put two explosive characters together, but to tamper with someone's sanity... wow! Yet another replay of Adam thrashing the rugby player ran through Nate's mind. Without his medication, Adam could – and had – hurt others. Now Nate really *was* anxious about the plan for tonight.

He pushed aside his worry. It was one thing to let someone outside the show get hurt, but Silver wouldn't injure someone connected with the show, would she? She needed Adam and Mattie – at least until the sold advertising segments ran out on Friday. Counting today there were only three days left, and now that Nate knew exactly what was going on, he'd keep an eye on the two of them; make sure everything was under control.

'Nate! Ready to go?' Baz burst into the caravan.

Nate logged off the computer and got to his feet.

'Yes,' he said. 'Ready.'

*

Mattie hadn't thought it possible to be so bloody bored. Even listening to Stuart wax poetic about his toenails was nowhere near as dull as this.

She sighed for the millionth time and watched the rain streak down the windows of the caravan. Mid-morning on day three and there was no sign of Baz. Ram had barged in earlier, shrugging when she asked what the plan was, and telling her he only had instructions to film.

Not that there was anything for him to film. Mattie had been sitting for hours, fidgeting. The stone-aged TV didn't work, there weren't any books to read and Adam had been sleeping non-stop since they'd returned from the rugby field yesterday. Thank God,

Mattie thought. After what she'd witnessed, the less time spent with him, the better.

Out of desperation, she and Ram had even played a few games of Crazy Eights. But even that had worn thin and now they were just staring out at the grey sky.

'Hiya!' Baz burst through the door looking as if he'd gulped one too many Red Bulls.

Mattie would have loved to push him into the ever-expanding mud puddle outside the caravan, but that would involve finding energy she didn't have. 'Where have you been?' Mattie asked. 'We're decomposing here.'

'Well, don't you worry.' Baz popped her patronisingly on the nose. 'We've got a great Relationship Repair planned for you this evening.'

'*Great?*' Mattie eyed him suspiciously. 'What is it?' Bear baiting? Hang-gliding? She could only imagine.

'Do you know what the date is today?' Baz asked.

She stared back at him, refusing to play his little game. Actually, she didn't know what the date was, anyway – time seemed to stretch forever here.

'It's February the fourteenth! Valentine's Day!' Baz did a twirl. He waited for her to respond, but she just kept staring. Valentine's Day, so what? She shook her head, sure The TweedleDuo would conjure up some vomit-inducing romance horror show.

'Tonight's activity will focus on *romance*. We've arranged for you and Adam to have a very romantic dinner at Carisbrooke Castle,' he said.

Mattie didn't react. Dinner at a castle? Seemed rather tame. She was sure Baz had something more sinister planned.

'Carisbrooke Castle!' he huffed, looking annoyed at her lack of response. 'Built in, er, well, ages ago. The grounds are normally closed at night but they've opened them up just for us. We've laid on a lovely meal for two in the Great Hall. We'll leave in a few hours.' He glanced at her. 'You might want to start getting ready now, eh?' He sniggered.

'Back off, Spaz,' Mattie said. The nerve of him! She knew she looked a state – her hair was a mess and with all the clothes she had on to keep warm, the Michelin Man cut a svelter figure than her – but she was beyond caring. Psycho Adam didn't deserve the effort it'd take to pretty herself up and she couldn't give a toss about the cameras and her TV image. Funny, the real world seemed so far away she was actually beginning to forget what she did *would* end up on television.

Baz rolled his eyes. 'Fine, whatever.' He turned to go.

'Baz, is that rugby guy all right?' Mattie couldn't get the image of Adam smashing his fist in poor Aussie's face out of her mind.

'Yeah, he's okay, don't worry. Just a broken nose and a couple of busted ribs. No biggie. He signed a disclaimer, anyway.'

Mattie stared. No biggie? A broken nose and ribs and it was fine and dandy because of a signed disclaimer? Wait a second! She'd signed a disclaimer, too, in the packet of papers Nate had brought over with the contract. Did that mean they didn't care what happened to her, either?

'See you in a bit! And Happy Valentine's Day.' Baz smirked.

'Happy Valentine's Day, right,' Mattie muttered, watching Baz run through the rain to whatever hole he'd crawled from.

God, Valentine's Day. Before she could block it out, memories of one year ago invaded her head. She and Kyle had been working late on a big account and Kyle had snuck over to her desk with a bottle of champagne.

He'd popped the cork beside her ear, nearly scaring her half to death, then swung her chair round and planted a kiss on her lips, saying he'd booked them a late dinner at Nobu – one of her all-time favourite restaurants.

She had been starving – her stomach had grumbled at the very thought of hot food, let alone Nobu – but there was still a mountain of work to get through that night and Kyle's expectation she could run off with him at the drop of a hat made her angry. She was just about to shove away the champagne and tell him to bugger off when he put a neatly wrapped gift on her desk.

She couldn't help swallowing her words and smiling as she pulled off the paper to reveal a De Beers box. Lifting the top, a gorgeous diamond Luck & Love bracelet winked at her in the dim light of the computer monitor. Kyle fastened it around her wrist and – with a tender look – told her how happy he was and how much he loved her. She'd worn that bracelet almost every day afterwards until . . .

Mattie wrapped chilly arms around her knees and dropped her head onto them. She missed Kyle. They *had* been great together. So why had she pushed him away? She bit her lip as the realisation flooded in. She'd been scared. Scared he'd leave her . . . like her father. But what good had come of being afraid? In the end, the outcome was still the same. She was without him, whether it was her doing or not.

She shook her head to dislodge the memory. She was here and Kyle was there – back in London, miles away. Even if she *did* miss him, nothing could be done now.

The sound of the rain tapping gently at the windows made her look up. The sky was darkening from grey to black, and Mattie struggled to her feet.

One thing was for sure: with Adam Android and the TweedleDuo, this would definitely be a Valentine's Day like no other.

*

Adam pulled on a shirt, anger swirling inside as it became apparent how crushed it was. Stupid shirt. He beat at the fabric but the wrinkles remained. How could he woo Mattie looking like he'd just crawled out of bed? Which he had.

Glancing down at his bruised hand, he flexed his fingers and grimaced, barely able to recall what had actually happened on the field yesterday. He just remembered feeling so angry when that bloke pawed Mattie. *His* Mattie.

He stopped thrashing his top when he heard Baz bang inside the caravan and start blabbering on about the day's activity. Adam cocked an ear. Oh, a Valentine's Day dinner? At a castle? Brilliant! He couldn't think of a better location to show Mattie his true feelings. So far she'd only seen the tough side – he could tell his show of strength on the battle-field yesterday had impressed her, despite her silence on the way back to the holiday park.

Now it was time to demonstrate his sensitive side. He'd be caring and attentive yet still in control . . . the perfect man.

How could she resist?

CHAPTER TWENTY-FIVE

Half of men attribute their bad date decorum to
drinking too much alcohol,
compared with eighty percent of women.

'HAPPY VALENTINE'S DAY!' Adam said as he leaned down to kiss Mattie's cheek. She almost choked – what was that hideous aftershave he was wearing? *Eau de loo?*

But at least he appeared to be back to normal. His face had returned to its neutral mask, traces of yesterday's hysteria all but gone.

'You look nice,' he said.

Mattie raised her eyebrows. Had yesterday's incident damaged his head? She looked anything but nice, although after Baz's sniggering she had made an effort to comb her hair. Her body still bulged from all the layers she was wearing, but a long-sleeved cotton top managed to smooth out most of the lumpy contours.

'Come on, let's get going,' Baz shouted from outside the caravan, a honking horn adding extra emphasis.

She followed Adam out into the dark night, surprised to see a gleaming limo waiting.

'Where's the oh-so-romantic Land Rover?' Mattie asked as she crawled into the plush leather interior, closely followed by Ram. 'Oh, look. There's champagne too!' She peeled off the gold foil and started twisting the top.

'Let me do that,' Adam said, prying it from her

grip. He opened the bottle with a flourish, handed her a glass, then poured one for himself.

'I thought you didn't drink!' Mattie said.

Adam looked uncertain for a minute. 'I don't usually. But it's a special occasion.' He took a big gulp and immediately slid a battered hand over to Mattie's thigh.

He was a persistent bugger, wasn't he? She lifted it off again and plopped it onto the seat between them.

Swigging more champagne, she realised she hadn't had a drop of alcohol since arriving on this bloody island. If ever there was a time and place for alcohol, then this was it. She poured herself another glass as the limo wound its way through dark country roads.

'Here we are!' Baz called out. The limo abruptly stopped. In the darkness Mattie could barely make out the line of the castle walls perched on a mound above the car park.

'Jesus,' Mattie said as they climbed out into the rain and whipping wind. 'Do we have to walk up there?'

Baz nodded. 'Yes, but there's supposed to be a guide . . . ah, here she is.'

A burly woman sporting a fluorescent orange vest ignored their greetings and gruffly handed them each a torch. 'Come on. This way.' She herded them through an arch, down a walled walkway and towards a yawning castle entrance up ahead. It looked about as romantic as a medieval torture chamber, Mattie thought as she pulled the sleeves of her shirt over her frozen hands.

'That's where you'll be dining tonight,' the guide said, pointing to a building across the courtyard with light streaming from the windows. Mattie picked up her pace, almost running towards it. By now she was so cold she couldn't think of anything but getting inside and warming up.

She swung open the door and looked around, breathing in the stuffy warmth of the room. Flames from the massive fireplace cast flickering shadows on the hall's lofty roof. A small table with candles was positioned directly in front of it. The scent of – Mattie sniffed – lamb? – drifted through the air and her stomach grumbled. It seemed ages since she'd had a proper meal, one that didn't involve garlic or toxic trans fats.

A tuxedoed man appeared from a side door. 'Welcome to the Great Hall at Carisbrooke Castle! If madam and sir would like to have a seat?' He went to pull out Mattie's chair but Adam flashed around the table and beat him to it, glaring wildly at the maitre d'.

'Here you are,' Adam said, pushing her down on the wooden seat.

'Tonight you will have a medieval feast,' the maitre d' said as he poured red wine into Adam and Mattie's goblets. 'We will start with roast goose, then haunch of venison, finishing with custard for pudding.' He placed a bell on the table. 'In the meantime, if you desire anything, please do not hesitate to ring the bell.' He smiled and backed away, disappearing into the shadows.

The lofty hall was silent except for the crackle of the fire and the shuffle of Ram and his ever-present camera. Mattie squinted in the dim light. Where had Nate and Baz scuttled off to?

'So.' Mattie cleared her throat awkwardly and tried to smile at Adam, who stared at her with a strange grin nailed to his face.

Adam raised his goblet. 'Cheers! Happy Valentine's Day. Here's to you and me . . . and what's waiting for us at the end.'

Yeah, keep that in mind, Mattie told herself as she

clinked his goblet. The stash of cash waiting for her at the end. Two hundred thousand pounds. Financial independence. She waited for the tiny thrill that always accompanied the thought of the money, but for some reason, it never came.

'Your roast goose.' The maitre d' appeared from nowhere and placed two delicious-smelling dishes in front of them, refilled Adam's wine, then disappeared. Adam gulped it down.

'Take it easy on the alcohol, Stumpy,' Mattie said as he wiped his mouth. He was psycho enough – she didn't even want to think about what he'd be like drunk.

'What did you say?' Adam slowly lowered the goblet until it thumped onto the table.

Mattie cleared her throat again. 'I said, maybe you should take it easy on the wine!'

Adam shook his head so forcefully he dislodged a piece of lacquered hair. 'No, I mean . . . What. Did. You. Just. Call. Me?' His voice rose with every word.

Mattie stared at the muscle jumping in his cheek. He really was mental! A finger of fear stabbed her gut and she forced a laugh.

'Sorry! It just came out.' She shook her head. 'Habit, you know?'

Ram was edging closer, as if anticipating conflict. For once, Mattie was happy to have him near – not that he'd help her, given what she'd seen yesterday on the rugby field. She pushed her chair as far from Adam as it would go.

Adam slammed his fist down on the table so hard the wine in Mattie's goblet leaped up and splashed on her arm. 'I'm *not* Stumpy!' he roared. His voice echoed around the room.

Mattie wiped at the wine and leaned back. This had gone too far. She wasn't going to sit here and be battered to bits like Aussie. Before she could move, Adam reached out for her, brushing the cuff of her sleeve. She jerked back. No way was he getting his monster mitts on her! Suddenly she was on her feet, racing across the Great Hall and out into the dark of the courtyard.

'Ouf!' she grunted as she smacked into someone. 'Baz, if that's you, we really need to talk–'

'It's not Baz.'

Mattie looked up slowly, squinting through the dark and rain.

The blond hair, square jaw, familiar cologne . . .

'Kyle?'

It couldn't be?

Her heart picked up pace as her mind raced. What was he doing here? Had he tracked her down to tell her it really wasn't over? Maybe it wasn't too late, maybe . . . In spite of what she told herself she felt about him, a rush of happiness flooded through her.

'Kyle . . .' She stretched out a hand.

He took a step back.

'Don't worry. I'm not here to harass you. This is the last place I want to be,' he said quickly. 'I was about to go away, clear my head. But then Baz rang and reminded me my contract said I had to be available for the duration of the show. I tried to get out of it but they threatened to sue. As much as I don't want to be here, it wasn't worth the hassle. So here I am.'

Mattie searched his face for the usual warmth, but it was empty of emotion. Her heart sank. Right. He wasn't here to get her back. He was here because he was legally obliged to be.

That's okay. That's fine. Great, even, she told herself. For a second there, when she'd been so excited to see him, everything else – even her business – faded from her mind. All she could see was him.

But now it was clear they were over; the door was closed. Her focus and ambition were safe. Mattie dropped her eyes from Kyle's face and looked down at his grubby Converse trainers. A sense of longing stabbed her heart.

'Right,' she said, turning away from him, trying to breathe through the weight on her chest. A million words jammed in her throat, but she couldn't grab onto even one of them.

'Guys!' She could hear Baz crunching across the courtyard. 'Come on, you two,' he said, sounding angry. 'You're not supposed to have met. Mattie, go inside with Adam. And act surprised when Kyle comes in.'

Mattie looked at Kyle over her shoulder as Baz frog-marched her back towards the Great Hall. Kyle's arms were crossed over his chest and his face was frozen into a cold mask she didn't recognize.

She tore her arm away from Baz as they neared the hall's entrance. 'Listen, there's no way I'm going back in there. Adam almost attacked me!'

Baz pressed his thin lips together, looking anything but pleased his big surprise had been blown. 'You'll be fine. We're watching at all times, you know. There's no way we'd ever let any violence escalate between contestants.' He gave her a big fake grin and grabbed her arm again. 'Anyway, Kyle's here now. I'm sure the three of you will get along great!'

'Yeah, right. That's why you brought him back again,' Mattie mumbled as they crossed the flagstones towards Adam. But the thought that Kyle was here – even if it wasn't for her – *did* make her feel somewhat better about being around psycho Adam. No matter how Kyle felt, he wouldn't let Adam hurt her.

She sat back down in her chair across from Adam and avoided meeting his bug-eyed stare.

'I'm sorry, Mattie,' Adam blurted. 'I'm not sure what . . . I just got so angry . . .' His voice trailed off in the annoying way it used to back in secondary school.

Mattie sighed. 'Don't worry, Adam. It's fine.' It was far from fine, but she was hardly going to poke him with a stick and rile him up again now, especially with Kyle about to enter.

'So what's happening?' Adam asked, looking around suspiciously.

'Serve the venison!' Baz's voice boomed through the Great Hall before Mattie could answer.

The maitre d' came out with two silver-domed platters. Just as he was about to place them, the doors to the hall burst open and Kyle strode through them.

Adam made a strangled noise and his face twisted. He gripped the side of the table so hard his fingers turned white.

Kyle approached them. 'Can you make that for three?' he said stiffly, in what was clearly a scripted line courtesy of Baz. Kyle kept his eyes level, not even looking in Mattie's direction. He nodded towards Adam, who stared unblinkingly at him.

'Of course, sir.' The maitre d' brought over another chair and scurried around setting an extra place. All three of them watched in silence.

'What are you doing here?' Adam asked finally in a tight voice, eyes bulging.

Kyle shrugged. 'You'll have to ask the producers that one, mate. They didn't tell me anything.'

Adam picked up his knife and fork and cut into the venison, his utensils shaking in his hands. He was tearing the meat apart as if it was about to attack him. Mattie shot a glance at Kyle, who was watching Adam with raised eyebrows.

'All right there?' Kyle said to Adam.

But Adam didn't answer; he just shoved a forkful

of food into his mouth and chewed it vigorously. The hall was so silent they could hear water dripping off the roof outside.

Mattie took a bite of her own venison, even though her stomach was churning. If Adam behaved like a psycho before, Kyle's presence now would have the same effect as a jumbo-sized taser – exactly what the TweedleDuo wanted. She hoped Kyle could handle Adam. She shivered, recalling again Adam pounding the rugby bloke, then stole a look at Kyle. He hadn't glanced her way once since he'd entered the Great Hall.

She sighed. Focus, Mattie told herself, trying to shove away the jumble of emotions. Just get the prize money. And get on with your life.

A few hours and several unexpected and torturous courses later, the limo pulled up to the caravan and Mattie fumbled for the door release, tumbling out into the clammy cold night air as fast as she could. Despite the car's roomy interior, Adam had somehow managed to weasel his way closer and closer, pressing up next to her until she was smashed against the car's rear airbag. Just like he had all through the painfully long dinner, Kyle had remained detached and distant, speaking only to Adam. At least Adam had managed to keep his lid on through the rest of the dinner – although judging by the way his jaw muscle was twitching, it wouldn't be long before he exploded once again.

'So, Kyle, welcome to your home!' Baz crowed, watching Kyle closely as he approached the caravan. Baz opened the caravan door and motioned him in, Ram following every movement with the camera. 'Come check it out. Guess you'll all have to make new sleeping arrangements. *Ménage à trois*, anyone?'

He leered at them.

Mattie noticed Adam stiffen but Kyle didn't rise to Baz's bait.

'Great, thanks,' Kyle said easily, mounting the steps and joining Baz inside. Mattie followed, shrugging off Adam's cold hand on her shoulder. Where would Kyle sleep? Surely he wouldn't stay in the lounge with Adam. With all those murderous glares, there was no way Kyle could be oblivious to Adam's antipathy. But what would she say when Kyle asked to sleep in her tiny room? She couldn't stand to have him so close yet acting so cold.

'Can I crash here with you, mate?' Kyle was saying. Adam nodded jerkily as Baz tossed a bundle of blankets at Kyle.

Mattie spun around and headed down the corridor to her room, ignoring the liquid pooling in her eyes. If Kyle preferred to bunk with a man who obviously hated him over her . . . well, it was a good thing, right? Now she wouldn't have to listen to his even breathing as he slept, or remember the way his body was always warm next to hers . . .

She took a deep breath and sat down on the bed. God, she was tired. Sinking onto the saggy mattress, she closed her eyes and tried not to think about the man just a few feet away.

*

Jess's mouth fell open as Kyle entered a massive hall and sat down at the table with Mattie and Adam. So *that* was why he hadn't answered her call!

'Oh my God,' she said aloud as the camera cut to Adam's face, his eyes practically boring holes through Kyle. Completely oblivious, Kyle was eating his meal in silence and Mattie was sitting there chewing and staring off into space. The tension in the room was so strong it was almost like a ghostly presence.

Jess got up and paced back and forth across her small studio. The person at the show had told her Adam was fine. But she didn't believe it, especially with what she'd seen in his flat! And after his aggression on the rugby field, now she wasn't just worried for Mattie, she was worried for Kyle, too. Who knew what Adam might do to get to Mattie, if he thought Kyle was in his way?

She sank back onto the sofa. She could sit here fingers crossed and hope for the best, like always. But now two friends might be in grave danger. Waiting around to see what happened wasn't an option: she had to act. And fast!

Hang on – she still had the number for that reporter, Deniz. Deniz would jump at the chance for more contestant gossip. If Jess spilled the beans on what Adam had in his flat and how he'd stalked Mattie – and Deniz reported it in a national newspaper – then surely the show would *have* to stop broadcasting, right?

Jess picked up her phone and dialled Deniz's number, fingers shaking as she recalled how wrong her last conversation with the tabloid reporter had gone. But this time was different. This time, her friends' safety was on the line. And the information Jess had could help save them.

CHAPTER TWENTY-SIX

*Fifty per cent of men admit to feeling threatened
by other males in their partner's life.
Fourteen per cent of marriage break-ups involve these other males.*

NATE YAWNED AS HE AND BAZ sat holding their BlackBerries, waiting for Silver to ring. It was six a.m. on Thursday, and Ginny had texted around five to let them know Silver would be calling.

Baz jiggled his leg nervously. 'What do you think she wants?'

Nate shrugged, enjoying the tense expression on Baz's normally confident face. 'Who knows? To tell us to murder someone today, for added drama?'

Baz shot him a surprised look at the nonchalant reply, but Nate just sighed, tired from all the intrigue. Pushing Mattie out, denying Adam vital medication and bringing back Kyle to stir up the whole thing was so far from his original concept he could hardly muster any feelings of pride any more. What had once felt like *his* show had now become a car crash. The whole thing couldn't be over fast enough.

'Last night was great, eh?' Baz crowed. 'Did you see how Adam lunged at Mattie? And then when Kyle came in . . .' He shook his head and rubbed his hands together. 'I can't wait to watch them in action today.'

Nate grunted, staring at Baz. How did someone develop sadistic enjoyment of others' discomfort?

'So today we've got the sea kayaking,' Baz said, grabbing the schedule. 'And we need to ramp up the conflict between Adam and Kyle, get them to be really competitive and see if Adam explodes again! Like on the rugby field.'

Baz's BlackBerry rang and he lunged for it. 'Hello? Yes, hello, Silver, good morning. Yes, he's right here. I'll just put you on speaker.' Baz pressed a button and placed the phone in the centre of the table.

'Hello, Silver. Can you hear me? Silver, Silver?' Nate said.

There was an impatient noise, and then the sound of chewing. 'Of course I can hear you. Now run me through today.'

Baz jumped in before Nate could open his mouth but Nate didn't really care. He leaned back, stretched his legs and yawned again. 'We're going to really make sure Adam loses it this time!' Baz said confidently.

'And how exactly are you going to do that?' Silver asked.

There was silence. The two of them looked at each other, petrified.

'Nate has a plan,' Baz blurted out.

Nate stared. Bloody Baz! He knew Nate had nothing.

'Really? What is it?'

Shit. What could he say?

'Nate, have you gone deaf as well as dumb?' Silver's clipped tone screeched out of the small phone speaker.

Nate suddenly decided he would use this to his – and Mattie's and Kyle's – advantage. 'Actually, Silver, I don't think we should push Adam too far, at least not until tomorrow when the advertising slots run out. A little competition's good but I think we should leave it at that. X-ACT will lose revenue if Adam blows too soon.' Ha! He didn't think he'd ever openly disagreed with Baz, and Baz looked as stunned as if Nate had announced his impending marriage to Claudia Schiffer.

There was a long pause. More chewing, then: 'Thank God one of you has an ounce of brains hidden in your tiny little heads. Baz, why you'd want to jeopardise the show before the final day is beyond me.'

Nate shot a victorious look at Baz, who deflated as though someone had pulled his plug.

A loud gulp came though the phone and Silver smacked her lips. 'We need a bit of a lull, to build up tension for the final push tomorrow. I'll be over later tonight – I want to ensure everything's set for the big day tomorrow. Baz, get a caravan ready.'

'Sure.' Baz glared at Nate.

Silver hung up without saying goodbye.

'Can you make me a cup of tea?' Nate said, standing up. 'I'm going to have a shower.' He shuffled off towards the loo, smiling to himself as he pictured the expression on Baz's face.

*

Adam shook his head to clear it as Baz nattered on about their Relationship Repair activity that day: sea kayaking, meant to get them back in touch with nature and their basic survival instincts. Adam's temples throbbed from all the wine last night. But worse, his heart ached as he recalled what had happened. What a fucking disaster!

He'd meant to show Mattie his softer side and instead he'd ended up acting like a *lunatic*. It was just when she called him . . . Stumpy; it still brought back so many bad memories. He grabbed his head. Whatever happened to the calm hero he was supposed to be?

But losing his cool wasn't the worst. The worst was *Kyle*. Adam had always hated him, even back when

Kyle and Mattie had just been working together. He'd known Kyle had designs on Mattie even before Mattie knew herself – watching the two of them dance around each other for months, it was pretty obvious. Chloe Collins had been a godsend and when they were all over, Adam thought he might finally have a chance again.

But even though Mattie had gone through men like wildfire, she'd continued mooning over Kyle for months. He had several surveillance tapes full of Mattie ranting to Jess about it. The woman really *had* cared for him, and Adam had patiently waited on the sidelines for her to get over it.

He was sure she had moved on, especially after the Chloe business and Mattie rejecting Kyle on national telly. But now the blond mimbo was back and Adam couldn't help but notice Mattie acting strangely when he was around – an extremely bad sign, as far as Adam was concerned. Obviously those producers thought she still had feelings, too, or they wouldn't have brought Kyle back again to stir things up.

Whatever happened, Adam wasn't going to quit. Sure, he'd slipped up, but it wasn't too late to recover. He would be the hero of the hour, not Kyle. And what did heroes do? They rescued damsels in distress – not that Mattie had ever seemed to be that. But maybe he could *make* her be, somehow . . . An idea filtered into Adam's head and he sat up straight, hope pouring back into well-buffed limbs.

He looked over at Mattie, who even now was darting glances at Kyle. Soon she'd forget all about him, Adam was sure. Just wait until they got on the water.

*

Mattie followed Adam and Kyle down the slippery

bank towards the beach. The tight band of the headpiece holding the small portable camera pinched her scalp, and the beginnings of a headache pressed behind her eyes. Even wearing a wetsuit, the icy wind was almost paralytic.

'Come on, dudes. Everybody in!' the dopey instructor called, slapping his own kayak into the choppy waves and moving out to sea. Up above, a helicopter buzzed and Mattie could just make out the silhouette of Ram and his camera through the open door.

Adam and Kyle got into their kayaks and expertly paddled away from her. Her teeth chattered from the cold – the clammy wetsuit was freezing – but also from fear. Sure, the life-vest was supposed to save her if she fell into the churning water, but . . . she couldn't swim. At all. Survival instinct, her arse. If she really wanted to survive, she'd stay out of the water!

'Mattie!' the instructor called. He looked like he'd smoked a whole field of pot that morning – not exactly a dependable person to call on if need be. Kyle glanced towards her as he moved his kayak through the waves.

Mattie sighed. Kyle knew she hated immersing herself in any body of water that wasn't a bath, yet he hadn't stopped to help her – even to poke fun like he had in the past. In fact, he hadn't spoken to her all day, despite their near-collision in the corridor when he returned to the caravan after an early-morning run. This impenetrable Kyle was like a stranger.

Fuck it! A burst of anger replaced the fear and hurt inside of her and she grabbed the kayak and heaved it into the water. She'd show Kyle she wasn't afraid; that she didn't need anyone's help. Waves fizzed around her ankles but she ignored them, trying not to wince as the boat knocked against her shins in the foaming water. She climbed inside and positioned herself against the slanted seat, grabbing the paddle and stabbing it at the sea.

Hey! She was moving! This wasn't so bad, she thought as she glided across the water. A wave crashed into the boat and the salt stung her eyes. Shit. Okay, it was relatively bad. She wiped her face and forced the boat forward. Her heart pounded and she tried not to estimate the depth of the water below. Finally she managed to pull alongside Adam, Kyle and the droopy-eyed instructor.

'Right. We're going to paddle along the cliff there,' – Mattie gulped at the sight of the white cliffs jutting out into the sea, a million miles away – 'and back again,' the instructor said. 'If you do flip into the water, just stay calm. I'll come get you and help you back in the kayak.'

'What do you mean, flip?' Mattie squeaked. How was that even a possibility? She eyed the angry-looking waves rolling towards shore.

'No worries,' the instructor drawled. 'These kayaks are really big and stable, meant for beginners. It takes a lot to flip them over. It's just the waves are pretty huge today so it might happen. But you've got the life vest on so it's not like you're going to drown. Let's get going, dudes.' He pushed away from her and started moving smoothly across the water.

'Wait!' Mattie called but the wind tossed away the sound. The waves bobbed the kayak up and down like crazy and she was drifting further away from shore. Sighing and pushing the paddle in the water again, she tried to catch up with the others.

After what felt like ages, she managed it, panting like crazy. Although the temperature had to be less than ten degrees, sweat was breaking out on her forehead. Mattie knew her curls must look as crazed as Adam's weird stare, and catching Kyle looking, she pushed one behind her ear. As soon as their eyes met, he turned away.

The instructor manoeuvred them into a row, with Adam on one side and Kyle on the other. 'Catch your breath,' he commanded. Annoyingly, she seemed to be the only one panting. God, the gym was a number one priority the moment she got back. Nevertheless, the physical pain helped minimise the horrible fact they were miles from land. She gulped, trying not to think about it.

'Oh, look! Seals!' Adam pointed far out into the ocean.

Kyle and the instructor turned to look. Mattie let go of the side of the instructor's boat to shield her eyes as she scanned the waves. 'Where?'

'Just there. Don't you see them?'

No. There were just waves, waves and more waves. Turning back to ask the instructor if they could head to shore, Mattie discovered with a shock she was a good thirty feet from the group and drifting fast out to sea. Reaching for her paddle brought another shock. It was gone!

'Adam! Kyle!' She waved her arms, feeling like an idiot. Where had that paddle disappeared to?

The wind whipped away her voice and the men were so busy examining something else Adam was pointing at, they didn't even notice her.

Shit! She was bobbing further and further away from them, almost out of the sheltered cove and into the open sea where – she shivered nervously – the waves appeared twice as big. Definitely large enough to flip the boat. Fear clogged her throat.

'Help!' she screamed again. Then suddenly Adam looked over, saw her, and peeled away from Kyle and the instructor. Thank God someone had spotted her.

Adam surged through the ocean towards her, quickly bridging the gap between them. But just as he closed in, a rogue wave rolled across the bay, slamming into the side of his boat and flipping him over.

'Oh my God!' Mattie screamed. She could only see the flat bottom of Adam's kayak, bobbing on the surface. Finally Adam's dark head emerged.

'Are you all right?' she yelled.

Adam didn't answer. Not that Mattie could hear, although the movement of his lips indicated a reply of some sort. Thank God he was okay.

Kyle and the instructor had finally given up on the seals – about time – and were now moving towards them, but the current was briskly pushing both her and Adam out of the cove. And all Mattie could do was sit, helpless.

The instructor stopped beside Adam and hauled him onto the closed-in front of the kayak; Adam's own boat was miles away now. Then Kyle glided through the water towards her.

'Thank you,' she said, as he pulled his kayak alongside. Relieved to be safe, she reached out and put a hand on his arm. He felt so solid. Swallowing hard against the rising emotion, she looked into his eyes: 'Kyle–'

'Where's your paddle?' he interrupted, deliberately avoiding her gaze.

Mattie lifted her hand and tears formed, wind stinging the release. He still sounded so distant. 'Um, I don't know. I must have dropped it.'

'Well, just hang on to the side. We've got to get moving. If we drift past those rocks, there's no way to get back under our own steam. The current's too strong.'

Mattie nodded and grasped the side of his boat for dear life as they inched towards the shore. After a few moments, Kyle turned towards her. 'Okay?' For a split second, she saw a trace of the old, familiar softness in his eyes and hope shot through her frozen body. Maybe it wasn't too late? Perhaps he *did* still care.

Mattie nodded and after a brief glance he turned away to battle the waves. Certainty surged through her. She loved him. What that meant for the business could be worked out. But for once she wouldn't wait until all the questions had answers, until things were black and white. There was surety in one thing: she wanted Kyle.

And that was all she needed to know.

*

Adam shook with anger, watching as Kyle pulled Mattie's boat across the water, the tall blond surging through the waves with clean, short strokes. Bloody Kyle got to be the hero, while he was like a wayward chick being carried to the nest! Grabbing Mattie's paddle and letting her drift out to sea – with the intention of being the hero who brought her back to safety – was a brilliant idea, but somehow Kyle had managed to foil his plan.

If only he could get mobile in the water again; maybe flip Kyle's boat?

No way was this over.

Heroes didn't let the villain triumph. Adam struggled against the instructor, who was holding him firmly by the neck of his wetsuit. To his annoyance, the instructor's grip didn't slacken.

'Just hold still, will you!' the instructor said. 'We're almost there.'

Adam jerked again but the instructor's grip was firm. Soon they'd reached the shore and Adam had no choice but to roll off the kayak and into the shallow swells, watching Kyle triumphantly carry Princess Mattie back to solid land.

It wasn't fair. He was the one who'd put in the time; waiting, watching for a chance. *He* was the one who'd transformed himself from zero to hero. He couldn't let her fall for Kyle again!

Time to get tough.

Real heroes did anything necessary to ensure the right outcome.

And so, by God, would he.

CHAPTER TWENTY-SEVEN

*One in two believe they know best when it comes to
choosing their friends' partners,
but wouldn't dream of letting their friends select a partner for them.*

JESS SWITCHED OFF THE TELEVISION and paced back and forth. What was Deniz playing at? Already twenty-four hours had passed since Jess had rung to tell her about Adam. Deniz had said she'd look into it and get back to her, but Jess had heard nothing. For what felt like the zillionth time, she picked up her mobile and checked the display. No missed calls, no new messages.

Well, screw that. Jess was tired of waiting around for people to call her back. Her friends were in danger, and if Deniz wasn't the answer then Jess would just go to the Isle of Wight herself. Sure, she didn't know the location of the holiday camp . . . or even how to get to the Isle of Wight. But she'd figure it out.

She'd give Deniz a final try, though.

'Deniz Grady.' The familiar nasal tone sounded peeved.

'It's Jess McKenzie. Did you find out anything?' Jess was through with wasting time.

'Oh, yeah. Sorry, hon. I was meant to ring you back, wasn't I?' Jess could hear her chomping chewing gum.

'That's all right,' Jess said. 'So what's going on?'

'Got the okay from my editor for a story, done a bit of digging – talked to a doctor who apparently examined the contestants, and yeah, that Adam bloke is a fucking psycho.'

'He's not a psycho . . .' Jess said automatically, before remembering that actually, he was.

'So I'm headed to the Isle of Wight now. Get the lowdown first-hand, you know? Just about to leave, in fact. Look, I'll talk to you later, yeah? Got to catch the last ferry.'

'Wait!' Jess couldn't leave the fate of her friends in the hands of a tabloid reporter. 'I'll come with you! I can . . .' Jess's mind worked frantically. 'Give you an exclusive on Mattie and Kyle! Tell you exactly what happened with Adam! And just think how cool your article will be – on the road with the star's best friend, trying to uncover the truth behind the reality show!' Jesus, where had that come from?

'Okay,' Deniz said finally, after subjecting Jess to a few more seconds of heavy mastication. 'Meet me outside Victoria Station in an hour.'

'Sure, absolutely, is there anything I can–'

But Deniz had already hung up.

*

'This place is a fucking tip,' Silver said, looking around the mobile production unit at the caravan site.

Nate shrugged as Baz grabbed a few empty tins of Red Bull and chucked them in the overflowing rubbish bin. It was pretty disgusting in the luxury van – the air was fuggy with the scent of grease and unwashed bodies, and you could almost sense the sleeplessness as the techies hunched over monitors showing live feeds from the contestants' caravan. Nate glanced at the screen – no one was moving and the caravan was silent. It *was* almost midnight.

Nate yawned and didn't even bother covering his

mouth. One more night until Silver planned God-knows-what to push Mattie out. And one more day of doing his best to make sure the contestants didn't kill each other and then he could . . . What? Do another show? A thread of uncertainty ran through him. The thought of doing all this again on yet another series made him feel sick.

He tried to tune in to what Silver was saying. Having only been present for five minutes she'd already issued about twenty thousand orders.

'So I hear there was high drama on the seas today, boys!' She tore open a fresh packet of sausages and Nate grimaced as the odour mingled with the stench in the caravan. 'What happened? I thought we agreed we'd tone it down, let the tension rise until the final day tomorrow.'

Baz looked over at Nate, obviously expecting him to answer, but Nate stayed silent.

'Baz?'

'Well, um, Adam had his own plans, apparently. From what we could see, he took Mattie's paddle and–'

Silver impatiently waved a hand clasping two sausages. 'I couldn't really care less about the details, Baz. What I do care about is keeping things under control. *We* dictate the storylines, not the contestants. *We* tell them what to think and do. Got it?'

Baz's head was moving up and down like a nodding dog riding speed humps in the back of a bus. 'Right, right. Of course, Silver.'

Silver narrowed her eyes. 'I'm worried about you boys not being on top of things. We've only got one more day – and it's the most important.' She gnawed at the double-sausage snack in her fist.

'So what exactly is the plan?' Nate asked, trying to sound casual.

Baz had been surprisingly quiet about the whole thing.

Silver smiled slowly. 'Well. You've arranged for the zip thing, right?'

Nate nodded. 'Yes, tomorrow's Relationship Repair activity is the zip-wire. You slide between trees on a cord. Really trendy these days, you know. The site is just up the track there. I can show you after if you—'

Silver cut him off with another wave. 'Well, boys, let's just say we have a little midnight mission beforehand. Or rather, *you* do.'

Nate stared. Midnight mission? 'What do you mean?'

Silver cocked her head. 'It's fucking brilliant. When you boys were faffing around in the waves, I had our cafeteria cook slip a sedative into the contestants' evening meal.' She looked at her watch. 'Given that they ate a few hours ago, they should out cold for the next six hours or so. You two will go in, move Kyle into Mattie's bed. Come morning, you'll wake up Adam first. He'll see the two of them, and then . . .' She bit into yet another sausage, raising her eyebrows. 'I wouldn't even worry about the zip-wire, lads. There'll be no need.'

'That's incredible!' Baz breathed, looking at Silver as though they were in the presence of the goddess of all game shows.

Nate's brain couldn't even form words. Sure, Silver was the queen of ratings, grabbing at any opportunity for drama. But to drug the contestants? And put them in compromising positions – literally?

'Oh, don't worry, Nate,' Silver sneered at his distraught expression. 'The sedative's perfectly safe. And no one will get hurt, we'll be watching at all times. We just need Adam to go mental enough to scare Mattie off the show.' She pointed the sausage in his direction. 'It's critical you rouse Adam first, before Mattie or Kyle moves out of position. One of you needs to watch the monitor all night, keep an eye on them.'

'Sure, sure, no problem, you can count on me,' Nate babbled, feigning enthusiasm as his heart thumped in his chest. Adam was really going to lose it if he caught Kyle and Mattie in bed, and Nate wasn't so sure Silver *would* intervene to stop the violence. Given what he'd seen, she would probably be the first one to hand Adam a knife and encourage him to go for it 'to add extra colour'.

Maybe he could sneak out during the night and somehow thump on the bedroom side of the caravan to wake up Mattie and Kyle before Adam saw them?

'Come on, then,' Baz said, springing to his feet like a spaniel. 'Let's go move Kyle.'

'Remember,' Silver said as they left the caravan, 'we all get a bonus if we pull this off. So. Don't. Fuck. Up.' The sausage wobbled as she stabbed it in the air for extra emphasis.

Nate gulped as he followed Baz's spiky head out the door and into the cool night air, unable to believe he was actually taking part in the ludicrous plan. But it was better to play along now, to be on the contestants' side if they needed him – or an ambulance. If he protested too much, Silver would just chuck him out, leaving the contestants completely at her mercy.

One more day, he repeated again. One more day.

*

A few hours and a ferry ride later, Deniz and Jess hurtled along the dark and deserted roads of the Isle of Wight. Inside Deniz's battered Corsa, all was silent except for the reporter's incessant gum-chewing. The machine-gun questions directed at Jess, covering everything from Mattie's childhood to what she ate for breakfast, had finally ceased. Jess gave as little detail as possible, but it was exhausting.

'You sure you know where you're going?' Jess asked, yawning and trying to peer through the fog.

'Unless that idiot Baz lied, yes. I knew shagging him would prove useful at some point. Plus he owed me one, after such a dud night.' Deniz glanced at the map beside her. 'We should be on the right road. Hard to tell with this bloody fog though.'

A bright sign up ahead loomed through the gloom – the only lights they'd seen for miles. Garlic Farm, the letters spelled out. Deniz abruptly swung the wheel and the small car squelched in the mud lining the bumpy track.

'I recognize this. They filmed here a few days ago!' Deniz exclaimed, pulling up in front of a shop and restaurant. They parked and got out, trying the door to the shop. It was locked, but the lights were still on inside. Jess rapped hard on the door and prayed someone would answer. The fog was rolling in even thicker and the plaintive cry of a faraway foghorn was downright eerie.

'Can I help you?' An old man opened the door, peering at them through ancient reading glasses. 'We're closed.'

'Sorry to disturb you,' Jess said. 'Just wondering if you can tell us how to get to Cliff Top Holiday Park?'

The old man took off his glasses. 'Where they're doing that show?'

'Yeah.' Deniz pushed forward. 'And if you don't mind, I need to ask you a few questions.'

'And who are you?' the old man asked, raising his eyebrows.

'I'm a friend of Mattie, one of the contestants,' Jess said, before Deniz could scare the man away.

'Well, come on in!' The old man swung open the door. 'I'm Gordie. And any friend of Mattie's is a friend of mine. She's a good girl.'

Jess wondered if the old guy was touched in the head. Mattie hadn't been nice to any man since Kyle had left her. But hey, no point in contradicting him. 'Sorry to have disturbed you,' she said. 'We just want to make sure we're on the right track to Cliff Top.'

Gordie rubbed his chin. 'Yes, you go down the road about ten miles, then turn left, take the first right . . . But it's too late to go there now. You'll never find it in this weather, anyway.' He indicated the window and the girls looked out to see that visibility was down to zero. 'Come on, sit down, have a cuppa. You can stay here for the night if you want.'

Jess hesitated and glanced at Deniz. She didn't want to waste time – Mattie's life may depend on it – but it was awfully dark and foggy outside and the thought of sweet warm tea and a comfortable bed was almost irresistible. Better to wait until morning than risk getting lost in the labyrinth of windy roads.

'What do you think, Deniz?' Jess asked.

Deniz shrugged. 'I guess we can stay here.' She turned to Gordie. 'But do you have any coffee? I hate tea.'

Gordie smiled. 'Of course. Come in, come in. I'll put the kettle on.'

CHAPTER TWENTY-EIGHT

*Five per cent of people claim they can't cope with the
mental strain of dating,
but ninety-five per cent say they would date until
they found true happiness.*

NATE JERKED AWAKE, BRUSHING OFF bits of crisps stuck to his cheek. Sunlight was streaming through the windows, and the digital clock said it was already six a.m.

'Fuck, fuck, *fuck*,' he muttered, looking over at the monitor in front of him. He'd meant to creep out and wake up Mattie and Kyle. Somehow, though, his eyes had sagged closed. Thank God inside the caravan was still silent and unmoving.

He wiped his mouth, grimacing at the thought of last night's antics. Together, he and Baz had dragged a comatose Kyle from the lounge through the narrow caravan corridor, banging his lolling head on the walls, then heaving the deadweight into bed beside Mattie. Nate had turned to go but Baz hissed at him to pull back the covers, rolling Mattie's body into the crook of Kyle's arm and stretching her leg over his.

Nate squinted at the monitor. Mattie and Kyle were still snuggled up and if anything, they were closer now than when he'd left – Kyle even had his hand clasped with Mattie's. There was no sound from the lounge, and the hunched form that was Adam wasn't moving, thank God. Just how much of that sedative had Silver put in their meal?

At least he could still save the situation, he thought,

standing and stretching his stiff legs. Now was the time to wake Mattie and Kyle, before Adam saw. Opening the caravan door, he breathed in the fresh morning air. Thankfully, the weather had improved its disposition.

'Morning! How're the love birds?' Baz appeared from around the corner, hair and natty outfit perfectly presented as always. He pushed past Nate into the caravan, then squinted at the monitor. 'Good. They're all still sleeping. Still on track for our bonus, mate!' he said, clapping Nate on the back.

'Yeah,' Nate grunted. *Bugger.* How would he alert Mattie and Kyle now, with bloody Baz tailing him?

'Ready to go rouse Sleeping Beauty?' Baz nodded towards the monitor showing the lounge. 'I've got Ram all set to film the action . . . Oh, shit! Kyle's moving!'

Nate swung towards the screen, watching as Kyle eased Mattie out of his arms, sitting up slowly. He swung a leg over the side of the bed with a dazed expression, then crept out of the room.

'Aw, fuck!' Baz sputtered. 'Silver's going to kill us!' He narrowed his eyes. 'Or you, anyway. You were supposed to be watching them.'

Nate shrugged, happy Silver's plan had failed despite falling down on his life-saving duties. 'Come on, let's just go tell Silver it didn't work.' He pushed up his specs, praying this would be the end of it.

Baz stared at him. 'Are you off your head? We can't tell Silver we fucked up – she'll choke us with a sausage.' He was silent for a moment, then a sneaky expression slid over his face. 'Come on.' He shot out of the caravan and up a path, disappearing into the trees. Nate huffed behind, wondering what the hell Baz was planning now.

Finally, he spotted Baz ahead, at a clearing in the dripping forest. Nate looked up at the trees. Half-way up the largest one, a small platform was erected and a narrow metal cord hung between it and the next largest oak, about fifty feet away. This must be the zip-wire site. Why the hell was Baz here?

'Look, you want that bonus, right?' Baz said in a low voice when Nate reached his side.

Nate nodded, eyeing Baz. 'Er, yes . . .' He glanced at the wire, high in the sky. Just what was Baz thinking?

'Well, I think we should plan for a little equipment malfunction.'

Nate stared. 'Equipment malfunction? What do you mean?'

Baz smiled slowly. 'Fucking brilliant, I am. We'll arrange for the straps on the contestants' harnesses to be frayed, just enough to carry their weight on the first few wires. And then . . .' He waggled his eyebrows.

'Then what?' Nate couldn't believe Baz was actually contemplating this. He was worse than Silver!

'Oh, don't worry, mate,' Baz said, noticing Nate's incredulous expression. 'No one's going to get seriously hurt. All we need is a few broken limbs, concussions, just enough to get them off the show – or insist they need to be in hospital under observation. The zip-wire won't be high enough for serious damage. You with me?'

Nate swallowed. That cord *was* pretty far up there. If someone fell . . . No way was he going to sabotage a harness, sending someone on their way to certain hospitalisation. But if he said no, Baz would probably do it – or something worse – on his own.

'It's a great idea,' he said finally. This way it would be possible to keep an eye on what Baz was up to, and warn the contestants.

'I know, right?' Baz's eyes lit up. 'I'm spending the bonus on a deposit for a little flat near Ladbroke Grove. Only a studio, but it will be mine.' Baz narrowed his eyes. 'And if you get cold feet, don't even *think* about telling Silver. If you do, I'll just say it was your idea. As EP, aren't you the one running the show?'

He smirked.

'Hey there!' A skinny man with a forest of pulleys and crampons attached to him jangled down a tree towards them. 'You must be from SiniStar Productions? Here to check the safety equipment?'

Nate and Baz nodded in unison. 'Yes, especially the harnesses and pulleys,' Baz said with gravitas. Nate raised his eyebrows, certain Baz had no more idea about zip-wires than he did.

'Sure. I'll just talk you through the course first,' the instructor said. 'They'll start there' – he pointed up to the higher platform – 'swing on the zip-wire to the next platform. There are five zip wires and three rope bridges. Nothing to worry about,' he said, spotting Nate's anxious expression. 'Safety is ensured at all times.'

That's what he thought.

Handing them a bundle of complex loops and buckles, the instructor continued: 'These are the harnesses they'll be using.' He pointed to a large metal ring attached to a nylon loop. 'This is where we attach the harness to the cable, and then the cable to the zip-wire.' He gave it a hard tug. 'See. Everything is completely secure.'

'Great, great,' Baz said smoothly. 'Do you think you could do a demo for us?'

'Sure, no sweat.' The instructor walked over to the tree and scampered up monkey-style. He slid on his own harness, secured the buckles and attached himself to the zip-wire then launched off the platform, sliding along the line and disappearing among the trees.

'What the fuck are you doing?' Baz hissed at Nate. 'For Christ's sake, get busy while he's outta sight!' Baz handed Nate a knife, then took up another and began slicing his way through the nylon loop the instructor had pointed out earlier. Nate grabbed a harness and pretended to be hard at work cutting through nylon. Luckily, his workmate was so caught up in destruction he didn't notice how ineffectual Nate's actions were.

'Hurry up! He's coming!' Baz observed, frantically sawing away at the loop. 'There.' Setting the harness aside he snatched up the third. 'I think I've done enough to make sure it'll tear all the way through.'

Shit. Baz had picked up the next one before Nate could even think to move it out of his reach.

'How're you doing on yours?'

'Fine, fine,' Nate said. 'There, done!' At least one harness would be untouched. Not that it would mean much to the two contestants who ended up in a fractures' ward.

Nate swallowed hard. What would happen if he *did* tell Silver? Baz would stick him with the blame, and then . . . Silver would try to distance SiniStar from him as much as possible. He pictured himself behind bars in a lumpy orange jumpsuit, shovelling prison muck into his mouth, and quivered with disgust.

No, he'd just have to warn the contestants, do something to make them see he was telling the truth. But what? There was no way Mattie would believe him after everything he'd pulled. Kyle hated his guts right now and Adam . . . There must be a way, somehow, to stop this whole thing.

'And that's how it works,' the instructor said as he marched towards them, chest out.

'Good stuff!' Baz handed over the harnesses and smacked him on the back. 'You looked great up there, mate. Everything appears to be in order so we'll return in about an hour or so with the three contestants.' He stood up. 'Come on, Nate. Let's get this day started.'

*

Sun filtered through the thread-bare curtains and Jess opened her eyes, taking in the floral wallpaper. The usual noise of buses and traffic was missing. Where was she?

Oh yes. The Isle of Wight, on the garlic farm, with Deniz. She cocked an ear, listening for any sounds coming from the rest of the house, but all was quiet.

Jess grabbed her mobile from the bedside table. Shit! Almost nine! She and Deniz had meant to get an early start and head over to the holiday park before anyone had a chance to wake up. By now, the contestants and crew could be anywhere!

Quickly pulling on yesterday's clothes and sweeping back her thick hair into a ponytail, Jess padded down the silent hallway to the bathroom to scrub her face. Through the window, Gordie could be seen in a distant field, already hard at work tending to his garlic. What a glorious day, she thought, taking in the sun over the fields with the sea glittering in the distance.

Now it was time to wake Deniz.

'Deniz?' She rapped softly on the door. 'Deniz, we need to get going.'

There was no reply. 'Deniz?' Jess twisted the knob and pushed open the door. The room was empty.

She must be having a morning brew, Jess thought as she ran downstairs and into the kitchen, but there was no sign of her. She peeked out into the car park in front of the shop. The Corsa was gone.

Unwilling to believe what her eyes were telling her, she pondered whether Deniz had moved the car for some reason? Or gone off for an early-morning spin? Surely she hadn't ditched her?

Pulling on her boots, Jess ran out onto the field towards Gordie, who stopped working and leaned on his hoe as she got closer.

'Gordie!' Jess could barely breathe. 'Where did Deniz go?'

'Well, now, she took off a few hours ago. I gave her directions to Cliff Top, and she said she'd be back in the afternoon to pick you up since you were still sleeping.'

'Oh,' Jess puffed, slightly mollified. Well, it was nice of Deniz to let her sleep, but she was hardly going to stick around here!

'Gordie, can I borrow your car or truck or something? I know it's a massive favour, but I really need to get to that caravan site. Mattie might be in danger.' Jess hated to ask someone she barely knew, but there was no way of trusting Deniz to stop whatever might go down today.

But Gordie was shaking his head. 'No can do, I'm afraid. It's in the garage at the moment. New carburettor, you know.'

Jess didn't know – or care. She just needed to get to that site before it was too late. 'Please, Gordie. Is there any way I can get there? Do you have . . . a bike, or anything?' She hadn't ridden a bike for years, but needs must, as her Gran used to say.

Gordie chewed his lip. 'Tell you what. Follow me. Might take awhile, but we'll get you there. '

*

Mattie opened her eyes and stared in groggy disbelief as Kyle padded out of the room. What on Earth was he doing – watching her sleep? He always used to tell her she seemed so peaceful in slumber. A whoosh of emotion warmed her chilly bones and she couldn't help smiling. He *must* still have feelings for her.

She sat up, even more determined to tell Kyle how she really felt. Today she would fight for their future.

Back at the caravan after sea kayaking, she'd tried to get him alone, but he'd continually managed to manoeuvre himself away and towards Adam, who in turn looked as if he'd happily strangle him. And then . . . Mattie squinted as she tried to recall the rest of the day. Dinner in the grungy cafeteria, some foul-tasting concoction the warthog cook tried to pass off as spaghetti. God, all that exercise had really knocked her out – she couldn't even remember going to bed. Well, yesterday didn't matter; nothing in the past did. Today, Mattie wasn't going to give up. She would tell Kyle how she felt if it required pinning him down and shouting in his ear.

A few minutes later, the door rattled with an accompanying knock. 'Morning, gang!' Baz's voice cut through the thin caravan walls.

Her heart sank. Now she'd have to wait until later to talk with Kyle.

'Come on, guys!' Baz banged down the corridor. 'Let's go, Mattie! We've got a real treat in store today.'

'I'm sure.' Mattie sighed and swung her heavy legs to the floor, trying to pat her hair into some kind of order. After attempting miracles in the loo, she headed out to the lounge. Millions of people watching her every move, and she couldn't even have a hot shower.

'Morning,' she said to Kyle, who was already dressed in jeans and a black T-shirt. He shot her a funny look, and her heart flipped. Would he believe her when she told him how she felt? Would he want to start again? She stared, trying to read his thoughts. He'd always been so open, but now . . .

Kyle nodded and glanced away.

'Morning, Mattie,' Adam said calmly. Sitting on the

sofa he looked surprisingly cool and collected. Thank God for that – Mattie had been sure he was going to have a meltdown after the kayaking incident.

'So what's the treat, then, Baz?' she asked.

Baz rubbed his hands together. 'You're going to love it. Today's Relationship Repair will focus on risk taking, because relationships are all about risks. So . . . you're all going zip-wiring!'

Mattie looked over at Kyle. He'd always said he wanted to go zip-wiring in the Amazon; she'd rolled her eyes and answered that she'd rather undergo Chinese Water Torture care of fifty rabid chavs. The Isle of Wight wasn't exactly the Amazon, but still, he'd love it. Kyle glanced at her and smiled. A glimmer of something resembling hope pinged Mattie's heart.

Baz herded them out of the caravan and into the bright sun where Nate stood waiting, shifting his weight from one foot to the other, looking anxious and nervous. God, that man really had to learn to relax – he never actually appeared to be was enjoying anything.

'The zip-wire site's just a few minutes' walk from here,' Baz announced, leading them away from the holiday camp and deep into the woods.

Mattie breathed in the clean scent of the trees. It wasn't so bad now that the monsoon-like rains had stopped and the weak February sun had made a halting appearance. The smell of damp leaves reminded her of the last time she'd been in a forest, when Kyle had asked if she could trust him.

Nate sidled over. 'Listen, can I talk to you for a second?' His voice was low.

'No. No you can't! You've said and done enough to last me a lifetime!'

Mattie tried to walk away but Nate grabbed her arm and tugged the cord of her mic out of the battery pack clipped to her back.

'What the–?' His forcefulness surprised her.

'Just *listen*,' Nate said, owlish eyes serious behind his specs. 'They're trying to get you all off the show. Today. They've tampered with the zip-wire harnesses.'

Mattie rolled her eyes. 'I'm not an idiot, Nate. Get real. After everything you've pulled, do you think I'm going to believe a production company has "tampered with my harness"?' She mimicked his tentative voice. 'It's not *CSI*.'

Unusually, Nate didn't scurry off with his tail between his legs. 'It's not the production company. It's Baz! Mattie, you have to–'

'What's going on over here?' Baz interrupted. 'What are you two whispering about?' He gave Nate a suspicious look.

Nate fiddled with the mic cord. 'Oh, nothing. Mattie had a problem with her mic. Just helping her fix it.'

'Come on, Nate.' Baz motioned him forward and Nate looked back at her over his shoulder, puppy-dog eyes pleading for understanding and belief.

Tossers, Mattie thought as she followed them up the path. Surely the pair of them could have come up with something better than 'we've tampered with the harnesses'? Not exactly unexpected, though, given that their combined IQ barely equalled that of the average dinner plate.

They came up into the clearing where a skinny man was standing, a tangle of metal hooks hanging off him, seemingly about to fall over under the weight of it all.

'Welcome to Cliff Top Zip-Wire!' he said, handing them each a harness. 'Now, I want you to listen to me very carefully. Health and safety is of the utmost importance . . .'

Mattie tuned out and turned the harness over in her hands, pulling on the hooks and tabs. Looked fine to her. Bloody Nate and Baz, trying to wind her up.

Just to be sure, she carefully observed the demonstration on fitting the harness. 'Pick up your right leg; place it carefully through the loops...' Mattie rolled her eyes. If Baz and Nate wanted to make the whole scenario believable, they could have at least got an instructor who wasn't Mr Safety personified!

Mattie slipped on the harness as best she could over all the layers of clothes and looked up to where the zip-wire was hanging between the trees.

God.

It *was* kind of high up there.

'Come on.' The instructor waved them all over to a ladder attached to a tree. Mattie watched as Kyle and Adam scampered up ahead of her and onto an open wooden platform, half-way up the tree.

'Come on, Mattie!'

'What does it look like I'm doing?' Mattie grunted, swinging onto the ladder. Don't look down, she told herself, climbing one careful step at a time.

She reached the platform, panting hard, and finally looked down. Ram was crouched, camera pointing up at them. Nate was mouthing something at her but she couldn't make it out.

What if Nate wasn't lying? What if something *was* wrong with the harnesses? She leaned over the edge of the platform and the ground loomed up at her. But no, Mr Safety definitely would have spotted it. Nate and Baz couldn't get the better of her this time.

'So who wants to go first?' the instructor asked the three of them as they stood lined up on the edge of the platform.

Mattie threw a defiant look at the TweedleDuo on the ground.

'I'll go!' She'd show them she wasn't afraid.

'Okay.' The instructor attached the cord hanging

from the zip-wire to the front of Mattie's harness. 'Ready?'

'Wait! Mattie!' Nate's voice boomed out and Mattie made a face. How long was he going to keep the ruse going? She was just about to launch off the platform when she saw Adam reach out and give Kyle a hard shove forward.

She watched in horror as Kyle struggled to keep his balance on the edge of the platform. Mattie tried to grab onto his harness but her hand grasped empty space. As if in slow motion, Kyle toppled off the platform and fell through the air, landing with a thump on the ground below.

'Kyle!' Mattie screamed, unclipping her harness and pushing past Adam on the narrow platform so she could get down the tree. Please don't let him be dead, she muttered with every rung. *Please don't let him be dead!* It felt like it took forever to reach the ground. She ran over to where he was lying, motionless. Ram and Nate were already at his side.

'Is he okay?' she asked. She touched his arm. 'Kyle, can you hear me?' Then, she noticed the faint movement of his chest rising and falling. Thank God! He was still alive.

'Keep filming!' Baz was yelling at Ram. 'You bloody big idiot, just keep filming!'

Ram ignored him and crouched over Kyle. 'Doesn't look like anything's broken,' he said to Mattie and Nate. Ram let out a low whistle. 'He's lucky. Must have fallen thirty feet.'

'Don't move him,' the instructor yelled from the platform above, where he was struggling to keep hold of Adam. 'Have you called 999?'

'Just now,' Baz yelled, holding up his BlackBerry. 'Should be here soon.'

Mattie knelt over Kyle. 'Kyle,' she said softly into his

ear. She touched his face, feeling the stubble scratch against her hand. 'Please be all right. Please. I want another chance with you. We need another chance.'

There was a noise nearby and she turned to see Baz shoving Ram's camera in her face.

'Get away from me!' she hissed. She couldn't believe the slimy fool was still filming.

Nate sprang up, grabbed Baz's arms and the camera crashed to the ground. 'That's *enough*!' Nate bellowed. Mattie stared at him, surprised. Nate had never sounded so angry.

Suddenly there was a shout from the platform above them and Mattie looked up to see the instructor and Adam rolling around, perilously close to the edge.

'Mattie!' Adam was screaming. 'Mattie! I love you!' He clawed at the instructor.

'Jesus Christ,' Mattie breathed, praying the instructor could hang onto Adam. He looked possessed.

Ram lumbered up onto the platform. He grabbed Adam's arms and hauled him upright, pinioning him against the tree trunk. Adam struggled, fists flying, but Ram held him tight. Seeing he couldn't escape, Adam sagged and rolled into the foetal position, whimpering and shaking.

Mattie shivered. There had never been any doubt in her mind, but now she was certain: Adam was one hundred per cent crazy. She couldn't believe he had pushed Kyle! Thank God Kyle was still alive but . . . who knew how injured he really was?

Kyle groaned and stirred on the ground beside her. 'You're going to be okay. The ambulance will be here any second.' She looked around frantically. Where the hell *was* it?

To her left the glint of a thick lens caught her eye. 'Baz!' Mattie was astonished he had the nerve to grab the camera and start filming again, even with a determined Nate still struggling to contain him. 'Check how far away those paramedics are, will you?'

'I told you, they're on the way,' Baz puffed, holding fast to the camera and kicking Nate away. 'Get lost, you useless moron!'

Kyle's eyes flickered open. Mattie tuned out Baz and Nate as she met his gaze. 'Kyle? You'll be fine. Everything will be fine.' She wiped a trace of dirt off his cheek as his eyes sunk closed again.

Had he heard her? Did he know she wanted a second chance? It didn't matter. She'd tell him again and again, until the words finally got through. This time, she wouldn't give up.

CHAPTER TWENTY-NINE

Seventy per cent of people believe their perfect soul mate exists.
In reality, fifteen percent find him or her.

NATE PRAYED THE AMBULANCE would come soon. He'd finally got a firm hold on Baz but he could only hang on for so long – it was like trying to grip a squirmy ferret.

'What the fuck, mate?' Baz said as he attempted to twist out of Nate's grasp again. 'We have to get this on film or Silver will kill us!' He lowered his voice. 'Remember our bonus.'

'Fuck Silver!' Nate said. It felt good to finally say that. 'And fuck this show!'

'I'd be careful what you say, Nate.' Silver's voice drifted into the clearing. Surprised, Nate relaxed his hold on Baz who scurried over towards the approaching production boss.

'You got it all, right?' she said to Baz. 'You got it all on camera?'

Baz nodded. 'Most of it. Before Nate grabbed me.'

'Well, well.' Silver looked up at the platform where Adam was lying curled on his side, then over to Mattie and Kyle. 'On behalf of SiniStar Productions and X-ACT TV, I'd like to thank you all for participating in the show. With today's unfortunate incident, I'm afraid we'll have to end here. But we will arrange for your free transport back to London and a certificate of participation.'

She flashed a big grin around the clearing.

'Cut the crap, Silver,' Nate said, unable to keep his thoughts to himself. He couldn't believe Silver would spew such lies to people she'd manipulated and drugged – all for ratings. 'You *made* this happen. It might not have gone according to your original plan, but you got what you wanted out of Adam, didn't you?'

Silver shot him a look. 'If I were you, I'd stop talking, Nate. *Right now.* Remember, you signed a non-disclosure agreement. I'll sue if you reveal anything else, you can bet on that.'

Nate shrugged. He was beyond caring now. 'So if I've already broken the NDA, who cares? I might as well keep talking.' He turned to Mattie. 'There was never going to be any prize money, you know. They were trying to push you out before you could get to the end. Baz even tampered with your harness.'

Mattie still didn't look convinced.

'If you don't believe me, check your harness.' He held up a hand as Mattie started protesting. 'Yours might be fine. But have a look at Kyle's.'

Mattie ran her hands over Kyle's harness, noticing the neat cut in the nylon loop attaching his harness to a metal clip. She looked up at Nate. 'Oh my God. You were telling the truth!'

Nate nodded. 'Yeah. I can kind of understand why you wouldn't believe me, though.'

'No one will believe you, Nate,' Silver said, striding over to where he was standing. 'I'll just say you were a disgruntled employee trying to get back at the company for firing you. In fact, *you* were the one who fiddled with those harnesses. The rest of the production crew knew nothing about it.'

The woods rustled, and someone stumbled out from the thick branches. A woman, dark and attractive, was brushing off her tightly fitting jeans and dark blazer in disgust, making tutting noises as if the forest was at fault for the dishevelment.

Nate squinted. Who was that? Not a member of the crew. He'd definitely never seen her before.

The woman raised a mobile phone high in the air. 'They might not believe him,' she said. 'But they'll sure as hell believe me. I've got the whole thing right here, on video.'

'Deniz?' Baz said, staring at her. 'How did you know we were here?'

Deniz snorted. 'You told me, you idiot. Remember? Right after you cried because you couldn't get it up?' She shook her head.

'Who the hell are you?' Silver asked, shooting Baz a furious look. He took a step away from her.

'I'm a reporter from the *Daily News*,' Deniz said, chomping on her gum. 'And I can't wait to break this story!'

Nate looked over at Silver, delighted to see fear mixed with anger flash across her face. Finally, the sausage bitch was caught in a web of her own making.

'Baz, get that phone from her!' Silver commanded.

Baz shuffled his feet, and looked over at Deniz. 'Um, I'm not sure . . .'

'Now!' Silver shrieked.

Deniz starting backing away into the woods as Baz advanced on her. Just as the slick producer reached her side, arms outstretched, a loud rumbling noise filled the air and the ground started shaking.

'What the hell?' Nate said as the noise got louder.

*

'Can't this go any faster?' Jess said to Gordie as they

powered up the path towards a clearing in the woods. It felt like they'd been on the tractor for hours, and she didn't even know if they were heading in the right direction.

They'd got to the holiday park only to find it deserted. No sign of life anywhere; just row upon row of identical-looking caravans. With no clue where to go, Gordie had done a loop around the compound. Then Jess spotted Deniz's car, parked off the side of the road, at the start of a narrow dirt track. Gordie had swung the tractor around fast.

'Oh my God!' Jess said as the clearing came into view. She brought her hand to her mouth, unable to believe what she was seeing. Mattie was kneeling over Kyle, who was stretched out on the ground, motionless. Adam was curled up on a tree-top platform, two men keeping watch. Deniz and a bloke with spiky hair were squaring off like they were about to start wrestling.

Gordie cut the engine. Jess jumped off the tractor and ran over to Mattie.

'Is he okay?' she said. Kyle's face was pale and a massive gash on his cheek oozed thick blood.

'I hope so. Adam pushed him off the platform.' Mattie sounded more scared than Jess had ever heard her, but she managed to give Jess a quick hug.

'Thank God you're here!' Mattie said, as Jess tried to hide her surprise at the unexpected show of affection.

To the right of the clearing, Deniz edged away from Baz and backed up against the tractor. Baz faced the group, scanning the clearing. 'Where's Silver?'

Jess shook her head. 'Silver? Who's that?'

'You're on your own now, Baz,' a chunky man with large specs called. 'But don't worry, I'll be sure to fill everyone in on what you've done.'

'And I got the video – with sound!' Deniz crowed, holding up the phone again.

Baz looked around the clearing like a hunted animal hiding out in a gun factory. 'Good luck waiting for that ambulance,' he spat. 'I never called one, you know.'

Then he turned and ran away from them down the track.

Jess's mouth dropped open. How could someone play around with people's lives like that? She looked down at Kyle. If possible, his face was even paler than before.

'We need to get that lad to the hospital,' Gordie said from the tractor, nodding towards Kyle. 'If we call an ambulance now, it'll probably take longer than if we just head there on the tractor, given the state of that track.' He looked up at the two men on the platform and over at the chunky man. 'Come on. Help me get him on here.'

The two men made their way down the platform, each gripping onto a glassy-eyed Adam. Jess swallowed hard.

'Will he be all right?' she asked. Adam's eyes stared blankly ahead and tears made tracks through the smudge of dirt on his cheeks. He didn't even remotely resemble the man she'd known. It was like the old Adam had totally disappeared. So sad.

The chunky man with the specs let out a big sigh. 'I hope so.'

Jess shook her head as they manoeuvred Adam into a sitting position against a tree, then attended to Kyle. Adam had still managed to hurt Kyle, but at least she'd done as much possible to stop it. This time, Jess hadn't sat back and let someone else take the lead.

*

Mattie squeezed Kyle's hand as they loaded him

carefully into the cab of the tractor. His eyes were closed but the up and down movement of his chest let her know he was still breathing, at least.

'He'll be fine,' Gordie said, patting her hand. 'I'll get him there as fast as I can.'

'Thanks, Gordie,' Mattie said, unable to take her eyes off Kyle's ashen face. Gordie slammed the tractor doors closed and rumbled down the path, the noise gradually subsiding. Finally all they could hear was the sound of the wind in the tree-tops overhead and the occasional birdsong.

Mattie sank back down to the ground, trying to take it all in. Adam's hand shooting out. Kyle falling hard to the ground.

And then . . . there was never going to be any prize money. She'd sacrificed her dignity, her privacy – for *nothing*. But even if there had been money, her business and her ambition weren't enough to keep her happy. She wanted Kyle.

It wasn't too late, was it? Kyle would be fine; he had to be. And he'd want to be with her again – she hoped. The alternative was unthinkable.

Mattie got to her feet. She wasn't going to give up this time; not until Kyle rejected her outright. He'd have to push her away to get rid of her!

She turned to Jess. 'Come to the hospital with me?' It was so good to see Jess. Mattie hadn't realised how much she'd missed her. There were a million questions that needed to be answered – like how on Earth Jess had turned up here – but right now, all Mattie could do was focus on Kyle.

Jess nodded and put an arm around Mattie's shoulder. 'Of course.' She looked around the clearing. 'But how are we going to get there? Wherever there is.'

Mattie glanced over to where Nate and Ram were

sitting beside Adam. 'Have you called an ambulance for him?' She nodded towards Adam, who was staring blankly into space. He needed more than an ambulance. The memory of him pushing Kyle made her shiver.

Nate nodded. 'I've just rung one. It's on its way. About forty minutes or so, they said.' He lowered his voice. 'And I called the police, too. They'll meet us at the hospital, to file a report on Adam's actions.'

Mattie nodded and took a deep breath. Forty minutes. Forty minutes to find out if Kyle was all right. And forty minutes to the continuation of the biggest – and most important – fight of her life.

CHAPTER THIRTY

*One in ten of all broken relationships reunite;
one in five of these ends within two months.*

MATTIE STRODE THROUGH THE CORRIDORS of St Mary's Hospital, Jess following in her wake. Every step made her more determined to convince Kyle to give their relationship another try.

'I'm here to see Kyle Cook,' Mattie announced to the nurse behind the reception desk.

The nurse didn't lift her double chin from the *Heat* magazine she was reading. 'Sorry, visiting hours are over for the day.'

'Right.' Mattie backed away.

'You're not going to give up that easily?' Jess asked, looking incredulous.

Mattie shook her head. 'No way. Wait here,' she said in a low voice. She walked a few paces, then raced down the corridor in what she hoped was the right direction. No silly nurse would stop her! Heart thumping, she glanced back to see if anyone was following. The corridor was empty.

Her heart sank as she passed a million identical doors with miniscule windows. How was she ever going to find him here? Feeling like a peeping Tom, she peered through one glass slot, getting an eyeful of an ancient man having a sponge bath. Jerking away, Mattie glanced through another small window, then another, resolve flooding through her. She'd happily encounter a whole colony of wizened sponge-bathing men if it meant finding Kyle!

Finally she spotted him through the narrow window. Tucked under a white hospital sheet, his face was drained of colour and his eyes were closed. Slowly, Mattie opened the door to the room and tiptoed over to the cracked plastic chair beside the bed.

Reaching over, she took his hand, holding her breath as his eyes slowly opened. Her heart beat faster as he blinked, focusing in on her. She tightened her grip, afraid to let go.

'Hey,' she whispered.

'Hey.' His voice was hoarse and scratchy. 'What are you doing here? Thought you hated me.'

She shrugged, moving her eyes away and staring down at the sheet. 'How are you feeling?'

Kyle tried to nod, grimacing with the movement. 'I'll live. Just a concussion. The doctor said I was lucky to escape at all. Medical miracle, apparently.'

'Thank God you're okay.' Mattie exhaled. She didn't know what she'd do if he had been seriously injured; it didn't even bear thinking about. Her fingers fiddled with a stray thread on the edge of the sheet.

'Look, Kyle.' Raising her eyes, she met his again. 'There's something I need to tell you.'

'All right,' he said, holding her gaze.

'I messed up,' she said quickly. 'I was using my business – and everything else – to protect myself against what I was feeling for you. I was scared to trust you.'

Kyle smiled. 'I know.'

'But I'm ready to take that leap now.' She reached out and covered his hand. 'With you.'

Kyle's eyes went soft and his fingers closed around hers. 'Well, I kind of liked how you said it the first time better.' His mouth twitched.

Mattie's jaw dropped. 'You heard that? But you were unconscious!'

'I heard,' he said. 'I just couldn't answer at the time.' His smile got wider. 'And, you know, I figured if you meant it, you'd say it again.'

'Bastard!' Mattie said, but she was grinning so hard her face felt as if it might split in two.

'Come here.' Kyle winced as he tried to raise an arm and Mattie moved towards him, leaning into the warmth of his body. He slid a hand onto her back. 'From now on, it's us, together. I'm on your side, no matter what.'

Mattie put her head gently on his shoulder. '*Second Chance for Romance*, after all?' she smiled.

Kyle pulled her closer. 'Second chance for love.'

T*W*O *M*O*N*T*H*S* L*A*T*E*R*

'QUICK!' JESS TURNED UP THE VOLUME on Kyle's TV and plopped down on one of the sofas. 'Mattie! Kyle! It's starting!'

Mattie smiled over at her friend as she and Kyle came in from the small garden of their Castle Combe cottage. Jess's cheeks were bright red. Mattie hadn't seen her so excited since she'd got the invite to the Staines Secondary School reunion. That seemed like another life now – so much had changed. *She* had changed. For the first time in ages, Mattie was actually happy.

Her thoughts flicked back to the aftermath of *The Hating Game*. Unwilling to leave Kyle, she and Jess had camped out at the hospital until Kyle's release the next day. Deniz had long since made her way back to London, so after several long conversations with the police about Adam, the three of them rented a car and made a beeline to the city, not even bothering to collect their things from the caravan. Mattie couldn't bear the thought of setting foot back in that place again.

At home, her voice mail was stuffed full of calls from media companies who'd seen her on television and wanted to discuss their needs with someone who 'understood the industry from the inside out'. It was ironic: she hadn't got one penny of the prize money, but it looked as if the show might save her business after all.

There were too many new clients to handle alone,

so Mattie and Kyle made a decision: they'd form a partnership. She'd be in charge of new business and he'd handle client services – much the same way they'd done before, but on equal footing now. The new partnership was going from strength to strength and the two of them were now thinking about buying larger office space.

'Quiet, it's starting!' Jess said again, turning up the telly even louder.

Reality Shows: the Reality flashed across the screen. They sat in silence as Deniz took them through a blow-by-blow account of what had actually happened on *The Hating Game*. Mattie shook her head as she watched Deniz explain that no prize money was ever intended; that the contestants had been lied to, manipulated and even subjected to physical harm.

'One contestant, Adam Higgins, is still recovering in hospital. Higgins experienced a psychotic episode after failing to be provided with the medication his doctor recommended,' Deniz said as a slow-motion video of Adam pushing Kyle played out on the screen. 'Once able to stand trial, lawyers say he will likely be faced with charges of attempted murder.'

Mattie closed her eyes, not wanting to see Kyle fall to the ground again or Adam's twisted face as he called out for her from the zip-wire platform.

'This documentary tried to contact Silver Hatchett, the former managing director of SiniStar Productions, at her home in the Cayman Islands. She declined our request for an interview,' Deniz was saying.

Mattie opened her eyes. 'Yeah, I bet she did! I still can't believe she managed to get out of the whole thing unscathed.'

'Former producer Baz Jonson – now working as second assistant clown co-ordinator for children's show *Clowning Around* – also refused to speak to us.' The television showed video of Baz pushing the camera away from his face, then ducking through a circle of clowns as a group of children jeered in an attempt to get away.

Mattie snorted. 'At least someone got what they deserved – worse than prison!'

They watched in silence for a few more minutes as Deniz explained the class-action lawsuit launched by the contestants against X-ACT and the lobbying for new government legislation to regulate future reality shows. Finally, the credits scrolled across the screen.

Instead of switching it off, Jess leaned closer. 'There it is! There's Nate name!' Her cheeks increased their rosy hue as the words *Nathan Reilly, Executive Producer* appeared.

Then Jess picked up her mobile and punched in a number. 'Congrats on your documentary debut!' she sang out before scurrying off into the garden.

Kyle and Mattie smiled at each other. It was lovely to see Jess so happy – and with Nate, of all people! When Nate got in touch with Jess to research his documentary on *The Hating Game*, the two of them had just clicked. They'd been together ever since, and despite Nate's ex-girlfriend breaking into his place one night and begging him to 'start fresh, like', they were even talking about Nate moving into Jess's scruffy Clapham flat.

Mattie had to admit she was impressed with Nate's determination to make his documentary production company a success. He'd already produced two or three meaty shows and he was on location God-knows-where right now, filming something about an evil dictatorship.

'Look, there's Ram's name!' Mattie pointed as the credit for principal cameraman came on-screen. Funny how *The Hating Game* had brought her and Kyle back together, saved her business and launched Nate's documentary career with Ram on camera and Deniz as host. Who would have thought it?

Jess came back in from the garden. 'Nate says hello. He'll be home from his shoot tomorrow. I can't wait!' She plonked down on the sofa across from them and grinned.

Mattie snapped off the TV, birdsong floating in from the soft April twilight. Kyle and Jess looked up at her expectantly. She smiled and raised her glass high in the air. 'Here's to reality!'

'To reality!' Kyle and Jess clinked their glasses with hers.

Right now, Mattie's reality was better than anything she – or any producer – could ever have imagined.

THE END